ALSO BY RYAN WINFIELD

Jane's Melody

JANE'S HARMONY

A Novel

RYAN WINFIELD

ATRIA PAPERBACK
New York • London • Toronto • Sydney • New Delhi

ATRIA PAPERBACK
A Division of Simon & Schuster, Inc.
1230 Avenue of the Americas
New York, NY 10020

First Atria Paperback edition August 2014

ATRIA PAPERBACK and colophon are trademarks of Simon & Schuster, Inc.

For information about special discounts for bulk purchases, please contact Simon & Schuster Special Sales at 1-866-506-1949 or business@simonandschuster.com.

The Simon & Schuster Speakers Bureau can bring authors to your live event. For more information or to book an event contact the Simon & Schuster Speakers Bureau at 1-866-248-3049 or visit our website at www.simonspeakers.com.

Manufactured in the United States of America

10 9 8 7 6 5 4 3 2

Library of Congress Cataloging-in-Publication Data is on file.

ISBN 978-1-4767-7125-0
ISBN 978-1-4767-7126-7 (ebook)

For lovers everywhere

PART ONE

Chapter 1

Jane lay awake, searching for the secret of all existence in Caleb's sleeping face. She was certain if she just looked long enough, she would find it there. And if there was no secret to be found, she would be perfectly happy to just go on gazing at him for an eternity anyway.

The constant clamor of music coming from the street below seemed not to bother him at all, as if he had been born from the belly of a snare drum and meant for no other world than the world of song—sweet melodies instead of blood pumping through his veins. The neon light filtering through the blinds painted red slats across his youthful face, and she watched as his eyelids flickered to the rhythm of some dream. When his lips curled into a slight smile, it was all she could do to keep herself from kissing him. But she knew he needed sleep, so she prayed to the music and to the night that his dreams might be dreams of her, and then she closed her eyes to dream of him.

She woke to the soft touch of Caleb's lips on the back of her neck. He must have dreamed of her after all, she thought.

Jane kept her eyes closed and listened to her heart throbbing in her chest. She knew if she could live a thousand years, she would never tire of being woken like this. And it wasn't just the primal, sexual pleasure of it, either. No, it was something more. It was the conscious awareness deep down in her soul that they were connected in every possible way—physically, emotionally, spiritually. That he was her, and she was him, and together they were all that mattered in this world or any other. They were entwined and unbreakable.

His hair hung down over her shoulder, tickling her chest, and she shifted onto her back and brought her mouth to his.

When he finally pulled away, she said, "I love you."

He motioned to his ear, as if he couldn't hear her.

"I said I love you," she repeated.

He reached and pinched her earplug and pulled it free. "I love you too, baby," he said, laughing. "But there's no need to shout it at me."

Jane laughed and fished the earplug from her other ear. "I keep forgetting they're in."

He just smiled and kissed her again. Then he rolled over and got up from the bed, and headed for the bathroom.

"Do you use them because of the neighbor's dog?"

She heard his question but was too transfixed by the view of his naked figure walking away to process an answer.

"Because I'll talk to her if you want," he added.

"The earplugs? No. These are for the music."

She wanted to tell him she hadn't had a good night's sleep since she'd been in Austin. His apartment was just off the main strip, and the music and crowds raged on in the streets until at least three in the morning. Then she had to be up by eight to feed the parking meter.

The parking meter!

Jane glanced at the bedside clock—8:10 a.m.

She jumped out of bed, shimmied into her jeans, pulled on Caleb's T-shirt, and rushed barefoot into the hall and down the apartment stairs.

The parking enforcement vehicle was just pulling away when she rounded the corner in a mad dash for her car. And there was the ticket, tucked beneath the windshield wiper, just like the dozen others she'd received in the last three weeks.

She heard laughter and looked up to see their neighbor sitting on her apartment balcony, wearing her tacky pink robe and smoking a cigarette. She seemed to relish Jane's battle with the meter as much as she did pounding on their bedroom wall whenever she thought their lovemaking too loud.

Jane flipped her off. She was almost to the apartment door when she turned and trudged back. "I'm sorry," she called up. "That was childish of me."

The neighbor stubbed out her cigarette, gathered up her little yapping dog in her arms, then went inside and pulled the slider closed without a word.

Caleb was already showered and drying his hair when Jane returned to the apartment. He tossed the towel and pulled her to him and kissed her. His lips were warm and soft, and she could smell the soap on his skin.

"How do you shower so fast?" she asked.

"Easy," he replied. "I turn the water on, soap up, and rinse off." Then he kissed her again and added, "I'm happy to get back in with you for a demonstration."

"Yeah, right," she said. "Like two people could fit in that tiny shower."

She placed her hands on his naked chest and pushed herself free, heading for the kitchen to see about breakfast.

"Men, men, men," she said under her breath.

"What's that, babe?"

The apartment was so small, they could practically hear each other's thoughts.

"I said I miss my bath."

"You do?"

"I do. You boys have it made. Society accepts you with all your hair just the way it grows. I've got to shave and pluck and polish just to be presentable."

"You could go bohemian," he called from the bedroom.

"Go bohemian?"

"Sure. We've already got the poverty thing going."

"You wouldn't mind?"

"Baby, I'd love you if you looked like Sasquatch."

"Yes, but would you make love to me if I did?"

Caleb leaned out from the bedroom and looked at her, considering her question. Then he smiled. "Yes. Answer's yes."

Jane chuckled and went back to making coffee and toast.

A minute later, Caleb called from the bedroom, "Although our kids might have a tough time in school."

"What's that?"

He stepped into the kitchen, dressed for the day in his signature jeans and T-shirt. Jane had bought him other shoes, but for some reason he insisted on wearing his old boots that he'd worn all those months ago while working in her yard back in Washington.

"I was just saying that if you looked like Sasquatch, our kids might have a hard time."

Jane glanced up at him from the toaster and frowned. "I thought we made a deal not to talk about that."

"Sorry. It's just that every time I look at you, I wonder what our kids would look like. Don't you wonder too?"

Jane turned away and pulled down two coffee mugs from the cupboard, speaking with her back turned as she filled them. "I wonder about a lot of things. Like what it would feel like to parachute off a building. Or backpack across Africa. Or swim the English Channel. Or get a sleeve tattoo."

"See," he said. "I knew you were bohemian."

She turned and handed him a mug of coffee. "That doesn't mean I'm going to do any of those things."

"Well, let's talk about it later."

"Let's not," she said.

He grabbed a piece of toast from the toaster and ate half of it in one bite, not bothering to butter it.

"Not even the tattoo?" he mumbled, choking down the dry bread. "It'd look good on you."

The twinkle in his green eyes was so charming, she couldn't help but smile. "Maybe someday," she said. "You want eggs?"

"No, I gotta run."

"I thought you didn't work until noon."

"I don't, but I'm meeting Jeremy to go over the set list for tomorrow's gig." Caleb glanced at the time on the microwave. "And I'm late already."

"You haven't even finished your coffee."

He went to the cupboard and pulled down a large plastic cup, poured his coffee in, added cream, turned the tap on, and filled it the rest of the way with cold water. Then he gulped the entire concoction down and put the empty cup in the sink. Jane just shook her head.

"Take the car," she said.

"You sure?"

"Please. I can't be running out to pay the meter all day. And put the parking ticket in the glove box with the others."

"I'm going to get you a monthly spot if I have to set someone's car on fire," he said.

"I'd rather you put your energy into finding me a place with a bathtub. Or how about air-conditioning?"

Caleb stepped up and wrapped his arms around her waist, no trace of impatience in his embrace, despite his being late. "Come on, it's not that hot here, is it?"

"Are you kidding?" she asked. "You're never here in the afternoons. This place is a sauna. And the few plants I bought for the balcony are already brown. Even the cactus."

"Maybe you should hang a sign in the window and offer hot yoga classes," he suggested.

She chuckled at the thought. "Yeah, right. I've taken one lesson and was nearly brought home by ambulance. All I can remember beyond the first fifteen minutes is coming to in the studio lobby and mumbling to the instructor that downward dog is not a resting pose."

"I agree with you there," he said. "It isn't. Although I'd love to see you demonstrate your technique for me in those jeans. Or maybe without them, even."

"Aren't you late, mister?"

He leaned in and kissed her. "I love you."

"I love you too."

He grabbed another piece of toast, snatched the car keys from the hook, and turned to leave. He stopped at the door and looked back. "Hey, babe. Would you mind letting me use the apartment this evening? To rehearse with the guys. My gig this weekend is an important one."

"Sure," Jane answered, a little surprised, since he hadn't mentioned it before now. "How late will you be?"

"Just until nine or so. Then maybe we can get a bite."

"Yeah, no problem. I'll go and see a movie or something."

Caleb flashed a smile. "Thanks, babe. And I'll see about finding us a used AC unit."

She meant to tell him not to bother, but before she could, he was gone. She stood in the kitchen with her coffee mug in her hand, looking at the door and listening to his steps fading down the stairs. A familiar and unwelcome silence enveloped the small apartment, as if his very presence generated some beautiful sound that left with him each day.

She carried her coffee to the couch, opened her laptop, and went through her daily ritual of deleting spam, hoping that she might have a message about a job from one of the many sites where she had posted her résumé. There was nothing. Just twelve messages inviting her to use LinkedIn, whatever that was, and an e-mail from Esmeralda letting her know that her home sale had closed. She shut her laptop and sighed.

Jane looked around at the tiny apartment. The faded paint. The awful track lighting. The clouded window that seemed to get worse with each cleaning. Funny, she thought, but she never missed her home on Bainbridge Island when Caleb was around. It was only when he left that she even noticed her sad surroundings.

She leaned back on the couch and closed her eyes, recalling the beauty of her island backyard. She remembered Caleb out there working in the rain, his wet shirt clinging to his body, wildly hacking down blackberries and ripping them from the ground. She remembered the day she had come home and found him constructing a Slip 'N Slide down into the creek. She remembered the new grass. The fountain. The silly old goat. And she remembered making love to Caleb for the first time, how excited and nervous she had been. She remembered the baseball game later, his ripping off her clothes when they had returned home, and bending her over the kitchen table like a man possessed. There were earlier memories too. Memories of her life, long before Caleb. Memories of her daughter, Melody. Of her best friend, Grace. But she kept that box closed on most days, today being no exception.

The ancient refrigerator whirred loudly to life, rousing Jane from her memories. She stood and looked out the window. At least they had a view, she thought. Even if it was of parked cars and dingy bars. She watched the daytime machinery of old Austin working in the street below. The booze delivery trucks. The traffic going by. The people. She knew she should be out there pounding the pavement, job hunting again. But she just couldn't stomach another day filled with rejection.

Maybe a little nap first?

No, it was already too hot for that.

She glanced down at her laptop, a thought playing at the edges of her mind. If her house sale had closed, that meant she had some money again. And even though she intended to save it for another house someday, and she wasn't working just yet, there wasn't much she wouldn't pay for the luxury of a warm bath and a cool room to rest in.

❧

Jane opened her eyes in the dark room.

She listened to the alarm, wondering for a moment where in the world she was. She had just been driving down the most dreamy country road in an old Mustang convertible with sunglasses on and her hand out the window, riding the breeze.

She rolled over and silenced the hotel alarm clock, glad that she had set it before lying down. She used the bathroom, freshening up her makeup in the mirror. Then she gathered her purse to leave and paused at the door to look back into the room—the comfy bed rumpled and waiting, the bath she had soaked so luxuriously in, the room-service tray sitting on the table. She felt somewhat guilty, as if she'd had some secret rendezvous with herself. But she also felt more rested than she had in a long time. It seemed a shame to leave when the room was paid for, so she kept the key, thinking maybe she'd surprise Caleb later. It had been a while since they'd had a queen mattress to play on.

"Thank you, Hilton," she said. Then she stepped out and gently pulled the door closed.

The night sky outside was warm and electric. To Jane, Austin was more a city of sound than anything else. The old church bells tolling the hours. The great-tailed grackles calling in chorus from street-side live oaks and ancient pecan trees. The constant wail of distant sirens patrolling the edges of downtown, as if there were always some emergency on its borders. And the music. All night long, the music. She passed bar after bar with every form of amplified sound pumping from their open doors, the dim light inside showing just a smear of drunken, hypnotized faces swaying to the beat. So much music and so little time. How could any man, woman, or band hope to make it when so many talented ones had already tried and failed, and settled on covering old hits for free drinks and a little money to pool toward making rent? It made her worry for Caleb. But then he seemed perfectly happy just producing music, whether anyone cared to listen to it or not. And if any talent might stand out above the crowd, it was Caleb's; she'd never heard a better voice than his. But then she might be biased.

The blocks passed in a blur beneath Jane's thoughts, and before long she was standing in front of their building. The lights were off in their apartment, even though Caleb had said they'd be rehearsing there. She looked at her phone—thirty-five minutes after nine and no missed calls. She shrugged, fishing her keys from her purse. The dog was yipping away behind the neighbor's thin door when she reached the landing, and she cursed the little devil under her breath as she hurried inside to close out the shrill sound.

The apartment was dark, save for a lone candle burning on the coffee table. She called Caleb's name, but there was no answer. She set down her purse and crossed the small living room to the candle, and found a single long-stemmed white rose and a card. Was it their anniversary? she wondered. They didn't even really have a date to go by, did they?

She opened the envelope and pulled out a note.

I know you're not a fan of flowers with thorns, so I stripped them off by hand. The other eleven roses are waiting for you on the roof.

She'd never been to the roof and wasn't even sure how to get there. Carrying the rose and the card with her, she went into the hall again and up the stairs, so curious about what awaited her that she didn't even hear the barking fading behind her. Three flights seemed to be thirty tonight, but at last she was standing at the roof-access door. For some reason she expected it to be locked, but the handle turned and the door opened easily and swung away. When she saw the scene before her, she clapped a hand over her mouth, as if to keep her heart from leaping out.

A path of white rose petals lined by candles burning in crystal urns led to a table covered with white linen and topped with a vase of white roses. And beside the table stood Caleb, freshly shaven with his hair slicked back, wearing a suit and tie. She'd never seen him in a suit before, and the silhouette he cut standing there in the candlelight, together with the roses and the rooftop table for two, made her eyes well up with tears of joy until the entire scene blurred together into one gorgeous and shimmering vision of something she might have dreamed. It wasn't until she blinked the tears away that she noticed Jeremy standing off to the side with his electric violin cradled beneath his chin, the bow ready on the strings. They seemed to be waiting for her, so she pulled herself together and walked the rose-petal path toward Caleb.

When she reached him, she opened her mouth to speak, but he pressed a finger to her lips. Then he took her hand in his and knelt before her. Jane felt a tear run down her cheek to the tip of her nose as she looked at him there. He smiled, and she noticed that his eyes were wet too. They were still for several moments, him on his knees looking up, her standing and looking down. There was a silent promise in that pose and in his eyes that wasn't lost on Jane, an intimate gesture of the position he wished for her in his life. A covenant to always place her above himself in all things from now until forever if she would only accept him, here, now, as he was, however he would be, together in joint harness wherever this ride might lead.

He had hardly asked, "Will you marry me?" before Jane nodded yes and pulled him up, kissing him and running her fingers through his thick hair. She could have kissed him there forever, but the electric violin began to play, and she remembered they were not alone on the roof.

She pulled free and smoothed his hair back with her hands, feeling slightly embarrassed. Caleb smiled his charming smile, and then he held up the blue felt box and opened it to present her with the ring—the ring he had worked so hard for all those long afternoons at Mrs. Hawthorne's place. He lifted Jane's hand to slip it onto her finger. It fit so well that she knew he'd had it sized. She took his hand in hers, interlaced their fingers, and held them up together to look at the yellow diamond, sparkling in the candlelight. The rooftop and the city seemed to fall away, the sirens and street noise fading, until only she and Caleb were standing there among the stars, floating on the sounds of an electric violin, their entwined forms cutting from the firmament a new constellation dedicated to love.

Jane was still lost in the dream of it all when Caleb pulled out her chair. She sat, and he uncorked a bottle of sparkling cider and filled their glasses.

"I hope it's a good year," she joked, remembering his saying it once at dinner.

He just smiled and stepped away from the table.

"Aren't you going to join me?" she asked.

He reappeared with a serving platter. "Yes, but I'm also your server," he said. "The friend I had lined up couldn't make it."

"Well, at least the music made it."

"Isn't Jeremy great?"

"Yes. I've never heard anything like it, and I love it."

Jeremy seemed to have heard them because his smile stretched a little wider and he played a little louder. After seeing that everything was set, Caleb joined Jane at the table and held up his flute of cider to toast.

"To love," he said.

"Okay," Jane replied. "To love. And to me becoming Mrs. Caleb Cummings."

"You sure?" he asked.

"Hell yes."

"Not about marrying me," he clarified. "About taking my name. Because it's fine if you want to keep yours, or even hyphenate them. McKinney-Cummings sounds nice."

Jane laughed so hard, cider splashed out of her glass. "Do you have any idea how long I've been waiting to get rid of my stupid family's name? Now, can we toast before the food gets cold?"

"I'm afraid it's already cold," he said, raising an eyebrow. "I was expecting you at nine."

"Look at this," Jane said. "We're not even married yet and we're already arguing. To Mr. and Mrs. Caleb Cummings, and that's final."

"You wanna know something?" he asked, holding back his glass. "I'm crazy in love with you."

Jane smiled. "I'm crazy in love with you too."

She clinked her glass against his and held his gaze as they sipped. The violin played on, the candles flickered in their crystal urns, and never before had a cold meal and warm sparkling cider tasted so great to anyone anywhere on earth.

"Ooh," Jane said after they had finished their main course. "He even has chocolate-covered strawberries for dessert."

"No"—Caleb shook his head—"this is pre-dessert."

"Pre-dessert?"

"Yes, because when we finish with these, I plan to take you down to our bedroom and have my way with you."

"I've got a better idea," Jane said.

"You do? Please tell."

She pulled out the Hilton room key card. "How about I take you back to my suite at the Hilton and have my way with you?"

"Your suite at the Hilton?"

"Well, it's a regular room, really. But it has a queen bed."

"And why do you have a room at the Hilton?"

Jane bit into a strawberry and grinned. "I'll explain it on the way, my sweet fiancé."

Chapter 2

Chris Cornell, without a doubt."

"I say Kurt Cobain."

"No way. Not even close."

"Get out. You know Nirvana wrote way better songs than Soundgarden ever did."

"The question was greatest voice of all time. Not greatest song. Ask yourself this—which of them would you rather be?"

"Easy. The one who's still alive."

"Chris Cornell. See, I rest my case."

"What do you say, Jane?"

Jane looked up from the camcorder she had in her lap. There was a crowded table of young faces staring at her. "What's that?" she asked.

"Chris Cornell or Kurt Cobain?"

"Neither," she said.

"Neither? Who's your favorite voice of all time, then?"

She smiled. "Caleb Cummings, of course."

There was a moment of silence; then they all nodded.

"She's good," one of them said.

"Hey," another kid cut in. "Did anyone notice that they all have the initials CC?"

"No, they don't, stupid. Kurt is spelled with a K."

Jane just smiled and enjoyed listening to their banter. In the short time Caleb had been in Austin, he'd amassed a misfit collection of friends, and Jane loved him for it. Some were musicians; others were friends from the warehouse where he worked. But they all admired Caleb. Jane could see it in the way they looked at him, how they hung on his every word. But if he was aware, he never let on . . . And maybe his humility was why everyone fell for him the way they did.

"There's the lights," someone said. "He's coming out."

Jane checked the borrowed video camera again, making sure it was ready. She didn't know exactly why, but she was nervous. Maybe because this was Caleb's first major solo gig. And on a Saturday night at Sherman's too. But if Caleb was nervous, Jane couldn't tell. He walked out onstage and stood in the lights, smiling at the crowd. Then he plugged in his guitar and proceeded to tune it, as if he were standing in his own living room without another soul around.

One by one, the crowd fell silent.

His quiet nonchalance onstage drew every eye and ear in the place. They were all waiting to see what this kid could do. His tuning somehow worked itself into a mini riff, and the riff somehow worked itself into a full-on guitar solo, and before Jane even knew what was happening, his fingers were running on the strings and the amps were wailing, and the entire place lit up with a kind of electricity that raised the hairs on Jane's neck.

Caleb's head hung, his hair dangling, and Jane was struck by how unaffected he was by the stage and the lights and the people. She could almost picture him as a boy, playing away by himself in some garage somewhere. He was an artist with something to say, a man baring his soul without fear, and the absolute absence of any fake showmanship was a huge turn-on to Jane.

Caleb played on—one minute, two minutes, three.

The crowd was so mesmerized by the sound of his guitar that Jane heard a surprised cheer erupt when he finally leaned in to the microphone and began to sing.

Baby, baby, baby. Baby, yeah, you know I'm singin' to you.

Then Caleb lifted his head and looked right at Jane. The crowd dissolved away and she sat in the spotlight of his green-eyed stare, listening to the voice she so loved.

Maybe I'll lay down this pen
Never write a song again
Baby, if only you ask me to
Maybe I'll smash this old guitar
Get me a job sellin' cars
Baby, if that's what real men do
And maybe I'll rise before the sun
Be home when the workday's done
Oh, baby, if it proves my love is true
But if you'll have me as I am
The moody poet, the broken man
Then, baby, I'll write every song for you
Because baby, baby, baby
I don't care nothin' 'bout no maybes
And I can't wait to fuckin' marry you

Fortunately for Jane, her shriek of delight was muted by the outrageous guitar riff Caleb unleashed to punctuate his engagement announcement. The boys at the table all turned their heads toward Jane to see if it was true. She grinned and held up the ring on her finger for them to see.

"Holy bling," one of them shouted. "You could signal the space station with that thing."

Jane blushed, saying, "It isn't that big," but her comment was covered up by another wave of guitar music from the stage.

She suddenly realized that the camcorder was still in her lap and that she had forgotten to start recording. She picked it up and turned it on, then settled back into her seat to record the rest of Caleb's performance.

This is twice now that I've been caught off guard by him, she thought, smiling from behind the viewfinder.

But Caleb wasn't the only one who could pull off a surprise. At least, she hoped not.

❧

Caleb was still sleeping the following Monday when Jane sat down with her morning cup of coffee and her stack of parking tickets, then logged on to the Austin Municipal Court website to pay them. At least there was one good thing about getting up early to go job hunting, she thought. She wouldn't have to worry about paying the meter.

As Jane entered the citation numbers and paid each ticket, annoying announcement banners kept flashing on the screen with various boring bits of city business that only a civics buff would care about or even read. New deferred disposition rules. Warrant roundup warnings. City vision and values. She had just paid the last ticket and was about to close the laptop when one of these banners caught her eye. Under the heading *City Jobs*, the notice read: *Parking Enforcement Officer opening. Click to apply.*

Jane clicked it just for kicks. A new window opened with a brief online application.

Oh, what the hell, she thought. At least she'd be able to hit the streets with her first job application of the day out of the way. Her résumé sure didn't seem to be drawing any interest.

She typed her future name into the application just to see how it would look: Jane Cummings. She liked it. But they had been engaged for only a week now, she reminded herself, and it wasn't officially her name yet. She reluctantly changed it back to McKinney. Then she entered her birth date: January 21, 1973.

"Nineteen seventy-three."

When she said it aloud, it seemed so damn long ago already. Another era even. A time you'd tell today's youth about as they sat slack-jawed with dumbfounded disbelief at all the things you had had to get by without. Like iPhones and Snapchat. But who needs any of that crap anyway? Jane wondered. Give her real letters to keep in a box, not an e-mail on some hard drive. Give her back the excitement of a dial tone, the kitchen cord stretched around the corner and under the bedroom door as she fell asleep on the phone with her first true love, whose name she couldn't even remember now. It was sometimes strange to think that she had had a driving permit by the time Caleb was born in 1988. Although from this side of the millennium, both those dates seemed equally ancient. And if he didn't care about the age difference, why in hell should she?

Jane finished the application, pressed Submit, closed her laptop, and tossed the paid tickets into the kitchen trash. She doubted she'd hear anything back about the job, and that was just fine with her. If she never saw another parking ticket, it would be too soon.

❧

Jane spent the day walking the streets of downtown Austin, at a loss for what to do.

She had been with the same Pacific Northwest insurance company selling individual and supplemental health insurance policies for almost twenty years, but her company had no affiliate in Texas. So here she was, forty years old and in a strange town, looking for work for the first time in two decades. She kept hearing her late sponsor's voice in her head, telling her that sometimes what seemed like lousy luck might just be a blessing in disguise, the universe doing for her what she couldn't do for herself. And hadn't she always found the insurance business to be boring anyway? But she had been good at it. And it had allowed her to pay her mortgage all those years. She'd even earned enough to save a little extra each month in her IRA, all while raising her daughter alone. Her daughter. Just the sound of it in her head brought up a world of pain. It already seemed so long ago—that day when everything in her life had forever changed, that day the phone call came.

She walked for several hours, killing time and thinking about her daughter. She'd catch her own reflection in a building as she passed, and for just the briefest moment, she'd see Melody instead of herself there in the glass. A stab of grief, perhaps even of guilt, would pierce her belly and she'd tell herself that it was just the heat, then silently say the Serenity Prayer and keep on walking, mother and daughter shadowing each other in the hot Austin streets. Once, the likeness was so striking that she stopped and stared at her reflection for a long time, but when she raised her hand to the window to touch her daughter's cheek, a tapping on the glass shattered the illusion, and a man in a necktie was looking out at her from a conference room full of suits, waving her away as if she were some insane street woman interrupting their business.

She finally worked up enough courage to stop outside the Jackson McFey Insurance Annex building. This time she paused and intentionally looked into the mirrored doors to ask Melody to wish her luck. But it was only her reflection that she saw now, once again alone. Her blouse had come untucked and a strand of hair was hanging in her face. She tucked them both back and entered the cool, dim lobby.

The only sounds inside were the whoosh of air-conditioning

and the gentle clack of her ballet flats on the worn marble floors. It seemed to be a place long abandoned. She looked at the directory, found the floor number, and entered the elevator. When it stopped, she stepped off and followed the sound of laughter to a reception desk on an otherwise empty floor, where a young man was talking on his mobile phone. As Jane approached, he glanced at her with an annoyed expression, swiveled in his chair to face away from her, and kept on talking. Jane stood there for several minutes, feeling uncomfortable, before she finally crossed to the small seating area to wait.

"Hello. Excuse me. Can I help you?"

Jane looked up. She'd drifted off for a moment. She stood and approached the reception desk again and handed the young man her résumé.

"I hope so, yes. I'm Jane McKinney. I recently relocated from Washington State and my company said you might have a sales territory opening up. I've sent a few messages, but I'm not sure if I even have the right e-mail address."

He took her résumé and set it on top of a stack of other papers without even looking at it. "I'll pass it on to human resources," he said. "But we're actually closing the office here in another two weeks, so things are a little, you know, crazy right now. Maybe you could check back in a couple months with the main office in Houston."

"Houston," Jane repeated, sighing.

"Tell me about it. They offered me a position, but there's no way I'm dealing with that humidity. Austin's bad enough."

❧

"Howdy, Jane!" the familiar voice called.

Jane stopped midway across the parking lot and looked up at Mr. Zigler. He was sitting on a lawn chair set atop one of the beer delivery trucks, wearing sunglasses and no shirt, the thick hair on his oiled chest glistening in the sun.

"How about this weather?" he asked.

"I do believe I miss the rain," Jane said, feeling the heat waft up from the blacktop.

"Nonsense," he said. "This is paradise."

"Yeah, right," Jane replied. "If it gets any hotter, maybe this blacktop'll melt and you can dive off that silly truck and go swimming in it."

Mr. Zigler laughed. "It's asphalt."

"What's that?" Jane asked.

"You ain't far from right. Used to be blacktopped, but the trucks kept sinking into it. Asphalt's better. People think they're the same, but they're not."

Jane smiled and was about to walk on when he pointed to the deli box in her hand.

"That for me?"

"No," she said. "You know it isn't."

"Shit," he said. "You can't blame a man for wishin'." Then he thumbed his glasses up on his nose and sat back in his chair. "If you're looking for that boyfriend of yours," he called as Jane walked away, "I fired him for drinkin' on the job."

Jane just laughed and kept on walking.

She found Caleb in the warehouse, off-loading cases of beer from a pallet. He didn't notice her right away, and she stood watching him work. He wore a simple white T-shirt that he had sweat through and it was clinging to his back. She could see his lean muscles working beneath the wet cotton as he hefted the heavy cases onto the stack. She noticed how his jeans hung low on his waist, and she worried that all this laboring in the heat was causing him to lose weight.

When he saw her, he froze and smiled at her over the case

of beer cradled in his arms. "Well, aren't you a cool drink of something to look at."

"That's funny," she replied, "because I was actually just getting all hot and steamy standing here watching you."

Caleb set the case down and wiped the sweat from his brow with his forearm. "How'd you get past old Mr. Zigler?"

"I told him I was in love with him, even though I'm marrying you."

Caleb laughed and stripped off his gloves. "Get over here and let me kiss you."

He pulled Jane to him, wrapped his arms around her, and laid a passionate kiss on her grinning mouth. The taste of salt on his lips and the sweet smell of his sweat turned her on more than a little.

"I've been thinking about you," he said, resting his forehead against hers.

"You have? In what way?"

They were so close she couldn't see his face, but she saw the flash of a smile in his green eyes.

"In every possible position and way," he said.

Jane dropped her jaw, pretending to be shocked. "You dirty, dirty man, you."

"You wanna hear a confession?" he asked.

Jane nodded. "They're my favorite things to hear."

Caleb looked around, then leaned his mouth to her ear and whispered, "The other day I thought about you so much I had to go into the storeroom alone just to get some relief."

Jane's jaw really did drop this time. "Caleb, tell me you didn't."

He grinned as if he had been caught doing something naughty and was torn between feeling guilty and proud of it at the same time.

"Hey, it's your fault. You're up and gone looking for work by the time I wake up. I miss our morning time."

"It's hardly been worth the bother," she said. "Tomorrow I'll sleep in with you, okay? I promise."

"I can't wait that long," he said, taking her hand and leading her away. "Come with me, sexy girl. Let me show you what I was imagining in the storeroom the other day."

Jane planted her feet. "Caleb, you're working."

"I'm due for a break. And besides, everyone's gone out on their daily deliveries already."

Jane hesitated, recognizing the mischievous glint in his eye. She held up the deli box. "But I brought you a box lunch."

He took the lunch and set it on the stack of beer cases. "It can wait. I've got a hunger for a different kind of box lunch right now."

As he pulled her toward the storeroom, she followed along, pretending to protest, saying, "If you think objectifying me is sexy, then you've got another think coming, mister. I'm not some teenager that you can—"

No sooner was the storeroom door closed than he had her pressed up against a rack of boxes and had silenced her with a kiss. She felt him unbuttoning her blouse.

"Caleb, what are you doing? The last thing we need is for you to get fired. Stop it."

But even as she said it, she was kissing him back and struggling to find the buckle to his belt. It slipped from her grip as he opened her blouse and pulled down her bra. He had one hand on her breast and the other between her legs now, and she could feel herself already soaking through her panties at his touch. His mouth moved down to her neck, and she looked over his shoulder and down his long, lean back, and she knew she would be powerless to stop him, not that she wanted to. She closed her eyes and heard herself moan. Desperate to feel him, she reached and hooked her fingers in his belt and pulled him toward her. He was bulging against the denim jeans and she needed more than anything to get him out of them and inside her, but for the life of her she couldn't manage to undo that stupid belt.

Finally, he stepped back and unbuckled the belt himself, then dropped his jeans to the floor. The sight of him standing there in that storeroom wearing just his sweaty T-shirt and a huge hard-on drove Jane mad with desire. She kicked off her shoes and unbuttoned her pants, then bent and stripped them off, along with her panties. Caleb was on her before her last foot was even free while he pressed his naked body against hers and picked her up as if she weighed nothing at all. He rested her against the rack of boxes and lowered her gently until he was inside her. Then he lowered her more until there was nowhere left to go, except maybe heaven.

"Oh, God," she heard herself say involuntarily.

She had her legs wrapped around his waist as her feet dangled behind him, her full weight upheld by nothing but her arms draped over his strong shoulders and the rock-hard muscles of his inner thighs. He was warm and hard and huge, and she thought maybe she could sit like that forever.

"Right there, right there," she said, panting. "Don't move."

But she felt his impatient hands gripping her ass, and then her back was free from the shelf of boxes and she was spinning in empty space, moving up and down on a carousel of guilty pleasure as his strong arms held her against his wild thrusts. Everything went white. She heard Caleb's muffled scream of pleasure, coming as if from far away. When the white faded and the room reappeared, they were lying on the cool concrete floor, entwined in each other's arms and panting.

"That was hot," Caleb said after he'd caught his breath.

"Yes, it was. But I wasn't done yet, Mr. Selfish."

Caleb laughed. "Sorry, babe. I'm on the clock. But I'll have all the time in the world to attend to your needs tonight."

Jane brushed the hair away from his green eyes.

"You know something, Caleb," she said, "I never knew I could be so in love with anyone in all my life."

"You sure?" he asked. "Because it isn't too late to take Mr. Zigler out there up on his offer. He's got a house with air-conditioning. And a pool too."

Jane pretended to consider this. "Hmm . . . air-conditioning and a pool, you say? Sounds nice. But tell me this—if it's true, if it really is, then why is he always up sunning himself on that stupid truck in the parking lot when he could be poolside at home?"

"He says he likes to keep an eye on his inventory so it doesn't walk out the door."

Jane pressed her finger playfully on his nose. "That's good advice, fella," she said. "You should keep an eye on your merchandise too."

"Oh, I plan to keep more than just my eye on it," he replied, kissing her with a grin.

A quiet moment passed and Jane looked around at the boxes of booze stacked against the wall. "I guess old Mr. Zigler doesn't have to worry about you running off with his inventory. Do you ever miss drinking?"

"Not really," Caleb said. "Why do you ask?"

"I don't know. Working around it all the time, I guess. Here at the warehouse. In the clubs where everyone's getting lit. It just seems like it's all around, you know?"

"Yeah, well, some people get to have all the fun, I guess."

"But don't you think it's bad?"

"What? Drinking? For me, yes. And maybe for you too, after

seeing you that night back in Seattle." He smiled to let her know he was joking. "But it isn't anyone else's fault my folks were drunks. I say, do whatever gets you off as long as it isn't hurting anyone."

"I agree," she replied. "And what gets me off is you."

"You know what's really bad for you? Look at that there."

Jane lifted her head from his chest and followed his gaze. Apparently, they had knocked several boxes off the shelf during their escapade, and one of them had broken open and was leaking a pool of sticky black soda syrup all over the floor.

"Now, that shit will kill you," Caleb said.

"What? Soda pop? Come on."

"I'm not kidding. Dave dropped one off the back of his truck last week and didn't know it. By the next morning, it had eaten a hole right into the blacktop."

Jane laughed. "Asphalt," she said, correcting him.

Caleb looked at her. "What?"

"It's asphalt," she said. "Some people think they're the same, but they're not."

Caleb shook his head. "What am I going to do with you, Jane?"

"I'll tell you what," she said, kissing him. "You just keep on doing what you're doing with me, and we'll be just fine."

"I see no trouble there," he said, his lips lingering on hers. "But right now I had better get my ass back to work."

"So you just have your way with me in the storeroom and then send me off, is that it?"

"That's right. And you had better be cleaning the apartment in lingerie when I get home too."

"But you haven't bought me any lingerie yet."

"Well, I'll have to fix that, then, won't I?"

After they had dressed and kissed and said good-bye two or

three more times, Caleb let her out and then stayed behind in the storeroom to clean up the mess they had made.

As Jane left she passed Mr. Zigler, now down from his truck and inside the warehouse. He didn't say anything. And she didn't dare say anything either because the knowing smirk on his face made her blush even more than she already was.

Chapter 3

Jane was in line at the grocery store when the e-mail came in on her phone. She read it quickly, then pumped her fist in the air and shouted, "Yes!"

The checker looked up at her. "Good news to start your morning?"

"The best news," Jane replied.

She was so excited to tell Caleb that she sped home and nearly clipped another car while parallel parking. She was juggling both bags of groceries in one hand and sliding her credit card into the parking meter with the other when the neighbor appeared on her balcony in her pink robe like some crazy cuckoo-clock figurine marking Jane's arrival. She lit a cigarette and blew the smoke out her nose.

"Don't you know it's Sunday?"

Jane looked up. "What's that?"

"You have to be stupid to pay the meter on Sunday."

But Jane was in such a positive mood that she smiled and thanked her before heading inside. She climbed the stairs at a run, fumbling with her keys, and entered the apartment in a rush. She had just set the bags on the counter and was turning for the bedroom to wake Caleb when she saw him sitting on the couch with his hair disheveled, as if he'd just gotten up.

"Oh, hi, babe," she said. "I'm glad you're awake because I've got—"

"What are these?" he asked, cutting her off.

He pointed at the coffee table in front of him, where Jane had left out her laptop and her morning ritual of paperwork, including her stack of apartment and home guides.

"They're just my magazines and stuff. Why?"

Caleb picked one up and flipped through its pages. "They're not just magazines. You've got tabs marking your favorite houses in here. Notes about taxes and payments."

"Boy, someone sure woke up on the wrong side of the bed this morning."

"This isn't funny, Jane. What the hell are these for?"

She didn't like being questioned like this, especially about something so trivial. So she turned her back to him and began putting away the groceries. "They're just dreams," she said. She heard him toss the catalog down on the table.

"We talked about this already, Jane. You said you were fine living here as long as we were together."

She slammed the cupboard closed and turned to face him. "I love you, Caleb. You know that. But I hate it here. I hate it. I don't have any room to breathe in this tiny apartment, let alone relax. And the fucking noise drives me mad. You sleep like you don't even hear it, but the stupid music plays all night long, all week long. And don't even get me started on the heat. By noon, you can't even go into the bedroom, it's so hot."

Caleb looked down and shook his head, mumbling, "The truth comes out at last."

"What's that supposed to mean?" Jane asked.

"It means I had no idea you hated living here with me."

Jane rested her hands on the counter and sighed. "I don't hate living with you, Caleb. I just hate this place. Why can't we look at other apartments? My home sale closed. I have some money now."

He stood from the couch and stormed off toward the bedroom. Then he stopped and turned and came back to face her. Jane had never seen him look so angry before.

"You know damn well I signed a six-month lease here, Jane. It was all I could afford. And it probably will be for a while.

Don't forget that I didn't ask you to sell everything and chase after me. You made that choice yourself."

Jane was floored by what he was saying. Did he mean he wished she hadn't come?

"You don't want me here?" she asked.

"I didn't say that."

"Then what are you saying?"

"I'm saying you ran me out of your house and off the island because I was too young. I needed to chase my dreams, remember? Isn't that what you said? Then you come all this way and tell me you love me just the way I am, but now here you are, trying to change me already."

"I'm not trying to change you, Caleb."

"Yes, you are."

"No, I'm not."

"Then what's this?" He reached and smacked the grocery bag with his hand. "We shop at Whole Foods now? Like we're East Austin yuppies or something? The guys I know don't call it 'Whole Paycheck' for nothing, Jane."

"Oh, come on," she said. "Lighten up."

"And don't think I didn't notice that you threw away my dishes and bought new."

"Now you're just being silly," Jane said.

"Silly? Didn't you think to even ask me before you threw my cups away?"

"They were old and they were plastic, Caleb. And besides, you said you got them from Goodwill. Life's too short not to drink out of something nice."

"Damn it, Jane. It isn't about the cups."

"Then what's this about, Caleb?"

He slammed his fist onto the counter so hard that the bag jumped. "It's about me being a man!"

The expression of anger mixed with pain on his face left Jane lost for a response. Silence fell over the small kitchen and she stood staring into his sad eyes. She heard the neighbor's dog barking.

Caleb dropped his head. "I'm sorry," he said. "There's no excuse for yelling at you."

Jane came around the counter and wrapped her arms around him, then rested her head against his chest. "I'm sorry too," she said. "I guess I'm just having a harder time adjusting than I thought I would. And you're right. I did come down here on my own and it isn't fair of me to try and change everything."

Caleb put his finger under her chin and lifted her face so she was looking at him. "I'll make you a deal," he said. "When you find work, and when my lease is up here, we'll go look for a new apartment together, okay? But it's got to be fifty-fifty or nothing. Rent, utilities, everything. I have to pay my own way."

Jane smiled at him cutely. "Can it have a bathtub?"

Caleb nodded. "Yes, it can have a bathtub."

"And a queen bed?"

"You're impossible," he said, grinning.

She rose up on her tiptoes and kissed him. "You're more impossible," she said. "Now do we get to have makeup sex?"

"Makeup sex?" he asked, gently biting her lip.

"Of course. What's the point of fighting if you can't have makeup sex?"

"Well, as much as I hate to reward your bad behavior," he replied, "maybe just this one time."

Caleb bent and picked her up and carried her toward the bedroom. No sooner had her feet left the ground than she remembered the e-mail.

"Wait," she called, "put me down."

"Too late now," he replied.

He had turned sideways to pass through the bedroom doorway with her and she reached out and grabbed the doorjamb and brought him to a halt.

"Oh," he said, looking down at her, "now you want to play like that, huh?"

"No, I mean it. Put me down. I have good news."

"What good news?" he asked.

"Put me down, and I'll show you."

"Fine," he said, backing from the doorway and setting her down. "But I'm holding you to your offer of makeup sex, just so you know."

She hurried to her purse and pulled out her phone. Then she scrolled to the message, opened it, and handed the phone to Caleb. She watched as he scanned it, trying to guess his reaction by the expression on his face. He finished reading and handed her back the phone.

"Isn't it great?" she asked.

"No," he said. "It's stupid."

"What do you mean, stupid?" She held up the phone as if it were some kind of proof that it was anything but stupid. "This is a once-in-a-lifetime opportunity."

"I can't believe you did this without talking to me, Jane."

"You never would have let me, babe."

"That's exactly why you should have asked me," he said. "Is this why you borrowed Mr. Zigler's video camera? You told me you wanted to document my gig for us, Jane. Not for some bullshit reality TV show singing competition."

Jane shook the phone at him. "Caleb, this is an amazing break. You know how hard it is to get chosen for a live, on-camera audition? Well, it's almost impossible. And they picked you."

"There you go trying to change me again."

"I'm not trying to change you, Caleb. I'm trying to help you. Isn't this what you want? To make it. To succeed. To be a real musician."

"Oh, I'm not a real musician now? Why, Jane? Because I don't make a lot of money yet?"

"Come on, babe, you know I didn't mean it like that."

"And you think the people on those shows are real musicians? They're frauds, Jane. They're wannabes. They're not artists. They don't have anything real to say. They're fame chasers. Karaoke kids with good skin and perfect teeth and doting parents who drag them around to these stupid auditions and tell them how great they are. That ain't me, Jane."

"But this is a new show, Caleb. This one is different."

"Why? Just because it has *songwriter* in its name? I saw the flyers too, Jane. It's called *Singer-Songwriter Superstar*. I'm not interested in being a superstar, and anyone who is doesn't know the first thing about what it takes to be a real musician."

"Oh God, Caleb." Jane sighed, dropping her phone back into her purse. "Get off your high horse."

He narrowed his eyes at her. "And what's that supposed to mean?"

She knew she should stop. That she had crossed into territory where sharing her opinions had the potential to do irreparable harm. But she had put so much work into this surprise—learning video editing software so she could send in just the right clip, writing the perfect bio for him—and she had been so excited to see that they had chosen him for an audition, so eager to tell him, that she just couldn't help but be angry.

Jane tried taking a deep breath. "It means it's just an opportunity to get some exposure."

"No, what did you mean, 'get off my high horse'?"

"Nothing, Caleb. Nothing, okay? But just so you know,

there's no law of song that says you have to be broke and struggling all the time to be a real musician."

Caleb walked away from her and stood looking out the window. Several quiet moments passed, and when he spoke again, his voice cracked with emotion. "I see now what this is really about."

"Come on, Caleb. That's not fair."

"No, it's not fair," he said. "But it's true."

Then he went into the bedroom and came out again a moment later, carrying his guitar.

"Where are you going with your guitar?" Jane asked.

"Out," he answered, passing her by.

"But what about our makeup sex?"

He paused at the open apartment door with his back to Jane. Her mind raced to find something to say that might erase the damage that she had done. But before she could, he was gone.

Jane just stared at the door. She thought maybe it would open and he would come back in, that they would apologize to each other, then make love. This had been their first major fight, and she was so overwhelmed with emotions that they seemed to all collide in her chest and cancel one another out so that she felt nothing at all. Eventually, she noticed the bag of groceries still on the counter and finished putting them away, almost in a trance, mumbling to herself that there was nothing at all the matter with Whole Foods.

Then, for reasons she didn't really understand, she began cleaning the apartment. She cleaned the bathroom and the kitchen. She moved the furniture and vacuumed. She washed the windows, even though she knew it was a wasted effort. Hours went by, and still he didn't come home.

She collected their dirty clothes and went down the hall to start a load of laundry. An hour later she went back to put them in the dryer, but her wet clothes were piled on top of the washer, and someone else's load was already spinning in the dryer. When she opened the dryer to see who had bumped her, a familiar pink robe tumbled out and she was hit with the sour odor of warm puppy pee.

"Unbelievable," she mumbled, taking the robe and storming down the hall.

She pounded on her neighbor's door for five minutes, but the only answer was the constant barking that already haunted her dreams. When her hand was tired of knocking and the anger had finally subsided, she went back to the laundry room, threw the robe in the trash, and carried her damp laundry into her apartment and draped it over the furniture to dry.

She replayed their argument as she worked. First she was mad at herself. Then she was mad at him. But by the time she had played it out six or seven times in her head, she felt nothing but sad. There wasn't anything left to clean, so she started again. She made and then remade the bed. Then she finally ran out of steam, sat down on the fluffed comforter, and cried.

∽

They passed without talking like strangers in the night.

Caleb came home late, crawled into bed, and slept with his back to her. Jane rose before the sun and sneaked away with her laptop to do her job hunting from a café. She felt as though they were caught in some kind of childish standoff where the next person to speak would lose the fight.

She walked the town all day, not wanting to go home and face him, not wanting to stop moving and face herself. She had intended to continue her job search, but her confidence was shot, and by late afternoon the count of résumés in her bag hadn't diminished by even one.

When the sun had dropped behind the buildings and the streets had grown shaded and cool, she came upon a kid in a doorway playing a guitar. She stopped to listen. He reminded her of a younger version of Caleb, cool and calm and lost in his song. She reached into her purse and held out a twenty-dollar bill. The kid just smiled and shook his shaggy head and went on playing. She would have been embarrassed if his simple gesture hadn't broken her heart. She remembered when she had first met Caleb, playing that lonely song on that lonely Seattle street. He was right. He did make music because he had something to say, not because he wanted to be some kind of pop star. And she had been wrong to meddle in his career and in his art.

She put her money back in her purse, left the young man playing, and headed home to make peace. She stopped along the way for a box of Caleb's favorite doughnuts, just in case.

❧

Jane was shocked when she walked into the apartment.

The first thing she noticed was how dark and cool it was inside. Then she noticed a loud popping noise coming from the bedroom. She set down the doughnuts and her purse, then went and opened the door to investigate. Caleb was standing on a stepladder, attaching empty egg cartons to the bedroom ceiling with a staple gun. More than half the ceiling was already covered, and it looked as though he had enough egg cartons stacked against the wall to finish the job.

"Oh, hi, baby," he said, pausing with the staple gun in his hand and looking down at her.

"Hi," she said. "What's going on?"

"Well," he said, looking at the egg cartons and scratching his head, "I was watching *Cool Hand Luke*, and I got inspired by

Paul Newman to see how many eggs I could eat. Now I've got to do something with all these empty cartons."

Jane stood looking up at him, wondering if maybe he had finally lost his mind.

"I'm just kidding."

He tossed the staple gun onto the bed and stepped down from the ladder. "Boy, you didn't think I was serious, did you?"

"Of course not," Jane said, laughing. "What would you know about *Cool Hand Luke*? You weren't even born when it was made."

Caleb bent and kissed the top of her head. "And neither were you. Come on and let me give you the tour."

He walked her into the living room and swept his arms out to indicate the dark blue curtains he had hung. "These keep the sun out when it drops below the roofline in the afternoon."

"It feels much cooler already," Jane said.

Caleb smiled proudly. "That's because of this," he said, crossing to the main window and pulling back the curtain.

A window-mounted air-conditioning unit was installed, trimmed out and plugged in, and quietly pumping cool air into the room.

Jane threw her arms around Caleb. "I love you, I love you, I love you."

"Wait," he said. "There's more."

He walked her back into the bedroom and pointed out the curtains there. "I made sure they were thick enough to block some of the noise. The egg cartons are ugly, I know, but Mr. Zigler had a pallet of them at the warehouse from some old Easter deal, and they really do help mute the sound in here. And then I got you this."

He stepped over to her side of the bed and switched on a sound machine. The sound of ocean waves filled the room, and

Jane couldn't have been happier if she were sitting with Caleb on a beach somewhere, sipping on a virgin piña colada.

"And if you get tired of waves," he said, "there's rain and birds and even a waterfall too."

Caleb switched the sound machine off and looked at Jane with a hopeful expression on his face. She knew this was his way of apologizing and that he was waiting to see if she might accept it.

But it's me who needs to be apologizing, she thought, even though her doughnuts now seemed wholly inadequate.

"Oh, Caleb, I love it. All of it. Thank you."

He came to her and wrapped his strong arms around her and hugged her tight. When he pulled away and looked at her, his eyes were sad even though he was smiling.

"I'm sorry, Jane. I never want to yell at you like that ever again. I remind myself of my dad when I raise my voice, and I hate it. I promise to try and do better."

"No," she said, shaking her head, "it's me who should be sorry. I never should have been so ungrateful about this place to begin with. And you've been so kind to not even charge me rent while I'm looking for work. But mostly, I'm sorry about meddling in your business and sending your tape to that silly show. I just wanted to do something for you, you know? I should have asked first. Can you forgive me?"

When she finished talking, he didn't answer right away, but stood there instead, just looking deep into her eyes. Then he said, "I decided I'm going to do it."

"The audition? Really? Are you sure?"

"I'm sure," he said, nodding.

"What changed your mind?" she asked.

"Do you remember when you told me what your friend Grace had said? In Paris. She asked you what would you do if you weren't afraid, or something like that."

Jane nodded, remembering it clearly.

"Well, I asked myself that same question, and the answer is, if I weren't afraid, I'd do the audition. You were right. I have nothing to lose. And being on a show, or being discovered or whatever, none of that has to change one thing about who I am or what I do with my music."

Jane reached up and took Caleb's cheeks in her hands, then planted a long, slow kiss on his lips. "I love you. You're a wise and sexy man, and I love you."

"Does this mean we get to have that makeup sex now?"

She nodded. "That's exactly what it means." Then she saw Caleb's eyes widen at something he saw over her shoulder.

"Hey," he said, "are those Gourdough's doughnuts?"

"Yes. They were going to be my peace offering."

"Did you get a Funky Monkey?"

"Three. And a Fat Elvis and a Mother Clucker too."

"Oh, this is on," he said, stepping past her.

"Oh my God," Jane said, shaking her head and following him from the bedroom. "We're not even married and the honeymoon is officially over, I guess."

"Why would you say that?" he asked, lifting the lid on the box of doughnuts.

"Because you just passed up sex with me for doughnuts."

"No, not for doughnuts, baby. For Gourdough's doughnuts."

Jane laughed, then flopped down on the couch and switched on their small TV.

"Well, bring them on over here so we can get fat together. Maybe *Cool Hand Luke* is still on, and we'll see how many doughnuts we can eat without puking."

Chapter 4

Jane hadn't expected a line of people stretched around the block. And judging by the disappointed look on Caleb's face, he hadn't either.

The convention center had been turned into a circus—thirty-foot banners had been draped from the roof advertising the show, media trucks lined the street with satellite dishes extended, and men in yellow "Crew Member" shirts hustled in and out of service doors with cartloads of equipment off-loaded from idling trucks. Several off-duty cops stood in the street, blowing whistles and directing traffic, even though it was at a complete standstill. Jane stood next to Caleb on the faded outdoor red carpet that marked the entry line, fanning herself with the printed e-mail that was their ticket inside.

"What's that thing say my call time is again?"

Jane unfurled the e-mail. "Says ten fifty-five."

"Why do you suppose they do that?"

"Do what?" Jane asked.

"They always make it a really specific number, and then they just make you wait anyway. It's like the doctor's office. Why can't it just be eleven?"

The line inched forward and Jane inched with it. Caleb slid his guitar case up with his foot, sighing. "What time is it now?" he asked.

Jane glanced at her phone. "Eleven twenty."

"Maybe we should just go," Caleb said.

Jane turned to look at him and saw that he was frowning. "Oh, baby," she said. "You're nervous, aren't you?"

"I'm not nervous. I just don't have all day to stand here and wait on these clowns."

"Is Mr. Zigler expecting you at the warehouse later?"

His shoulders slumped and he looked at his feet. "No."

Jane reached and pushed a strand of hair away from his face and tucked it back behind his ear. For just a moment, she could see the boy he had once been.

"You'll be fine. They'll love you. Everyone loves you."

The people in front of them fell quiet, and Jane looked up as a fat man with a clipboard emerged from the building and began walking up and down the line, checking call tickets while shouting instructions like a carnival barker.

"Running a little behind, people," he called, "so have your tickets and your ID ready when you get to the door. They'll have a waiver for you to sign at the desk—nothing special, just says that any part of your audition today can and may be edited in any way and broadcast on national or international television, cable, Internet, or via any other means, whether you're selected to participate in the show or not. But that's why you're all here anyway, right? No biggie. Standard waiver. Nothing special. If you need to read it before signing, please step off to the side so that others can go ahead. I'll say it again, if you don't want to be passed up, have your call tickets and ID ready . . ."

It was thirty more minutes before they made it into the convention center, where they were sorted and grouped and given a colored lanyard. Then they had to wait another thirty minutes before being herded along with the others into a large room. They took seats in front of an enormous projection screen, and a woman told them to pay close attention to the video, then she dimmed the lights. The screen blinked on and a sheet of music appeared and caught on fire. When the paper had burned away, these flaming words remained:

SINGER-SONGWRITER SUPERSTAR

The video went on to explain the show.

Today they were filming acoustic or a cappella auditions in front of their panel of five music industry executives. The judges would vote with thumbs-up or thumbs-down, and each artist needed a perfect score of five thumbs-up to advance. The winning artists from each city would then be flown to Los Angeles the following month to participate in the show, where they would compete against the other acts for America's votes and a half-million-dollar recording contract. The acts could be solo artists or duos but had to perform only original material.

When the video finished, they were hustled through another door just as a new group was being ushered in behind them. It reminded Jane of livestock being moved at the fair. Next, they were corralled into a windowless room and asked to sit and wait again. Caleb leaned forward with his elbows resting on his knees and his chin resting on his hands, an unnatural pose for him. Jane sat beside him and gently rubbed his back. She wanted to encourage him somehow, if she could only find the right words, but she decided that maybe it was best to just let him feel whatever he was feeling.

Jane looked around the room. You could tell the musicians from their families because the musicians were all nervous. Some had their heads bowed. Others were silently mouthing their lyrics, as if worried they might forget them. A few cocky ones were bouncing around and jabbering on about how they couldn't wait to get to the live show. One nervous punk rock girl with a black lace dress and sparkly red shoes had a large plastic clock hanging around her neck, and she kept holding it up in front of her face and closing one eye and looking at it, as if she might be late for something.

Everyone froze when the door opened.

An energetic man entered and called for all the musicians to come with him. Caleb stood and picked up his guitar.

Jane threw her arms around him. "I'm proud of you."

"But I haven't done anything yet," he replied, kissing the top of her head.

She pulled back and looked into his green eyes. "Yes, you have."

Caleb smiled at her and she knew that he would be just fine. He glanced back before leaving, and Jane gave him two thumbs up. He grinned and walked through the door.

Several minutes later, a woman came and took the family and friends out to an area not far from the soundstage marked off with yellow ropes. She ordered them to silence their cell phones and be quiet. Several LCD monitors showed what the stage looked like on camera, and Jane had to admit that it was a slick set—the panel of judges sitting in an elevated and ornate theater box looking down on the polished and gleaming stage backed by a wall of old-fashioned bulb lights that spelled out the show's name. But when Jane looked away from the monitor, the perfectly framed camera shot disappeared and she saw it for the illusion that it was—the walls propped up by ugly metal stands, the flimsy false ceiling hung from wires, the makeup artists standing just off camera with their powder and brushes ready. So this was what you didn't see on TV.

"Everyone quiet on the set! Three, two, one, rolling."

Even though they could see the actual stage from where they were standing, Jane and everyone else turned to watch the screens. The young girl with the clock around her neck trotted out onto the stage first. Jane couldn't believe it, but she was actually chewing bubble gum.

"Well, hello," one of the judges said. "What's your name, young lady?"

"Amanda," she said meekly. "But people call me Panda."

"Okay, Panda," the judge said. "You don't happen to have the time, do you, dear?"

She shook her head no, and all the judges laughed. Her cheeks turned as red as her shoes, and she looked down at her clock and then at the stage. She was obviously nervous.

"Where are you from, Panda?"

"Selma, Texas."

"And you're going to sing a cappella for us today?"

"Yes, sir."

"Well, you've got five pairs of ears here dying to hear it."

The girl was still looking down at the stage as she took the gum from her mouth and wedged it behind her ear. Then she began to quietly hum. When she finally looked up, her mouth opened wider than any mouth Jane had ever seen, and she let loose a note that shook the house. The song she sang was almost operatic, and Jane could hardly understand a word, but the emotion of it was unmistakably beautiful. While she was singing, her crazy clothes and her clock seemed to fade away with her shyness and she was transformed into something else entirely, as if she belonged to her voice rather than it belonging to her, just a red pair of shoes to carry it around and a clock to tell it when to sing.

As soon as she finished her song, she looked down at the stage again, so she didn't even see the five thumbs that turned up. The judges held them there until she did finally lift her head, and when she saw them, both hands leaped to cover her mouth, and she looked as if she might cry.

"Congratulations, young lady," a judge said. "You're going to the City of Angels, where that voice of yours belongs."

"Thank you, thank you," she said, her grin so big she looked to be all teeth. "I can't believe I'm going through." Then she turned and left the stage, and only her wad of pink gum that had fallen from her ear while she was singing remained. A stagehand scurried out and collected the gum, then carried it off cradled in his hands as if it might be precious.

When the judges had finished chattering about her, and after the handler had called again for quiet, an awkward pair of twins stepped out onto the stage with matching ukuleles.

Jane wondered how she had missed them in the other room. They were each at least six and a half feet tall and as thin as fence posts, their hair thick and as blond as straw. They gave their names as Buford and Billy-Ray, and their accent was so thick Jane could hardly understand them. One of the judges asked them where they were from, and they answered in unison.

"Sir," they said, "we're from L.A."

The judge laughed. "Come on, if you two are from Los Angeles, then I'm from Mars."

"Not Los Angeles," the one drawled. "The other L.A. You know, Lower Alabama."

"That's right," the other added. "Down around Mobile."

Jane couldn't help but chuckle.

"Okay, boys," one of the judges said. "Let's hear it."

They had hardly begun playing their ukuleles and singing before the judges all turned aside and shook their heads, squinting as if they were in pain. And Jane could understand why. The twins were terrible. So terrible, in fact, that she wondered if they hadn't come with hopes of their audition making it into the show just for the shock value of it. The judges all stuck out their thumbs, pointing down, of course, but the boys kept on playing anyway.

"Enough, enough!" the main judge cried. "Stop already."

They stopped and blinked up at the judges as if stupefied. "We could play somethin' else," one of them said.

"I think not," the judge replied. "We've heard too much."

"Maybe jus' a little gospel piece we wrote together?"

The judges all shook their heads, but the boys began pluck-ing their ukuleles and humming anyway.

"Will someone get them off the stage, please?"

Two handlers appeared and took the twins by their bony elbows and led them off. They never did stop playing, and Jane could hear the sound of their ukuleles fading across the audito-rium until a door slammed somewhere and shut the sound out. When Jane looked back to the screen, Caleb was already out in front of the judges. He was standing center stage with the guitar she had bought for him in his hand, and he looked so at home and perfectly made for the setting that she would have sworn he'd always been standing there, and that they'd designed and built the entire set around him.

"Tell us your name and where you're from, fella."

"Caleb Cummings," he said simply. "Seattle."

"Seattle? We were just up there."

"Well, I'm here in Austin now."

The woman next to Jane nudged her with an elbow. "This one's really cute," she said.

"I know," Jane replied. "And he's all mine."

"And how old are you, Caleb?" the judge asked.

"Twenty-four," Caleb answered. Then he cocked his head and scrunched his brow as if he were thinking. "Wait. Today's the thirty-first, isn't it? Today's my birthday. I'm twenty-five."

Jane almost had a heart attack. How had she forgotten his birthday? She had even made a note of it back in the spring, when she had signed him up for his health insurance.

"Happy birthday, then," the judge said, chuckling. "I like a guy who doesn't take himself so seriously. And it says here in the bio you sent us that you're a synesthete."

When Caleb nodded but didn't say anything, Jane was a lit-

tle worried that maybe she shouldn't have mentioned that part
in the bio she wrote for him. That maybe it was private. She
silently scolded herself for writing something so personal but
then forgetting his birthday.

"Did you know Billy Joel has synesthesia?"

"No, sir, I didn't know that."

"He does. And so did Duke Ellington, I believe. How did
you learn about your condition?"

"I think of it as a gift," Caleb said. "Not a condition."

"Okay. And how did you learn about your gift then?"

"I told my fourth-grade teacher that I hadn't been doing
my homework because I'd been up at night writing music. She
didn't believe I knew how to write music, so she asked me to
bring it in and show her, so I did."

"And how did she know from your music that you had synesthesia?"

"She didn't, but the counselor she sent me to did."

"And how did the counselor know?"

"He had an uncle with it. He guessed it because my music
was all written out in crayon lines of color instead of notes."

A female judge at the end of the panel was staring at Caleb
through narrowed eyes as he spoke, as if he might be lying. "And
are you seeing any color now?" she asked. "As we sit here and
talk to you?"

"Yes, ma'am," he answered. "I'm seeing yellow."

"And why are you seeing yellow?"

"Because that's the color of this giant light you've got pointing in my face."

All the judges laughed except her.

"Well, then, young man," the middle judge said, "let's hear
what you've got for us."

Caleb draped the guitar strap over his head, took the pick

from the frets, and began playing. It was a catchy melody that
Jane hadn't heard before, and it built layer on layer until it was
ringing loud from his guitar to fill the set with sound. Then he
fell to strumming and began to sing. His voice was crisp and
clear, and it resonated through the auditorium in a way that was
hard to describe. Not nasal at all, but somehow throaty and rich
and pure. And then he hit the chorus and broke into a falsetto
that made Jane shiver, it was so beautiful.

> *I love you will never cross my lips*
> *'Cause it isn't ever really true.*
> *And if you'd never said it, honey*
> *I might not feel so blue.*

The judges looked at one another and nodded. Jane closed
her eyes and said a quick little prayer.

"I think I love this one," the woman next to Jane said.

"I love him too," Jane mumbled.

When Caleb finished, he let the guitar fall against his chest,
suspended by the strap, and he clawed both his hands through
his hair to pull it away from his eyes. Then he stared right at
the judges with a sincere but stoic expression, looking to Jane
like some sexy Roman warrior in the center of the Colosseum,
gazing up to Caesar for his fate. The five thumbs came up from
the judges and a huge smile erupted on Caleb's face. Then the
female judge on the end slowly turned her thumb down, and
Jane heard herself shout, "No!"

The handler waved erratically at Jane to get her attention,
holding a finger to his lips and signaling for her to keep quiet.
When she looked back to the screen, the judges were arguing,
and Caleb was standing there tight-lipped and gently nodding,
as if he had expected it to go this way all along.

"Sorry, young man," the middle judge finally said. "I think most of my fellow judges up here would agree that you have a unique style and an amazing voice. And you're obviously a very talented songwriter too. But unfortunately, it has to be a unanimous decision. The answer for you is no."

"Thank you for your time," Caleb said. Then he walked off the stage with his shoulders pulled back and his head held high.

Jane was so heartbroken and so proud of him at the same time that she forgot they weren't supposed to leave the viewing area until the last act in their group had performed. She rushed right through the yellow rope and knocked down the stanchions that held it up, ignoring the sound of them clattering on the floor behind her as she ran around to the stage exit and caught up to Caleb, then threw her arms around his neck and kissed him.

He was obviously embarrassed, because when she pulled her lips away to look at him, he just looked away sadly. "I forgot it was my birthday."

"I know," Jane said. "I forgot it too. I'm sorry. But Caleb, you did so great. I loved it. Everyone loved it. And don't worry about that stupid bitter-beer-faced judge. She's probably just upset because you reminded her of some guy who dumped her sorry ass in high school. Let's get out of here and go celebrate."

Caleb smiled and nodded, then took her hand as they walked toward the exit.

"You know what I wanna do?" he asked when they were midway across the auditorium. "For my birthday, I mean."

"We can do anything, sweetie. Anything at all."

"I wanna go to the water park."

"The water park?"

"Yeah. My aunt used to take me on my birthday. I think there's one in New Braunfels that's supposed to have a six-story slide that you go doubles down."

Jane squeezed his hand in hers. "You're just a big adorable kid, aren't you?"

"Hey," he said. "I'm twenty-five."

～

The thermometer in Jane's car read 107 degrees when they arrived, and she believed it. After cooling off in the wave pool and making two trips around the lazy lagoon on the kiddie canoe, Jane finally plucked up the courage to tackle the six-story drop from the park's highest slide, the one that Caleb had been itching to ride. The Black Knight, it was called.

Wearing their gift-shop bathing suits and surrounded by hundreds of laughing and screaming kids, they got in line and slowly climbed the steps.

"It really is high," Jane said.

"You going chicken on me?" Caleb asked.

"No," she said, crossing her arms. "I'm not chicken."

A small boy, who couldn't have been more than ten, turned around and looked at her with enormous eyes. "There's nothing to be afraid of, lady," he said with great authority. "My grandmother even did it."

Jane's jaw dropped, but the boy turned back around before she could respond. "Did he just compare me to his grandmother?"

Caleb at least attempted to contain his laughter, which Jane appreciated.

When they reached the platform at the top, Caleb took a two-person inner tube from the pile and led Jane to the launch line, where they stood looking down the mouth of the slide.

"Hold on a minute," the man said. "Okay, now go."

Jane panicked and stepped aside.

Caleb waved her back. "Oh, come on, baby. You can do it."

Jane stood her ground and shook her head. She had always

been fearful of heights, and six stories up a rickety old water-slide counted as heights to her. She stood there for at least a full minute, refusing Caleb's pleas to return to the slide, until the children in line grew restless and pressed forward, chanting, "Go, lady, go! Go, lady, go!"

"See," Caleb said. "Even they want you to go."

"I'm not taking orders from a bunch of kids," Jane said.

The man working the slide laughed and shook his head. He'd seen this before. He pointed to a tiny girl anxiously waiting in line and called her forward. "Sweetie, would you show this nice lady how easy it is?"

The little girl grabbed an inner tube, stepped up, and launched herself down the slide without a moment's pause. All Jane could see were her tiny legs and waving feet disappearing around the corner along with her happy scream.

Two more child demonstrations and a pep talk from Caleb later, and Jane was finally ready. She felt her heart thudding in her chest as Caleb counted down from ten. She decided to put her trust in him, and in the children, and in the engineers who had built this devil ride. When he said, "Go," she dove with him—racing down into the blue blur, whipping around turns, rising and then dropping, faster now, steeper, and she felt the cool spray of water, the whoosh of air, and she heard her own cries of joy echoing in the tube behind them as they launched out into the air and landed in the pool with a splash.

She was clinging to Caleb's shoulders and laughing when they surfaced.

"That wasn't so bad, was it?" he asked, spitting water.

"Let's go again!"

They rode the Black Knight six more times before Jane had had enough. Then they bought hamburgers and onion rings and an enormous strawberry milkshake each, and sat with them in the cool shade of the gazebo, beneath the magic mist machine, and ate and laughed and watched the children playing in the pools just beyond.

"I'm sorry they didn't have any birthday cake," Jane said.

Caleb popped another fry into his mouth. "That's okay. I think I'm getting fat."

"Yeah, right," she said. "You're sitting down and I can still see your abs."

He stood and inhaled deeply, sticking his belly out like a Buddha. Then he rubbed it against Jane's cheek. "Does this make me look fat?"

"No," she said, trying not to laugh and pushing his belly away from her face. "It makes you look pregnant."

Caleb exhaled and dropped back into his chair. Then he looked at Jane with a mischievous smile on his face. "I'd like to see what you look like pregnant," he said.

"Come on, Caleb. We already talked about this."

"No. We already talked about how you don't want to talk about it. But we never really talked about it. Don't all these cute kids running around here make you want one?"

"No," Jane said. "They maybe make me want to have a friend with kids. You think it's easy, but it isn't. It's hard work raising a child. You have no idea."

"But you were alone when you raised Melody. You're not alone anymore, Jane."

The very mention of Melody's name brought tears to Jane's eyes. She felt silly about it, embarrassed even. As if she should be over it by now. But she would never be over it, and maybe only a grieving mother could understand that. She turned away so Caleb wouldn't see her crying, and she watched a little girl feeding ice cream to her younger brother.

Caleb leaned forward and took her hands in his, waiting for

her to look back at him. When she did, there was nothing but love and understanding in his green eyes.

"I know it still hurts, baby," he said. "And I won't ask you to talk about it. But I want you to know that I'm here to listen if you ever do want to talk. All right? I'm a good listener."

"I know you are," she told him, nodding.

He smiled. "I promise I won't mention kids again, okay?"

Jane reached and placed her hand on his sweet cheek. The sounds of the children faded to just a beautiful murmur, and she and Caleb sat like that for several quiet moments—she with a hand on his warm cheek, he smiling at her with his kind eyes—and she knew that if she ever did want to have another child again, it would be with him. She wanted to tell him so, but the silence seemed too perfect to spoil with words.

When the moment had passed, the noise faded back in and Jane returned her gaze to the kids playing in the pool. She picked up her milkshake and polished it off.

"Just so you know," she tossed out, "if you ever do want to bring up us having a kid again, mister, then you had better start planning a wedding."

❧

The sun had set by the time they finally left the water park, and Jane stretched her legs out and relaxed into the passenger seat, thankful that Caleb had offered to drive.

Her muscles ached in that wonderful summer way; her skin was flushed and pink and warm. The smell of chlorine in her hair took her back and reminded her of some fleeting time when she'd been sixteen or seventeen and everything that lay ahead of her had yet been empty road, limited only by her imagination, all the endless possible futures, and where that road might lead. She glanced over at Caleb. He was looking ahead and lost in his own thoughts. For the first time in my life, she mused, I don't think I'd go back. She wouldn't risk one wrong turn that might lead her somewhere other than here. Here now with him.

She rested her head back and turned to look out the side window at the dark hills and the silhouettes of cedar trees sliding past. She must have napped, because her phone vibrating against her makeup compact in her purse startled her awake. Caleb had the radio playing softly, and the sky was darker, with a crescent moon riding now just above the hills. She reached in and fished her phone from her purse. The bright light of its screen momentarily blinded her, and then her eyes adjusted and she read the first line of the e-mail she had just received.

Caleb slammed on the brakes when she screamed. He held out his arm to keep her in her seat, a gesture Jane would have thought only mothers did instinctively.

"Is everything okay?" he asked.

"You made it!" Jane shouted. "Oh my God, you made it."

"What do you mean?"

"I just got the e-mail. You made the show, Caleb! You're going to Los Angeles, you superstar you."

"Let me see that," he said.

"You had just better look at the road and drive, buddy. I need you to live long enough so I can cash in on all your new-found wealth and fame."

"Then you read it to me," he said, obviously excited.

"Only if you promise to make love to me as soon as we get home," she replied, clutching the phone to her breast.

He put the blinker on and drifted onto the shoulder.

"Hey, what are you doing?"

"I'm pulling over."

"But why are you pulling over?"

"So I can read the e-mail myself, and then make love to you right here in the car."

Chapter 5

I thought I told you I fired him for drinking on the job."

Mr. Zigler had moved his chair down from the beer truck and was reclining in the shade just beneath the open warehouse door. As Jane approached, he reached and turned off his radio, then picked up a spray bottle and misted himself.

"What happened to paradise?" Jane asked, nodding toward the truck in the parking lot.

"Shit," he said, "this is too hot even for me. And my wife's worried I'm getting skin cancer. Says she doesn't want me to die. Which surprised the hell out of me, because I thought she'd been trying to poison me with her cooking all these years."

"I didn't know you were married," Jane said.

"Hell, neither did I for the first few years. That turned out to be a problem. But seriously, we've been hitched now thirty-two years and there's nobody on God's good earth I'd rather come home to. Speaking of which, when are you and Caleb tying the knot?"

"Oh, I don't know. We've talked about it a lot, but it's hard to plan anything with this L.A. music show coming up. That's kind of all we have time to think about right now."

Mr. Zigler nodded. "I'm sure gonna miss that kid around here. He's a good worker, and it'll take me two guys to replace him. But I knew when I hired him on it'd be temporary. I've got a few guys here who've been with me better'n ten-plus years. But Caleb's meant for bigger things. You can see it in his eyes. You just can. When do y'all leave?"

"He leaves next Tuesday."

"You're not going with him?"

Jane shook her head. "He wants me to, but I can't."

Mr. Zigler raised his eyebrows, as if to ask why not.

"It's just . . . well, I've got to find work. They're covering his expenses but they don't pay him anything. Not unless he makes it through this first round of eliminations and onto the live show. They pay him then. That's why he's been working all this overtime with you. But anyway, you don't care about all this. Is he in the back?"

Mr. Zigler turned in his chair and looked back into the warehouse, as if to check. "I think he's out with Brad doing deliveries all afternoon. Bars are stocking up for Hot Austin Nights."

Jane saw him eyeing the sack in her hand. She smiled and handed it to him, saying, "There are two sandwiches in there. I expect Caleb to get at least one of them when he gets back."

He smiled guiltily and took the sack. Jane heard the crinkle of a bag opening as she walked back to her car.

"And one of the bags of chips is for him too," she called to him over her shoulder.

❧

Jane woke before Caleb and lay in bed, looking up at the egg cartons on the ceiling and listening to the waves from her sound machine. It dawned on her that this was their last weekend together before he left.

Weekends were her favorite because Caleb usually didn't have to work, and she didn't have to feel guilty about not job hunting. It was their uninterrupted time to spend together— walking Lady Bird Lake, seeing matinee movies, or even just staying in bed all day and making love. Some nights, if Caleb didn't have a gig, she'd go out with him into the street and sit nearby with her arms wrapped around her knees and listen to him play for tips. He said he did it mostly just for inspiration, but it was always fun to go spend the money in his guitar case on a late-night ice cream cone or an early breakfast at an all-night diner. Jane wondered what she'd do to fill the time when he was gone.

She unplugged her sound machine and took it with her into the bathroom for her ritual Saturday-morning shower. She lit a vanilla candle, turned on the shower, and looked at her reflection in the mirror. Faint stretch marks from when she had been pregnant with Melody remained on her belly. She remembered how frightened and abandoned she had felt when Melody's father had taken off and left her to deal with her pregnancy alone, just shortly after she had begun to show. These feelings had lain dormant for many years, and she guessed that Caleb's leaving was bringing them back up. But she knew Caleb was different. Oh, so very different. But she also knew that although she had accepted her stretch marks long ago, she wasn't ready yet to face the other scars that remained unseen beneath the surface.

Jane opened the cabinet and removed her ingredients. Next, she took out the small mixing bowl and the whisk. She uncapped the coconut oil and poured it into the bowl. Then she added sugar and the used coffee grounds she saved every day. She whisked this odd mixture into a sticky brown sludge and then used her fingers to smear it all over her naked body. She was almost completely covered in the strange concoction, crouched and rubbing it onto her calves, when the bathroom door opened.

"Hey, babe, you mind if I . . . ah . . . sorry."

"Caleb! Don't you know how to knock?"

He had his hand covering his mouth, and she could tell he was trying not to laugh. "Sorry, babe. I heard the shower and just assumed you were in there. I have to pee."

"Well, go pee somewhere else."

"But this is the only bathroom."

"You're telling me?" she asked, standing there exposed, wearing only her coffee rub.

He smiled and slowly backed from the bathroom. He had the door nearly shut when he opened it again and leaned in. She could see the question on his lips before he even asked it.

"I saw it on *Dr. Oz*," she said. "Now get out!"

He had made them both a big breakfast by the time she joined him in the kitchen. An apology of sorts, she assumed. She didn't say a word as she pulled a stool up to the small bar that they used for their table and waited for him to serve her. He laid everything out and then sat down and joined her.

"I thought you had to use the bathroom," she said.

"Oh, I did, but I peed already in the sink."

She slugged him on the shoulder. "Caleb! Tell me you didn't."

"Okay, I didn't."

"Did you, though? Because that's a deal breaker if you did."

He laughed. "Of course I didn't. I ran downstairs to the convenience store. Here, I got you some oranges too, because he wouldn't let me use the restroom unless I bought something."

"How romantic of you," she said sarcastically. "Did you brew coffee?"

"I did. Would you like some?"

"Yes, please."

"Okay, but only if you promise to drink it and not wear it."

He burst out laughing at his own joke, and Jane shoved him so hard he fell off his stool.

"You set me up for that, you jerk."

He picked himself off the floor, still laughing, and poured them each a cup of coffee. "Seriously, though," he said, setting her coffee in front of her, "how was the Dr. Oz skin treatment?"

Jane buttered a piece of toast, still refusing to make eye contact with him. "Fine," she said. "He claims it only takes seven minutes, but he doesn't say anything about the thirty-seven minutes it takes to clean the shower after."

"But does it work?"

"I don't know," she said. "I can't tell yet."

Caleb moved around behind her and leaned in to brush his lips against her neck. "Let me have a look," he said softly. "Maybe I can tell."

Jane tried to ignore him, still buttering her toast.

"Mmm . . ." he said, kissing his way around her neck. "Still not sure, though. Maybe I need a better look. Maybe here. Oh, yes. I think this Dr. Oz of yours must be a real genius. I can't remember ever seeing skin so smooth."

"I didn't put it on my ear, you goofball."

"How about here? I know you put it here."

His lips moved down to her collarbone, and she could feel his thick hair drop into her shirt and tickle her bare chest. The butter was an inch thick on the toast by this time, and Jane set it down along with the knife and leaned her head back.

"I was wondering if it worked a little lower," she said.

Caleb spun her around on her stool to face him. Then he kissed her. When his lips left hers, he moved lower, pulling the loose T-shirt down and flicking his tongue over her nipple.

"Maybe here?" he asked.

"Yes, maybe right there."

"I wonder if this magic potion works everywhere," he said, moving his mouth to her other breast. "Maybe I need to inspect you thoroughly so we can give this TV doctor of yours an honest appraisal."

"Maybe you're all talk," Jane said.

Caleb lifted her shirt over her head, and Jane reflexively raised her arms. He tossed the shirt aside, then cupped his hands beneath her chin and leaned in and kissed her, and soon all she could think about was him. His sexy smile; his haunted eyes. His lips. His body. Oh, dear Lord, his body. And those hands. Hands that did a real man's work. Hands that made music. Hands that made love to her. Hands that were right now tugging on her shorts.

"What are you doing?" she asked, her voice trembling.

But he pressed a finger to her lips to silence her. Then he continued to pull her shorts free. She lifted herself off the stool slightly to help him, and when she straightened her knees he slipped them free. They landed on the floor next to her shirt. He stood back a moment and looked at her in the light slanting in from the partially drawn curtains. Any other man and she would have been uncomfortable sitting naked on that stool. Not so with Caleb. The way he looked at her, with desire and appreciation in his eyes, made her feel like some kind of prize that he would spend his entire life winning again and again.

He pulled his own shirt off and tossed it down with hers. His skin was golden in the morning light. She could see the striations of muscle between his ribs, the cut of his obliques. Then he pulled his shorts off and stepped out of them. His thighs were long and strong, and she could see between them that he was already swollen for her with his need.

She wanted him on the bed now, and she started to rise from the stool. But he shook his head and stepped toward her and forced her back down. Then he bent and kissed her gently, and when he pulled his mouth away, he dropped down onto his knees before her. She felt his tongue on her inner thigh, his thick hair there too. Then she slid forward on the stool and parted her legs to make room for him to come closer, and she shuddered with pleasure when he did—his tongue now teasing her. He wrapped his arms under her legs and around to grip her thighs, then pulled them apart, working his talented mouth there between them. She opened her eyes and looked down on him, kneeling before her, lost in the intricate details of her most intimate flesh, and she felt for a moment on that stool like a queen on her throne with the world taut and trembling before her, and all her kingdom safe between her legs.

She buried her hands in his thick hair and pulled him up to her mouth. Not because she'd had enough, but because she needed more. He tasted sweet and salty and it drove her mad with desire. He was standing before her now and the stool was high and their waists were at the perfect height. She wrapped her hand around him and felt him pulsing in her grip. Then she reached behind him with her other hand and gripped his ass, pulling him toward her, guiding him to where she needed more than anything else for him to be.

He moaned as soon as he was inside her and so did she. He was gentle and rhythmic at first, but his tempo quickly built. Jane reclined against the short back of the stool and looked down and watched—his quads were flexed, his abs were tightened, and he was hard and long and disappearing inside her with each thrust.

"Fuck, yes," she said. "Just like that."

She felt herself blushing because she never spoke like that. But then Caleb smiled.

"You like that, baby?" he asked. "You want me to fuck you like this?"

"Yes, please. Yes."

He grabbed her thighs and spread her legs farther and drove himself deeper, thrusting like a man in need of relief. She knew she was close when she began to feel weightless and every nerve in her body seemed to scream with pleasure. Then he was driving into her harder and the stool was wobbling and Jane reached her arms out and spread them on the counter behind her, pushing their breakfast aside, and she leaned back on the stool with her arms spread and her legs spread and Caleb rising between her, his chest slick already with sweat, his mouth half-open and moaning, and they looked into each other's eyes and fucked until she heard herself scream—

"Oh God, yes! Yes! Yes! Yes! Don't. Stop. Now."

And then pleasure flooded over her like light and she was speechless and shaking and Caleb must have felt it because he came too. The stool had half tipped, so Caleb lifted her and kicked the stool over, then gently laid her on the floor, their legs and arms tangled and him still inside her. When Jane's heart stopped thudding in her ear, she heard the neighbor pounding on their bedroom wall, her dog barking in the background.

"That woman needs to get laid," Caleb said breathlessly.

"If it'll shut that damn dog up," Jane joked, "then I say you go do it."

"I'll have to do it later, you wore me out."

"Don't you dare, mister," Jane said, kissing him. Then she wrapped her arms around him. "You're all mine."

He scooted slightly on his back, and Jane rested her head on his chest and lay quiet for a minute or so.

"I'm going to miss you, Caleb."

"I'm going to miss you too, baby. But I'm not gone yet."

"No. But you will be soon."

"It'll only be a few weeks."

"An hour is too long. And it's three weeks and two days if you go all the way to the live show."

"You know I want you to come. Why don't you?"

"We talked about this, Caleb. I need to get to work. My savings are draining away. And besides, what would I do all day? Sit around in the hotel and wait for you?"

"I could stay here, then."

"Hell no," she said, lifting her head and looking at him. "This is your big break."

Caleb smiled, brushing her hair away from her eye. "And it was all because of you."

"Don't thank me yet. I'm worried you might hate it."

"I won't hate it," he said.

"Then I'm worried you might love it."

"I love you, you silly freak," he said, laughing. "Now we had better get up off this dirty floor and eat our breakfast."

"But it's cold now."

"How about Magnolia for breakfast, then? My treat."

"I'd like that," she said. "But I'll need to take another shower first."

Caleb laughed.

"What?" Jane asked.

"Nothing."

"You laughed about something."

"You want me to bring in the coffee grounds for you?"

❧

"This is worse than that nail salon you brought me to."

"Oh, zip it," Jane said. "You don't need to pretend to not like it for us. We both know you're secretly enjoying it, and we don't consider you any less manly because of it."

"She's right," the hairstylist said, painting bleach onto another piece of foil. "And you know what they say about those who protest too much."

Caleb just scowled into the mirror. His head was nearly covered now in foil, and Jane had to admit to herself that he did look a little ridiculous. She couldn't contain her chuckle.

"See, I do look like a dolt," he said. "And what's with this damn tinfoil? I swear I'm picking up a Russian radio station."

"That's on the speakers in the salon, silly," the stylist said. "The owner's Ukrainian."

"Think how great highlights'll look on TV," Jane said.

The stylist winked at Jane over Caleb's head. "TV?" she asked. "I had no idea you were going to be famous. We better dye your eyelashes and wax your eyebrows while we're at it."

Caleb shook his head so violently that a few of the foils fell out. He started to rise from the chair, but the stylist laughed and pushed him back down.

"I'm kidding, handsome. Your eyebrows are perfect."

When they finished at the salon, they stopped at Hoffbrau Steaks for an early dinner. The sign said the restaurant had been there since 1934, and by the look of the small space and the worn tables set end to end, Jane guessed they hadn't updated the decor since then either. But for less than fifteen bucks you got a garlic salad, potato wedges, and a grilled rib eye swimming in a pool of lemon butter with free soda bread to mop the butter up, which they both did. After they had eaten, they sat and sipped Diet Cokes and made each other laugh by passing notes back and forth on a napkin with wild guesses about the other oddball patrons eating on their left and right. When the server dropped off their check, they both grabbed for it.

"You bought breakfast," Jane said.

"I know, but I figure if I pay for dinner too, I can expect you to put out later."

"Chauvinist much?" Jane asked, smiling. "I'll tell you what. I'll let you treat, but only if you use this." She tossed a card across the table.

Caleb picked it up and looked at it, obviously confused. "What is this? And why does it have my name on it?"

"It's a credit card I got for you. It's linked to my account."

"But I like to use cash."

"I know you do, but you'll be in a strange city and you'll need something in case of an emergency. I don't want to worry about you. I love you."

Caleb smiled and tucked the card away in his pocket. "I'll only use it in an emergency then," he said, pulling out his cash for the check. "But buying you a twenty-dollar steak is not an emergency. And I love you too."

"I also got you this." Jane opened her purse and slid the box across the table.

"There's more? Wow. I would have gotten highlights in my hair a long time ago if I knew it would have the ladies handing me credit cards and gifts."

"Oh, zip it and open the box, Fabio."

"Let me guess," he said, making a show of struggling with the paper. "Socks for my trip?"

"Yes," Jane said, "because it's so cold in L.A."

He laughed, then opened the box and pulled out the phone. Jane watched for his expression, a little worried that he might feel as if she were trying to put a leash on him.

"I know you don't like phones and Facebook and all that crap, but you might need to start, now that you're going to be famous. And this one does everything. Plus, I wanted you to be able to get ahold of me in case you needed to tell me you missed me or something."

"This is really sweet, Jane. Thank you."

"I programmed my number in already."

"Oh, I've already got your number, babe," he said.

"Turn it on. Go ahead. The button's right there."

Caleb turned it on and the welcome screen lit up. When it faded, the screensaver was a picture of him and Jane, taken with her phone at the water park on his birthday.

"Aw, I love it, honey."

"There are a few others of me in a folder marked Private," she said. "But those are for when we have phone sex."

Caleb laughed so loud the restaurant got quiet. "Now I see why you got me the phone. You want to call and talk dirty to me." Then he smiled at her mischievously and added, "I hope you're ready for a big bill."

❧

"You sure you won't let me drive you to the airport?" Jane stood in the bedroom doorway, watching Caleb stuff his clothes into his duffel.

"You know I'm terrible with good-byes, babe. Plus, why waste all that gas and fight all that traffic when the bus takes me there for a buck?" He cinched his duffel closed and looked up at her. "Baby, why are you crying?"

Before she could respond, he stepped around the bed and wrapped his arms around her. "I'm going to miss you too. But I'll probably get kicked off the show and be home before you know it anyway."

Jane brushed a tear away from her cheek and laughed. "Yeah, right," she said. "You had better not. I bet Mr. Zigler lunch every day for a month that you'd go all the way."

"Now I have no choice but to win," he said. "The way old Zigler eats, that bet could bankrupt you."

He reached and lifted her face to his again, then cupped her cheeks in his palms and kissed her. She felt safe and complete there in his arms—the strength of their connection, the heat of their kiss, the love beating back and forth between their two hearts like a Möbius strip. She knew that the bond they shared would carry them past any obstacles, was worth any temporary inconvenience. She knew it with every neuron firing in her brain, and she knew it with every cell in her body. A hundred trillion tiny voices all screaming, He's the one!

She just hoped she'd still believe it when she was alone.

"Well, I better get moving or I'll miss the bus."

"Okay. I'll come out with you to the stop."

Caleb slung his duffel over his shoulder and picked up his guitar case. "At least I'll have my Jane guitar with me. It always reminds me of you."

"I'm glad," she said, following him from the bedroom. "But that guitar had better be the only thing with a woman's name that those fingers of yours strum while you're away."

They were nearly out the apartment door when Jane ran back to the bathroom for something. "Here, you'll need this."

Caleb looked at the mini bottle she handed him. "Really? Hair conditioner?"

"Yes, you've got to take care of it now that we put highlights in."

He smiled and tucked the conditioner away in his duffel, mumbling, "Why do I suddenly feel like I'm heading for the set of *Glee*?"

The sun had yet to rise and the Austin skyline stood black against a rim of golden light to the east that marked the promise of another coming day. The world just kept on spinning, despite everyone's hopes and fears, or so it seemed to Jane. They crossed the street together and stood at the bus stop.

Caleb took out his new phone and checked the time. "I hope I didn't miss it."

"You want me to just drive you?"

"It's okay. It should be along."

They stood there quietly together, both looking down the empty street to where the bus would come from. Jane felt strangely shy. As if this were the parting at the end of a first date and she didn't know whether to hug him or kiss him or just shake his hand and say farewell. The yellow light of the bus sign grew out of the gloom and was upon them before Jane was ready to even admit that this was good-bye.

The brakes hissed. The door popped open.

Jane threw her arms around Caleb. "I love you, you silly so-and-so. You know that?"

Caleb hugged her back. "I know you do. And I love you, baby. Bunches and bunches."

Then he kissed the top of her head and was gone. She stood and watched him climb the step and feed his dollar into the pay slot. Then he walked to the rear of the bus and sat down next to his guitar and his duffel. His eyes were forward and he looked to Jane like a young man scared to be leaving everything he knew and loved, and determined not to look back and show it.

The motor whirred, then the bus lurched away from the curb. Jane saw Caleb turn and look out the side window at her, his hand pressed up against the glass. Then all she could see was the back of the bus painted with an Austin nightlife public safety service announcement that read: FRIENDS DON'T LET FRIENDS LEAVE ALONE.

Digging in her purse for her keys, Jane sprinted across the street to her car. She jumped in, started the engine, and pulled away, still latching her seat belt. She whipped a U-turn and sped after the bus. She caught up with it half a mile down the street and flashed her headlights. The bus kept going. It turned onto Congress Avenue, where there were four lanes, and she pulled alongside it and laid on her horn. Caleb looked up and saw her and smiled. He reached and yanked the cord for the next stop, and Jane fell in behind the bus.

When the bus stopped, Caleb hopped off with his duffel and his guitar and jogged to the car, tossing them into the backseat before he got in next to her. He smelled like his shower soap and the outside. He looked at her and he was grinning from ear to ear, but he didn't say anything.

Neither did Jane. She just put the car in drive, took his warm hand in hers, and eased back onto the road to take her fiancé to the airport.

PART TWO

Chapter 6

Caleb watched Austin shrink away beneath him.

His heart seemed to remain down there somewhere, tethered to Jane, and he imagined a giant silver cord unspooling from his chest and trailing the plane to California. The feeling came in the form of a song lyric, and he went to write it down before realizing that his notebook and pen were stashed away with his duffel in the overhead bin. He pulled out his cell phone instead, found a notepad app, and typed out the line. It worked, but it wasn't the same.

"Is that in airplane mode, sir?"

Caleb looked up at the flight attendant. "What's airplane mode?"

"There's no cell phone use allowed on the aircraft."

The big man seated next to Caleb leaned into his personal space and tapped the phone's touch screen, navigating options.

"What are you doing?" Caleb asked.

"I used to have this same one."

"Maybe just turn it off," the flight attendant suggested.

"Sorry," Caleb told her, jerking the phone away from the man and powering it down. "I've only flown twice in my life, and this is the second time."

The flight attendant smiled and passed on.

The man next to Caleb let out a belly laugh and said, "Only your second time flying, eh? I hope you're not nervous, because when I was boarding, I think I heard the pilot say the same thing to one of them stewardesses."

The flight attendant reappeared in the aisle. "Excuse me,

sir," she said, addressing Caleb. "You look a little cramped in there. Would you like to move to an exit row where there's more room for those long legs of yours?"

"Yes, please. That would be great."

Caleb unbuckled, and the big man stood to let him out and watched him go with a look of disappointment.

"Thank you," Caleb whispered as he settled into the emergency row seat.

The flight attendant winked at him.

It was a race between the plane and the rising sun, but the sun won, and it was well up and boring a hole in the hazy Los Angeles skies when they landed and taxied to the gate. Caleb already felt a million miles away from Jane, and it seemed strange to him that with the time change there were only a few hours between them. He got out his phone and turned it on, then composed and sent a text:

Landed safe and sound in Tinseltown. Missing you already, baby.

He pocketed his phone and stood to deplane.

"Welcome to Los Angeles," the flight attendant said.

He had expected it to be nicer. Glitzy even, like it looked in the movies. But if LAX was any indication of the city it served, Caleb thought, then the city needed a face-lift. He was on his way to claim his checked guitar when he passed a huge man in a black suit scanning the crowd and holding a sign. Caleb stopped and stepped back to read the sign again.

"I'll be damned," he said.

"Are you Mr. Cummings?" the man asked.

Caleb nodded. "I'm not used to being called Mr. anything, but I guess I am."

"Great. I'll be your ride. Do you have bags checked?"

"Just my guitar."

"Wonderful. I'll accompany you to baggage claim."

The luggage was a long time coming, so Caleb stood at the carousel watching the people milling about. It was a mix of faces the likes of which he'd never dreamed of seeing—the poor and disheveled, curiously unaware; the rich and beautiful with their noses in the air; the glam girls with their heels and their makeup, their knockoff purses clutched in their arms. And many of them kept glancing at Caleb. A few even pointed and whispered. As if maybe he were someone they should know. Then he looked to his right and saw why. His driver was standing beside him with his arms crossed and his mirrored sunglasses on, looking like Secret Service, or maybe private security. Caleb couldn't help but chuckle to himself.

After he had gotten his guitar and opened the case to check that it was okay and to retighten the strings, he followed his escort out to the limo lot and climbed into the back of a black Cadillac SUV. They left the airport and sat in traffic for what seemed like hours, starting and then stopping again. L.A. had its own sound and Caleb leaned back to drink it all in.

The commuters beyond the dark windows, honking horns and revving engines, shouting at one another from their yuppie convertibles. The Cadillac's radio quietly droning on about news of war and Wall Street. The air conditioner blowing. And the huge driver navigating this madness, as relaxed and placid behind the wheel as a man born to the job who couldn't possibly care less about any of it.

He glanced in the mirror at Caleb. "First time in L.A.?"

"Yeah. First time in California."

The man nodded as if he'd suspected so. Then he looked back at the road.

He dropped Caleb off at a studio lot in Culver City and handed him a pass to get inside. He said he'd take Caleb's luggage on to the hotel, but Caleb refused to part with his guitar. Then he decided it was silly to send him with just the duffel, so he took it too and thanked him, then walked on toward the gate with all his possessions and his entry ticket in his hand, feeling like a carpetbagger come to claim a prize.

The guard looked at the ticket and waved him through, mumbling something about Lot B. Caleb followed the signs. Soon he began to see others who seemed to equally not belong there, mostly young people standing about near the studio entrance, trying not to look lost.

He noticed the punk rock girl from his audition and wondered why she hadn't been on his flight. But then he remembered she'd said she was from Selma, and he figured she must have flown out of San Antonio. She was standing by the door, chewing gum and kicking at a weed in the cracked sidewalk with her sparkly red shoes.

"Hi there," Caleb said. "I remember you."

The girl looked up at him. Then she looked around as if to verify that he wasn't speaking to someone else. "You do?"

"You're the singer from Selma with the amazing voice."

She blushed and looked down again. A full half minute later, she said, "I'm sixteen."

Caleb stuck out his hand. "Nice to meet you, sixteen. I'm Caleb."

"Oh, funny," she said, catching the joke late. "My name's Amanda, but people usually call me Panda."

"Well, Panda, do you know where we're supposed to be?"

"A man came by a little while ago and said we should wait here. That's all I know."

"Well, it's more than I know. Thanks."

Caleb set down his guitar, then dropped his duffel onto the sidewalk and sat on it. The girl kicked at the weed.

"I'm not nervous," she said out of the blue. "My stepmom says I should try not to look so nervous—she says it looks bad on camera—but I'm not nervous, I'm just shy."

"Shy, huh?" Caleb asked. "I just figured you were angry."

"Angry? Why would I be angry?"

"Maybe you should ask that weed you're kicking."

She pulled her foot back midkick. Then she stepped over and sat down next to Caleb, and hugged her knees to her chest.

"Are you?" she asked, after a minute or so had passed.

"Am I what?"

"Are you nervous?"

"Yeah," he said. "I'm nervous."

There were at least thirty of them sitting or standing around by the time the big bay door rolled open and a man in linen shorts and a Hawaiian shirt stepped out. He was followed by a small retinue of eager assistants. The man clapped his hands and everyone who was sitting stood, except Caleb.

"Listen up, chuckleheads," he called. "My name is Garth and I'm your producer. Today is going to be a full day with lots of information, so pay attention. A few ground rules first. I'm sure many of you have heard from teachers and parents and other well-meaning sorts of folks that there's no dumb question except the one you didn't ask. That's a lie. Don't ask questions. There's going to be forty of you total here and another twenty of us working with you at any given time, and if you waste one minute with a question, you've wasted one minute times sixty people, and in my world that makes an hour. And you don't want a bill for an hour's worth of production costs, trust me."

He looked to one of his assistants and motioned for her clipboard. He scanned the paper on it and handed it back.

"Douglas Carpenter," he called.

A young man with bad acne and curly red hair stepped forward from the crowd.

"You're excused, Douglas."

"I'm sorry, sir?" the young man said.

"I said you're excused."

"But what does that mean?"

"What did I say about questions? It means you lied about your criminal background on your application, young man, so you're gone. Layla here will take you back to the hotel and arrange for your flight home."

The young man dropped his head, obviously ashamed, and the assistant led him away.

"That's the second rule," the producer said to those who remained. "Don't lie. Not to me, not to any of us, not ever. Third rule is don't spike the cameras. We won't be filming today's orientation, but every other day there will be cameras in your face. Lots of cameras. Including when you're working on your songs at the hotel. Don't look at these cameras. Don't play to these cameras. Just pretend they're not there. Ignore them. Works for me to imagine them to be my wife. But you're all too young yet to understand that. Anyway, don't worry, you'll get used to the cameras and you won't even know they're there."

One of his assistants leaned in and whispered something to him. He nodded. "Where's Caleb Cummings?" he called.

Caleb's heart jumped just a little. He looked up at Panda, and then he looked at the producer and raised his hand.

"Why are you sitting down?" the producer asked.

Caleb pulled his legs up from where he had them stretched out in front of him and stood.

"That's better," the producer said. "Now, do you know what plagiarism is, young man?"

"Yes, sir, I do."

The crowd of contestants was dead silent and the producer stood in front of them, staring at Caleb for what seemed to him like forever. Caleb heard a truck somewhere in the street.

"Well, kid, aren't you curious why I asked you if you know what plagiarism is?" he finally asked. "It's a heavy word."

"Of course I'm curious," Caleb replied. "But you said not to ask any questions, sir."

The producer smiled. "So I did. So I did. Well, the reason you're here is because one of the contestants they originally passed through in Austin decided to get cute and borrow his melody from someone else's Top Forty song."

Then his eyes left Caleb and he scanned the crowd before continuing. "So let that be a lesson to you all. The title of this show is *Singer-Songwriter Superstar*. We won't be covering other artists' hits like all those other shows do, and we sure as shit won't be stealing from other artists' work."

He paused to look at his assistants, as if to be sure he wasn't forgetting anything. Then he clapped his hands again.

"Grab your things, boys and girls, and follow me. I'll give you the tour of the set that will be your home away from home. For how long, nobody knows."

As they fell in with the crowd to follow him into the studio, Panda slid up next to Caleb and said, "I have to use the bathroom, but now I'm afraid to ask."

Caleb caught up with one of the assistants and asked for her. Then he pointed Panda to the bathroom and watched as she trotted off toward it with her dress bouncing and her red shoes clicking across the polished concrete floors. He couldn't decide if she wasn't yet ready for Hollywood or if Hollywood wasn't yet ready for her.

The set and soundstage were similar to the one they had auditioned on in Austin, only much bigger and much more intimidating. There were forty contestants, and they were told that over the next several days they would perform on camera for the five judges. The judges would then select one artist each in turn, much like a lottery, until each judge had eight contestants on their team. Over the following weeks they would compete against their own team, with their judge sending half of them home each week until only one remained. That one would then go on to the live show and compete against the other four for America's votes and the half-million-dollar recording contract. It all sounded like a scripted long shot to Caleb, and any ideas he had had about this show being different from the others seemed to flee, along with his hope of winning.

A tattooed youth wearing eyeliner and giant disks in his ears nudged Caleb as they stood receiving yet another set of instructions from yet another production assistant.

"Hey, guy," he said. "You seen Jordyn yet?"

"Who?" Caleb asked.

"Jordyn. Jordyn-with-a-*y*."

"Your guess is as good as mine, kid," Caleb said. "There aren't any of us wearing name tags here that I've seen."

"I know, man," the kid said. "I just haven't seen her yet, so I was asking you."

Caleb ignored him, pulling his phone from his pocket and checking it on the sly. Still no reply to his text to Jane.

"Where you from, guy?"

"Austin," Caleb told him, slipping the phone back into his pocket. "Via Seattle."

"That's cool, man. But I can't believe you don't know who Jordyn-with-a-*y* is. She's only got like four million YouTube hits. I don't even know why a hit indie chick like her is doing this show anyway. She doesn't need it, that's for sure. Not like the rest of us. Of course, she'll probably win. Isn't that how it always goes? I wasn't sure whether to be pissed when I saw her name or excited that I get to meet her. Maybe she'll dig me, you know. Stranger shit has happened, right?"

Caleb ignored his rambling until he finally fell quiet.

A minute later, the kid asked, "What's your name again? I'm sure I Googled you too. I Googled everyone on the sheet."

Caleb left him without an answer and stepped over to stand next to Panda. As he walked away, he heard the kid say, "Nice chatting with you, guy."

⟡

It was dark by the time the bus brought them to the hotel.

The show had rented an entire floor. The handlers gave each contestant a welcome packet, then took them up the elevators in groups and showed them to their rooms. Caleb was hardly inside with the door closed when he set down his guitar, tossed his duffel, and flopped down on one of the beds, so exhausted that he didn't even care that they'd given him a room with two doubles. He was used to hard work, but it had been a long and taxing day. And he had a sinking feeling things would only be getting worse.

He pulled out his phone, but there was still no response from Jane. He was about to dial her when he remembered her trip to France with her friend Grace. She had shown him a picture of the two of them jumping together on the hotel bed.

It took him a few minutes, but he found the phone's camera app. Then he kicked off his boots and jumped up onto the bed and began bouncing on it, trying to catch a shot of himself in the wall mirror. He was bouncing and kicking and making funny faces for the camera when the door opened, and the kid with the eyeliner and tattoos walked in holding a key card. They froze and looked at each other—the kid in the doorway, Caleb on the bed.

"I know there's a joke here somewhere," Caleb said, "but I wouldn't recommend making it. I've had a long day."

"I was thinking of that old song about monkeys jumping on a bed," the kid said, "but I'm not saying it."

"You sure you have the right room?"

"They didn't mention anything about us having to double up, but this is the key they gave me and there's two beds."

"Well, it's a surprise to me too."

The kid looked at him standing on the bed and grinned. "You want me to wait in the hall or something until you finish your trampoline?"

"It's just a fun photo for my fiancée back home," Caleb said, holding out the phone. "Would you mind taking it?"

The kid dropped his suitcase and took the phone, then framed up the shot. Caleb jumped and kicked out his legs.

"You get it?"

"Hold on," the kid said. "Do it again."

"Did you get that one?"

"A little higher. Maybe stick your tongue out again."

"Is that one any good?"

"Just a couple more," the kid said, suddenly doubling over and breaking into fits of laughter.

Caleb jumped down from the bed and snatched the phone from his hand. "Give me that, you clown."

He sat on the bed and scrolled through the pictures to pick one to send to Jane. As he did, the kid wasted no time, laying out his suitcase and proceeding to meticulously unpack. He hung shirts in the closet and tucked folded pants away in the dresser. He even made several trips to the bathroom to set out his toiletries.

"Looks like you're moving in permanently," Caleb said.

"Have you seen these other jokers we're competing against?" the kid asked, stowing his empty suitcase in the closet. "I plan to be here until the grand finale. Shit, I plan to win."

"You think you're that good?" Caleb asked.

"I think I'm even better."

"Well, you think you're good enough to show me how to send a photo from this thing?"

❧

Caleb came out from the bathroom after a long hot shower and found both beds turned down with chocolates on the pillows, but the kid was nowhere to be found.

He checked his phone again, but still no response from Jane. He was worried something was wrong, so he sat down on the bed in his towel and dialed her. He put the phone to his ear, but nothing happened. Then he looked at the screen again and saw a message box that read: *Turn airplane mode off to make calls.*

Then he remembered the man on the airplane meddling with his phone, and he laughed at himself and his technology challenges. When he hit the button to disable airplane mode, the phone searched and found a signal. Almost immediately the messages began to come in—one, two, three of them.

Hi, baby. I hope your flight went well. I love you.

Not trying to bother you, babe, just want to make sure you made it.

You must just be busy. Call me when you can. Love you!

He dialed her and she picked up on the first ring.

"Hi, honey. How are you?"

"Hey, babe. Gosh, it's good to hear your voice. I had my phone on airplane mode and just now figured it out."

"I guessed it was something like that," she said, laughing.

"I was sitting here reading your message that just now came in. Nice bed-bounce shot. Grace would have loved it."

"Thanks. My roommate took it."

"You have a roommate?"

"Yeah. Some kid from who-knows-where. But he isn't here right now."

"Is it nice there?"

"No. It's terrible. I mean, the hotel's nice. But the people? The show? I don't know. How was your day?"

"It was okay. I went job searching all afternoon. You'd be proud of me. I went into at least a half dozen places and refused to leave until I talked to someone with the power to actually hire. Anyway, I'll be back at it tomorrow. Hey, have you seen my favorite T-shirt? The pink one I sleep in."

"Yeah, I've seen it."

"Where was it?"

"It's in my bag."

"Oh my God, you brought my shirt along. How cute. Are you planning to sleep with it?"

"I'm not sure how it got in there, actually. I must have packed it by mistake."

"Yeah, right. You have so many size-small pink shirts."

There was a pause in the conversation.

"What are you wearing now?" Caleb finally asked. "Since you don't have your shirt."

"Nothing," Jane replied. "I was actually just lying here naked and thinking about you."

Caleb sighed. "I sure wish I could see that."

"But you can see it, baby," she purred. "Just go to your photo album and click on the folder marked Private."

"Okay, hold on, you little temptress, you."

Caleb took the phone from his ear, scrolled through to the

photos, and opened the album. It was nearly a full minute later before he remembered that she was on the line.

"Holy shit, babe."

"I thought I had lost you. Do you like them?"

"Like them? I effing love them. But I didn't even know you had one of those things."

"Well, I have a few things stashed around here that you don't know about. Maybe when you get back, we can play with them together."

"You're a dirty girl and I love it. Although, to tell the truth, the size of that thing makes me feel a little inadequate."

"Oh, you're anything but inadequate, baby. Maybe we could get you to rise to the occasion now, if you know what I mean. Send me a photo to look at while I'm lying here all hot and bothered and naked."

"You really want a picture?"

"Pretty please."

The photos of her had already sent most of the blood rushing from Caleb's head. But then the sound of her pleading voice and the mental image of her stretched out on their bed wearing nothing made him so hard, the towel tented at his waist. He was reaching to unwrap the towel and take a shot when he stopped himself and glanced at the room door.

Once caught, twice cautious, he thought.

"Hold on just a second, babe. Don't move."

Then he got up, hurried to the room door, and latched the privacy lock. When he picked up the phone again and dropped the towel, the only thing bigger than his hard-on was his smile.

❧

Caleb woke to pounding on the door.

Sitting up in his bed, he tried to remember where he was and why. It all came flooding back when he heard the voice calling through the door that was now open a crack, held back by the privacy latch.

"Come on, guy. Let me in."

He rose and went to the door to release the privacy latch he had forgotten to undo before going to sleep. The kid was leaning against the door and the latch wouldn't budge.

"You've got to let me close it," Caleb said.

"No, man," the kid cried. "Open it and let me in."

"It won't unlatch unless you get off the door."

"I'm not sleeping on no floor, guy."

Caleb shook his head and leaned all his weight against the door and forced it closed. Then he flipped the privacy latch free and quickly stepped back. The kid burst into the room.

"Shit, man. What's up? I thought I was gonna have to kick that thing off its hinges."

Caleb glanced out into the bright and empty hall before shutting the door and returning to his bed. He noticed the time.

"It's four in the morning, kid."

"I know it," he said, flopping onto his bed with his clothes on. "And you should see the creatures that come out in this city after about two. I feel like I survived the apocalypse."

"What did you get into?"

"I went all over Hollywood. I had to go see Canter's."

"See what?"

"Canter's Deli, dude. The Kibitz Room? Don't you know anything? Guns N' Roses. The Wallflowers. They all got their start there, man. It's legendary."

"What do you know about Guns N' Roses?"

"I know they got their start at Canter's, which seems to be more than you know. And quit calling me kid. I'm twenty-one. And I'd bet you're not much older."

Caleb could just make out the kid's silhouette in the light cast by the alarm clock. He was lying on top of his covers with his hands clasped behind his head, staring up at the dark ceiling like someone very satisfied with himself.

"What should I call you then?" Caleb asked.

"My name's Sean," he replied. "Sean Tess. You're Caleb Cummings, right?"

"How'd you know my name?"

"I looked you up on the sheet and Googled you again in the hotel business center, dude."

"Did you find anything?"

"No. Nobody's heard of you."

Caleb laughed. "Is that good or bad?"

"Bad," he said. "Or maybe good. I don't know. Maybe it means you can make yourself into whoever you want for the show, you know. Like reinvent yourself."

"Maybe so," Caleb said, thinking about this. A minute later, he asked, "Where are you from, Sean?"

"I'm from Waterloo."

"Where?"

"Iowa."

"Shit. You don't look like you're from Iowa."

"Good," he said. "I've worked hard not to."

Caleb smiled at him, even though he couldn't see him. Then he said good night and rolled over to go to sleep. Five minutes later, the kid asked a question and he rolled back over.

"What's that?"

"Jordyn. Did she show up?"

"What are you asking me for? I've been in here sleeping. You're the one running around all over Hollywood. Now, we've got to be up in a few hours, so go to sleep."

"Okay," he said. "Sorry."

There was silence in the room, but Caleb was somehow sure it was too good to be true. And he was right.

"Hey, did your lady like the photo you sent?"

He knew Sean meant the bed-jumping photo he had taken, of course, and not the ones he'd sent later, but that didn't stop Caleb from grinning like a Cheshire cat in the dark.

"Yeah," he said, "she liked it."

❧

"Wake up, Sean. We're gonna be late."

Sean rolled over and looked up at Caleb. His eyes were bloodshot and his hair was plastered to one side of his head.

"Come on, guy," he said. "Let me sleep."

"That's how I felt last night. Get up. The bus is coming."

"Just a few more minutes."

"I thought you told me you were in it to win it."

"I am, man. But I need a full eight hours to perform."

"Well, that's too bad, then," Caleb said. "Because if you're late they'll probably send you home, and I heard in the hall that Jordyn's here."

"Jordyn-with-a-*y*?"

"I didn't ask them how she spelled it, but I'm guessing so."

There was an explosion of bedding as the kid leaped up and bolted for the bathroom, calling back over his shoulder and asking, "How much time do I have?"

"Maybe ten minutes."

"Shit. It takes me that long just to put my eyeliner on."

Caleb shook his head and laughed. He wasn't quite sure what he had gotten himself into, or even where it would lead, but he was committed to making the most of it while it lasted.

Chapter 7

Jane had gotten to know the streets of downtown Austin better than she had ever wanted to. And when she ran out of places to hand out résumés, she turned instead to scouring the jobs section of the daily classifieds. There wasn't much there either, but at least she could kill a couple of hours at the coffee shop, poring over the listings with her highlighter. And she was doing just this when her phone rang.

"Hello, Jane McKinney speaking."

A robotic voice replied, "You have been selected . . ."

Jane assumed it was another annoying political survey or an automated telemarketer pitch, and she pulled the phone away from her ear and was about to end the call when she heard the words *city of Austin*.

She put the phone up to her ear again.

"Thank you for your recent application. You have been selected to take a civil service exam. You can take the exam at your earliest convenience between the hours of nine a.m. and two p.m. at any of the following city locations . . ."

Jane got out her pen and took down the addresses. She knew it was silly to get her hopes up, but having an actual next step to take was a huge relief.

❧

It was so difficult to tell the blocks of brick and stucco buildings apart that Jane passed by twice before she spotted the small monument sign:

CITY OF AUSTIN
DEPARTMENT OF HUMAN RESOURCES

The door closed behind her, sealing out the sunshine and the birds, and it was quiet inside. Too quiet. Quiet in that strange and timeless way that only libraries and government buildings can sometimes be. There was an old letter-board directory on the wall that listed the civil service examination room on floor three. Jane rode the old elevator up, listening to the soft hum of the motors and the squeak of the cables over their pulleys.

When she walked into the testing room, a woman sitting at an old metal desk looked up at her and asked in a voice so low it was nearly a whisper, "May I help you?"

"I'm here for the civil service exam."

"Your ID, please," the woman said.

Jane opened her wallet and handed the woman her license.

"How long have you been in Texas?" the woman asked, checking her sheet.

"Just a few months now."

"You do know you're applying for a position as a parking enforcement officer, I assume. The job requires knowledge of Austin's streets and traffic laws."

"I've received two dozen parking tickets driving around looking for work," Jane said, smiling. "Does that qualify me?"

The look on the woman's face when she handed Jane back her license made it clear that she was not amused.

"You'll need to go to the DPS office and get a Texas license. Here's the civil service exam. I'm assuming you studied. There are number-two pencils and a sharpener on the table over there. Pick any desk and take as long as you'd like, as long as you're done by two. But please don't leave the room without checking in here first. Even for the restroom. And no cell phones or computers. Good luck."

There were two other people already taking the test on either end of the room, and Jane took an empty desk an equal distance between them so as not to appear rude. Then she filled in her name and birth date, and sat looking at the first question, wondering what on earth it had to do with civil service.

Q. If you had three watermelons in one hand and two bananas and a coconut in the other hand, what would you have?

Jane giggled quietly as she wrote, *You'd have very large hands.* Be serious now, she told herself, erasing the answer.

She flipped ahead to see how many pages were in the test. Then she looked up at the wall clock—tick-tick-ticking away the seconds, one at a time. She sighed. She had a feeling this was going to be a long morning.

❧

The Department of Public Safety was packed wall to wall with unhappy patrons, and none of them appeared at all shy about letting it be known. Jane took a number ticket and found a seat. A woman with two crying children, bouncing one on each knee, looked at Jane and rolled her eyes.

"You'd think they'd have more people working."

"How long have you been waiting?" Jane asked.

"Maybe an hour," she said. "But an hour with these two seems like forever."

Jane sat and waited and watched the clock, then waited some more. The woman next to Jane was eventually replaced by a man wearing sixteen layers of clothing, despite the heat. Fortunately, he was too busy conversing with himself, as he searched his countless pockets for something, to engage Jane. She heard drums on the street, and she looked past the man and out the window. Outside, a noisy group of protesters marched by with shotguns and AR-15s draped over their shoulders, waving enormous flags that read: DON'T TREAD ON TEXAS.

When her number was finally called, Jane approached the counter and handed across her Washington driver's license and the form she had filled out while waiting. The clerk asked her a series of questions and then waved her over to an eye test machine. Jane placed her face to the machine and read off the rows of letters as best as she could. She finished and looked up.

The clerk handed her back her Washington license.

"Sorry, ma'am," he said, "you failed the eye test."

"What do you mean, I failed?"

"I mean you need glasses."

"That's not possible."

He shrugged and hit the button to call the next number.

"Let me try it again," Jane pleaded. "Please."

He shook his head firmly.

"Sorry, ma'am, no license for you today. Next!"

"Oh, that's cute," Jane mumbled, tucking her license away in her purse. "No license for me today, huh? Who do you think you are? The soup Nazi of driver's licenses?"

❧

She found Mr. Zigler in the warehouse behind the wheel of a forklift. He was racing one of his employees around an obstacle course made of beer cases. He pulled over and braked, then smiled down on her from the forklift's seat.

"Hi there, Jane. How's our boy?"

"He's doing great. They've got him putting in longer days than even you did, so I don't get to talk to him much. Plus, I can't bring him lunch there, of course."

He switched off the idling forklift and jumped down.

"Well, you know I'd never turn down lunch if you'd like to keep up the practice," he said, winking. "I'm guessing you came by for Caleb's check since he asked me to make it out to you."

"Yes, sir. I'm going to cash it and go shopping."

He led Jane to his office and went around his desk, then opened a drawer and handed her an envelope. Then he cocked his head and looked at her funny.

"Is there something different about you?"

"What do you mean?" Jane asked.

"Did you change your hair or something?"

"Oh God," Jane said, removing her glasses. "I'm supposed to wear these when I drive, but I keep forgetting to take them off. It's only been a couple of days."

"Well, they look good."

"You think so? I haven't told Caleb yet."

"He's the one who ought to be worried."

"Caleb should be worried? How so?"

"What if you've been seeing him blurry all this time? Now maybe you put your glasses on, see him for the toad he is, and realize you're really in love with me."

Jane made a show of putting her glasses back on and looking him over. "You are really handsome," she said, taking them off again. "But I'm going to stand by my man, Mr. Zigler. Toad or no toad."

He grinned. "He's lucky to have you."

They had said good-bye and Jane had turned to go when Mr. Zigler called her name. She stopped and looked back.

"You used to sell insurance, didn't you?" he asked.

She nodded. "Twenty years."

Mr. Zigler waved his hand to take in the office. "I could sure use help in the sales department around here if the job market isn't looking too good out there."

Jane knew his offer was as much out of kindness as it was out of genuine need for a salesperson, but that alone wouldn't have made her say no. She'd just had too much pain in her life caused by booze to be out peddling it to bars for a living. It was a fine job for someone, just not her.

"I appreciate your offer, Mr. Zigler. I really do. But I have an actual job interview tomorrow with the city of Austin."

"Congratulations," he said, smiling at the news. "If they have any sense at all, they'll make you mayor."

"If they do," she replied, "my first order of business will be naming a street after you. We'll call it Harry Zigler Avenue."

His smile was so proud and so sincere, he looked to Jane to be fifteen instead of fifty-five.

"You tell that man of yours we're all pulling for him here. Shit. The guys are already running around saying they knew him when. And don't forget to mention I'm expecting to hear my name in his acceptance speech when he wins. You tell him."

❧

Jane sat in the Austin city hall lobby, waiting.

She'd been waiting a lot lately, but then so had everyone else, it seemed. And who was she to expect special treatment? She was lucky to even be considered for the position. She took out her phone and checked her messages. Nothing from Caleb since his text early this morning. She read it again.

> Hi, babe! They put us on teams yesterday. Guess who my coach is? That lady who gave me a thumbs-down. Ha-ha! As the kids here say, FML! Apparently it means Fuck My Life. I should be home soon.

She reread her reply to him, questioning it now.

The bed's lonely without you, but don't hurry home for
me. She'll fall in love with you just like everyone does.
Just be yourself and have fun.

Jane had to admit that she had felt a twinge of excitement at
the proposition of his leaving the show early, but she had tried
to mask it in her text. She was torn between wanting him to succeed and wanting him home. She was only human, after all. She
kept hearing Grace's voice saying, *You're not responsible for your
thoughts, honey. You're only responsible for what you do with your
thoughts, which ones you choose to ignore and which ones you choose
to act on.* Of all the crazy voices inside her head, it was always
Grace's she knew she could trust.

"Mrs. McKinney."

Jane looked up at the woman addressing her. "Miss McKinney, but yes. Or Jane's fine."

"Right this way then. Mr. Blanco will see you now."

She brought Jane back to a simple office, adorned with one
photo and one plant. But in the center of the office, and standing out against the simplicity of its nearly bare walls, was a gorgeous carved-mahogany desk with matching chairs. Behind the
desk sat a slender, olive-skinned man in a well-pressed suit. He
stood and motioned with his hand for Jane to sit. When she had
done so, he reseated himself and picked up a piece of paper from
the desk and studied it.

Jane watched him scanning the paper. He had dark, quick,
intelligent eyes. His shiny black hair was touched with gray at the
temples and it was slicked back against his head. Jane thought the
look might work for Caleb, and she was trying to guess whether
he used a cream or clay to style it when he cleared his throat to
get her attention. He was still holding the paper in his hand, but
he was looking at her. She blushed with embarrassment.

"So," he said, "you're from Seattle."

"A little island just west of it, actually, but yes."

"You must be a fan of the Seahawks, then."

"No, not really. I don't follow football much."

"That's a shame," he said. "I've picked them in the office pool to win the Super Bowl."

"That's great. And I am a fan, of course. Especially if they go to the Super Bowl." Jane laughed uncomfortably. "I mean, they're my home team and everything."

"Are you nervous"—he paused to read the paper in his hand—"Mrs. McKinney?"

"Miss McKinney. But please, just call me Jane."

He glanced at the ring on her finger. "Sorry, I just assumed."

"Oh, yes. I can see why you might. But not yet. No."

"No you're not yet married, or no, you're not yet nervous?"

Jane looked at the ceiling, replaying the last question and determined to get it right. "Let me try again. Married? No, I'm engaged. Nervous? Yes. Very nervous."

"Well, I'm always a little nervous doing these interviews myself, if it helps."

"Yes, but . . . it's been about twenty years since I've had an interview, sir."

"Please, Jane, call me Manuel or Manny."

"Okay, thank you. Manuel."

He set the paper down and patted it with his open palm. "There's nothing to be nervous about. I'd much rather interview someone who's out of practice because she's kept a job for twenty years than some of the professional interviewees we get in here. And besides, your test scores were very good. Especially in language and communication skills, which are important. This is a people job. Some think it's about writing tickets and raising revenue, but they are wrong. It's all about the people."

"Thank you, sir. I mean, Manuel. I like people very much."

"Besides liking people, what made you want to apply to be a parking enforcement officer, Jane?"

"Truthfully? I was paying a ticket online and I saw the link to apply. I've been looking for work in my field, but with everything changing in the health insurance world right now, there aren't any jobs to be had."

"Do you blame the Affordable Care Act for this?"

"I don't know. I mean, it's all part of it, I guess."

"And do you think this new law is good? Or do you think it is bad?"

Jane bit her lip. There were two things she tried to get through this life without talking about, and those two things were politics and religion. And this fell under both, depending on who you asked. Still, he was looking to her for an answer.

"I think time will tell," she said. "But I will say this—I've spent most of my adult life working to make sure people have health coverage. And I've seen what happens to people who don't. So I'm all for anything that leads to more affordable coverage, if it works."

"Even if it means you're out of a job?"

"Even so," she said. "But as I said, we'll have to see."

"A very good answer," he said, nodding. "I see why the high scores in communication."

Jane smiled. "It's all about the people, right?"

"Yes," he said, smiling back. "It is all about the people. And people are what the city of Austin is preparing for. You might have read that there's a new speedway here in Austin. This fall we will be hosting Formula One racing for the second year, and we expect many, many people. That and our music and film festivals have been steadily growing. And more people mean more cars, and more cars mean more need to enforce our parking laws. Do you feel you know the downtown area fairly well?"

"Yes, I do. And what I don't know I'll learn fast."

"And you have a valid driver's license?"

"Yes, sir. Fresh off the press just the other day."

"And can you drive a standard transmission if asked to?"

"I might be a little rusty, but I'm sure it'll come back."

"And you have no problem being on your feet for long periods of time, walking?"

"I'm a walking fool. I'll walk this city silly."

"And you have no complaints about working nights in the downtown area? Just on the weekends."

"I'm up late anyway."

"And who will win the Super Bowl this year?"

"Why, the Seattle Seahawks will win, of course."

He leaned back in his chair and smiled. "Good. You start Wednesday for orientation."

❧

Jane was still so giddy when she got home that she didn't even notice or care that the neighbor's dog was barking. She ran into the apartment, kicked off her shoes, and jumped on the bed. There was no mirror, so she was bouncing and trying to take a photo with her arm extended when the bed collapsed on its frame and slammed onto the floor.

"Oh shit," she said, standing on the collapsed mattress with bent knees and outstretched arms like a mattress surfer in some college comedy skit. Of course, the neighbor was now pounding on the wall to go with the dog's barking.

The picture she had taken showed only her feet and the broken bed, but she flopped down on the mattress to send it to Caleb anyway. The caption she sent with the photo read:

Hi, babe. I've gained so many pounds eating chocolate since you left that I broke the bed. But the good news is . . . wait for it . . . wait for it . . . I GOT A JOB! Can you believe it? I know you're super busy, but call me when you can. You'll never guess what I'll be doing. I love you.

Chapter 8

Caleb was hiding in a corner backstage, tuning his guitar, when the makeup artist finally found him. She hooked her hands on her hips and shook her head.

"I've been looking for you. Didn't you hear the call?"

"Come on, is this really necessary? I'm a guy."

"You at least have to get some powder, unless you want to look all shiny on camera."

"I don't mind if I look shiny."

"Well, the producers do, mister. So get up and let's go."

Caleb followed her to her makeup chair, then sat and looked at himself in the mirror. He still wasn't used to the highlights in his hair, and he hoped he'd never get used to the glamour lights and powder.

The makeup artist brought her brush to his face. "Close your eyes and hold still, doll."

Caleb sighed and did as he was told. When he opened them again, Sean was standing in front of him, smiling.

"Hey, roomie. Sure you don't wanna borrow my eyeliner? It'll give you that pop factor out there onstage."

Caleb laughed. "No thanks, Sean. There's only room on the show for one vampire Avril Lavigne look-alike, and you've got the role all sewed up."

"Hey, Avril Lavigne is the shit."

"You're right," Caleb said. "I'm sorry. I shouldn't have insulted her by making the comparison. Or vampires either."

Caleb started to rise from the chair, but the makeup artist pushed him back down. Then she began styling his hair, carefully layering each piece and spraying it into place.

"Sean, why are you still here? This is awkward enough without you standing there and staring at me."

"Maybe I'm just trying to get inside your head. Get an edge on you in the competition."

"Sean, we're not even on the same team. We won't compete against each other unless we both make the live show. And I highly doubt either of us will. No matter how much you might look and sing like Avril Lavigne."

"I don't sing like Avril Lavigne."

"I thought you said she was the shit."

"If you have to keep talking," the makeup artist said, "could you at least sit still?"

Sean stepped up closer and lowered his voice. "Say, how are things on your team?"

"They're fine, Sean. Everyone's just trying to make it to the next round."

"Is there anyone you're particularly worried about?"

"No, not really. We've only had group rehearsal once. And I try to focus on my own performance."

"Well, okay, then, but maybe what about Jordyn? Have you talked to Jordyn?"

Caleb saw the look in his eyes and realized why Sean was over here harassing him. He decided to play with him a little.

"Jordyn who?" Caleb asked.

"You know—Jordyn from New York. What's she like?"

"You mean Jordyn-with-a-*y*?"

"Shit, Caleb, how many Jordyns are there on your team?"

"Just the one, I think."

"Then I meant her," Sean quipped.

"Okay, sure," Caleb shot back. "What about her again?"

"Has she said anything to you?"

"Only that she's not into dudes who wear eyeliner."

"Just forget it," he said, turning and storming off.

Caleb grinned and watched him go. Sean hadn't quite left the makeup and dressing area when he called back.

"And everyone knows chicks dig eyeliner."

After he had disappeared, the makeup artist looked at Caleb in the mirror.

"He's right," she said. "Chicks do dig eyeliner on a guy."

Caleb just shook his head.

⟨⟨⟩

When Caleb stepped out onto the stage, everything in his head went quiet. Quiet and white. It had always been that way. It didn't matter to him whether he was playing for passersby in the street, a bar full of drunken music lovers, or a reality TV judge backed up by a crowd of fake fans in a Hollywood studio soundstage; once he plucked the first chord, the result was the same. He wasn't playing for anyone, he was playing for everyone.

He sometimes imagined a great mythic cloud passing by overhead and in the cloud was every story ever told and every song ever sung. And if he was lucky, he got to reach up into this cloud and pull something down and shape it in his own way and show it to someone so that they might see for just one fleeting but magic moment the greatness that they themselves were capable of. Then he'd strum the last chord and his song would drift back to join the ether from where it had come. And he was just fine with that. He wouldn't have it any other way.

"Listen up," the producer shouted from the edge of the stage. "This isn't being broadcast live, but we have a full afternoon and we'd like to get this filmed in one take. Those of you in the audience, please pay attention to the applause sign. It's very important that you cheer at the right moment. And for our artist . . . let's see . . . Caleb, right? Caleb, you need to let a few beats pass after they call action. Don't play right when the curtain lifts, okay? Just a pause to set the mood. And do the same when you finish the song. You can react naturally to the applause, of course, but don't look too happy to be through with the performance. Stay in the moment. Got it?"

Caleb nodded that he understood, even though he wanted to walk off the stage. And he probably would have if he hadn't been worried about disappointing Jane.

The producer called for the set to be readied and the partition dropped in front of Caleb, blocking him off from the audience and the judge. He stood alone with his guitar, listening to the producer bark out his final orders.

Caleb had known before he came that these reality shows were mostly scripted. But now that he had looked behind the curtain, he saw that they weren't just scripted, they were total bullshit. He actually felt relieved that he'd probably be going home. There were eight artists on his team, and by the end of the week, only four would remain. He didn't have a lot of hope for himself, considering his judge had already given him a thumbs-down.

Caleb heard the director call, "Action!"

Then he heard applause as the partition lifted away on its cables, revealing the crowd. He looked into the lights and listened to the applause, and he knew that this was what every musician dreamed of. And hadn't he secretly dreamed of it too? But not like this. Not with phony fans and an LED sign that told them when to cheer.

He pushed these thoughts from his mind and looked to the crowd for inspiration. He hadn't decided yet which of his songs to sing, but when he glimpsed a woman in the front row who reminded him of his aunt, his fingers moved, striking a familiar melody in a minor key.

"This is for everyone out there who has lost someone," he said. "Especially if that someone happened to be a soldier."

Then he sang.

> *They came in full dress*
> *But you already knew*
> *They handed you the letter and left*
> *But no medal could comfort you*
> *Another hero lost*
> *Another coffin draped in red, white, and blue*
> *Now you stare into the past*
> *Remembering love that was true*
> *I know today you hate the sun*
> *Oh, it pours down love*
> *Love on everyone*
> *But it slips beneath your blinds*
> *Onto memories you rerun*
> *The letters you meant to write*
> *But were never begun*
> *You cry, Give me rain instead*
> *Or even snow*
> *Cold to numb my pain*
> *A flood to drown my sorrow*
> *'Cause if you've ever lost true love*
> *The person you knew was the one*
> *Then I'm sure you know*
> *What it's like to hate the sun*
>
> *Now the sun's turned to rain*
> *And everyone's gone*
> *They left with their condolences*
> *And it's just you here alone*
> *Oh, the sweet love you made*
> *The promise of years yet to come*

But even the best memories fade
Just like the sun
I know you used to hate the sun
But now rain pours down
Down on everyone
It drips from your gutters
Onto the memories you rerun
The letters you meant to write
And should have begun
You cry, Give me pain instead
Or even sorrow
A wind to blow away the rain
A ray of hope for tomorrow
'Cause if you've ever lost true love
The person you knew was the one
Then I'm sure you know
What it's like to miss the sun

You finally visited today, Auntie
I know you were there
I saw you put your ear to his grave
I wonder what you heard
You decided love isn't gone
You said, It's right here with me
You knew your heart was his home
And always will be
I know you used to hate the sun
Oh, it pours down love
Love on everyone
It drips into your heart
And onto the memories you rerun
The letters you meant to write

And have finally begun
You cry, Give me peace instead
Anything but tears
Warm memories to keep
Faith to pass the years
'Cause if you've ever lost true love
The person you knew was the one
Then I'm sure you also know
Love just keeps going on

The audience was quiet when he finished—too quiet. They stared at him, and so did the judge, but no one was clapping.

"Cut!" the director yelled.

Then the producer appeared at the edge of the stage. "Damn it!" he shouted out to some distant sound booth. "Why didn't you throw the applause switch?"

"Sorry, boss," a voice from the booth said. "I got wrapped up in the song and forgot."

The producer shook his head. "Get someone less sentimental to run the sign this time. Okay, people, let's do it over. Caleb, perfect pause. So let's do the same thing again. Just take it from the top."

Caleb shook his head. "I can't do it again."

The producer had half turned away, but he heard Caleb and spun back around. "Excuse me?"

"I said I can't just play it on command."

"Why not?"

"I felt it, but now it's gone."

"But that's your job, son."

"Sorry."

"I'm afraid you're going to have a real hard time in this business if you can't perform when you're asked to. This isn't some art house gig where you get to call the shots, pal."

"I can probably play you something different."

"Fine," he said. "I don't really care what you play."

"No," the judge said. "I don't want another song."

Everyone turned to look up at her in the judges' box. So this is it, Caleb thought. She's not even going to wait for the eliminations to send me home.

"Why not?" the producer asked.

"Because that one was perfect," she said, smiling at Caleb. "Let's just reshoot the applause, can we?"

The producer threw up his hands. "I guess so, sure. Caleb, do you think you could stand there and look like you just played the song again, or would that be too much to ask too?"

Caleb nodded that he could. Then he watched as they got everyone back in their places like so many set pieces in a play. When the director called action again, Caleb strummed the last chord, the sign lit like it was supposed to, and the crowd went wild with the kind of applause that seemed slightly tone-deaf, given the song he had actually played. But this wasn't his show, so whatever.

After depositing his guitar backstage, Caleb rejoined his group in their assigned section to watch the remaining artists he was competing against perform. He had hardly sat down when Sean leaned his head over Caleb's shoulder from the seat behind.

"Nice work, guy. Really nice."

"You think so?"

"I sure wish I could write shit like that."

"Thanks," Caleb said. "That one still cuts deep for me."

"I could tell. Anyway, screw the producer. The judge liked it, so that's good news for you."

"You think she liked it enough to pass me through?"

"I'm thinking so, man. Although I could guaran-damn-tee you there'd be no doubt about it if you'd listened to me and worn a little eyeliner."

"What's with you and the eyeliner, dude? It's like you own stock in Maybelline or something. Next thing you know, you'll be trying to get me to put those disks in my ears too."

"They're called gauges, man. And they're the shit."

"Well, if you don't lay off me about the eyeliner, I'll put a padlock through them while you're sleeping and chain you to the hotel bed. How about that?"

"That's just plain mean," Sean said.

One of the other contestants turned to them and scowled. "Do you mind? I'm trying to listen."

"Listen to what?" Sean shot back. "The producer barking orders at the light guys? Get over yourself, Carrie Ann."

Less than two minutes later, Sean leaned forward again. "Check her out, man. There she is onstage. Jordyn-with-a-*y*. I told you she's fucking beautiful. Admit it, she's a knockout and you dream about her at night."

"Sorry," Caleb said, "but I dream about my own lady."

"Fine. But you can at least admit she's gorgeous."

"Jane? She's the most gorgeous woman on earth."

"No, not Jane, guy. Jordyn. Check her out."

Caleb looked at her on the stage. Dark blue dress, wavy auburn hair, red lips. She was sitting on a stool with an electric slide guitar on her lap, and even the sound crew guys plugging her in and setting her microphone were having a hard time keeping their eyes off her.

"Okay, I'll admit she's pretty. In a Lana Del Rey sort of way. But anyone can show a little skin and make pouty-lipped love to the camera these days, and become an Internet star. I'd be more impressed if she could really sing."

Sean sighed. "Man, are you in for a big surprise."

When the director finally called action, Jordyn came alive. It was as if the camera changed her. Something in her posture, or maybe just her eyes. She looked beyond the camera into the audience, as if seeing someone or something there that she loved, and then she began to play the slide guitar with a smoothness that Caleb had only seen in old-time steel players. Her voice was rich and husky and sensual, and her song was so haunting and beautiful that Caleb could hardly believe she had written it.

When she finished, the applause light hadn't even gone on yet and the entire audience was on their feet. Then even the contestants all stood to clap and to cheer, and only Caleb was still sitting—watching, wondering, worrying.

Sean put a hand on his shoulder and leaned down. "What do you think now, guy?"

Caleb was still looking at her when he answered. "You were right. She's the one to beat."

⁊∾

"A meter maid? Are you shitting me?"

Jane laughed on the other end of the phone. "The proper term is parking enforcement officer, young man. And unless you want to see a bunch of unexplained tickets with your name on them when you return, I'd suggest you not call me a meter maid from now on."

"But I don't even have a car."

"Maybe I'll use my handcuffs on you, then."

"You get handcuffs?"

"No. I was only kidding. It's not a bad idea, though. Kind of turns me on. Where are you right now?"

"I'm lying on my bed."

"What are you wearing?"

"Sorry, not tonight, babe. Sean's here. He's in the shower. Seriously, though, this is great news about the job, Jane. I'm so excited for you. But are you sure it's safe?"

"Why wouldn't it be?"

"I don't know. You said you'd be doing the night beat downtown, right? That can get kind of rough, don't you think?"

"The night shift is only Thursday through Saturday. But don't worry. I'll be with a trainer for the first week. And we're issued a radio and can summon police if anything happens. Plus, I've got pepper spray."

"You do?"

"Uh-huh. Got it this afternoon at the gun store."

"The gun store?"

"Yep. The guy there tried to sell me a thirty-eight instead, but I stuck to the MK-9."

"MK what?"

"That's the agency-recommended pepper spray."

"Shit, Jane. I'm gone for less than a week and you're putting on a uniform and gun shopping. What's going on down there?"

"Maybe this would be a good time to tell you that I have glasses now too."

"What? You do? Like eyeglasses?"

"Yeah, but I only really wear them when I'm driving. But they're sexy, I promise."

"I'm flying home," he teased. "You can't be left alone."

"You just miss me and you're looking for any excuse to come back."

"I do miss you."

"You do?"

"Yeah. Like a lot."

"But you're doing good, right? I mean, you made it through to next week."

"Yes, I made the cut. But I don't know, Jane. These kids, they're good. You remember that little punker girl from my audition? The one with the clock around her neck?"

"The girl with the voice? How could I forget her?"

"Did you know she's classically trained? And she writes music too. All I can do is write tabs for my guitar. I've always had to have Jeremy or somebody else write for the other instruments. And Sean's really good, as goofy as he is. And then there's this girl from New York on my team. I say team, but really I'm competing with her. Anyway, she's got like millions of YouTube followers and an album out on iTunes already, and she looks like some kind of pop princess. But get this, she's got rich parents or something and she went to Juilliard, Jane. Fucking Juilliard." He paused to take a breath. "I guess I just feel out of my league."

"A pop princess from Juilliard, huh? I'm feeling out of my league too. What's her name?"

"Jordyn-with-a-*y*."

"Shit, even her name trumps mine."

"How so?"

"It's like Jane except with an extra syllable."

"Jane, seriously, I'm worried I can't beat her."

"I'll tell you what, baby. You stop worrying about her and focus on just being you, okay? I know you, and you wouldn't want to win any other way. And if you do get sent home, I'll be waiting here with open arms. And maybe even a pair of handcuffs too."

"You're right, babe," he said. "You always are. And I love you so much. I have no idea what I did to deserve you."

He could tell Jane was smiling on her end of the phone.

"You gave me multiple orgasms, for one thing," she said.

"Oh, I did, did I?"

"Yes. Just this morning, in fact."

"Wow, I must have mad powers to be dishing out multiple orgasms from a thousand miles away. Are you sure you're not just using me for sex?"

"No way. I'm using you as a handyman too. Don't forget, you need to fix the bed frame when you get home. The mattress is still on the floor."

The bathroom door opened and Sean came out wearing his towel and brushing his teeth. "Tell Dane I said hi."

"Did your friend just call me Dane?"

Caleb laughed. "He knows your name. He's just got a toothbrush jammed in his mouth. Anyway, they expect us to be on the bus before the sun's even up, so I better get off the phone. I love you, babe."

"I love you too," Jane said. "You rest up for tomorrow."

"If you go to sleep too," he offered up, "then maybe we can meet in our dreams."

"Are you kidding?" she asked. "I'll be up for hours yet. I've got work to do."

"What kind of work do you have to do at this hour?"

"I've got to get busy leaving negative comments on Jordyn-with-a-*y*'s YouTube page. What else?"

Chapter 9

Jane's uniform had certainly shrunk in the wash, so much so that she could hardly walk. It didn't help, of course, that she was juggling her afternoon latte and a notebook and map while trying to keep up with the fastest-moving woman she'd ever seen outside of the summer Olympics. She finally gave up and tossed her latte in a trash can. Then she ran stiff-legged to catch up with her trainer, who had thankfully stopped to issue a ticket.

The trainer looked up from her handheld ticket dispenser and eyed Jane. "You should've finished your coffee. The four-to-midnight shift's a grind."

"Oh, I've had enough," Jane said, wiggling to readjust her tight uniform shirt.

The trainer eyed her with a slight smile. "Did you get that uniform in the kids' section?"

"No," Jane said, pulling at it. "It was actually too big, if you can believe it. I washed it in hot water to shrink it."

"Looks like maybe you overshot the mark just a bit."

"You're telling me," Jane said. "I feel like I'm suffocating in this thing."

"It'll loosen up," the trainer said, printing the ticket and slipping it inside the envelope. "Maybe don't wear your vest for a day or two until it does."

"My vest?" Jane was confused. "What vest?"

"You didn't get a stab vest yet?"

"A stab vest? Really? What would I need that for? All they mentioned was pepper spray."

"Oh, you'd be surprised, honey. We're not exactly winning

any awards with folks out here. Especially not on night patrol. It might be smart to get some of these swabs to carry in your belt too."

She held up a clear plastic tube with a test swab inside.

"And what's the swab for?" Jane asked.

"Spitters."

"Spitters?"

"Yep. I've heard of one officer getting hit with feces, but that's rare."

"And spitting's not rare?" Jane asked.

"Oh, it's rare too. Especially since they made it a felony to discharge bodily fluids on a public safety worker. But you need a swab for DNA to prove it."

"Oh, great," Jane said. "Anything else I might need that they didn't tell me about?"

The woman laughed. "Just comfortable shoes and maybe a uniform that fits. Here, put this ticket under the wiper there. We've got to keep moving."

She dragged Jane all over downtown, explaining the ins and outs of enforcing parking. Which streets garnered the most offenders; how to spot an expired meter receipt with just a glance; how to chalk tires on blocks without pay stations. She taught Jane to punch a plate number into the handheld, print a ticket, and slip it under the wiper in less than thirty seconds.

"You've got to serve it fast or you'll end up holding."

"What do you mean, holding?" Jane asked.

"If you've already entered the plate and they drive off before you can serve it, you're left holding the ticket. Then you have to manually cancel it. You don't want too many of those. It looks bad. Plus, it wastes time and you need to keep up your pace. The downtown routes see about a hundred tickets a shift. You don't want to come up short."

"But I thought there weren't any quotas."

"There aren't, technically. But there sure are expectations."

"That's not what they said in my orientation."

"Well, they didn't mention getting a stab vest either, did they? Listen. Forget about human resources and what they said. This is the real deal. You stick with old Kristine here and work real hard for me this week and I promise to give it to you straight. Okay? Now let's finish these last few blocks before the sun sets, because then we get to go down to Sixth Street and I'll show you a few reasons you'll want to get a vest."

They were walking a quiet block on the edge of downtown when she stopped in front of an outdated old coin meter, laid her hand on it, and bowed her head as if she might be praying to it. Then she looked up at Jane.

"This is the end of an era here. But I guess even the best have to be retired sooner or later. We just don't have any say in the matter."

She looked so sad and depressed that Jane didn't know quite what to say.

"I had no idea when they assigned me to you that you were retiring," Jane finally said. "I hope you're not being forced to leave. I hope it isn't awkward training me."

"Me?" she asked, laughing. "Retiring? No way. I'm moving up to the morning shift and getting a car. That's right. The only walking these old feet will be doing any longer is my Saturday-morning mall walk with the ladies from church."

"I'm sorry," Jane said. "I must have misunderstood you."

Kristine nodded to the meter that her hand was resting on. "These here are being retired. This little block's the last stretch of the old guard. These spring-loaded coin meters were all there was when I started. Now they've been replaced with the fancy electric pay stations that bring in a million dollars each year.

But I've been stopping and saying hello to this same meter here every day now for twenty-two years. They're going to let me have it, you know. When they take them out. My husband says we should make it into a lamp, but I plan to park it right in the living room just as it is."

Jane looked at her skeptically. "You stop and say hello to a parking meter?"

She nodded. "I know it sounds crazy, but it's not. You'll see. We all have our thing. Our rituals. Harold takes pictures of lost and abandoned shoes. He's going to do a series of photo books when he retires. Victoria's been working mornings on restaurant row for years, and she has a collection of beer bottle caps she glues to her house. You'll come up with little routines of your own to break up the weeks and pass the time."

"Shoot," Jane said. "Between the stabbings and the spitting, I didn't think there'd be a dull moment in the day."

"Listen, I told you I'd give it to you straight. The job's boring as hell and everyone hates you for doing it. But it's thirty-six thousand a year plus benefits. And if you keep at it like I have all these years—meet your expectations, don't cause any grief—then you might just end up with a morning shift and a car. Then it's smooth sailing all the way to retirement."

"Then what?" Jane asked.

"What do you mean, then what?"

"After retirement. Then what?"

She looked momentarily confused, as if perhaps it had never occurred to her to think about it before. Then she looked at the old parking meter again and laughed.

"I guess you just park yourself in the living room and watch TV until it's time for God to come and get you."

It was well after midnight when Jane got home.

She went straight to the shower, turned the water on, tied her hair up on her head, and got in, still wearing her uniform. She spun a slow circle, soaking herself front to back. Then she poured hair conditioner into her hands and rubbed it onto the tight fabric at her thighs, hoping it would encourage it to give.

She thought of that morning when Caleb had barged in on her while she had coconut oil and coffee grounds smeared on her skin. She remembered his grin as he tried desperately not to laugh. She remembered his making her breakfast, and then making love to her in the kitchen before she even had a chance to eat.

But mostly, she remembered his eyes. She missed those eyes. She missed looking at them when he was sleeping. Watching them move behind his closed lids, wondering what they were seeing in his dreams. And she missed his eyes looking at her when he woke. She missed the desire, the passion. She missed seeing the spark there when he spoke. The joy. The pain when something hurt.

She turned the water off and patted her uniform just enough to keep from soaking the floor when she stepped from the shower. Then she went into the living room and began doing lunges across the floor with her arms outstretched. The fabric seemed to be giving a little and she thanked the Internet and Pantene for small miracles. She was on her fourth or fifth pass when she caught her reflection in the window—a middle-aged woman in a too-tight, soaking-wet meter-maid uniform, lunging across her apartment living room like some crazy cougar getting ready to go out on Halloween.

See the humor of it, Jane. Not the sadness. Not the shame.

She had started to lunge again when she heard a dog barking outside her window. But then the bark turned to a growl, and she heard a woman scream for help.

She rushed to the window but she couldn't see anything except shadows. On the other side of the small garden fence, a terrible noise rose up—a combination bark, snarl, and scream.

Jane pulled on her shoes, grabbed her purse, and bolted from the apartment. By the time she descended the stairs and burst outside with the safety pin pulled from her pepper spray canister, the barking had ceased. But the woman was still screaming for help.

She rounded the fence at a run and stopped in her tracks, momentarily at a loss for what to do. The dog was on its back, turning circles on the patch of dead grass, locked in a death match with an enormous raccoon. The neighbor was standing over them and screaming, holding her pink robe closed with one hand and whacking at the raccoon with the slipper she held in the other. The raccoon seemed to either not notice the neighbor hitting it or not care, because it just kept snarling and snapping and slashing the poor pup to shreds.

"Stand back!" Jane shouted, pointing the pepper spray.

The neighbor looked up at her and Jane could see that her face was white with fear.

"Step away," Jane said as she unleashed a stream of spray, aiming as best she could for the face of the raccoon but hitting them both. The raccoon paused on top of Buttercup and looked up at Jane. For a moment, she thought the spray might not have worked. She was about to hit it again when it lifted its paws into little fists and rubbed at its eyes, looking like some cartoon raccoon just waking up. Then it sneezed and coughed and left Buttercup lying there on the dead grass as it lumbered off, wheezing. The last Jane saw of it was its tail slipping beneath a parked car.

The neighbor rushed to her dog and knelt beside it. "Oh, Buttercup. My sweet baby. What did he do?"

"Be careful," Jane said. "You'll get pepper spray on you."

But she didn't care. She lifted Buttercup in her arms and stood and turned to Jane, panic written on her face. The dog was so limp and so bloodied that Jane would have sworn it was dead if it hadn't whimpered and kicked one leg.

"You have to help me get him to the vet," the neighbor said. "There's a twenty-four-hour one in South Austin on Lamar."

"Of course," Jane answered. "We'll take my car."

As Jane drove, the woman sat in the passenger seat with her head bent over her mangled dog, sobbing and saying over and over again, "He was protecting me. My little hero. He was protecting me."

Jane hadn't even parked the car in front of the animal hospital before the neighbor was out and running. She had her dog in her arms and her pink robe was open and flapping behind her as she raced for the door. She disappeared inside the building.

Jane sat in her car for a moment, wondering what she should do. She knew she couldn't leave them, but she hadn't signed up for a night at the animal hospital either. She sighed and turned off the engine.

It was the brightest lobby Jane had ever seen. Fluorescent lights in white ceilings. White floors, white walls, white chairs. The only color was an orange beanbag in a corner with some children's books next to it.

The reception desk was empty and her neighbor was nowhere to be found. Jane thought about going to see where they were, but then she figured she'd done her part and now she'd just be in the way, so she sat on one of the chairs. She instinctively reached for her phone to text Caleb, but she realized that in her rush she had left her purse in her car. All she had were her keys. She was tempted to go back out for it, but the wall clock said it was after midnight, and Jane knew that even with the time difference Caleb would be fast asleep.

As she sat waiting, she noticed a book lying beside the bean-bag. It had a familiar cover and she rose to get it. She stood with it in her hand, smiling at the title. *The Little Prince*. It had been her favorite growing up. She used to look up at the stars and imagine that wonderful little towheaded prince up there among them, laughing. It was a sweet memory. But memories were a funny thing, and Jane was soon lost in her reminiscing.

She was fifteen again and standing in the waiting room of another hospital, where her father lay dying. She hadn't been sad then. She hadn't known what she was supposed to feel. She had hated her dad. She had had reason to. She had hated his abuse and his booze. But mostly, she had hated that he was dying and she had hated the waiting rooms. They were always the same. The fear-infected and sterile hope. The worry. The guilt. The people slumped in chairs, silently praying. The coffee machine. The squeak of the nurses' shoes. The friendly janitor. There had been more waiting rooms later, after her daughter Melody's first overdose. The first of many. She had had no idea that Overlake Hospital would become as familiar to her as her living room. But as much as she had hated that waiting room, what wouldn't she give to be back there now, to be with her daughter? Her daughter sick, but still alive.

"Why'd you have to die, baby? Why'd you have to die?"

"No," she heard a voice say. "He's not dead yet."

Jane looked up through teary eyes and saw her neighbor looking down on her. She glanced around and realized that she had sat down on the beanbag. The book was in her lap and she had been crying.

"He's going to be okay?" Jane asked, because she couldn't think of anything else.

"They won't say for sure, but they're working on him. Vet says he got cut up maybe the worst he's seen. They're worried about rabies too. I came out to let you know it's going to be a long night and that you should go home. Thank you for driving me. And thank you for showing up when you did. For me and for Buttercup."

Jane didn't know what to say, so she just nodded that she understood. Then she started to rise from the beanbag but stopped when she noticed her neighbor's feet.

"You're missing a slipper," Jane said.

The neighbor looked down as if just now realizing it. Her hair was wilder than ever and her pink robe was covered in blood. She looked as if she'd been through hell, and Jane guessed that she had.

"Why don't I go and get you some shoes and something clean to wear?" Jane asked. "If you're going to stay."

"I wouldn't want to trouble you," she said.

"Oh, it's no trouble. I'm a night owl anyway. Well, as you know. Since we're neighbors."

The neighbor glanced up from her feet, and Jane thought she looked momentarily ashamed. Whether it was because of her appearance or because of the silly little feud they had been having as neighbors, Jane couldn't say.

"You wouldn't mind?"

"Not at all. Really. It's no trouble."

The woman reached into her robe pocket and handed Jane her keys. "There's a pair of Crocs with socks stuffed in them beside my bed. And if you wouldn't mind grabbing me the thin coat out of the hall closet too, that would be great. I was just out letting Buttercup pee. I had no idea we'd be here. Well, you didn't either, I guess."

She looked at Jane's clothes when she said it, and for the first time Jane realized how crazy the two of them must look, her in her damp work uniform and her neighbor in her bloody robe.

Jane laughed. "Aren't we a pair? Okay, I'll go get your things and be right back."

Jane's uniform had stretched quite a bit and was dry by the time she drove home, so she didn't bother changing. She went upstairs and straight into her neighbor's fusty apartment instead. It was dim, and it smelled of mothballs and of dog. The layout of the apartment was an exact mirror of her and Caleb's unit, and she felt as though she had entered some alternate universe where left was right and right was left, some other possible future where she had grown old alone with nothing but the junk she had collected to keep her company.

When Jane entered the bedroom, she saw that the bed was up against the wall their apartments shared, and she could see in the lamplight the wear marks in the wall's paint where the neighbor pounded on it when they were too loud. Jane saw the Crocs beside the bed and bent to pick them up. She paused when she noticed the picture frames crowded on the small nightstand—a dozen or more, and all of them of her neighbor when she was younger, smiling in the arms of a handsome man. Jane could only guess that it was her husband and that he had passed away. She left the bedroom carrying the Crocs and stopped at the hall closet to collect the coat.

On the way back to the animal hospital, Jane pulled through a Jack in the Box and picked up two Sourdough Jacks and two fries. The kid in the window looked at her uniform and the patch on her shoulder and scowled.

"Hey, you're a parking copper. I got a parking ticket from one of you the other day and the meter was broken."

"I'm sorry," Jane said.

"Can I contest it?" he asked.

"You can do anything you want," Jane said. "Just don't spit on me, please."

He looked at her as if she were crazy and handed out the bag of food.

The animal hospital lobby was empty again when Jane returned. She set the coat down on a chair and the Crocs down on the floor beneath it. Then she took a seat herself and ate a burger while she waited for her neighbor to appear. The wall clock said it was one thirty in the morning, but it felt much later to Jane. The food and the quiet of the lobby conspired to make her drowsy, and despite the glaring lights, she closed her eyes and went to sleep.

When she woke again, the clock said seven ten, which meant Jane had been sleeping in the chair for hours. And she felt it too. Her neighbor was sitting across from her wearing the thin coat and the Crocs, but no evidence of the food remained.

"Is he going to be okay?" Jane asked.

She smiled and nodded. "Thank you," she said.

Jane wasn't quite sure if she was thanking her for going back for the shoes and coat, or for saving the day with her pepper spray. She supposed it didn't matter either way.

"You're welcome," she said, sitting up and rubbing the sleep from her eyes. Then she added, "Who knew raccoons could be so vicious?"

"The vet said he read in the paper just last month that one had moved into a woman's attic, and fell through the ceiling onto her bed in the middle of the night and mauled her. He said the police had to shoot it."

This sounded like a tall tale to Jane, but she didn't say so. "Good thing we're not on the top floor, I guess."

The neighbor nodded agreement.

"Do you need a lift home?" Jane asked.

"No. I'm going to wait until they release him. You go on ahead. You've done too much already."

Jane wasn't about to argue with her. "I put your keys in the coat pocket there."

The neighbor put her hand into the pocket to check and then nodded. Jane turned to go, but then stopped and turned back. It seemed odd to just walk out after everything they'd been through. She looked at the woman in her chair: her puffy red eyes, her wild hair, her bloodstained pink robe showing beneath the jacket.

"You know," Jane said, "we're neighbors, but I don't even know your name. It just says 3B on your mailbox."

"Marjorie Johnston."

"Jane McKinney."

They both nodded, as if simply saying their names was truce enough and everything that had happened in the past could now remain there.

"Stop by and let me know how he's doing, won't you?"

"Oh, yes. I'll bring him by when he's feeling better and we'll give you a proper thank-you. I'm sure Buttercup will smother you with kisses."

Oh, great, Jane thought. I can hardly wait.

Jane pulled out of the animal hospital in the gray light of dawn and drove the deserted streets toward home. She could see the traffic already moving on the highway in the distance, but the back roads of town were still quiet. The car clock said seven twenty-five, which meant it was almost five thirty in L.A. She wondered if Caleb was up.

Her purse lay on the seat next to her and she reached over as she drove to fish her phone out. She dialed him but it went to his voice mail. She hung up and tossed the phone back into her purse. A minute later it rang, and she reached into her purse again, excited to catch his call, but in her rush her hand closed on something else. She heard an aerosol spray and almost instantly her eyes began to water.

"Oh, shit, I didn't just do that."

She jerked the wheel and pulled the car over. By the time she was stopped, her eyes and lungs were burning, and she slammed the car into park and jumped out. She stood with the door open, taking deep gulps of cool morning air. When she looked back into the car, she could see a fine red mist still lingering above her open purse. She hit the buttons to roll the power windows down, and then went and sat on the curb to wait for it to air out. She was crying from the pepper spray and laughing at the insanity of it all when her phone rang again from inside the car. She got up and went to the passenger window, then held her breath and closed her eyes as she reached inside with her head turned away to carefully pluck her phone from her purse. She took it back to the curb and dialed Caleb on speaker to keep from touching the phone to her face.

"Hi, babe," he answered. "We're playing phone tag."

"Oh, Caleb. It's so good to hear your voice."

"Is everything okay?" he asked.

"Everything's fine now," she said.

"Good," he replied. "I've got a few minutes before I have to get ready to go. I want to hear all about your first official day on the job. Tell me everything."

Jane glanced down at the curb she was sitting on and at her shrunken uniform, noticing a mayo stain from her Sourdough Jack. She laughed.

"Since you've only got a few minutes," she said, "why don't you tell me about your day instead."

Chapter 10

Caleb was in the hotel rehearsal room working on a new song when Jordyn finally came over to introduce herself. The ever-present camera crew followed her, but Caleb had learned to ignore them by now. She walked up and stood in front of him as if she expected him to stop midsong and acknowledge her, but he pretended she wasn't there, just like he did the cameras. Only when he had finished singing and had strummed the final chord did he look up at her from his chair.

"Can I help you?" he asked.

"Actually, I came over to help you," she said.

Caleb laughed. "Oh, you did?"

"Yes. I couldn't help but hear you playing and it's good. But you need a key change."

"A key change. Why?"

"It's missing something. Your verses are in A minor, and that's fine, but you should switch up the chorus to C major."

"That won't work."

"It worked well enough for David Bowie."

"David Bowie?"

"You know the song 'Let's Dance,' I'm sure."

"Of course I do."

"Well, you're no David Bowie, but that song has similar pacing to the one you were just playing, and it's B minor in the verse and A major in the chorus."

"But you said I should go A minor to C major."

"You're exactly right, you should. Don't you think?"

"That's not even a real key change. They're relative."

"Here," she said, reaching and taking his guitar from his hands. "It'll be easier if I just show you."

Then she stood there in front of him and the cameras and played and sang his song, note for note, word for word, making the key change she had suggested on the chorus. He couldn't believe it, but it was better. Much better. But even more unbelievable was that she could remember the chords and the lyrics after only having heard them once. She finished and handed him back his guitar. Then she stuck out her hand.

"I'm Jordyn," she said. "Jordyn-with-a-*y*."

He shook her hand. She had a firm grip. "Nice to meet you, Jordyn-with-a-*y*. I'm Caleb-with-an-*e*."

"Are you going to play that song this week?" she asked.

"I was thinking about it."

"You should. It's really good."

"Aren't you worried that I'll beat you with it? Now that you gave me the secret David Bowie key change and all that."

"Not at all," she said, shaking her head. "We'll both go through this week."

"Oh, you think so, do you?"

Caleb looked into her eyes and found the confidence he saw there both interesting and unsettling.

"I know so," she said. "And then it will be down to just the two of us next week."

"And since you know everything, what then?"

"Then I beat you out for the live show and there isn't a key change on the planet that will save you."

❧

"Did she really say that?"

Caleb turned in his bed to look at Sean. "She did. Can you fucking believe it? Took the guitar right from my hands and played the song like she'd written it too. I'll tell you, that chick's a trip."

"Maybe she just wanted to help you," Sean suggested.

"Oh, come on. She was trying to intimidate me."

"You think so?"

"Either that or she was playing for the cameras. But you never know how they're going to edit this crap together in the show anyway, so 'why bother' is my view."

"Yeah, I guess so," Sean said, gazing up at the ceiling. Then he asked, "Did you say anything to her about me?"

"No, I didn't say anything about you. What the hell would I say anyway? 'Hey, my crazy roommate wants to compare eyeliner and earrings with you'?"

"That's not all I'd like to do with her," he said.

"Dude, that girl would eat you alive."

"I know it," he conceded, shaking his shaggy head on his pillow. "But I've always had a tough time telling the difference between fear and attraction. A buddy back home took me skydiving with him, and it was so fucking scary I fell in love with him on the trip down. I swore by the time we landed I was gay and wanted to marry him. Fortunately, it didn't stick."

Caleb laughed. "That's funny. But they kind of frown on that in Iowa, don't they?"

"You'd be surprised," he said. "Iowa's ninety percent white but they're pretty diverse in their opinions of shit."

"Well, where do they come in on men wearing eyeliner?"

"They mostly hate it. Why do you think I wear it?"

Caleb smiled and reached to turn off the lamp. After a few quiet minutes, he heard Sean roll over on his bed, and he knew he was looking at him even though it was dark.

"Can I ask you a question?"

"Sure," Caleb said. "As long as it isn't about Jordyn."

"No, not about her. It's about your music. How do you write those songs?"

"What do you mean, how?"

"I mean, all my shit feels like pop rock stuff to me. Almost too formulaic. I know I get some raw emotion down, and I make it my own and everything, but I don't ever feel like I'm telling a story. You tell stories. That one the other day knocked everyone flat. But you're not that much older than I am, and I don't see where you get them. The stories, I mean."

Caleb thought for a minute about how to answer. "I guess people just give them to me."

"They give you stories. Like in interviews or something?"

"No. I just watch them and they give them up. Or maybe I watch them and make them up. I don't know. But it doesn't amount to much difference, I guess."

"What do you mean by 'watch them'?"

"I just get quiet and watch people being themselves. It's one of the reasons I love playing on the street. People think you're homeless. Which I've been. Or they treat you like you're a streetlamp or something. Like you're not there. You know what else I used to do?"

"No, what else did you do?"

"I used to go to funerals."

"Funerals?" Sean asked.

"Yeah," Caleb said, "funerals."

"Whose funerals?"

"Strangers' funerals."

"That's creepy," Sean blurted out.

"No, it's not creepy. It's part of life, man. And besides, they didn't have anybody else to go."

"Why not?" Sean asked him.

"Because they were transients and nobody cared."

"You went to homeless people's funerals?"

"Yeah. I started because I had made friends with this cat who used to collect cans all up and down Chinatown. Old Jumping Johnny, they called him. He was a proud man too. Wouldn't take a handout for nothin'. I got him some boots at the Goodwill, and I had to wait until the bastard was passed out to put them on his feet because he wouldn't accept them. Anyway, he died and I wanted to pay my respects. But I paid hell finding out where he'd gone. It turns out if you die and there isn't anybody to claim the body, then they hold you for about six months in one of those refrigerators, and then the state gives you a simple burial."

"They do?"

"Yeah. They put the date and name, if they even have the name, in the paper, but nobody reads them or cares. So I started looking for the announcements and whenever they'd have one, I'd show up and see them buried."

"Did you pray over them or something?"

"No, it wasn't really a religious thing. I just figured nobody should have to be alone when it comes to that. You know? I sure wouldn't want to be."

"But what's this got to do with writing songs?"

"That's what I'm trying to tell you. I didn't know anything about them so I had to sit there while they were being put in the ground and make up a whole life story. What they loved. What they lost. How they ended up there all alone. And then sometimes those stories would turn into songs."

"So you'd write songs for dead street people you didn't even know?"

Caleb thought about this for a moment in the dark.

"No," he finally said. "They write the songs for me."

A minute or two of silence followed and Caleb rolled over and shut his eyes. He was nearly asleep when Sean spoke again.

"Can I ask you another question?"

"What's on your mind now?"

"It's about your lady. Jane. You two are engaged, right?"

Caleb smiled in the dark just at the mention of her name. "Yep. And I'm hoping to save up enough to give her a real wedding. And if I win this show and get the money, that's the first thing I'll do."

"Well, how did you know?"

"How did I know?"

"That she was the one."

"I knew it as soon as I saw her."

"Yeah, but how?"

"Haven't you ever looked at someone for the first time and instantly known them? Not known them by their looks. But really known them. The real them. The thing that makes them who they are."

"You mean like love at first sight?"

"Yeah, but more than that. And your dick getting hard when you look at Jordyn doesn't count. It's more like meeting an old friend, but for the first time. Like you were made to understand this one person, and they were made to understand you. And when you finally do meet, you look at their face, you look into their eyes, and you just know."

"Do you think it can happen for everyone?"

Caleb thought about this for a minute. "Yes," he finally answered. "I do. As long as you're not busy looking at the wrong things."

"What's that mean?"

"I don't know. Just that I was playing my guitar in a doorway when Jane came looking for me. And I know if I'd had my eye on chasing tail, or chasing money, or chasing anything at all instead of just being right there and doing what I love to do, then I would have missed her."

There was another moment of silence when Caleb knew that Sean was pondering what he'd just said, and Caleb began to question having said it since he was really just guessing himself.

"I like everything you said about love and all that," Sean finally replied. "But then what are we doing here?"

"What do you mean?" Caleb asked.

"Aren't we here chasing a prize? Chasing fame? Maybe I should be at home just doing what I love. Painting and making music. Maybe while I'm here I'll miss my soul mate."

"I didn't know you painted."

"Yeah, I do watercolors."

"Nice. But I think you're taking what I said a little too literally."

"Well, hell," Sean said. "You're the one who said it."

Caleb laughed. He was really beginning to like this kid.

"Remind me not to get into conversations with you before bed. Now go to sleep. Those damn cameras will be in the hall in a few hours, and if anyone needs their beauty rest, it's you."

〜

Garth was more upset than usual, over something as silly as craft services arriving late.

"What are we paying you people for if you can't even show up on time?" he shouted, pacing in front of the poor caterers setting up. "It's not like the food's worth the prices."

He stopped in front of Caleb and Sean where they stood waiting to get their breakfast. "Are you onstage today?" he asked.

"No, I play tomorrow," Caleb answered.

"Not you, chucklehead. This one here with the girly lashes and holes in his head."

"They're gauges," Sean said.

"I don't care what they are, take them out."

"But the stylist said they were fine. She said they go well with my look."

"Well, the stylist works for me and I say your look sucks. We're filming a family-friendly show here. So take them out."

"But if I take them out there's just holes and loose skin."

"Cute," he said, looking disgusted. "So, what are you going to do when your parents stop wiping your ass for you someday and you have to get a job in the real world? March into the interview with a couple of vaginas hanging from your head?"

"Maybe cut him some slack," Caleb suggested, stepping between them. "He'll be fine how he is."

"Yeah, what do you know about the real world, kid?"

"I know that you reap what you sow."

"And what's that, one of your cute lyrics or something?"

"No. It just means that in the real world someday you'll be old and incontinent and having to have your ass wiped for you. And probably by a guy with earrings and tattoos too."

He looked as if he wanted to punch Caleb in the face. "You better hope you sing as well as you mouth off, kid."

Then he glared at them both once more before marching off and yelling at various people he passed.

"Thanks," Sean said, looking relieved.

"I didn't do it for you."

"Then what did you say that for?"

"I was hoping he'd send me home."

Sean laughed. "That talk we had last night has you missing your woman, doesn't it? I found your weakness. Now if we both make it to the live show, I know to keep on talking."

"If we both make it to the live show," Caleb said, grabbing a plate from the stack, "I'm getting my own room."

"That hurts, man. That really hurts."

"Oh, shut up. What are you playing today?"

"I don't know. I've been thinking about a song I wrote after a breakup, but I've never played it for anyone before, so I think I'll go with something else to play it safe."

"Why not sing it?"

"I don't know. The emotion's still too raw, maybe. She said I wasn't going anywhere with my music, and she married this dickhead high school jock because his dad owned a chain of restaurants. It fucking broke my heart, dude."

"You should sing it," Caleb said.

"You think so?"

"I do. It's been my experience that the best way to get over hard stuff is to sing it out and leave the emotions on the stage."

"I'll think about it," Sean said.

⌘

Caleb sat with the other contestants, waiting to watch Sean's group perform. First up was Panda, the young girl from Selma. She stepped onstage and sat at the piano. Her clock was gone from around her neck and she was no longer chewing gum, but she was still wearing her sparkly red shoes.

One of the contestants from another team nudged Caleb. "It's Cyndi Lauper's mini-me up there."

"Her name's Panda," Caleb said. "And you better prepare to eat those words."

The song she performed was about a young summer love coming to an end, and Caleb thought it had all the innocence and nostalgia that a song about love and summer should. The audience applauded, and Panda stood from the piano and bowed.

The judge waited for the crowd to quiet before addressing her. "Dear, you play the piano with the nuance of Chopin, and you sing like the angel who must have sat on his shoulder when he composed. If his heart weren't floating in a jar of cognac in Poland, I'd swear it was inside you. Thank you."

Panda beamed with pride as she trotted offstage.

There was a brief break while the piano was wheeled away and the stage reset, and then Sean stepped out with his guitar. He looked the polar opposite of Panda up there.

The director called, "Action," and Sean took a deep breath.

"I wasn't going to sing this one, but a good friend of mine convinced me that the best way to get over something painful is to let it all out and leave it on the stage. So here goes."

He played a biting guitar intro that roused the crowd and made even Caleb forget about Panda's piano piece. And then Sean sang an edgy song, the lyrics laced with anger and heart-ache, the final lines driving it home . . .

> *But you didn't get far, did you, you pretty little liar*
> *The tears are coming, sweetie; the screams of soft regret*
> *But you're too late, Katie, you'll never pay off your debt*
> *Because I wake each morning in my own prison cell*
> *Sentenced to solitary confinement in a lonely lover's hell*

When he finished, he looked as if he'd unloaded a burden he'd been carrying for a long time. He glanced toward Caleb and smiled, and Caleb knew that he was thanking him.

∽

Caleb stood backstage, waiting his turn and watching the moni-tors as Jordyn performed. The camera loved her, that was for sure. She had a presence offstage too, an almost intimidating air, but the camera picked up something else, something vulnerable, and it turned her into a star.

She finished her song and smiled flirtatiously into the camera. Then she glided offstage and was gone. Caleb was still looking up at the monitor and the empty microphone where she had stood when he heard her speak beside him.

"Was it any good, or do you think they hate me?"

"I have reason to believe they don't hate you," he said.

"And what reason would that be?"

"Because everyone was kind enough to wait until you left the stage to take their earplugs out. Even the judge."

"Now, that's just mean-spirited," she shot back, pretending to be hurt. "Are you a mean boy, Caleb?"

"I've been told I'm direct, if that's what you mean."

"I'd agree with that," she replied. "But women like a man who's direct. And I'm sure you know that, don't you?"

"I know my fiancée does."

One half of her mouth curled up in a sneaky kind of smile, and she said, "Oh my, you think I'm flirting with you."

"Aren't you?" Caleb asked.

She batted her eyelashes at him, purring her response. "Maybe just a little."

"Well, it won't get you anywhere."

"Maybe not with you," she said, implying by the look on her face that it had gotten her plenty of other places with plenty of other people. Then she said, "Besides, you're not really my type. But you are cute, you know. You should do videos and put them up on YouTube. I might even do you a favor and share your first one with my fans and get you some exposure."

"No thanks," Caleb said. "I'm not interested."

"Not interested in exposure? That's a first."

"I've heard there's a first for everything."

"Then what are you interested in?"

"I'm interested in making music."

"Oh, you're a purist. Let me guess, you listen to vinyl records and hang out in local coffee shops. Probably belong to a microbrew-of-the-month club too. I know your type, honey. You're still naive. But you'll see. Someday you'll see. The only thing pure about the music business is that it's pure business."

"If that's what they teach at Juilliard, then I'm glad I never went. It's been nice chatting with you, Jordyn."

As he walked away, she called after him. "What are you playing today?"

"My new song," he called back over his shoulder.

"With the key change I gave you?" she asked.

"Yep, with the key change."

❧

They stood lined up on the stage as if waiting to be executed. But only half of them would be, and even then it would only mean the end of their time on TV, not the end of their lives, as it might have seemed.

They were separated into five groups of four, one group for each judge, and the judges sat in their elevated box looking down on them like gods. The producer called for quiet on the set, the director called action, and the hackneyed Hollywood host put on a fake smile and took to the stage.

"Welcome back to *Singer-Songwriter Superstar*," he said, flashing a grin at the camera and waving his arm expansively to take in the contestants. He was reading from a teleprompter. "In the next hour, half of these artists will be going home. The other half will go on. Who will stay and who will leave? We'll be right back to answer that after these short commercial messages."

"Cut!" the director called. "That's in the can."

"Let's move on to eliminations," the producer said. "We'll edit in the close-ups and the bios later."

The director nodded. "Fine by me."

"And we've got one chance to get this right, because once they know who's going home and who's staying, we'll never get a real reaction from them twice."

There was a brief commotion while the camera crews reset, the boom operator moved the microphones, and the gaffers adjusted the lights, and then the producer called again for quiet on the set.

There went the teleprompter, here came the hotshot host.

"We're back again with our first round of eliminations. We'll start with your team, Cynthia. Please tell us the name of the first of your four artists you intend to save."

Great, Caleb thought, my judge would go first. But then he thought maybe it was better, because then at least he'd know and could enjoy the rest of the show.

The judge looked down upon the four of them, sweeping her eyes over them slowly as if hers was an impossible decision to make and she just didn't know. But it was all for the camera.

"I need the name," the announcer said.

"I know," the judge said, feigning distress. "It's just that I've come to love all of them so much. It's hard to choose . . ."

Caleb could hardly believe his ears. She'd come to love them so much? She had hardly said hello to any of them.

"But," she continued, "the first artist I choose to go forward with me is Jordyn."

Jordyn placed both hands on her chest and opened her mouth as if she were shocked. Caleb thought she was a better actor than even the judge. The host congratulated her and had her move over to one of ten chairs waiting for the ten finalists.

Then he turned back to the judge. "Now, we need the name of the first artist you're sending home."

"My, oh my." The judge sighed. "This is in no particular

order, by the way. As much as I think you're all amazing, I must cut two of you. The first artist I'm sending home is Joshua."

"Sorry, Joshua," the host said. "We've enjoyed having you. Good luck out there."

Joshua thanked the judge and walked awkwardly off the stage in the direction he was pointed by the host. So now it was down to two. Caleb had mixed emotions. He liked the girl standing next to him. She was sweet. And she was a fine singer too. But he wanted to move on. He wanted it for himself, and he wanted it even more for Jane.

"There are two artists remaining," the host said. "And only one spot. Please give us the name of the second contestant who will sit in that chair. The other will leave the stage forever."

The girl next to Caleb looked at him nervously, so he reached and took her hand in his and held it. Then he looked back up at the judge.

"I wish I could keep you both," the judge said. "I really do. And this is just the beginning of the road for each of you, whether you go on or not."

"I hate to rush you," the host said, "but I need the name."

"Okay, okay. The second artist I am keeping is . . . is . . . Jen—no, sorry, I'm going to go with my gut and keep Caleb."

Caleb hadn't realized he had been holding his breath until she said his name and he let it out. But then he felt terrible for the girl next to him. She had jumped with excitement when the judge said her name, and then he had felt her hand go limp once his name was uttered. And he suspected the judge had done it all for the cameras too.

He hugged the girl and wished her well, and then watched her walk off the stage.

"Congratulations," the host said, pulling Caleb toward the chair. "Take your seat with the winners, you've earned it."

Caleb sat next to Jordyn. He could smell her perfume, and he could feel her staring at him. He finally looked over at her. There was a sparkle in her eyes and she was grinning.

"I told you it would be down to us."

"Yeah, well, so what?" He shrugged. "Even a blind squirrel can sometimes find a nut."

She laughed loudly but then cut herself short when the producer called for quiet on the set.

"Cameras are still rolling, people!"

Once the focus was off them and back on the host, she leaned in to Caleb and whispered in his ear. "Pick another team and I'll tell you who goes through."

Caleb looked at the other four teams still standing, one of them nervous and in the spotlight now. "Okay," he whispered, pointing. "That one there. The one with my roommate, Sean."

She looked for a few seconds, biting her lip cutely. Then she put her mouth so close to Caleb's ear that her lips tickled him as she whispered her answer.

"That's easy," she said. "Your roommate goes through and so does the adorable little girl with the red shoes."

Chapter 11

It was only the beginning of Jane's first week alone on the job, and already everyone loved her. The employees of the businesses on her blocks would see her and run out to bring her coffee or slices of pizza, or sometimes simply shout her name and wave hello. At first she thought they were just being kind. But when she noticed their cars, she began to understand.

She saw a hat first. Left out in plain view on the dash. It belonged to the guy from the sandwich shop around the corner. Then she saw a stack of menus from the pizza place, also perched on the dash. A T-shirt from the pub; a coffee-shop apron. And all of these cars had one thing in common—expired meters. Jane was conflicted. She knew they were local employees working hard to make ends meet, but she also had a job to do. She decided to try leaving notes, writing them out and placing them in ticket envelopes left under the wipers. The notes read:

Hi. I noticed you work on the block and I decided to leave you a warning first. Please help me do my job and either pay the meter or find a more permanent parking solution. Thanks! —Jane

The next day came, and no one said hello and most of the cars were gone. One car remained with a ticket envelope still under the wiper, and when Jane stopped to check it, she found a twenty-dollar bill tucked inside. She left the envelope and the money where she'd found them and added an actual ticket. That'll teach them to bribe me, she thought.

But it wasn't just the local employees she had a hard time ticketing. It was lots of other cars too. If she came upon an expired meter and the car parked there looked run-down, its owner likely struggling financially, Jane would leave a note instead of a ticket. She did the same thing if a car had infant seats or if a vehicle had a war-veteran plate. But once she started leaving notes for some people, it didn't seem right for her to choose who she would ticket and who she wouldn't, so she began making rules for herself to follow. She decided she'd leave notes on every other block and then switch the blocks up the next day to be fair. Then she'd make an exception, of course, and she'd have to remake the rules again.

On the afternoon of her third day, she came upon a yellow Porsche double-parked. Finally, a citation she could write without remorse. She had just printed the ticket and was stuffing it into the envelope when she leaped back because the Porsche's alarm sounded. She looked up and saw the driver jogging toward her with his remote in his hand.

"I'm just leaving!" he shouted, jumping into his car.

She remembered what her trainer had said about serving the ticket and she rushed to put it under the wiper. But the driver peeled away in his Porsche and left her standing at the curb with the ticket in her hand.

Jane sat for lunch at a local deli. When she'd finished eating, she tallied up her tickets for the day. She'd written fifteen and served only ten of them. A far cry from the hundred or so her trainer had said was normal.

"How many of those do you write in a day?" the server asked, eyeing the tickets in Jane's hand as she refilled her tea.

"Not enough," Jane replied.

"Are you on commission?"

Jane shook her head.

"That's good," the server said. "My husband's an auto mechanic, and he always says people are about as happy to see him as they are to see the meter maid or the dentist."

❦

Jane had been home from work less than an hour and was just getting out of the shower when she heard a knock on the door. She pulled on her sweats and a T-shirt and went to answer it. Her neighbor was standing there with Buttercup in her arms.

"Hi, Marjorie," Jane said. "How is he?"

"Just Marj is fine. He's doing much better, thanks to you."

The dog had several patches of shaved fur where he had received stitches, and he looked at Jane from the opening of the silly cone on his head and let out a thin bark.

"He's happy to see you."

"Well, don't stand out in the hall. Come on in."

Jane stepped aside so they could enter and then shut the door behind them. Marj stood, looking around at the apartment.

"It's just like mine but backwards."

"I know," Jane said. "I had the same feeling when I went into your apartment to get your shoes."

Marj looked back at Jane and smiled. "Well, we didn't want to bother you, but Buttercup insisted on saying hello. Didn't you, Buttercup?"

She leaned her face down to the cone opening and Jane saw Buttercup's little tongue lick her nose. Then she held the dog out to Jane, but Jane shook her head.

"That's all right," she said. "I wouldn't want to hold him wrong and open a stitch or something."

"Oh, don't be silly, he loves to be held."

Jane relented and took the dog from her and cradled him in her arms. She rocked him gently and looked down at his tiny face staring up at her from the cone like some kind of alien baby in a bonnet. The brown snout, the black button nose.

"He really is cute," she said. "What kind of dog is he?"

"A min pin. That's short for miniature pinscher."

"Like a Doberman?"

"No. People think that, but they're different. They call these the 'kings of the toys.' Although he sure defended me like a Doberman the other night. Didn't you, Buttercup?"

"I've noticed he's not barking as much lately."

"That's because of the pain medication the vet sent home with us. That and I'm walking him more. He barks because he misses his yard."

"You used to have a yard?"

She nodded. "We moved in here six years ago, but I've had Buttercup going on ten years now. He used to love his yard."

"I miss my yard too," Jane said.

She remembered the photos of the handsome man on Marj's nightstand and was tempted to ask her about him, but she didn't want to pry. Instead, she looked back down and spoke to the dog.

"You're a little cutie, aren't you, Buttercup? A tough little cutie too. You sure showed that crazy coon. I'll bet he's still licking his wounds. Oh, baby, look at your eye. I'm sorry about the pepper spray, if that's why it's red. I got a little on myself, so I know what it's like."

When Jane glanced back up, Marj was standing at her shelf of books. She reached and took one down, then flipped it open.

"I have this same book of daily reflections," she said.

"Is that right?" Jane asked. "Are you in recovery too?"

Marj set the book back down on the shelf. "I used to be in Al-Anon. When my husband was alive. But I just quit going when he died. I'm not really sure why. I miss it sometimes."

"I miss it too," Jane replied.

Marj turned to look at her. "Al-Anon or A.A.?"

"Al-Anon. I went for years."

"Why did you stop going? If you don't mind me asking."

"My daughter's an addict. Well, she was an addict. She's passed away now. Then I moved here and it just seems so hard to get reconnected, you know?"

"Well, isn't this a coincidence," Marj said. "The two of us meeting up like this. And all because of a raccoon."

"Maybe it's a coinci-God," Jane said.

"What's that?" Marj asked.

"Oh, just something my old sponsor used to say. When something really random and coincidental would happen, I'd say it was spooky and she'd always correct me and say it wasn't spooky, it was spiritual. 'There are no coincidences, Jane,' she'd say. 'Only coinci-Gods.'"

Marj laughed. There was another silence between them when it was obvious that each was lost in her own thoughts and neither knew what else to say. Eventually, Marj stepped over to take Buttercup from Jane's arms.

"It's almost time for his medication, so don't be surprised if you hear a little barking coming from next door."

Jane was closing the door after them when she had a thought.

"You know," Jane said, "there's an Alano Club on my work route. I was thinking about popping in for a meeting, if maybe you wanted to go together. Maybe even tomorrow."

Marj didn't answer right away, and Jane thought maybe she had overstepped a boundary. Her neighbor looked down the hall at her apartment door, as if recalling the loneliness that waited inside, then she looked down at Buttercup in her arms. She looked back at Jane and nodded.

"I think that's a great idea."

"Don't you have to work today?" Marj asked, buckling in.

"It's my day off," Jane said, pulling the car away from the curb. "Then tomorrow I start my first night shift. Or my first one solo anyway."

"Friday night downtown. That's got to be rough."

"Yeah, but at least I've got my stab vest now."

"What's a stab vest?"

"Oh, nothing."

They drove the rest of the way in silence and when they reached the Alano Club, Jane parked and paid the meter with her credit card.

"Don't you get a special pass or something?" Marj asked.

"Nope. I've got to pay like everyone else."

"I'm really sorry about laughing at you that one time."

"What time?" Jane asked.

"From my balcony. When you got that ticket. The day you gave me the finger."

"Oh, yeah," Jane said. "I'm sorry for flipping you off."

"I guess I get angry at the noise because I miss my home. It was so quiet there. And the apartment walls are so paper thin. But maybe it's more than that. I don't know. Maybe I get mad at everything because I miss my Rob."

With the meter transaction completed, Jane looked up and saw that Marj was staring at the ground. Jane glanced at the entrance to the Alano Club, where a few men stood smoking. Then she looked back at Marj.

"Is this hard for you?" Jane asked. "Because we can just go get a coffee or something instead. Or maybe ice cream."

Marj looked up, and Jane saw that her eyes were wet.

"No, I should do this," she said. "It's not hard because of what you might think. My Rob was a good man and he'd been sober for a lot of years. It was his heart that got him, not the booze. It's just that we used to go to meetings together. That's all. But this is good. I need to do this."

Jane took Marj's arm in hers and they walked together toward the door. The two men there held their cigarettes away in an effort to keep them clear of the smoke, then both nodded and one welcomed them. Framed sobriety slogans lined the walls of the foyer and a short hallway led them to an open door and the meeting already in progress. They slipped inside and sat in two empty chairs. The chairs were metal and circled up so that everyone faced one another, maybe twenty people in all. The man who was sharing had paused briefly when they entered, but as they sat, he began speaking again.

"I know they say a meeting is a meeting no matter where you are, but I guess I'm just getting used to the meetings here in Texas still. They're so different from meetings in Maryland. Yesterday I was down at the Last Chance Saloon—they've got a seven a.m. meeting there before the bar opens—and this guy came in . . . let's see, how do I say this? He was a guy but he wasn't, which is fine, of course. But anyway, he or she was still drunk and smelled like booze, and when she sat down, she dropped her purse, and you'll never guess what fell out."

"A vibrator," someone guessed, joking.

"Why a vibrator?" someone else asked from across the room. "Did you lose one?"

A silver-haired gentlemen sitting next to the first man who had spoken out of turn elbowed him gently in the ribs.

"No cross talk, John."

Jane and Marj looked at each other, suddenly realizing that they were the only two women in the room and simultaneously guessing they had stumbled into the wrong meeting.

The man sharing continued. "No, it wasn't a vibrator. She dropped her purse and a pistol fell out. Right there on the bar floor. And no one even said a word. A guy just leaned over and picked it up for her, and she put it back in her purse. I knew then I was really in Texas. But I guess a sex addict is a sex addict, no matter where you are."

Everyone laughed and nodded at this as if it were true. Then the man who had been speaking looked right at Jane. "I'd like to pass to the newcomers," he said. "Ma'am, would you like to share?"

Jane was struck momentarily speechless. She pointed at her own chest, as if to verify that he was in fact asking her to speak. He nodded that he was, and she nodded that she'd guessed so. She glanced at Marj, but Marj just raised her eyebrows and shook her head.

Jane looked back to the man who had called on her to share and said, "I think maybe we made a mistake coming."

"Everyone's welcome," the man replied.

"Yes, but I mean . . . well . . . it's just that . . . we're not sex addicts, you see. Not that there's anything wrong with being sex addicts, or love addicts, or any kind of addict. I mean, it's great. Well, obviously it's not great or you wouldn't be here. I didn't mean that. Not like it sounded anyway . . ."

All twenty pairs of eyes were locked dead on Jane, but not one face seemed to contain an expression for her to speak to. She glanced at Marj, as if looking for a safety line, but Marj was staring at her hands in her lap.

"Ah, we're the ones who fall in love with addicts," Jane continued. "We thought this was . . . we were looking for—"

"Al-Anon's across the hall," the silver-haired man said, chuckling. "But we're glad you stopped by."

"Oh, God," Jane said. "Thank you. I'm so sorry."

She stood and tugged on Marj's sleeve. They both waved awkwardly good-bye and made the uncomfortable walk to the door. As soon as they were in the hallway, they burst out laughing. When they finally stopped, they could hear the men in the room laughing too.

"Should we go barge into the Al-Anon meeting now?"

Marj was still giggling and trying desperately to catch her breath. She shook her head. When she could speak again, she said, "I think we've embarrassed ourselves enough for today. Let's go get that cup of coffee. We'll have our own meeting."

Jane thought that this was the best idea she'd heard all day, and she smiled at Marj to let her know it. They walked out together toward the car, arm in arm and still laughing.

Jane was already in bed with the lights out when her phone went off. She reached for it on the nightstand and felt her spirits lift when she saw Caleb's picture on the screen.

"Hi, baby. I was hoping you'd call."

"Sorry it's so late," he said. "We're rehearsing like crazy."

"It's okay. I was just lying here in an existential depression, thinking about the time we've been apart. Did you know if I only have forty years left to live, then forty years times twelve months is four hundred eighty months? So, say five hundred. And if you've been away from me for almost a month by the time you get back, then that's one–five hundredth of the rest of my life I've spent away from you. That's like point-two percent."

"Oh, baby, you need to turn on the TV or something."

Jane laughed. "I think that's the problem. I was watching the Science Channel. From now on I'll stick to *Dr. Oz*. I miss you, Caleb. But I'm so proud of you, honey. So proud."

"Don't get too excited, I haven't made the live show yet."

"Not yet. But you'll beat her."

"You think so?"

"Absolutely, I do. I've watched all her videos on YouTube at least twice. I hated her at first, of course, but she's growing on me. She's good. But she's not as good as you."

"That's nice of you to say. I guess I'll be home next week whether I make the live show or not."

"I know," she said. "I'm marking off the days."

"Okay, but stop freaking yourself out with the math. Now, tell me what you've been up to. Besides saving neighbors and calculating the percentages of our lives. I'm missing my Jane."

"Let's see . . . I pepper-sprayed the raccoon and then myself, but I told you that already. Oh, this is fun. I had a really obese guy chase me three blocks and almost collapse of a heart attack just to tell me that he saw someone who wasn't disabled parking in a disabled spot."

"Was he handicapped?"

"No, bless his barely beating heart. Just a Good Samaritan. Then another lady told me she hoped I'd drop dead when I wouldn't take back her ticket."

"Drop dead? Doesn't sound ladylike to me. I hope you told her off."

"Even better. I smiled sweetly and pointed at the Jesus-fish bumper sticker on her car and told her I'd see her in heaven when I did. Then today I went to a Sex and Love Addicts Anonymous meeting. Otherwise, just an ordinary week so far."

"Wait a minute. A what meeting?"

Jane laughed. "It was an accident. I'll tell you about it when you get home. What's Sean up to?"

"He's out scouring the town for someone new to break his heart. I swear that kid's a vampire. He gets by somehow on like three hours' sleep."

"And since he's gone, what are you doing?"

"I'm just lying here in bed with your T-shirt, thinking about you."

"That's funny," Jane replied, "because I was just lying here in my bed thinking about you. Except I had something other than a T-shirt to remind me of you. Something between my legs."

"You filthy woman."

"Oh, you know you love it."

"Actually, yes, I do. Why don't you do it again and talk me through it on the phone?"

"I don't know," she said, sounding coy. "I might have to go back to that meeting if I do."

"Come on, baby. I'm dying over here. It's been weeks now and I can't stand it."

"Okay, tell me what you'd do to me if you were here."

"Really?"

"Yes, really."

"First, I'd light a candle to set the mood. Then I'd strip naked and climb on top of you. But I wouldn't let you touch me. Maybe I'd brush my lips against yours. But no kissing yet. Then I'd undress you with my mouth."

"Oh, really, with your mouth?"

"That's right. I'd unbutton your shirt with my tongue. I'm very talented, you know."

"Oh, I know. What about my bra? It clasps in the back."

"I'd just chew through it."

"Is that so? Now I'm getting turned on."

"Well, you'll have to wait because I'm not done teasing you yet. Next, I'd pull your panties off with my teeth and then I'd spread your legs and just lie there for a long time, my lips pressing ever so gently against your skin. Then I'd taste you. You'd arch your hips because you want more, but I'd only give you the tip of my tongue. But then I'm so hard now I can't wait to get inside you. My dick is just aching for it. And that smell. Fuck, your smell. It drives me crazy. I rise up and run my tongue over your nipples, and then I'm kissing you and you're moaning in my mouth for my cock because I've got just the head of it pressed against—"

Jane let out a huge moan into the phone.

"What was that?"

"Just a moan."

"No, the other sound. The vibrating."

"Sorry, baby. I couldn't wait for you. My drawer was too close. Go on. Don't stop. You're inside me now. Oh, you're inside me. Can you feel it? I can feel you."

"Mmm . . . I can feel it," he said.

She threw the covers back so she could work better with the hand that was holding the toy.

"Are you hard for me right now, baby?" she asked. "Tell me what you're doing right now. Tell me. Please tell me."

"I've got my cock in my hands and I'm stroking it, baby. I'm stroking it for you. It's so hard. I've never seen it so hard."

"Oh, yes. I like that."

"Now I'm massaging myself, but I'm holding back because it feels so good. Oh, Jane. I'm so hard for you— Oh, holy shit!"

Jane heard a loud thud, as if the phone had dropped. Then she heard someone apologize and the sound of a door closing. Then Caleb was on the line again.

"Sorry, babe. I've gotta go."

"Was that Sean?" Jane asked, laughing. "Did he just walk in on you while you were . . ."

"It's not funny, babe. I gotta go."

Jane was still laughing, even though she was trying not to.

"Babe, it's not funny."

"Sorry," she replied, still giggling. "Okay. I love you."

"I love you too," he said.

Before they hung up, Jane added, "But it is kind of funny."

"Okay, maybe it's a little bit funny."

"Good night, my long-distance lover."

"Good night, you sexy siren you. I'll call you tomorrow with the door locked."

❧

Jane sat in the lobby turning over in her mind all the possible reasons her boss could want to see her. She had a sneaking suspicion that it wasn't to give her a raise.

"Mr. Blanco will see you now," the receptionist said.

Jane rose and retucked her uniform shirt, then pulled her shoulders back and followed the receptionist to Mr. Blanco's office. He stood waiting for her behind his desk. He waved her to a seat, excused the receptionist, and then sat down. Jane was nervous, but then he smiled at her and she felt much more comfortable. He had an easy way about him. A calm energy.

"And how are you, Jane?"

"I'm doing well. Thank you, Mr. Blanco."

He flashed a smile. "Please. Manuel."

"Yes, I remember. Manuel."

"So, are you enjoying the job so far?"

"I think I'm getting the hang of it, yes."

"Good. Good."

He sat smiling at her for what seemed like a long time. Then he leaned back in his chair and sighed, his hands holding on to the edge of his mahogany desk.

"I like my job very much also," he said at last. "There's an unexplainable reward in doing work well. My father taught me that. He was a cabinetmaker, and he would have been happy to have had me become a cabinetmaker as well, so long as I took pride in the work. But we all find our own paths in life. When I graduated from college, he made me this desk."

"It's a beautiful desk," Jane said. "I noticed it before."

"Yes, he was very talented. Sometimes I wish I had chosen a profession where I could see the fruits of my work. But I digress. Forgive me. Do you have children, Jane?"

Jane tried not to look upset when she answered. She considered mentioning Melody but then thought better of bringing it up. She might lose her composure.

"No," she said, "I don't have any children."

"I have a son," he offered. "He's twelve. I hope to instill the same work ethic into him that my father did for me. I can't make him a desk such as this, but perhaps I will pass this one on to him as a reminder that any work is worthy work as long as it is done well."

"Excuse me if I sound blunt, Mr. Blanco. I mean, Manuel. But is all of this your way of telling me I'm doing a lousy job?"

He flashed a smile again and laughed. "Yes, I have been told I might benefit from being more direct. And I appreciate your bluntness with me. Otherwise we might be here all day. You must understand that much of my day consists of revenue projections and spreadsheets. And as boring as it is, I take pride in doing my job well."

"I understand," Jane said. "I can try to do a better job."

He smiled and reached across the desk and shook her hand. Then he stood, signaling that the meeting was over. Jane rose and said good-bye. She was at the door when he called her name. She stopped and turned back.

"Did you see the Seahawks beat the Panthers on Sunday?"

Jane shook her head. "Has the season started already?"

"Yes. My son and I always watch the games together. I told him I had met a real twelfth man from Seattle. Or twelfth woman, I should say."

"You mentioned me to your son?" Jane asked.

"He thinks everything from Seattle is cool," he answered, shrugging. Then he smiled and added, "I guess I do too."

Chapter 12

Caleb stopped playing midsong and shook his head.

"This isn't working," he said. "It's too hokey."

"Hokey," Jordyn repeated, her tone mocking. "What are you, like fifty years old? Nobody says *hokey* anymore. They say *lame* or *wack*. But I agree with you. The song sucks ass."

"Oh yeah, because *sucks ass* is so much more current than *hokey*. Did they teach you to talk like that at Juilliard?"

"What's your hang-up with my education?" she asked. Then before he could answer, she added, "Just because I didn't learn guitar in juvie like you did. Get off me about it."

"Sorry, but I just think you're fake. That's all."

Jordyn set her guitar down and leaned forward in her chair, looking straight into Caleb's eyes.

"Listen," she said, looking suddenly serious. "I don't like spending my Saturday writing a stupid duet with you any more than you like spending yours with me. But this is important."

"I don't see why," Caleb replied. "One of us is going to stay and the other is going home. Why sing together?"

She huffed as if he were a stubborn child. "You just don't get it, do you?"

"Don't get what?"

"What this is really about. You've got to see it in terms of marketing. You're right, only one of us is going through. But when we do, we'll be competing against four other singers on live TV. And it won't be up to the judge anymore, then it'll be up to America to decide. And those voters, viewers, whatever you want to call them, all they'll know about us is what they will have just seen on the shows we're recording now. Including this hokey duet. So, Caleb, you need to wake up and take this seriously. We want America to fall in love with us."

"I signed up to write and perform music. You make it sound like we're selling breakfast cereal or something."

"Aren't we?" she asked.

"I sure hope not."

"You know what? I like you, Caleb. And because I like you, I'm going to tell you something."

"Should I feel special?"

"Just shut up and listen. Will you listen?"

"Fine, I'll listen."

"I didn't really go to Juilliard. Well, that's not true either. I kind of did go, but not how I like to let people think. I was in their precollege division."

"What's that mean?"

"It means I was a freshman in high school when I went. I didn't officially graduate from there. I got a certificate, but it isn't the same. But that's not my point. My point is this. Here I was, learning music theory and solfège from the best."

"What's solfège?" Caleb asked, interrupting her.

"It's a method for sight singing and identifying pitch. It's why I could hear your song once and then play it back to you. But let me finish. What I'm trying to say is that I was there with the best and the brightest in the world, learning from the most accomplished musicians, and I realized something. I realized that most of those prodigy kids were going to go on to be great musicians themselves. But at the same time, I knew that almost nobody would ever hear them perform."

"So you're saying popular music means better music? Then explain Justin Bieber to me."

"He's actually pretty good, I think. And Usher obviously thought so when he discovered him. But I don't want to argue about Bieber. And I'm not saying popular makes better. But let me ask you something, Caleb. I've heard your songs. You really have something to say. Is it fair to let twits like Kesha take up all the airwaves? Don't you want your voice to be heard?"

Caleb shrugged. "Yeah, I guess so."

"Then you've got to get popular first so you can say what you want to say and have them hear it."

"That's what you think?"

"That's the lesson I learned. You keep hating me because my father's rich. But my dad doesn't care about money. He's a biologist. And a good one. He's rich because he helped found a biotech company that develops drugs that make people's lives better. And the more money they generate, the more research they can do; the more research they do, the more lives they can save. The money's just a nice bennie. Get it? So why not become famous, build an audience, and then speak your truth? That's what I learned at Juilliard. That's what I learned from my father. That's why I'm here. Now do you understand?"

Caleb sat quietly watching her, considering these things she had said. She looked different in jeans and a T-shirt with almost no makeup on. She looked young. Too young to be wise. But her eyes were bright and alive, and he knew she believed every word of what she was pitching him.

"You wanna know what my father taught me?" he finally asked. "He taught me that you can't drink just a little bit and still be sober."

"And what's that got to do with anything?"

"He convinced himself that he'd drink just a little to get through my mother's death. Then he drank so much he joined her. You better be careful you don't get addicted to the fame."

Jordyn leaned back and crossed her arms and looked at him. He thought he saw both sorrow and defiance in her eyes, and he was sure she was about to reply when the door opened and their judge walked in, followed by a camera crew.

"How are my two superstars doing?" the judge asked, speaking a little too loudly for the room, probably, Caleb thought, for the benefit of the microphones. He watched as Jordyn flashed the judge a huge Hollywood smile.

"We're getting on like old friends," she said. "So much so that I just can't imagine what I'll do next week when we're forced to part."

She looked to Caleb to confirm this, but he only laughed and picked up his guitar, then went back to rehearsing the song.

❧

Sean had a cut lip and one swollen eye when he came in at midnight. He closed the door and leaned against it, breathing hard. Then he opened it again and peeked out into the hall and looked left and then right, as if perhaps he were checking to see if he had been pursued. When he closed the door again, he latched the privacy lock and flopped onto his bed, where he lay looking at his knuckles and appearing somewhat perplexed.

"Well, fuck all," he finally said. "I didn't see that coming."

"What the hell happened?" Caleb asked.

"Shit, man. I was in the lobby bar trying to pick up this chick. She's in town with some girlfriends going to Disneyland. Who the fuck goes to Disneyland if they're old enough to drink? Anyway, some douche got all butt-hurt over my talking to her, and he came over to give me the what-for."

"So you got in a fight over a girl you don't even know?"

"No, dude. Screw the girl."

"Sounds like that's what you were trying for," Caleb said.

"Yeah." He laughed. "I was. I was trying hard too. But that wasn't it. There's way too many mice in the barn to fight some crazy cat over just one."

"I've heard of fish in the sea," Caleb interjected, "but mice in the barn?"

"It's something my old man says. It's an Iowa thing, dude. Anyway it wasn't about her. When Mr. Sunglasses strolled over and cut in, I was happy to tap out. I was gone. But then he had to jump in on me with a comment about the way I looked."

"Oh, no. What'd he say?"

"He called me Billie Joe Armstrong."

"The lead singer of Green Day? What's wrong with that?"

"That's what I said, man. I actually thanked him."

"So, what was the problem?"

"After I told him it was a compliment, the idiot goes on to say Billie Joe Armstrong can't sing for shit."

"So what?"

"So I hit him."

"Let me get this straight," Caleb said. "You won't fight over a girl, or even over the way you look being insulted, but you'll up and throw down on a guy for insulting Green Day."

"Dude, I grew up on Green Day. Some shit's just sacred."

Caleb laughed so hard he nearly fell off his bed. "Sorry," he said, regaining his composure. "But seriously, dude, I'm really going to miss the hell out of you if one of us goes home this week."

Sean got up and looked at himself in the wall mirror. "I'm sure as shit going home now," he said. "Look at me."

"Oh, that's nothing, pal," Caleb said, trying hard to sound reassuring. "The makeup gal'll fix you right up."

"You think so?"

"Sure. And even if it shows a little, just sing one of your edgier songs. You'll totally look the part. Everyone loves the bad-ass rocker."

Sean looked at Caleb's reflection in the mirror. "Thanks, man. How was your duet rehearsal with Jordyn? She ask about me yet?"

"Yeah, she asked me if you were single."

Sean whipped around to look at Caleb straight on with his one good eye open wide. "She did?"

"No, dude. I'm just screwing with you. She did give me a lecture on the nature of the music business. Truth is, there's no way I'm going to beat her. She's too commercial and I'm too alternative. Plus, I don't think our judge ever liked me."

"She passed you through this far."

"Only because it makes good TV. I swear, this show's as scripted as a movie. The whole thing's a racket."

"Yeah, well, what isn't?"

"That's what Jordyn said."

"See, we were meant to be together, her and I were." Then he sat on the bed and stripped off his shoes, saying, "I don't think I'm going through either. Makeup or no makeup."

"Why not?"

"We rehearsed our duet this afternoon."

"You and Panda."

He nodded. "That chick scares me."

"She's all of sixteen, dude."

"I know it. But that voice. Damn. It's like she opens her mouth and it comes from everywhere all at once. Like a ghost or something. Like the sky opened onto heaven and angels are singing. That girl makes me want to give up music altogether and work for my dad on the farm."

He tossed his shoes in the corner and rose from the bed. "I'm gonna take a shower. You want me to knock before I come out of the bathroom?"

"Why would I want you to knock?" Caleb asked.

"I dunno," he said, grinning with his split lip. "Maybe you wanna call your girl or something."

Caleb threw a pillow at him. "Get out of here."

Caleb was sitting in the makeup chair getting his face powdered when his judge walked by on her way to the set from her dressing room. She stopped to look him over. The makeup artists stepped back with an air of deference, letting the judge have an uninterrupted view.

"I thought your duet with Jordyn this morning was great, Caleb," she said. "But are you ready to wow me out there with your final solo act? Only one artist can go through, you know."

Caleb looked up at her from the makeup chair. "Would it make a difference if I do wow you?"

"Now, what is that supposed to mean?"

"I dunno. I just figured you must already know which one of us you're sending through."

"Well, that would spoil all the surprise, wouldn't it?"

"Maybe for the TV viewers, I guess, which is all anyone here seems to care about."

She crossed her arms and cocked her head to look at him, then let out a short laugh.

"You're a strange boy, Caleb Cummings."

"Is that good or bad?"

"Maybe a little of both," she said.

"Can I ask you something, Cynthia?"

"Fire away."

"Why did you give me a thumbs-down in Austin? And why did I end up on your team here?"

"That's two somethings," she said, "but I'll answer both. You ended up on my team because we picked names blindly out of a hat. I was as surprised as I'm sure you were."

"Well, that's encouraging," he muttered.

"I gave you a thumbs-down at your audition," she went on,

"because although I thought you were good, I didn't think you were ready."

"But you gave Panda a thumbs-up just before me. And she's only sixteen."

"Yes, well, some people are born ready."

"Do you think I'm ready now?"

She smiled and cocked one plucked and painted eyebrow. "I told you," she said, "I'm waiting to be wowed by your final performance to decide. Hopefully your roommate hasn't rubbed off on you too much."

"Rubbed off on me how?"

"Don't you think it's odd that he wears more eyeliner than the sixteen-year-old girl he's competing against? This is the music business, Caleb, and I've been in it a long time. America loves clean-cut and attractive people who are good at what they do. That's why Starbucks is so successful."

"But I'm not selling coffee in a cardboard cup."

"You see," she said, shrugging her thin shoulders, "that's why I gave Jordyn a thumbs-up. She's ready. The only question now is which of you I think America would love more."

As she finished talking she smiled and tossed her hands up, as if to say the outcome was anyone's guess, even though Caleb suspected that that was far from true. Then she turned on her heel and marched off toward the stage.

When she was out of sight, the makeup artist reappeared from the sideline, where she had been organizing her supplies while obviously eavesdropping the entire time.

"Wow," she said. "You're braver than I am. She mistook me for a set hand the other day and asked me to get her iced tea. I got it instead of correcting her."

Caleb laughed, closing his eyes for the powder. "It's just a show and she's just one of the judges."

"For you, maybe," the girl said. "But for me it's just a job, and she's just one of the bosses. Now, let's get this hair fixed up for you and then I think you'll be set."

~

The artists stood lined up on the stage, every one of them nervous as hell, while the judges laughed and talked among themselves. The judges would occasionally point down from their box and comment to one another on the contestants, as if this were just some other day, which Caleb guessed for them it was. For him it was anything but. If he made it through this round, there would be only four artists and four weeks between him and half a million dollars. Enough after taxes for a down payment on a house and one hell of a wedding.

Don't think about it, he told himself. You'll only get disappointed. Just think about getting home and seeing Jane. Think about that.

The producer eventually called for quiet on the set. Then the director called for action. And just like that, it was really happening. The host was onstage in his shiny suit and coiffed hair, gleefully reading from the teleprompter the rules that would determine the contestants' fates.

Caleb watched as the spotlight hit the first pair of artists. They were both girls with incredible voices, although Caleb figured Jasmine would be the one going through today. And he was right. The judge hemmed and hawed and eventually chose, and Jasmine jumped and jiggled and hugged the host so hard he dropped the microphone.

When Jasmine was seated in the chair and the losing contestant had gone, the spotlight moved. A guy and a girl this time—both young country artists. Caleb guessed the guy. He was wrong. The judge called Carrie Ann, and she curtsied and skipped over to join Jasmine. The losing kid went into a short speech to thank the judge and the show, but the host eventually cut him off and ushered him off the stage.

Next up were two folksy girls who could have been sisters. Caleb couldn't pick between the two, and it appeared the judge couldn't either. The host pressured the judge for a decision, a well-rehearsed and ramped-up sense of urgency played out for the camera, and finally the one named Erica went through.

Then the spotlight moved to Sean and Panda. Sean looked at Caleb and smiled nervously, in spite of his swollen lip. Then he dropped his head as if he knew. Panda was standing beside him in her sparkly red shoes, and she reached up a hand and patted him on the back as if she knew too. It was a strange, almost maternal gesture from someone so young. The host asked for a decision, and the judge spent so long complimenting Sean on his performances and on his growth as an artist that before the winner's name was even spoken, everyone on the set and in the audience knew he was going home.

"We need the name now, Judge. America's waiting."

"Panda," the judge finally burst out. "I'm choosing to put Panda through."

Sean immediately turned and hugged Panda, and told her she deserved to go on. A true bad boy through and through, Caleb thought, but one hell of a good guy too. Then Sean looked at Caleb, and Caleb could see by the spotlight in his eyes that he was crying. He smiled and gave Caleb two reassuring thumbs-up, and then he walked off the stage for his last time.

Caleb was still watching him go when the spotlight hit his eyes. Jordyn was standing next to him, and she reached and took his hand in hers. He would have rather faced the judge alone, but Jordyn's grip was tight and she wouldn't let go.

Oh well, he thought, she's probably just as nervous as I am.

Then Caleb saw the host speak, and he was aware that the judge had begun to ramble on about how great he and Jordyn each were, but for whatever reason, he couldn't understand a word. It was as if the stage and the judges and the people had retreated to some faraway place, his body standing there in the spotlight, but his mind and soul and heart were a thousand miles away with Jane. He heard her parting words: *I love you, Caleb. I love you no matter what. Rich or poor, win or lose. And I'll be waiting right here for you when you return.*

He could see Jane's face, the crease in the corner of her lips and the twinkle in her eyes when she smiled. He could taste her kiss good-bye. Smell the shampoo in her hair. And he wanted to reach out and touch her, to feel the skin of her cheek with his fingertips, caress the delicate flesh at the back of her neck. And he wanted to tell her that he loved her and that he always had and always would. Rich or poor, win or lose, no matter what the world threw at them, they would face it together.

"Caleb. Did you hear me, Caleb?"

"I'm sorry," he said, coming to and looking up at the judge. "Did I hear what?"

"We need your decision; we're running out of time."

"My decision?"

Caleb looked around, feeling very confused. Then Jordyn squeezed his hand and leaned in to him and rose onto her tiptoes and whispered in his ear.

"Just go along with me," she said. "You're going through. Nod if you understand."

He nodded and Jordyn lifted their joined hands into the air. "Yes, we'll do it! We'll go through together."

The applause sign lit up, and the audience rose to their feet and clapped and cheered.

Did she say *together*?

Caleb looked over at Jordyn. "What do you mean, together?"

But it was so loud now on the soundstage, none of the microphones caught his comment. And if Jordyn did, she only ignored his question and kept on smiling and waving for the cameras.

~

"Dude, did you have a seizure up there, or what? You really had no idea what she asked?"

Caleb splashed cold water on his face again, then raised his head and watched it drip off in the bathroom mirror. He could see Sean standing in the doorway behind him.

"I didn't hear a word, Sean. I was all wrapped up in a daydream, and the next thing I knew, everyone was clapping and Jordyn was lifting my hand up in the air like I'd won a boxing match or something. She said I was going through, but I didn't know it meant both of us as a stupid duo."

"Still, a duo's better than going home, dude."

Caleb dried his face with a towel, then turned to look at Sean. "You think so?"

"Sure. You still get the recording contract if you win, even if you do have to split the advance. And I don't know about you, but I sure wouldn't turn down a quarter million dollars."

Caleb tossed the used towel on the floor and sighed. "What did the judge say? Did you hear?"

"I was watching the monitors backstage. She just went on about what an impossible choice it was, same as they all do, but then she said she loved your duet so much that she had a proposition for you. She said you could go through together if you both agreed to be a duo. Otherwise, she'd choose one."

"I just wonder why she did it. And why did Jordyn agree to go through with me? She seemed like a lock to me."

"Maybe because she's into you, man."

"I don't think so. I think she's just smart and conniving, even though I can't see her angle yet."

"Well, whatever, dude. She's not bad to look at anyway."

"I've got a girl, Sean. And I intend to marry her."

"Yeah, but that doesn't mean you're dead, dude."

Caleb walked past Sean into the room and flopped down onto his bed with a sigh. He picked up his phone and checked it. He'd sent a text to Jane with the news, but she hadn't replied yet. He glanced at the clock and figured that she must still be out working since it was Friday evening.

He set the phone down and looked at Sean. "Hey, what are you even doing here? It's our last night. Shouldn't you be out running the town?"

Sean looked down at his feet and shrugged. "Nah, I've seen enough of L.A., dude. I'm looking forward to getting home."

Caleb could tell that Sean was depressed. He just wasn't sure if it was because they would be going their separate ways in the morning or because Sean wouldn't be coming back.

"Hey, I've got an idea," Caleb announced, hopping off the bed. "Let's get out of here together and go have some fun."

"Really? Where would we go?"

"You could show me Canter's Deli."

"You really wanna see it?"

"Sure. I love Guns N' Roses. And I wouldn't mind walking Sunset Strip. I've been here this whole time, and all I've seen is that stupid soundstage and the inside of this room."

"Sweet. We can hit up Jumbo's Clown Room too."

Caleb had his shirt half on when he paused. "Jumbo's Clown Room? I'm afraid to even ask."

"Dude, it's the land of milk and honey. They claim it's the best alternative pole-dancing club in Hollywood."

"What do you mean by 'alternative'?"

"The girls are insane. Big ones, little ones. There was a midget last week. And they're all tatted up and pierced."

Caleb laughed and pulled his shirt the rest of the way on. "Let's start with Canter's and see what happens."

⚬⚬⚬

They caught a cab in front of the hotel and had it drop them at Canter's Deli. Caleb had expected to be impressed, but it just seemed like an all-night diner with a bar attached, except that there were photos of the owner together with Slash on the wall above their booth. They ate thick pastrami sandwiches, and Caleb had a glass of cold milk while Sean had a Heineken. Then Caleb held the menu up for cover while Sean used his pocketknife to add his initials to the hundreds of others on the wooden booth.

When they left they walked up to Hollywood Boulevard, passing crazy cartoon-costumed street characters posing for pictures with tourists, passing Grauman's Chinese Theatre and its creepy concrete footprints from the past, passing Marilyn Monroe, and James Dean, and even Elvis twice, once young, once old. They walked on past the Roxy and the House of Blues, doubling back to stop into Musso and Frank, where they sat at the bar and pretended to be Hollywood bigwigs. Caleb had a club soda while he watched Sean down martinis and a dish of baked escargot, because they had neither in Iowa, or so Caleb assumed. Then they headed deeper into the Strip.

There they walked beneath the warm glow of a thousand billboards from a bygone era, and they talked about their lives and their hopes and their dreams, and about music, of course, music being the thing that connected all three. And they were not alone. Their shadows followed beside them with the ghosts of Janis Joplin and Jimi Hendrix and Jim Morrison, forever young, forever falling in love with life and with music and with one another, the voices of sweet poetry and endless possibility, their conversations still echoing just beneath the din and clamor of the clubs, if one were drunk enough, or brave enough, to put his ear to the sidewalk and listen.

"I hear Van Halen," Sean said. "How about you?"

"I've got Poison. No, wait. Mötley Crüe."

They pushed their way into a club and got lost in the neon fog and the electric sound. The crowd separated them for several sets until Caleb finally found Sean bent over a toilet and heaving between promises to never drink again. If he lived, he said. Caleb cleaned him up and they left the club, then walked arm in arm back to Canter's for coffee and eggs.

"It was coming out of both ends," Sean said, stirring sugar into his third coffee. "I think I've got Montezuma's revenge."

"Dude, you're in L.A., not Mexico."

"I think it was those snails."

"Might have been the martinis," Caleb suggested. "Or the shots of tequila, perhaps."

Sean shrugged and sipped his coffee. "Maybe," he said.

They sat for a while and listened to two drunken girls in the next booth, working together to craft responses to text messages from boys they'd met this very night who were already trying to bed them.

"How come you don't drink?" Sean asked, out of the blue.

"I used to drink a little," Caleb said. "But I started having a bit of a problem putting it down and it scared me sober. My dad and my mom both died from booze. Well, my mom died in a car wreck, but she was drunk."

"Don't you find it's hard to write songs sober, though? I seem to write my best stuff when I'm flying a little high. Not like tonight. But at least my feet off the ground, you know?"

Caleb nodded that maybe it was so. "I'm sure if you embrace the visions, alcohol or LSD or pot and all that shit help just the same. But there's a high to be had in turning it all down too."

"Turn it down to get high? What do you mean?"

"I dunno. It's kind of a trip itself being clear all the time."

"Like a Scientologist or something?"

Caleb laughed. "I think that's a different kind of clear. I'm talking about feeling everything because you're sober."

Sean nodded and downed the rest of his coffee. When he set his empty mug on the table, he leaned over and looked into it, as if by chance there might be something to be read there on the bottom.

"Well," he said, still looking into that empty mug, "I might have to try giving it up for a while."

"I thought you said the trouble was those snails."

Sean grinned and looked up. "What the hell did you think I was talking about giving up?" he asked. "You didn't believe I'd quit booze, did you?"

Caleb laughed and called for their check.

There was already a hint of gray in the sky when they left. There were no cars and no cabs, and it was a long walk back to the hotel. Even so, neither of them said much.

When they finally arrived at their room, Sean quickly showered and packed his bags, then called down to see about the shuttle. His flight was several hours earlier than Caleb's, and he said the sooner he could get to the airport, the sooner he could board the plane and pass out, then wake up back home. He stood at the door with his bag, neither of them knowing how to say good-bye.

"I'll just follow you down," Caleb said.

"You don't gotta do that, guy. Why don't you rest?"

"It's fine. I have a few minutes to wait before my morning call from Jane anyway. And besides, I need some toothpaste from the front desk."

They rode the elevator down, crossed the lobby, and walked outside together. The hotel shuttle was already idling out front. Sean stopped before getting on and turned to Caleb.

"They had a big fancy driver with a sign and everything for me when I arrived. Now that I'm leaving, I gotta ride the short bus." He sighed and looked past Caleb into the hotel. "You don't need any toothpaste, do you?"

Caleb smiled and shook his head.

Sean nodded, as if he'd suspected not. "I'm not very good at good-byes."

"Neither am I," Caleb replied.

"You know, I'm okay with being sent home. Truth is, I never thought I'd get this far. But you deserve to go on, dude. You're a hell of an artist and . . . you're . . . well . . . ah, shit. I'm not any good at this. Fuck it all. Well, it's been real, it's been fun, but it hasn't been real fun."

He stuck out his hand to shake, but Caleb batted it aside and hugged him.

"I'm glad I got to know you, Sean," he said, pulling away. "I wouldn't have wanted to room with anyone else."

Sean smiled and wiped a tear from his cheek with the heel of his hand. "I wouldn't have wanted to room with anyone else either," he said, nodding. "I'll catch you on the TV, dude. And maybe when you're famous, you'll come and tour Iowa." Then he picked up his bag and boarded the shuttle.

The door was closing when he wedged his hand in and opened it again so he could lean out. "Except Jordyn," he said. "I would have rather roomed with Jordyn."

Caleb watched Sean's grin disappear as the door closed. He could see his shadow through the tinted windows as he walked to the back of the shuttle. He took a seat on the opposite side, maybe so they wouldn't have to stretch out their good-bye. But Caleb stood and watched the bus drive away anyway. In fact, he stood for several minutes after, just watching where it had gone.

Chapter 13

Jane stood outside the flight gate exit waiting for him. She was so nervous that she hardly even noticed the odd glances from strangers as they passed her on their way to baggage claim. She knew she shouldn't be nervous, that she and Caleb had spoken nearly every day since he'd been away, but she was nervous just the same.

A pilot paused to look at her. He smiled and said, "I might be a frog now, but I know if a woman as beautiful as you are were to kiss me, I'd change into a prince."

Jane glanced down at the homemade glitter sign she had hanging around her neck—

PRINCE CHARMING

—and then she looked back up at the pilot and blushed.

"You're certainly very charming," she said, "but my prince is on his way."

The pilot grinned and carried on with his bag, replying as he passed by, "And he's a lucky prince at that."

When she saw him coming, it was from a long way off.

Caleb was taller than she remembered him being, his head above most of the others walking toward her. He had his duffel slung over his shoulder and he was wearing a black T-shirt and torn blue jeans. His hair was a little longer than it had been when he had left, but she could clearly see the highlights they'd put there catching the sun coming in from the high terminal windows. And even though she couldn't take her eyes off him, she didn't miss the looks he got from every girl and woman he passed, and a few others he even got from men.

She knew he had seen her when a smile flashed on his face and he quickened his step. A moment later and his duffel was on the ground at his feet and she was in his arms, being turned around in the air. She buried her fingers in his hair and looked down at his upturned face. His smile seemed wider and whiter than ever against the several days' worth of stubble around his gorgeous mouth, and his green eyes seemed to sparkle with a new intensity, a deeper happiness.

Perhaps, Jane thought, from having made the live show. Or maybe, she hoped, from having finally come home. She meant to ask, but then he set her feet on the ground again and kissed her.

His lips were softer than she remembered, even though his kiss was firm and filled with need, and his tongue tasted of coffee and of mint. He pulled his lips away, held her head between his hands, and looked into her eyes.

"Do you know how much I love you?"

"How much do you love me?" she asked.

"So much that I can't wait to marry you."

"Good," she said. "Because I was worried maybe now that you're famous and everything, you might have changed your mind about marrying a lowly old meter maid."

"Famous? The first episode hasn't even aired yet."

Jane smiled. Then she brushed his T-shirt with her hand. "I got glitter all over you."

Caleb looked down at her welcome sign. He laughed. "I'll bet you've had a few takers while you were standing here with that sign."

"I was going to write *Singer-Songwriter Superstar* on it but it wouldn't all fit. Plus, I didn't have enough glitter. Do you like it, though? After you told me about their driver with his sign, I didn't want to let L.A. show me up."

He smiled and kissed the top of her head. "It's a great welcome home. It couldn't possibly be better. Unless maybe you were naked, wearing nothing but the sign."

"Then I might have had more than a few takers," she said, laughing.

As they walked to baggage claim together to retrieve his guitar, Caleb handed her a small box.

"What's this?"

"Just a little present."

"You didn't have to do that, babe."

"Go on. Open it."

Jane removed the paper and opened the box. Inside was a necklace. A beautiful handcrafted silver pipe whistle on a chain.

"You like it?"

"I love it."

She draped it over her neck with the sign and looked down at it on her chest.

"I saw it and thought you might. And if you get in any trouble out there on the job, you can blow it. It's pretty loud. Plus, all the proceeds go to help bring peace to the Congo."

"It's beautiful, Caleb. But you shouldn't have."

"It wasn't that much," he said. Then he smiled and added, "Besides, I used your credit card."

Jane opened her eyes wide, pretending to be shocked.

"I'm only kidding. Let's get my guitar and get home. I've got an image of you in my head that I'd like to make a reality."

"And what image is that?"

"You wearing nothing but that sign."

"Can I wear the whistle too?"

"Sure. Maybe you can blow it when I hit the right spot."

He filled Jane in on everything while she drove them home from the airport. He told her all about daydreaming on the stage and agreeing to go through as a duet without even realizing it. But despite her reassurances that he had done the right thing, he must have sensed some of her doubts.

"You sure you don't mind?" he asked. "Because I don't have to go back, you know."

"Don't be silly," she said. "You have to go. This is your big chance for big money. And even if you don't win, they'll be paying you per episode now. I read the rules. You get to join the TV union and everything."

"Yeah, but what about Jordyn? Doesn't it bother you?"

"Should it?" she asked.

"No way."

"Then it doesn't."

She drove in silence for a minute or two. "But it's not a good sign if you have to ask me."

"What do you mean?"

"Well, would you be asking if it bothered me if it were Sean you were partnered with?"

"Of course not."

"Then see? Why are you asking about Jordyn? Either you think I'm insecure or you don't trust yourself around her."

"That's not fair, Jane."

"It isn't?"

"No. You know damn well it isn't the same thing as if I were paired up with Sean."

"Why isn't it?"

"Because he's a dude and Jordyn's an attractive girl."

"So you *do* think she's attractive."

"Oh, come on, Jane."

"It's okay. I think she is. I watched her seductive videos on YouTube, and I was almost ready to switch teams."

"That's not funny. Let's just change the subject already."

"Fine. And just so you know, I trust you, Caleb. I trust you completely. If you wanted to be with someone else, it would kill me inside, but I'd rather you be with them. I won't have you unless it's of your own free will. So I'm not bothered about Jordyn. In fact, I'm rather flattered."

"You are?"

"Yes. I'm pretty sure you could be with her or any other woman, and the fact that you're here with me makes me very proud. Proud of us. I want you with me because you want to be with me. Not because of some piece of paper or some ring."

"I want the same thing from you," he said.

Jane smiled. A mile or two later, she said, "But I'm still counting on a wedding, just so you know."

"We could turn around this minute and go back to the airport and fly to Las Vegas."

"Are you kidding me?" she asked. "I'm not getting married in Vegas. And besides, I'm taking you home to practice the honeymoon right now."

When they arrived, Jane had hardly put the car in park before Caleb was out and around at the driver's door waiting for her. She stepped out and he kissed her. Then he took her hand and pulled her toward the apartment building.

"What about your bag?" Jane asked. "Your guitar?"

"They can wait," he said, practically dragging her up the stairs at a run.

The apartment door hadn't even latched behind them before he had her up against the wall and was unbuttoning her blouse. Jane pushed him away and she saw him frown, thinking he was being rejected. Then the frown curled into a smile as she handed him the sign and unbuttoned her blouse herself and stripped it off. She took her bra off next. His eyes moved to her chest. She took the sign back and draped it over her neck, along with the whistle.

"Is this what you wanted to see?" she asked.

He nodded that it was.

"Good," she said. "Now take off your shirt."

He peeled his T-shirt off over his head and Jane flushed at the sight of his long torso. It looked as though he'd lost a little weight on his trip and she could see every muscle.

"Are you flexing your abs to impress me?" she asked.

"Maybe," he said, grinning.

"Come over here."

Caleb stepped toward her, and she took his head in her hands and kissed him. There was something about his taste that made her think of sex and only sex. She gripped his thick hair with one hand, pushed the sign aside with the other, and pulled his mouth down to her breast. She let out a soft moan when he took her nipple gently between his teeth. His hands feverishly worked on her zipper, but she pushed him away again.

"I want you on the bed," she said. "Now. Do as I say."

"Wow," he replied, looking shocked. "A girl gets a badge and some pepper spray, and suddenly she's a dominatrix."

"You can refer to me as Mistress," she said. "Now, get on the bed before I get my whip."

He paused at the bedroom door just long enough to say, "Hey, I thought you broke the bed and needed me to fix it."

"I fixed it myself," she replied, pushing him into the room. "If you think I need a man for everything, you're wrong. I'll show you what I need a man for, though. I'll show you right now. Get on the bed and lie on your back and close your eyes."

Caleb looked cautiously excited as he crawled onto the bed, stretched out, and turned to look at her. She waited for him to close his eyes, and then she took the sign off. When she caught him looking at her again, she brought the whistle to her mouth and blew on it.

"Busted, buddy. Now, I said close your eyes or else."

He smiled and closed his eyes.

Jane opened the drawer and took out the handcuffs she had purchased. He must have heard them rattle, because his eyes cracked open a slit and then opened wide.

"You didn't," he said.

"You address me as Mistress or you don't address me at all," she said, crawling on top of him. "Now, close your eyes and give me your wrists."

He laughed and offered up his wrists.

She clasped the cuffs around one, then fed the chain through the metal headboard and clasped them around the other. Her breasts were hanging in his face as she secured the cuffs, and when he lifted his head and licked her nipple, she felt her spine tingle. She pushed his head back down onto the pillow and kissed him. He instinctively moved to wrap his arms around her, but the cuffs caught with a clatter on the bed frame and he was trapped.

Jane giggled and kissed her way down to his neck. He tasted like the outside and like soap, and she was so turned on she could hardly keep up her little game. But she did. She moved her mouth down to his chest and tickled his nipples with her tongue, lying there and watching them go hard. He had just the right amount of soft hair that grew in just the right places, and it turned her on like crazy to feel it against her cheek. She traced his abs with the tip of her tongue, moving down to his belly button, his waistline. He was bulging against his jeans, and she cupped him with her hands and put her mouth to the denim and blew warm air through the fabric. She heard him moan, and then she heard the cuffs clatter on the bed frame.

"This is fucking torture," he said.

"Good. It's supposed to be."

She undid his belt slowly, first yanking it tight, then gently releasing it. Next, she undid his button. Then she pulled the zipper down. Caleb wasn't wearing any underwear, and as the zipper parted he rose from his pants and stood erect and throbbing in front of her face. She felt her insides tighten with anticipation, felt herself get wet.

Not yet, she told herself. Not yet. Make him wait.

Jane stripped off his shoes and pulled his jeans completely free, tossing them onto the floor. Then she stood back for a second to look at him, stretched out and handcuffed to the bed frame, completely naked. He was looking at her from between his upraised and cuffed forearms, and she thought she'd never before seen such a look of chained desire.

She bent and put her mouth to his calf and kissed her way up his long leg. When her tongue hit his inner thigh, she felt the muscle tighten and twitch. A tiny moan slipped from his lips. She had her hands now on either side of his waist, her thumbs resting in the *V* that ran down to become the crease leading to his erection, and she looked up at him as she teased him with her tongue. Just around the base. She saw the vein there thicken and she saw him harden even more, pulsing with spasms of need that seemed now to be beyond her control not to satisfy. She rose up and took just a taste. Salty and sweet and just like him.

"Oh, fuck," he said. "I need to be inside you right now."

She grinned up at him, flicking her tongue in and out against the object of his torture. "Maybe if you beg," she said.

"Please. Please. Please."

"Please, Mistress," she said, correcting him.

"Yes, Mistress. Please, Mistress. I need to be inside you right now. Take these cuffs off and let me make love to you."

He rattled the cuffs, but she shook her head.

"How about we leave them on and *I* fuck *you*."

"Okay," he agreed, nodding fiercely. "Yes, Mistress."

She backed off of him and stood and stripped down to her panties. Then she turned away and folded herself in half in one of the only yoga poses she could remember and looked at him through the gap in her legs. He was writhing in the cuffs like a man drowning.

"You like?" she asked.

Caleb nodded, but by the size of his hard-on she already knew the answer. She stripped off her panties and tossed them at him. Then she crawled on top of him and straddled him on the bed. She was resting with her ass on his thighs and her pelvis just beneath his, and he rose so far up her belly she couldn't believe all of him would fit. She raised herself up and leaned forward, resting her weight on one hand and reaching back behind with the other and wrapping him in her fingers—and then she lowered herself down, guiding him to her, down, down, guiding him inside her, down, down. He closed his eyes and exhaled the breath he had been holding, and she watched his face slacken with ecstasy as she rode him, up and down, sliding her hips forward and back, feeling him, deep and pulsing, the man she loved back inside her where he belonged.

Jane meant to go slow and continue his torture, but even for her the game was up. She placed her hands flat on his chest and fucked him like she'd never fucked another man. She was riding him hard, clutching his chest and flailing her hair, feeling her breasts bounce and letting herself go completely with wild moans of pleasure, when there was a tremendous crash and they both dropped. But she hardly could have cared. She was swimming in deep ecstasy, as if she were there in the room but yet she wasn't. Then every thought and fear she had ever had in her life was swept away, as if they had never been, as she was caught up in a flood of sweet relief so vast, it threatened to sweep her away to a place from which she would never wish to come back. Had she been able to think at all, she would have known without a doubt that it was the best orgasm of her life.

Jane was lying flat against his sweaty chest, quivering and panting, and when she finally looked up, she saw that his poor hands were caught up high above his head because the mattress had fallen again through the frame and was resting on the floor. And he was looking at her with an expression that suggested both admiration and fear. Then Caleb laughed.

"I'm so sorry, baby," she said. "Are your wrists okay?"

"I think my wrists are all right for the moment, but there's something else I need released."

"Oh, baby, what's hurt?"

"I didn't come yet, honey."

"Oh, gosh. I'm sorry. It always happens at the same time when they're doing it like this in the books I read."

"Is that where you've been getting these ideas?" he asked, laughing. "How about we get these crazy things off me so I can make love to you."

Jane rose on rubber legs, still reeling from her orgasm, then retrieved the key and freed him. He immediately took her in his arms and laid her out on the broken bed and kissed her. His lips were soft and his hands gentle, a sweet contrast to what she had just experienced. His mouth was still on hers when he slipped inside her. She was drenched from the flood and he was harder than ever, so they coupled almost without trying.

Caleb rested his weight on one arm and stroked her cheek

with that hand while he cupped her breast with his other, and she could feel the cold steel of the handcuff that was still attached to that wrist. He never stopped kissing her as he thrust himself deeper and harder, as if he might meld them together into one being so that no man or woman would ever again see either of them as just one, as if by some miraculous fusion they might conjoin there on the bed and lie forever embraced, nothing between them but the constant pulse of pleasure and the sweet dealings of private love.

He began to move faster, and his breath was pushing into her lungs with each thrust, and then she heard a kind of high-pitched cross between a scream and a whimper, and she felt his muscles clench and his entire body shudder and she was suddenly full and warm. It felt so good, Jane was sure she was going to come again, but she didn't.

He sighed and collapsed on the mattress next to her and laid his head on her chest. She could feel his breathing, still fast but slowing, and she could smell the salt from his sweat. The room seemed to float in empty space. She heard a siren outside somewhere, completely disconnected from her and his reality. Another world. Perhaps another time.

Remember this moment, Jane told herself. Lock it away with absolute clarity to recall someday when you're unsure of just what is this thing we call love. Because this is love and love is this. This feeling. This moment. This glorious afterglow.

They lay there together for a long time, neither of them speaking. And she would have willingly lain like that forever had she not glanced up at the clock.

"Oh, shit. I've gotta go, babe. I'm late for work."

He tried to pull her back down, but she was already scrabbling up out of the broken bed and rushing to the closet for her uniform. She had slipped on her panties and was pulling on the uniform pants when she realized that she had better hit the bathroom first to avoid an embarrassing emergency. When she came out again, she was dressed. Caleb was still lying on the mattress with a contented look on his face.

"Your uniform's way hot," he said. "I didn't know they fit like that."

"They usually don't," she replied, grabbing her work belt from the closet and strapping it on. "I shrank it in the dryer just to look cute for you."

"Well, I'll bet you've got guys lined up at expired meters just begging to get ticketed."

She laughed. "I wish. There's plenty of food in the fridge if you're hungry. Do you need your bag from the car?"

"Nah, it'll be fine in the trunk."

"Okay, I've got the bar beat tonight so I'll be home just after midnight."

"You sure you're safe out there?" he asked.

"I am now that I've got my whistle," she said, smiling.

She stopped at the bedroom door to take one last look at Caleb's naked perfection, something to carry with her on her shift. "I love you, baby. Welcome home."

"I love you too, Jane."

She turned to go and had grabbed her purse and made it as far as the door when she heard him call her name. She glanced back. He was standing in the bedroom doorway with the handcuffs dangling from his wrist.

"Where's the key for these?"

"I don't know," she said. "A girl can't be expected to keep track of everything. You'll probably find it on the floor when you fix the bed."

"Fix the bed? But I thought you didn't need a man."

She smiled at him. "Why fix something yourself when you can get a man to fix it? That's a woman's motto, you know."

Caleb had the bed apart and nearly fixed by the time he found the key and freed his wrist from the handcuffs. He laughed as he slipped them back into Jane's drawer. Then he took a hot shower.

It was quiet in the apartment without Jane. Too quiet. Now that he was back, he wasn't used to her having a job to go to, and he began to appreciate all those days she had spent alone while he had been working. He kicked around and picked a few things up, and then he decided to go out for a walk and clear his head.

The air was humid. Dark clouds had piled up on the horizon with tendrils of rain dropping down and catching the last rays of sunset, giving the horizon a strange and heavy appearance, as if the sky itself were bleeding. Caleb stuffed his hands in his pockets and walked on.

He heard chatter in restaurants that he passed and laughter in the bars. He heard bands warming up, street musicians banging plastic-bucket drums, and sirens crossing one another in the distance. He heard everything and it was all coming in as waves of color that he let wash over him as he trod the sidewalk at a steady pace, letting his footfalls keep the beat.

He thought about his childhood dreams of being a musician and escaping the constant longing that came with cold streets and having little or nothing to eat. He thought about all the lonely hours crashed in strange apartments, writing songs about heartache and injustice. He thought about the day he'd first seen Jane's daughter, Melody, and he remembered more than anything the look of impossible hope burning deep in those sad and tortured eyes. And he remembered seeing the same look again in Jane. Only her sadness had been more real, her hope more hidden.

He sometimes felt as though Melody had crossed his path

as a foreshadowing to his falling in love with Jane, the coin they had passed back and forth a talisman that would lead Jane to him. And he thought about the inequity of such a position, the injustice of fate. Oh, the hands that had passed that coin without knowing its ultimate purpose, the hands that worked somewhere still in the background, perhaps passing a talisman for each of us until it someday found its place.

These thoughts came crashing in on top of one another and he was powerless to stop them unless he gave them a voice in song, and so he began to hum a melody and work these rambling musings into lyrics. This was why he made music; this was his art. Not some silly TV show where he'd be competing with Twitter kids hoping for followers and fortune and fame.

He was torn. He didn't want to go back to the show. He feared it might ruin him. But he wanted more than anything to provide for Jane. To be a man she could both love and respect. To give her the wedding she deserved and had never had. To give her a home. To give her a child. To give her love. He wanted these things more than he had wanted anything in all the days since he'd found the courage to even dare to dream. But he was still torn, and he hoped above all else that whatever his decision, it wouldn't prove to tear them apart in the end.

The crack and rumble of thunder cut through his thoughts and they fell away somewhere behind him in the night. The first raindrops hit the ground in front of him, but he only hunched his shoulders and walked on.

❧

Jane walked the blocks surrounding Sixth Street, dodging the rickshaws and the drunks. She glanced routinely at the meter receipts on the cars as she passed them, but her mind was somewhere else.

Her mind was on Caleb.

She was happy to have him home, even if for just the next few weeks. And as sad as she knew she would be to see him leave again, she was happy that he had made the live show. But she feared his disappointment if he didn't win. She would never forget the defeated expression on his face when he had walked out of that audition after getting that judge's thumbs-down. And she knew that the rejection would only be worse the closer he was to success.

If she were honest with herself, she had to admit that she was equally fearful that he might win. She wanted it for him, but she feared it for them. She feared how everything would shift if he did.

Jane had been the breadwinner when they had met. Then she had followed him down here, and being unemployed, and, in a way, dependent, had been terrible. And as much as she hated handing out citations for a living, she was happy to be earning an honest wage and paying her part. She was in love. She was happy with their life. She didn't want it to change.

She thought she heard someone call her name and looked up. But she saw no face she recognized on the busy sidewalks, only people shuffling by with their hoods up and their heads bent. She hadn't even noticed that it had started to rain.

She closed the flap on her ticket pouch, zipped up her jacket, and kept on walking.

Chapter 14

Jane could tell Caleb was getting more and more nervous the closer they got to their destination. He kept fiddling with the car's climate control, even though the temperature was fine.

"Are you sure we have to go?" he asked.

"Of course we do. They're getting together to watch you."

"I know, but can't we just watch it from home?"

She shook her head. "Not after all the trouble Mr. Zigler went to."

"What trouble?"

"I think he's set up a projection screen in the warehouse and everything."

"Are you kidding me?"

"No. And he said he's got plenty of chairs and food, and that he might even crack open a few cases of beer for the guys to enjoy on the house. They're all very proud of you."

"Who's they? I thought just the guys from the warehouse were going to be there."

"No. Jeremy's coming too. And he's bringing your music buddies. After all, they were at the show I taped that landed you the audition."

Caleb sighed and looked out the window.

"Oh my," Jane said. "I've never seen you so shy. There's no reason to be nervous, Caleb."

"I'm not nervous."

"Yes, you are."

Jane pulled in and parked. She took the brownies she'd baked from the backseat, and they got out and walked together across the twilit parking lot toward the bright yellow glow of the open warehouse door. She had talked at length with Mr. Zigler about his plans for the evening, but even so, she wasn't prepared for what awaited them.

Clusters of colorful balloons were everywhere, along with an enormous arch of silver Mylar balloon letters strung together that read: CONGRATULATIONS! A WELCOME HOME banner hung on the wall. There were tables of treats, and coolers with soda and beer. An enormous projection screen hung from a high storage rack with folding chairs lined up in front of it, and behind the chairs a projector was mounted on the roof of a forklift. Power and cable cords were taped to the floor, leading to Mr. Zigler's office.

And there were people, lots of people. Mr. Zigler stood with a woman who Jane thought must be his wife. The warehouse workers were there, and Caleb's friends. As soon as one group ceased chattering to look at her and Caleb as they entered, there was a moment of intense quiet. Then someone clapped and they all followed with wild applause and even cheers.

Jane had never seen Caleb blush so much as he did in that moment. But his shyness and fear seemed to melt away beneath the warm smiles of so many friendly faces, and he soon rushed to say hello to everyone. Jane followed him, carrying her brownies and smiling with pride.

"We knew you'd do it, kid," Mr. Zigler announced, patting Caleb on the back. "You're the absolute top. First-class. The real deal. And when you get famous, I'm having custom beer labels designed with your picture on them. They'll fly off the shelves like hotcakes in a hurricane. I'll do a nonalcoholic version for you nondrinkers, of course." Then he turned to Jane. "Thanks for sharing him with us tonight, Jane. It's mighty generous of you. I don't believe you've met my wife, April."

His wife smiled and said, "So you're the one my husband claims has been fattening him up with all those lunches."

Jane laughed and nodded that she was in fact the one, offering Mrs. Zigler a brownie from her plate to prove it. She offered one to Mr. Zigler too, saying, "I've learned you've got to feed the troll to get through the door in this place."

"It's the same at home, dear," Mrs. Zigler joked. "I've taken to hiding my weekly ration of almond biscotti in the dryer, because laundry seems to be the one thing he's afraid of."

Mr. Zigler grinned and snapped his fingers. "Dang it," he said. "That's the one place I hadn't looked." Then he turned to address Caleb. "So, Caleb, catch us up on everything. Jane said you're going through to the live show, but she didn't say much else."

The others had drifted over to listen in, and by the time Caleb answered, he was addressing the entire crowd.

"Well, I think we're going to see the two-hour premiere tonight. But don't feel like you need to watch the entire thing just for me. In fact, I'm fine if we just visit and don't even turn it on. Anyway, the shows will air twice each week for the next few weeks, and you'll see artists perform and then either get passed through or get eliminated."

"But you went through, right?" Jeremy asked, pausing with his beer bottle at his lips.

"I did," Caleb answered, nodding. "Although they paired me up with another artist and put us through as a duet."

Jeremy almost spit a mouthful of beer. "A duet? I haven't seen you sing a duet since a hammered fan took the stage way back in Seattle's Shark Club days."

Caleb shrugged, as if to suggest that he wasn't happy about it, but that it was out of his control.

"Well, who is he?" Jeremy asked. "Who's your partner?"

"She," Caleb said. "It's a girl. Her name's Jordyn."

"Jordyn? Why does that sound so familiar? It's not Jordyn-with-a-*y*, is it?"

Caleb nodded that it was.

"Dude, I follow her on Facebook. She's crazy hot." Then he glanced at Jane and sucked air through his teeth as if he were in pain. "Sorry, Jane. I'm just a fan girl when it comes to Jordyn."

"It's okay," Jane said, shrugging off his comment. "I'm a fan girl now too. When they were competing, I checked out her music. She's good. And I think they'll make a great duo."

There were several seconds of awkward silence. Then one of the older warehouse workers stepped up and plucked a brownie off of Jane's tray. "You don't mind, do you, ma'am?" he asked. "I've been eyeing them from across the way there."

Jane smiled, grateful to have the subject changed. "No, I don't mind, Tim. And you know me well enough to call me Jane. Here, have another. And pass them around too."

There was a loud chirping sound and Mr. Zigler glanced at his wristwatch and silenced its alarm. He clapped his hands. "It's time, everyone. Grab something to drink and take your seats. And don't forget to turn off your cell phones. We don't want any interruptions during the show."

As everyone scattered to find seats, Mr. Zigler climbed up onto the forklift and fired up the projector. It flashed blue on the screen, searching for a signal. He called for someone to kill the lights, and one of the workers rose and went to switch them off. Then they sat in the dark, staring at the blue-glowing screen and listening to Mr. Zigler fiddle with the connections and cuss. Then the channel came through and they were watching a commercial for an erectile dysfunction pill. Everyone laughed.

"Better pay attention, boss," one of the workers called. "Couple more years and you'll be needing these for sure."

"He's already tried to get them," his wife replied from her seat. "Doctor won't give them up because of his heart."

Everyone laughed again.

"April, you hush up," he called from the forklift. "One more word and I'm eating all your biscotti when we get home."

The commercial ended and the screen went momentarily black. Then a single sheet of music appeared and caught fire, burning to the beat of a drum until only the *Singer-Songwriter Superstar* logo remained.

Jane was sitting next to Caleb and she reached and took his hand in hers. He leaned over and kissed the top of her head. The logo faded and the screen flashed through images of various cities while a voice-over announcer explained the show and the audition process. They seemed to be pitching themselves as a fast-paced *American Idol*, promising quicker results and gritty drama while searching for real talent who could both write and perform their own songs. Then they introduced the judges and explained their industry credentials. Then it was on to the auditions.

The first city up was Chicago, and they flashed through snippets of Windy City hopefuls, showing those who received five thumbs-up from the judges, and a few outlandish losers just to mix it up. After a commercial, they moved on to New York. When Jordyn walked onstage, they showed the judges all stop talking and pay attention. Then she played her song and they montage-cut to the big power-note finish and five smiling judges all with their thumbs in the air. Then on to Seattle. Then to Los Angeles. Then to Austin. They showed the line outside the convention center, and Jane thought she caught a glimpse of her and Caleb, but it flashed by so fast she couldn't be sure. Panda's audition stole the show. Even Jeremy leaned back in his seat to look at Caleb and said, "Dude, she's going to be tough to beat."

After Panda, they edited out the ukulele-playing twins who had come next and cut straight to Caleb. He walked out onto the stage and everyone in the warehouse watching clapped and cheered and turned to smile at him in the dark. Jane squeezed his hand. They showed quite a bit of the exchange between him and the judges, including Caleb's joke to the one judge that he was seeing yellow because of the stage lights and not because of his synesthesia. They showed a close-up of her scowling while the other judges laughed. Then they showed the opening of his song, cutting away to the judges' enthusiastic expressions, then cutting back to show Caleb's finish. The thumbs went up and everyone cheered. They didn't show the judge turn her thumb down or bother explaining that Caleb had been called back because another artist had been caught plagiarizing someone.

There was a long commercial break where everyone stood and stretched and grabbed something to eat or drink. A few of the warehouse workers stepped outside for cigarettes. Then the show was back on and everyone drifted back to their seats.

The final segment began as a fast-paced, drama-filled teaser for the episodes yet to come. They opened with a pair of contestants fighting in the hotel hallway, one girl pulling the other's hair and calling her a karaoke queen. They showed snippets of judges critiquing performances, segments of artists pulling late nights in the rehearsal room working on songs, and clips of tearful contestants worried they were about to be sent home.

And woven through it all, they showed what appeared to be a budding romance between Jordyn and Caleb. It started with apparent glances from across the room. Then they showed Jordyn walking up and taking Caleb's guitar from him and playing his song. They showed him laugh and smile shyly. They cut to the two of them rehearsing a duet together. They showed her touch his arm. They showed him blush. The editing was so seamless and masterful that Jane found herself almost believing it for a moment, wondering if it could possibly be true.

The show ended with a montage of tantalizing images and the voice-over announcer saying, "Tune in next Tuesday for more amazing singer-songwriter performances, more bitter rivalries, more angst, and more forbidden love."

When the announcer said this last line about forbidden love, Caleb's face flashed onscreen, his intense green eyes staring off at something, followed by a quick cut to Jordyn, batting her eyelashes and looking down as if she had been the object of Caleb's longing stare. Then the *Singer-Songwriter Superstar* logo appeared and the credits rolled.

The channel had just cut to a car commercial when Mr. Zigler killed the projector. The screen went dark and everyone sat quietly in the shadows. Jane could hear Mr. Zigler's feet crossing the warehouse floor to turn on the lights. They flickered, then stayed on, and they seemed to Jane to be altogether too bright.

"That was great," one of the warehouse workers said.

"That was total bullshit is what that was," Caleb replied.

"Come on, honey," Jane said. "It's just Hollywood drama."

"I can't fucking believe they did that to me, Jane. And to you. It's not right. Now I see why they sent us through as a duet. It's all part of some screwed-up reality TV ratings stunt."

"It's okay, Caleb."

"No, it isn't."

Mr. Zigler had crossed to the dessert table and was busy packing things up. "Anyone want to take these cream cheese bars?" he called over his shoulder. "My wife'll put them in the garbage and pour dish soap on them if I bring them home."

It was clear he was offering a change of subject, and most everyone jumped at the chance. They flocked to the table to gather leftovers, they moved to put away chairs, they crushed cans for recycling, each of them suddenly busy with something.

Each of them except Jane and Caleb, of course, who stood looking at each other in front of the blank screen.

❧

"I had nothing to do with that, Jane," Caleb stated firmly. "You have to believe me."

The headlights from oncoming traffic were nearly blinding her, so Jane resisted the urge to look over at him and kept her eyes on the road instead.

"Baby, could you—"

"They did that with movie magic or some shit, Jane. None of that was real. The glances. The blushing. I mean, they took entirely different footage and stitched it together—"

"Honey, I get it. But would you mind—"

"And I feel so bad that you had to watch that. And in front of all those people too."

"Caleb, I need—"

"I'm so sorry, Jane. Can you forgive me? I'm not going back. I'll sue them. I'll do whatever it takes to show you—"

"Damn it, Caleb!" she yelled, slamming her palm on the car dash. "Would you shut up for a second and listen to me?"

"I'm sorry. I knew you were pissed. I knew it."

"I'm not pissed. I just need you to open the glove box and hand me my glasses."

"Your glasses?"

"Yes, before I crash and kill us both. I need them when I drive at night."

Caleb opened the glove box and handed the glasses over to Jane. She slipped them on and sighed with relief as the blurry lights came into focus.

"Much better," she said. "Thank you."

She noticed Caleb leaning forward in his seat with his head turned to get a look at her with the glasses on. She held up her hand to block his view.

"Come on," he said. "Look at me."

"I need to keep my eyes on the road."

"You can look at me for a second."

"Fine," she said, dropping her hand and turning to look at him. Then she looked back at the road. "Satisfied?"

"I like them," he said. "They're cute."

"They don't make me look old?"

"Actually, they make you look young."

"Not as young as Jordyn, I bet."

"Jane, I'm so sorry. You have—"

"I'm only kidding, Caleb. I totally get it. I know you had nothing to do with it. I know it was all smoke and mirrors. I know it. I'm not stupid. Did you see your audition? How they made it look like you went right through with five thumbs-up? That's not how it happened. We know that's not how it happened. I knew right then that their editors were up to shenanigans. But who cares? It's just a show."

"But it looks bad, Jane."

"Bad for who?"

"Bad for you. Bad for me. What will people think?"

"Listen, Caleb. This is your big chance. I know you love me, you know you love me, and everyone in our lives we really care two shits about knows you love me. So forget it. I'm sure they'll have you two breaking up in next week's episode anyway. Gotta ramp up the drama before the live show, right?"

"Well, they can ramp it up without me because I'm not going back for it."

"Yes, you are," she said.

"No, I'm not," he shot right back.

Jane glanced at him again and said, "I thought you knew better by now than to argue with me."

Caleb crossed his arms and turned to look out the window. "You can't make me go."

"Oh, yes, I can."

"Maybe I'll cuff myself to the bed and swallow the key."

"I knew you liked the handcuffs," she said, smiling. "But it won't work. I'll borrow one of Mr. Zigler's beer trucks and drive you along with the headboard to L.A."

She could tell by his body language that he wanted to laugh, but she knew he wouldn't let himself.

"And besides," she added a minute later, "who's going to get me Jordyn's autograph if you don't go back?"

∽

Marj paused before getting into the car, glanced up at the apartment, and said, "Caleb didn't want to come? I wouldn't have minded, you know. And it's an open meeting."

"He's still asleep," Jane replied, climbing behind the wheel. Then, when Marj was sitting beside her, she added, "You know, I've never brought him to a meeting with me. I should ask him sometime if he wants to go."

They made certain they had the right meeting this time, arriving early and double-checking the schedule on the door. It was a simple room with one window, sea-foam green walls hung with recovery slogans, and two dozen folding chairs set out in a loose circle. They were the first to arrive, other than a very large man wearing a cowboy hat who was busy at the refreshment table arranging cookies on a plate to go along with the coffee and tea. He saw them and smiled.

"You better come get you some while the gettin's good," he said. "We get a lot of double winners at this meeting, and you know them alkies can rip through a plate of sugar cookies like they was laced with booze."

"Thank you," Jane said, rising. "I think I will. Marj, can I get you coffee or tea or anything?"

Marj shook her head. "No, thank you, dear. I had my Ovaltine this morning."

Jane chuckled to herself as she walked toward the coffee machine, finally having solved the mystery of who exactly drank Ovaltine. The cowboy nodded to her and slid out of the way, but he made no effort to introduce himself or ask any questions. And Jane liked that. It made her feel welcome without feeling overwhelmed. She heard chatter and caught glimpses of people filing in as she poured herself a cup of coffee and stirred in a Splenda and powdered cream. Then she took a sugar cookie from the tray and was turning to head back to her seat when she saw him and froze. She stopped so suddenly, hot coffee spilled over the brim of her cup and onto her hand, but she hardly noticed the pain. She wasn't prepared to run into her boss at an Al-Anon meeting.

Mr. Blanco seemed to be equally shocked, looking at her with uplifted eyebrows, then looking behind him to the door, as if to check that he had in fact come to the right room. When he looked back at Jane, he smiled. A boy stood beside him, fairer skinned and with fairer hair, but by the shared shape and color of their eyes, he was obviously his son.

"Hi, Jane. How are you?"

Jane was about to address him as Mr. Blanco when she remembered that the *Anon* in *Al-Anon* stood for *anonymous*. That and he had told her twice to call him Manuel.

"Hello, Manuel," she said. "What a coincidence."

"If you're here for Al-Anon, it's less of a coincidence than you might think," he replied. "There aren't many meetings on the weekends, and almost no others near downtown."

"Yes. I mean no." She laughed at herself. "Let me start again. Yes, I'm here for the meeting. And no, there don't seem to be many. I found this one on the Intergroup website and it just happened to be on my route. This must be your son."

Manuel put his hand on the boy's head, and the boy looked down shyly at the carpet.

"This is Chandler. Chandler, remember your manners."

Chandler looked up at her and stuck out his hand. "Nice to meet you, ma'am."

Jane went to shake his hand but realized she had her coffee in one hand and a sugar cookie in the other. She was momentarily at a loss for what to do, but then she clamped the cookie in her mouth and reached out to shake the boy's hand.

"Nice to meet you, Chandler," she mumbled past the cookie caught in her mouth.

"Chandler, this is the woman I was telling you about. The twelfth man from Seattle."

The boy's eyes lit up. "Are you really from Seattle?"

Jane nodded. "I am. And I've got the moss on my back from all the rain up there to prove it. Of course, it's getting a little dried out here in all this Austin sun."

The boy looked confused, but at least his father laughed.

"I hear you're into football," Jane said. "That's cool."

The boy smiled and shrugged, as if he knew it was cool and it wasn't any big deal.

"We're actually gearing up for the Seahawks game against the Forty-Niners this afternoon," his father said. "That's our little deal—he comes to the meeting with me, and I watch the football game with him."

"Yeah, but it's not really fair," the boy said to Jane, "because he'd be watching the game anyway."

Manuel laughed and gave the boy a squeeze. "Son, why don't

you grab us a couple of seats while I finish up talking with Jane here?"

The boy beelined for a handful of sugar cookies before marching off to claim them seats. Manuel watched until he was out of earshot, then he looked back to Jane.

"Thanks for being so nice to him. Things have been a little rough on Chandler since his mother got put away." He sighed. "She was a pretty bad druggie. Probably still is if they can get that junk in prison. I'm hoping to get him into Alateen soon."

"Alateen's a good program," Jane said. "My primary qualifier for Al-Anon was my parents, but I've been coming since my daughter started drinking."

He looked confused when she mentioned her daughter. Then she remembered telling him in his office that she didn't have any children.

"She's dead," Jane quickly added. "My daughter. Melody. She passed away from this disease."

He bowed his head. "I'm very sorry. I can't imagine your grief."

"Thanks. It never completely goes away, but it gets a little more manageable every day."

He nodded as if he guessed that what she said was true. "Chandler's mother tried to run away with him out of state, and it nearly destroyed me. Fortunately, I have custody now and she's locked away in a safe place."

"He's a lucky boy to have someone love him like you do."

"Thank you. I feel lucky to have him to love."

There was a moment when they just looked at each other, unsure of what to say, or maybe just not needing to say anything more. Jane took a sip of her coffee. Then she saw Marj wave at her, and she noticed the chairperson passing the basket to start the meeting.

"Looks like they're getting started," Jane said. "I'd better get back to my friend. It's her first meeting in a long time."

"Of course," he said, smiling graciously and letting her pass. "Say, Jane," he called softly after her.

She stopped and turned.

"You wouldn't be interested in watching the game with us, would you? Seahawks versus the Niners."

"That's such a kind offer," Jane replied. "Thank you. But I've got to get home to my fiancé after the meeting."

Jane thought she saw him blush, but it was hard to tell with his caramel-colored skin.

"You're welcome to bring him," he said, recovering.

"I'm afraid he's exhausted," Jane replied.

Then for some strange reason, she felt a strong desire to talk Caleb up, to somehow justify him as her fiancé, as if she might somehow be judged because she was engaged to a much younger man, even though Manuel didn't know his age.

"He's a musician and he just returned from L.A., where he's been filming a new music show. I'm not supposed to say anything yet, but he'll be on the live show in a few weeks."

Manuel looked genuinely impressed. "What's the name of the show?"

"*Singer-Songwriter Superstar.*"

"We'll be sure to watch it," he said before heading off to join his son. "The only thing Chandler likes from Seattle as much as their football is their music."

As soon as Jane reclaimed her seat, Marj leaned over and whispered in her ear, "Who's the Spanish heartthrob?"

"Marjorie," Jane said, shaming her neighbor with her eyes, but smiling at her at the same time. "You know I'm engaged."

"You're engaged"—Marj grinned—"but I'm not."

Chapter 15

Jane and Mr. Zigler pulled in and parked at the same time, rushing together from their cars toward the warehouse door.

"How long has he been here?" Jane asked.

"I'm not sure," Mr. Zigler said, pulling out his ring of keys. "The janitors called me and the first thing I did was call you."

"I'm glad I answered. I figured he was out playing a late gig and was about to go to bed. Did the janitors say what he was doing that scared them?"

Mr. Zigler shook his head and unlocked the door.

"I'll bet it was that stupid show again," Jane said, shaking her head. "It was on tonight while I was working."

They couldn't see him, but they heard him as soon as they were inside. Bottles rattling, heavy boxes slamming down. They rushed across the dark warehouse and around the corner to the delivery gate. He had turned the lights on in that section and was unloading several stacked pallets by hand, carrying two or three heavy cases at a time and walking them the length of the floor, then piling them on another stack he had going there. The pallets looked to be half-unloaded, and it seemed an impossible amount of weight for one man to have moved in the space of anything short of a week.

If he saw them, he paid them no mind as he walked back to grab another load. Jane could see that his hair was slick with sweat and his shirt had soaked through. Stranger yet, he wasn't wearing any shoes, and his bare feet left wet prints on the cool concrete as he walked. She watched them evaporate and disappear from behind him like the prints of some ghost chasing after him to do his work.

Mr. Zigler cleared his throat.

Caleb stopped with an armload of boxes and looked at them. Jane couldn't read anything of his mood in his stare.

"You know," Mr. Zigler said, "it'd be a lot easier if you used the forklift and moved them while they were still on the pallets. We've come a long way since the pyramids."

Caleb set the boxes down at his feet, then stood again and looked at the forklift as if he were seeing it for the first time. "Well, I didn't have the key," he said.

Mr. Zigler chuckled. "That sure didn't seem to keep you from finding your way in here in the middle of the night."

"Am I in trouble?"

"No, you're not in trouble. But you sure gave my cleaning crew the fright of their lives. They thought there was a madman in here stealing my booze."

"That doesn't make sense," Caleb said. "Who would carry cases into the warehouse if they were aiming to steal them?"

"I know it," Mr. Zigler replied. "Those cleaners sure are a funny bunch, aren't they? Hard to believe they thought this was odd at all. Of course, once they described the thief, I knew they were talking about you. And where's your shoes?"

Caleb glanced down at his feet. "I didn't have any socks and they were filling up with sweat. They're over there. I'm really sorry for making you come out here in the middle of the night, Mr. Zigler. I was just working off a little stress, I guess."

"It's not me you should be apologizing to," he replied. "I got a bunch of work done for free because of your little stress release. But poor Jane here was worried sick when I called."

Caleb looked suddenly very exhausted and very sad. "I'm sorry. Are you mad at me?"

Jane had been standing quietly, not wanting to interrupt, and she was so far from being angry, she couldn't even put into words how she felt when he asked. She just walked toward him and hugged him. His shirt was soaked, and he smelled like an odd mixture of cardboard and sweat.

"Let's go home, honey," she said. "Let's go home and rest. I'll give you a nice massage."

Caleb went and collected his shoes while Mr. Zigler clicked the bright lights off. Then they all walked together in the dim glow of the emergency lights toward the door.

"If you want your job back, it's always waiting," Mr. Zigler said, pausing once they were outside before closing the door. "But I've got to warn you, I'm not hiring for any graveyard shift, so you'll need to come at human hours."

"Thanks, boss. I appreciate it."

"But if you don't mind me giving you my two cents for free," he added, "I think you should listen to your lady here and chase your dream. You're a good man, and a good man can take a little setback like this and make it a springboard to bigger things. You know, I half expected we'd find you drunk and breaking bottles in here. That's what mostly happens in my business when I get a call about an employee in the middle of the night. But here you are, working off some steam. You need to direct that passion of yours into your art, young man. Not into moving boxes of bottles around."

He paused to put his hand on Caleb's shoulder. "I've not mentioned this before, and the only reason I'll say it now is because I think so highly of you and of Jane. But when I was a boy, I always wanted to be a musician. I played saxophone. Was pretty good at it too. Practiced three whole summers with my best friend while staying with my father in Rome. But my mother, you see, well, she hammered into me this idea that I needed to do real work, be a real man. She said there wasn't any-body ever who made a real living off being in a silly band. I guess she finally got to me. And now here I am with this warehouse and all these trucks with my name on them. But I'd give it all back in a second for a chance to play Casa del Jazz just one time with my old best friend."

He smiled, remembering. Then he removed his hand from Caleb's shoulder and wished him and Jane a good night. They were almost to the car when Caleb turned back.

"Hey, why don't you?"

Mr. Zigler looked up from his ring of keys. "Why don't I what?"

"Why don't you go and play with your friend in Rome?"

"Because his mother got to him too. He gave up playing and went to work at the port of Civitavecchia. He was crushed to death by a crane the summer we turned nineteen."

❧

They made love later that night, but Caleb seemed to still be somewhere else. Afterwards, he rolled onto his back and lay looking up at the ceiling, while Jane lay on her side, watching him. He hadn't been shaving or even trimming his beard since he'd been home, and he was beginning to look scruffy. He needed a haircut too. But his eyes were still bright and clear—almost too bright, almost too clear, the whites white, the irises a sparkling green—yet they seemed to look off at nothing and everything at once.

"Are you okay, Caleb?"

"I should have stuffed them with newspaper first."

"What's that, honey? Stuffed what with newspaper?"

"The egg cartons that I stapled to the ceiling. I think they would absorb more sound if I'd stuffed them with newsprint. Maybe tomorrow I'll take them down and do it."

"Caleb, do you want to talk? Something's eating at you."

"No, I'm fine, babe. I'm just tired."

"I'm sure you are. But honey, you've been moping around here since you've been home. Maybe you're depressed."

"I'm not depressed."

"Well, it sure seems like it."

He fished his jeans up from the floor beside the bed and stood and put them on. Then he walked from the bedroom to the bathroom.

Jane pulled his T-shirt on and followed him. The water was running in the sink when she got there, but he was just standing in front of the mirror, looking at his reflection. She leaned against the doorjamb and sighed.

"Caleb, you know you can tell me anything."

"I know," he said, looking away from his reflection. "I'm just not sure what I'm thinking, so it's hard to tell you."

"You don't have to go back if you don't want to."

"You wouldn't think less of me?"

"No, I wouldn't think any less of you."

He looked up at her and she thought she saw an immense sadness in his eyes.

"But I want to do it for you, Jane. I want to get you out of this lousy apartment and get us a house. Something with a yard. And I'd like for you to be able to quit this awful job."

"It's not that bad, Caleb. I'm getting lots of exercise."

"Yeah, running from assholes trying to spit on you."

Jane stepped into the bathroom and caressed his cheek. "Baby, I'm fine. We're fine. You can go back to working at the warehouse. Play gigs at night. Everything'll be like it was."

"Until what, Jane? You know all those times playing at the club, or outside the club, I convinced myself I was working for a break. And here one comes and it turns out to be bullshit."

"It's not bullshit, Caleb."

"Come on, Jane. You watched the last few episodes. And

tonight's was worse. They're making it seem like Jordyn and I are a couple. And not only that, it also looks like I wasn't good enough on my own."

"Is that what this is really about?"

"What?"

"You being good enough to be a solo artist. Because I'm okay with the Jordyn charade as long as you come home to me after the show, Caleb."

He turned the water off. Then he turned and leaned back against the sink and sighed. "Maybe it's both. I don't know."

"Well, the show might be bullshit, but the money's real. And so is the recording contract. And the exposure. Go for it if you want to. I'll be here supporting you and cheering for you, and so will everyone else. But if you want to stay, stay. You have to decide, Caleb. One way or the other. You can't keep torturing yourself, and you can't keep torturing me."

He reached and pulled her to him, then wrapped his arms around her. He wasn't wearing a shirt and she pressed her cheek against his naked chest. He felt warm. He felt safe.

"Will you come with me?" he asked.

"You know I can't, Caleb. I need to be working. We need the money right now." She lifted her head to look up at him. "I'll make you a deal. If you get to the finale, I'll find a way to get a few days off and I'll come then. Fair?"

She could see in his eyes that he was thinking, the gears of his mind working in those deep pools of green. Then he subtly nodded and leaned down to kiss her on the forehead.

"Okay, baby. You got a deal."

She hugged him tighter and snuggled her cheek against his chest again. He couldn't see it, but she was smiling. "I love you, Caleb."

"I love you too, Jane."

A few seconds later, she looked up at him again. "You want to take a shower together? Like we used to?"

"It's a pretty tight space in there," he said.

"Duh," she responded. "That's the point."

He grinned. "Okay, I'm in for a shower duo. But only if you rub yourself down with coconut oil and coffee grounds."

She pushed him away and stripped off her shirt. "Fine, but I'm rubbing you down with it too."

"Hmm . . ." he said, pondering this with a finger to his temple. "Maybe we should switch out the coffee grounds for maple syrup instead, and you can apply it with your tongue."

"I don't know," she retorted, smiling playfully. "I'm not sure Dr. Oz would approve."

He grinned and unzipped his pants and pulled them down. "That's okay," he said, "because Dr. Cock approves."

She looked at him and bit her lip and nodded. "Jane approves too."

❧

The day Caleb would leave her again seemed far away to Jane, hardly even a reality, until suddenly the eve of his departure had arrived. Time, she thought, sure had a funny way of changing up its pace if you weren't looking.

She had the afternoon off from work and they went shopping together. Jane picked him out two new pairs of jeans, a half dozen discounted designer T-shirts, new boots, and a leather cuff to wear on his wrist. He stepped out from the fitting room, looking to Jane like a real rock star, missing only a girl on each arm and a guitar.

"This is really fun," she said, rubbing her hands together. "I feel like I've got a life-sized Ken doll to dress up."

Caleb looked at himself in the mirror. "I don't know. I feel silly."

"You look hot. This is game time, baby. You've got to wow them in every way. And if you'll just drop the moody artist persona and smile for the camera, you'll win America's heart just like you've won mine."

He smiled at her in the mirror. "We could trade all this in right now for a three-piece suit and go and get married."

Jane wagged her finger at him and shook her head. "No, no, no, my love. I'm holding out until you're rich and famous, and then I want a Tristan-and-Isolde-themed wedding at a castle somewhere."

"Tristan and Isolde? Didn't he die a sad and tragic death before they even got married?"

"I don't know"—Jane shrugged—"I only saw the movie once. But the costumes were to die for."

"So you'd cast me as the doomed prince for the dress?"

"And a castle," she said. When he rolled his eyes at her, she added, "Hey, a girl's got to have her priorities."

She left him to look at socks while she went to the MAC makeup counter and restocked on the things she needed. Night cream, foundation, blush. The saleswoman was ringing her up when she asked Jane if there would be anything else.

"You know what," Jane said, "I could use some eyeliner. What's your best smoky look?"

The saleswoman turned to look at the selection. "I'd say MAC Eye Kohl in Smolder. The color really lasts."

"But is it edgy?" Jane asked. "Like the young kids wear."

"Are you kidding me? It's pure rock and roll in a pencil."

"I'll take two, then."

They lunched at a mall café and each tried to push their leftovers off on the other, arguing playfully about which of them had lost more weight. Jane blamed walking all over town; Caleb blamed nerves. After lunch, Caleb pulled her into a mall arcade and bought tokens for Dance Dance Revolution, then challenged Jane to a dance-off.

"You want an eighties remix or nineties?"

"Do you even have to ask? The eighties were so much more fun. Wait, you weren't born yet, so you wouldn't know."

He just grinned at her and set the machine. "Prepare to go down," he said.

The music started, the arrows lit up at their feet, and they were dancing to an electronic mix of "Do It Right." But Jane knew without a doubt that she was doing it wrong. Caleb was busy busting a move beside her like a pro, but while he racked up points, all Jane saw on her side of the screen was red. She was still laughing and having fun and by the time the song ended, they fell into each other's arms, both out of breath.

"You could have been a gentleman and let me win."

"I was trying, baby. But there's no way I could have lost to you unless I'd sat down."

Jane punched him in the shoulder. Then she noticed a boy standing in the corner watching them. He was very short and very heavy for his age, and he had a funny hat pulled down almost to his eyes. Jane got Caleb's attention and pointed.

"I think you've got a fan," she said.

"I'm not signing any autographs," he told her. Then he nodded to the kid. "Hey, kid. You wanna play a round?"

The kid nodded and stepped forward without a word.

"Let him win," Jane whispered in Caleb's ear. Then she stepped aside and let the kid take her place on the dance platform.

Caleb pumped tokens into the machine. "You got a song preference, kid?"

The kid shook his head.

"How about a level?"

The kid stepped forward and pointed at Expert.

Caleb chuckled. "How about we go with Difficult, okay?"

He set the machine and took his place on the dance pad. Then he sized up his young competition.

"Don't think I'm going easy on you because you're a kid."

The kid dismissed his comment with a shrug and pulled his hat down tighter on his head. Then the music began and the kid's feet took off as if he were standing barefoot on hot coals. He had one hand up on top of his hat to keep it in place, and he was dancing like some cartoon kid version of Fred Astaire, his feet moving so wildly and crazily that Jane could hardly take her eyes away. When the song ended, the kid had a near-perfect score.

Caleb shook his head. Then he shook the kid's hand. "You got a name?" he asked.

The kid pointed to the high-score player list. The top name read Tommy Two Shoes. Then he drifted back to his corner again, presumably to wait in the shadows for his next victim.

As Jane and Caleb left the arcade, Caleb must have heard the chuckle that Jane was trying desperately to contain.

"Knock it off," he said. "You told me to let him win."

"Yeah, right," she said, letting out her laugh. "That kid danced the pants off of you."

"He sure did," Caleb admitted, adding, "You'd think he'd be more fit, though, wouldn't you? Dancing like he does."

Jane elbowed him. "What's wrong with you? My Caleb doesn't go around insulting kids about their weight like some kind of caveman."

Caleb scooped her up and carried her through the mall, her legs dangling along with the shopping bags.

"Put me down," she said, kicking. "What are you doing?"

"I'm carrying you home to my cave so I can dance the pants off of you."

When Jane emerged from the bathroom after her shower, Caleb had candles lit and music playing. He took her hand and led her into the bedroom. He sat her on the bed, then crawled up behind her and massaged lotion into her shoulders. The lotion smelled of lavender, and his hands were warm.

"What's all this for?" she asked.

"I just want our last night together to be special."

"You make it sound like you're going away for good."

"No, baby. Not for good. But it'll be five weeks if I go to the finale, and even a day away from you is too long."

She turned her head around to look at him. "I'm going to miss you."

He kissed her, pulling his lips away just long enough to softly say, "Shh . . . let's not talk about me leaving. We have tonight, and tonight can last forever if we want it to."

Then he peeled away her towel and laid her back on the bed. She shimmied up until her head was resting on the pillow.

"This isn't fair. I'm naked and you're still dressed."

"I'll be naked plenty later on, trust me. But I want this to be about you right now. So close your eyes and relax."

She did as he asked. She lay on the bed with her eyes shut and her heart open, doing nothing and feeling everything. His hands roamed her body, gently massaging lotion into her skin. He slid his hands down her arms and worked the insides of her palms with his thumbs. He moved to her legs, massaging from her thighs to her toes. He was attentive and patient, as if he wanted to commit each section of her body to the memory of his touch, as if he wanted to leave some mark of his love on every inch of her flesh. It was nurturing and sexual, and it turned Jane on.

Caleb's hands roamed back up to her inner thighs, and she raised her hips to signal that he should work a little higher between them. Then his hands left her for a moment and the next thing she heard was vibrating. She smiled but kept her eyes closed. Whatever he had, when he put it between her legs, it sent shivers up her spine to the crown of her head and down to the tips of her toes. She let out a little moan to let him know she liked it. She could feel the warm lube, the silicone vibrating, and she could feel the fingers of his free hand working in tandem with the toy. He must have been watching with his face close because his hair grazed her thigh.

She reached down and showed him how to position it, and together, hand in hand, they worked it until she was lying there quivering with pleasure, with just the soft sound of the vibrating audible beneath her moans.

He crawled up and kissed her. When he pulled his lips away, she opened her eyes and looked at him.

"Where did you get that?" Jane asked.

"It's a little going-away gift I picked up for you. I've got another going-away gift for you in my pants when you're ready. Only this one doesn't vibrate."

She shook her head. "It's my turn to pleasure you. Get undressed."

Without getting off the bed, Caleb peeled off his shirt and shimmied out of his pants. Then he flopped down onto his back with his arms behind his head and smiled at her. She let her eyes roam the length of his naked body. Then she straddled him and uncapped the lotion.

"Close your eyes," she said. "And just relax."

Jane worked the lotion into his chest first, kneading his pecs. His muscles seemed larger when they were beneath her small hands. She worked up to his shoulders, marveling at the striations in the muscle there. She worked down to his legs, his thighs, his calves. He laughed when she reached his feet.

"Does that tickle?"

"Yes."

"Good. How about that?"

"Stop it."

She was working her way back up between his legs when her eyes caught sight of the pink toy sitting on the edge of the bed. She snatched it and turned it on.

"Hey now," he said.

"Just close your eyes and relax, baby. I'm in control."

She heard him suck in his breath the second it touched his skin. His legs kicked a little. She knew he had lube somewhere, but she didn't want to look, so she set the toy down and squeezed more lotion into her palm. Then she picked the toy back up and brought it to his most sensitive place, then wrapped her other hand around him and began to stroke. Caleb was like warm stone in her hand. She laid her head on his thigh and enjoyed the close-up view while she worked—one hand sliding up and down, the other working the toy, slowly inching it lower. She thought she heard him say her name above the sound of the vibrating, then his quad muscle began to twitch beneath her cheek. She expected him to protest, but instead she felt his legs spread slightly more.

She worked her other hand faster, enjoying seeing him lose control, and when he came it was in a flood that shot so heavy and high that she watched it rise into the air and turn to fall again. Some landed on his belly. Some landed on her cheek. She tried to reach it with her tongue. Then she just lay there, feeling him pulse in her hand and listening to the toy vibrating where she had dropped it between his legs.

Eventually, she picked it up and switched it off, then scooted up to join him at the pillows. She thought he looked more content than she had ever seen him, as if he had no care in the world. Smiling, she laid her head on his chest. She could hear his heart pounding in his breast, the thunder of a life she loved more than her own, a life she would do anything to protect. She stretched her arm over him and hugged him tight. Without intending to, she sighed.

"You okay, babe?"

"I've never been better."

"Then why the long sigh?"

"I'm just going to miss you. That's all."

He caressed her hair. "I'm gonna miss you too. But I'll be home soon. And lose or win, either way, it makes no difference to me as long as I have us to look forward to. And we'll find a way to have your big Tristan-and-what's-her-name wedding and live happily ever after."

"Do you think there is an ever after?"

"I suppose we all die someday. But until then, sure."

"But what about after we die? Do you think there's anything then?"

"Are you getting all existential on me again, baby?"

"I don't know. Maybe I should go back to doing Sudoku. It kept my mind off stuff like this."

She played with his fine chest hair, lifting it in her fingers, then blowing it away with her breath. "I guess sometimes I just miss Grace. And I miss Melody. All the time, I miss her. I wonder if I'll ever see them again."

"I'm sure you will, baby. I'm sure you will."

"You really think so?"

He kissed the top of her head, softly saying, "I do."

A few quiet minutes passed, and then she said, "I saw that you packed your bag already. I have to work the morning shift tomorrow, so I can't take you to the airport."

"I know. I plan to catch the bus."

"I can leave the car and have Marj drive you."

"I'm fine with the bus, baby. I like Marj, but not enough to sit in traffic with her."

Jane looked up at him, then glanced theatrically at the wall and held her finger to her lips. "Shh . . . remember, she can hear through these walls."

"I thought you got her earplugs."

"I did, but I have a suspicion she likes to listen."

"That's creepy."

Jane shrugged. "Wouldn't you if you were all alone?"

"Yeah, I guess so."

She laid her head back on his chest and almost on cue they heard Buttercup bark. Both of them started laughing. When Caleb wrapped his arms around her and held her tight, she closed her eyes and let the love in. She was right where she wanted to be. Right here. Right now. Forever. With him.

●

Chapter 16

She was gone when Caleb woke. He wandered into the kitchen and found the coffee already made, and next to the coffeepot he found a note:

You looked too peaceful to wake, so I whispered in your ear that I love you more than life itself. And it's true. I do. You smiled in your sleep. So cute! Go get 'em, superstar.

He drank his coffee and reread the note. The apartment was quiet; he missed her already. He flipped the paper over and wrote her a response:

To the angel who whispered in my ear, I smiled because I was dreaming of you. Thanks for the great send-off last night. I love you. Signed, your man in la-la land.

The airport was crowded and the security lines were long. He was exhausted when he finally boarded the plane. Nothing seemed right. The number of the seat he sat in was printed on his ticket next to his name, but he felt all wrong. As if he were the wrong guy in the wrong clothes heading to the wrong place to live the wrong life. Shouldn't he be excited? he asked himself. After all, he was going to be on live TV with a chance at a cool quarter-million dollars and a recording contract. Shouldn't he be thrilled at the opportunity?

He watched out the window as the tarmac slipped away beneath them, and all he could think about was Jane. His entire

life he had felt edgy and alone, but when he met Jane, everything had fallen into place. And when he was around her, he felt
fine. His breathing slowed to synchronize with hers, his mind
got quiet, and his entire being opened in a fundamental way.
It was as if their hearts beat a rhythm that rhymed, their souls
strolling together forever in some place beyond space and time,
step for step, humming a sweet tune of hope, her voice and his,
a harmony neither could deny.

As an artist, he had always been interested in love. As a man,
he had always been fearful of it. But when he thought of Jane, he
knew what true love was, and he knew beyond any doubt that it
had the power to see anything and everything through.

When the FASTEN SEAT BELTS sign turned off, he stood and
excused himself, and retrieved his pad and pen from his duffel
in the overhead bin. Then he returned to his seat and settled in
for the long flight. And when he finally heard the melody he was
listening for, he opened to a blank page and began to write. Two
voices composing in harmony, words that flowed straight from
his heart. It was a song he had always wanted to write but had
never had a reason or even the courage to start.

❧

Caleb set his guitar on the floor, tossed his bag on the bed, and
looked around the room. Same hotel, same floor, but everything
was different. A queen bed instead of two doubles. No dirty
socks on the floor. No crazy roommate to possibly barge in. He
considered jumping on the bed for a photo to send to Jane, but
he didn't feel up to it. He sent a text message instead to say that
he had arrived and that he missed her.

He decided to unpack this time, and as he opened his duffel
and laid his clothes out on the bed, he found a package from
Jane. A thin box with a piece of paper wrapped around it se-

cured with a rubber band. He pulled the note off and saw that it was eyeliner. The note read: *Just don't let Jordyn borrow it!*

He took the eyeliner into the bathroom and practiced putting it on. It was more difficult than he might have guessed and by the time he gave it up, his eyes were red rimmed and watering and he looked like some crazy crying clown. He knew Sean would never let him live it down if he were there, and the thought made him miss his roommate. He pulled out his phone and composed a text to him.

> Back in Tinseltown, but not the same without you, dude. I hope you're still making music and painting and raising hell and all that stuff. Don't get lost in all those Iowa cornfields. And don't have sex with any cows.

Almost immediately after he sent it, there was a response.

> Dude, I'm pissed. Been watching the show and apparently you've been having a thing with Jordyn right under my nose. Ha-ha. JK. I know they're full of shit. She only has eyes for me. You're gonna kill it, man. I'm playing a coffee shop tonight. Love my life. :-)

He was working on song lyrics later that evening when a knock came at the door. It was a production assistant with a welcome basket and instructions for the following day. As they spoke in the doorway, she kept staring at Caleb strangely. When he said good-bye and closed the door, he caught his reflection in the mirror and realized why. He went to the bathroom and washed his face, two passes with soap and water, until the eyeliner was gone. Then he settled in to eat the goodies from his welcome basket and watch some TV.

Later, he tried to sleep. But it was two hours earlier, Austin time, and he had a lot on his mind. He tossed and turned and stared at the ceiling. There seemed to be tiny lights everywhere in the dark room. A red dot on the TV, the green glow of the alarm clock, a blinking LED on the wall smoke alarm. And they all seemed to be eyes staring at him from the dark—watching him, judging him, tormenting him.

He sat up in the bed and reached for the phone, then called down to the front desk and asked if they had any electrical tape. The man spoke broken English and seemed to be confused. He said he could send up maintenance if there was an electrical problem. Caleb gave up and hung up, then pulled on his jeans and his shirt.

He was halfway to the elevator when he saw her and stopped. She was sitting on the carpet next to a room door with her back against the wall. There were covered room service plates on the floor next to her, as if she had been banished to the hallway to eat her supper alone.

"Hi, Panda. You all right?"

She looked up at him, her eyes red, as if she'd been crying. "Oh, hi," she said. "What's up, Caleb?"

"I couldn't sleep so I'm heading to find some tape."

"Find some tape?"

"Lights are bothering me," he said. Then he nodded to the room service tray. "What are you doing out in the hall, having a little party?"

She pointed a thumb at the door behind her. "My dad and stepmom are fighting."

"What about?"

"Same thing they always fight about. Money."

"Oh. That sucks. I think there's a vending machine down the hall. You want to get a soda or something?"

"Yeah, sure," she said, standing. "That sounds cool."

They walked down the hall to the nook with vending machines, and Caleb pulled bills from his pocket and fed them into the machine to buy them each a soda—she chose a Pepsi, he chose an Orange Crush—then they stood in the deserted hotel hallway and drank them. It was strangely quiet for so many people being so near. Like a hallway between worlds.

"That caffeine'll keep you up," Caleb said.

She looked at the can of Pepsi in her hand and shrugged. "I can sleep anywhere."

"You can?"

"Yeah. I can even sleep standing up."

"I don't believe you," he said.

She set her soda on the ground. Then she stood perfectly still and closed her eyes. Several seconds passed and nothing happened until she just tipped over. Caleb lurched to catch her with his free arm, balancing his soda in the other. She opened her eyes and looked up at him. Then she started laughing.

"You little sucker," he said. "You got me."

She pulled herself upright, using his arm, then retrieved her Pepsi and stood beside him sipping on it. A minute passed before she looked at him again.

"Do you really like Jordyn?"

"You've been watching the shows, huh?"

She nodded that she had.

"No, I don't like Jordyn. Not like they showed. They're just doing that because it makes for interesting TV."

"Good," she said. "Because she's not right for you."

"She's not?"

She shook her head. "No way."

"Well, then, who is right for me?"

She blushed and looked at her feet. "I dunno. Maybe someone more like me."

"Well, that's very sweet," Caleb replied. "And I think you're right because I'm engaged to be married to an amazing woman, and in some ways you remind me of her."

She somehow managed to look happy yet defeated at the same time. They stood quietly for a few moments. Then a door opened down the hall and a man's head popped out and looked around. He spotted them and called out in a hushed voice.

"Amanda. You get back in here right now."

She looked up at Caleb and rolled her eyes. "Thanks for the soda."

"You bet," he replied. "Thanks for the talk. It was just what I needed."

Her father watched as she trotted down the hall toward the room. But she stopped short of the door and turned back.

"What's her name?" she asked.

"Her name's Jane, and I hope you get to meet her."

She smiled. "I hope so too."

She disappeared into the room, and the father cast him a long look before pulling his head in and closing the door.

Caleb stood in the quiet hall and finished his Orange Crush.

❮❯

Caleb woke to someone knocking on his room door.

He sat up and looked around, but the room was pitch-black. He reached for the lamp and turned it on. Then he peeled the tape off the alarm clock and looked at the time.

"Oh shit!"

He pulled on his jeans and went to answer the door. The production assistant took one look at him and shook her head.

"I overslept," he said. "I'll be right down. I promise."

"Fine," she answered. "But don't bother doing your makeup, there's no time."

"Very cute," he replied, closing the door.

They were all down in the banquet-hall-turned-rehearsal-room, drinking coffee and snacking on fruit and baked goods from a continental spread on a table against the wall. He saw Panda and her parents. He saw the production assistant talking to members of the stage crew. He saw the other artists sitting together at a table, eating and chatting. And he saw Jordyn. She was standing by herself looking at her phone. He was torn between going to greet her and going to get something to eat. Each choice seemed equally awkward. He decided to get it over with, since they were going to be partners.

"Counting all your fans?" he asked.

Jordyn looked up at him. There was a moment when he couldn't read her expression, an uncomfortable silence when he wished he'd gone for a bagel instead. But then she smiled and leaned in to hug him with her free arm.

"Good morning, partner. I was actually just reading a Twitter thread about what a cute couple we make."

"Well, I'm glad I'm not on there to read that shit," he said.

"Oh yes, you are. I even tweeted at your handle last night, and you've already got three thousand followers."

"I don't have a Twitter account."

"Yes, you do. You've got a Facebook page now too."

"This is bullshit, Jordyn. I didn't give you permission to put me out on social media like some kind of stooge you can use to get more fans."

"Relax, Caleb. I didn't do it. The producers made accounts for you. Read the paperwork. You gave them permission to manage your social media during the show. Don't worry, though, you'll get it back when it's over."

"Well, I don't want it."

"You might."

"I don't think so."

"Hey, my album on iTunes has been selling like crazy since the first episodes aired. And now all my fans want to know about the hottie I fell in love with on the show."

Caleb looked at her for a moment—a cunning mind and a pretty face, a very dangerous combination.

"I hope you didn't have anything to do with the way they're portraying us on TV, Jordyn, because I don't know if I could forgive you if you did."

She shrugged his comment off. "I'm only playing around. I was as surprised as you were. But whatever gets us America's votes. That's what I'm here for."

"I'm sure," he said, believing that part at least.

Then her eyes lit up as she saw someone enter the room. She grabbed Caleb's arm and spun him around. "I want you to meet someone, Caleb."

She was a fair-skinned and dark-haired girl about their age, maybe a little older, and she looked to be all business in a pencil skirt and white blouse. She wore black-rimmed glasses and carried an iPad and an enormous purse. Ignoring Caleb, she went straight into talking to Jordyn about downloads and post conversion rates. But Jordyn cut her off and turned to Caleb, who was standing at her side.

"Caleb, meet Paige, my social media manager."

Paige opened her huge purse and dropped the iPad inside. When she looked up, she ignored Caleb and addressed Jordyn with something bordering on contempt in her voice.

"Social media manager? Is that what I am now?"

"Well, I had to give you a title."

"Nice to meet you, Paige. I'm Caleb."

Paige looked at his extended hand but didn't move to shake it, saying instead, "Yeah, I know who you are." Then she looked back to Jordyn. "I'll be working in the room."

Caleb watched her walk away, her big bag bouncing as she strode toward the exit. "She's friendly," he said.

"Don't worry, you two will hit it off, I'm sure."

Caleb doubted that very much, but he didn't bother saying so. He excused himself to go and get something to eat.

"Will you grab me a scone, honey?" Jordyn called after him. "We've got a big day ahead of us and I need my energy."

❧

The bus took them to the same studio lot as before. The exterior looked unchanged, but inside everything was different. Bigger, better, flashier. There were more lights and more backdrops and more seats for a larger audience. There was even a phony red-carpet staging area, complete with fake paparazzi snapping their photos as they entered.

They were led to a fitting room, where stylists began working on each of them for the shoot. Caleb's stylist liked his jeans and his boots but picked out a different shirt for him and made him lose the leather cuff.

"We want you more *American Bandstand* and less *Back to the Future* for this shoot," the stylist said, standing back and looking at Caleb. "Besides, the eighties are so over."

"I like the eighties," Caleb replied.

The stylist pretended to bite his fist, saying, "I can tell."

When they had all had a turn in the makeup chair, they were herded onstage for a photo shoot. The photographer was mounted on a platform at the end of a large boom, suspended out above the stage, and he barked down directions to his lighting crew from behind his enormous camera lens like some kind of crazed, one-eyed photography god riding on a cloud.

When they took a break to adjust the lights, Caleb looked at his competition. Panda, the shy punk rock flower child who seemed to surprise even herself with her talent each time she sang. Jasmine, an African-American woman with a voice that could bring down the house and a smile that could put it back together again. Carrie Ann, who was as country as they came, her blond hair curled just so, her skirt cut just above her knees, her boots covered in rhinestones and glitter. And Erica, the young, sad-eyed folk artist who looked to Caleb like every Sunday afternoon singer he'd ever seen in Seattle coffeehouses, her hair a little messy, her posture slightly slouched as if her natural position were cradling a guitar.

And then there was Jordyn. Jordyn and him. The indie rock couple, he presumed. The edgy artists filled with angst who sang about heartbreak and love. The mix was almost too perfect, as if they had each been handpicked by a casting director to play a part. And Caleb guessed that in a way, each of them had. He wondered if they already knew who would win, if the whole thing was rigged, or if at least the live show would be real.

A production assistant stepped in front of him and Jordyn and looked them over. Then she reached down and put their hands together, stepped back, and looked at them again.

"That's much better," she said.

Caleb dropped Jordyn's hand.

"She won't bite you. Just hold hands long enough for a few shots, okay? Since you two are one act."

Caleb relented and took Jordyn's hand again. Then he thought about the photo, about where it might be printed or shown on TV, and that made him think of Jane seeing it. She had said she didn't care. And maybe she didn't. But he did.

The photographer called for everyone to smile, but just before he took his first shot, Caleb pulled his hand away.

❧

Caleb waited for Jordyn in the hotel rehearsal room but she didn't come. When he finally went up to her room, he heard arguing inside and decided not to knock. He was walking away when the door opened and Paige rushed out and stormed past him toward the elevators. Jordyn was standing in the open doorway, and Caleb couldn't decide if she looked more furious or more frightened as she watched Paige leave. Then Jordyn noticed him and her disposition completely changed, softening into her usual easy charm.

"Hello, Caleb. I didn't see you there. Do you mind if we rehearse in my room? I don't feel like facing cameras today."

Caleb paused and looked back toward the elevator. Paige scowled at him as the door slid shut. He turned to Jordyn.

"I left my guitar in the rehearsal room."

"That's fine," she said. "I have plenty. Come on in."

It looked like a bomb had gone off inside her room. Clothes and costumes hanging everywhere, cosmetics taking up every inch of the dresser top, tangles of power strips and computer cords hanging from the laptops and phones that were set up on the small desk, and two acoustic guitars and one electric on stands against the wall next to a keyboard.

She handed him a guitar.

"There isn't anywhere to sit," Caleb said.

"Sure there is," she replied, taking up her guitar from its stand and sitting on the bed. Then she reached over and picked up the clothes off of the bed next to her and flung them away.

"You're not going to play standing up, are you?"

Caleb sat next to her and the soft hotel mattress sank beneath his weight, and she exaggerated its effect and leaned in to him and laughed. He ignored her and lifted his guitar into place but quickly realized that the way they were sitting wouldn't work. His guitar was hitting hers, so he flipped it the other way.

"You grew up poor, didn't you?"

"That's an awfully odd thing to ask," he said. "Rude too."

"Maybe. But who plays a guitar that way?"

"Yeah, so what? I'm left-handed. I play both."

"But who taught you to play upside down?"

"I learned myself."

"By ear and wrong side up on a right-handed guitar?"

"Yeah, you could say that."

"Wow," she said, appearing impressed. "I have southpaw friends, but their parents bought them left-handed guitars."

"Maybe they're all left-handed guitars," he said. "Did you ever consider that you're the one playing upside down?"

She placed her hand on his arm. "You know what, Caleb? You make me smile."

Jordyn held his stare for several quiet seconds, and he thought he saw something hidden there in her eyes, something she wanted to confess. But then she softly shook her head and took her hand away and began to play. He joined in and they sang their lines back and forth to each other, first him, then her. She played on for several bars after Caleb had quit. She seemed to be lost in the song. When he didn't come in with her for the chorus, she stopped playing and opened her eyes.

"Why'd you stop?" she asked.

"I'm just not feeling it."

"Not feeling it?"

"Sorry. A love ballad just isn't the right song for us. I want to play the song I showed you. The one I wrote."

"Caleb, we offered them both to the producers and this is the song they want. And it's also what America wants to hear."

"I'm not interested in playing what America wants to hear. I want to play what I want to say. This song doesn't feel real."

"Why can't you just fake it until you make it?" she asked.

"What's that supposed to mean?"

"Just pretend you feel it and maybe you will."

"Maybe I don't want to feel it," he said, setting the guitar down on the bed and standing to leave.

He had crossed the room and was reaching for the door handle when he felt Jordyn's hand on his shoulder.

"Please, don't go."

He paused but didn't turn to face her. A kind of quiet guilt was sitting in his gut like a bellyful of cold water, and although he wasn't entirely sure why it was there, he didn't like any of the possibilities that came to mind.

"Come on, Caleb. This is a big week for us."

He turned, but she kept her hand on his shoulder and let it cross over in front of her so that her forearm was now resting against his chest. She looked up at him and blinked her long black lashes, and her eyes pleaded for him to stay.

"Please don't go. I don't want to be alone right now."

They stood looking at each other.

Sunlight filtered in through the sheer curtains, illuminating the edges of Jordyn's hair, and an aureole of white light surrounded her face, giving her the appearance of some young angel beamed in through the window to beg him to return with her to heaven. He was searching for the courage to break the spell, willing himself to turn now and leave, when her computer rang and a face popped up on its screen. She looked back.

"Oh, this is perfect timing. My producer's calling on Skype and I wanted you to meet him."

She turned to answer the call, but the door was already closing behind Caleb as she said hello.

He paused for the briefest moment in the hall, with his hand still on the handle before he let it latch and walked away, headed for the rehearsal room to practice on his own guitar, the one Jane had bought for him as a gift.

Chapter 17

When the day had finally arrived, Caleb could never have guessed how much pressure and panic went on backstage in preparation to pull off a live TV show. There were handlers running everywhere, reminding people when they were due on-stage, and what their cues were, and when they should exit and how. The makeup artists were constantly on the move, touching up lip gloss and powder, and then circling back to start again. And the producer walked through it all, hollering at everyone to hurry up, as if they were all sitting around doing nothing and needed his motivation.

In the midst of all this chaos, Jordyn was the only one who seemed perfectly at home. She was standing in front of a mirror while a stylist pinned her dress, holding her guitar and striking different poses, as if to determine which angle might be her best.

"You sure seem to be enjoying this," Caleb said, stepping up beside her at the mirror.

"This is nothing," she said. "I used to do pageants when I was a kid, and they were way crazier backstage than this."

"Was that before or after junior Juilliard?"

"Hey, I told you that in confidence," she said, nodding toward the woman at her hem.

The stylist didn't even look up from the dress. "Don't worry," she said, taking a pin from her mouth, "we don't hear a thing. Just ignore us like everyone else does."

Jordyn looked Caleb up and down in the mirror. "You look silly in that suit."

"Yeah, well, you look equally ridiculous in that stupid dress," he retorted. Then he glanced at the stylist and quickly added, "Sorry, I didn't mean to dig on your costume."

"Don't apologize to me," she said. "I just make sure they fit, I don't design them. And I agree, it does look ridiculous."

Jordyn huffed and shook her head. "Oh, you two are great to have in my ear before I go out onstage in front of millions of people. I could have used you at those pageants to help lower my self-esteem when I was a girl. And the dress goes with the song, Caleb."

"Well, that's what I wanted to talk to you about. I'm kind of having second thoughts about the song."

"It's a little late now. It's already cued up and approved."

"But I like the one I wrote better."

"No way. It's too moody. We need votes, honey."

"Don't call me honey."

"Whatever. We need votes. You ever watch those other singing shows? I'll bet you do. You don't? Well, if you did, you'd know that the country girl always wins. Why? Because America loves country. And that means until we get Carrie Ann off the show, we need to pull some of that vote."

"Fine," he said. "But next week we sing mine."

She looked as if she wanted to argue but she didn't even get the chance, because the producer appeared at the door, waving his clipboard and yelling at them from across the room.

"Jordyn. Caleb. We need you stage-side five minutes ago."

They stood just offstage and watched from behind a partition as Jasmine finished a ballad that brought the audience to its feet. She bowed and smiled and faced the judges as if to see whether she was going through, even though the vote was now in the viewers' hands. The judges all threw her bouquets of praise, and then the host hugged her and looked into the cameras and told America to be sure to vote for her after the show.

Then the applause faded, the lights brightened, and sound technicians flooded the stage and reset the microphones for Jordyn's and Caleb's guitars. The digital backdrop switched to a country sunrise. The producer called for quiet on the set.

"Live in five, four, three, two, one."

The host bounded onstage and grinned into the cameras. "Welcome back, America. If you didn't already know this show was special, you will after hearing these next two artists perform live. They met on our set and formed a bond that couldn't be broken, a bond so strong they decided to go on together as a duo. Ladies and gentlemen, I give you the newly formed duo Jordyn and Caleb Entwined."

"That's your cue," the producer whispered. "Go, go, go!"

Jordyn switched her guitar into her other hand and took Caleb's hand in hers and led him out onstage. It happened so fast he had no time to think, let alone protest. They faced the cameras and the crowd, and bowed. Then they took their places on their stools and plugged in their guitars, just as they'd rehearsed.

The crowd had disappeared behind the bright lights but Caleb knew they were there. Just as he knew the cameras were there too. The background music started, the big camera panned across them slowly on its robotic boom, and Jordyn plucked the opening notes on her guitar. Caleb fell in behind the beat and joined her, and then even though they hadn't rehearsed it, she smiled into the camera and said, "This is for all you lonely lovers out there."

Then they began to sing.

$\approx$

Caleb sat on the edge of his bed with his elbows resting on his knees, one hand holding his bowed head while the other held the phone to his ear.

"Did Marj watch it with you? What did she think?"

"She loved it," Jane said. "She gave you a standing ovation right here in our living room. Buttercup loved it too. You got three yips and a bark."

"Did you vote?"

"Did we vote? We sat here texting for two hours. Or at least, I did. Marj has a landline and she ran over there and dialed the eight hundred number a hundred times. Don't worry, baby. I know without a doubt that you're going through. You sounded great. You looked great. Except, what was with that hat and that silly bell-bottomed suit?"

"Oh gosh, I know. It was terrible, right? Jordyn seems to think we need to court the country vote. Can you imagine? I've got mad respect for country music, but dressing like Jim Reeves is not really my thing."

"Well," Jane said, sighing into the phone, "when you're entwined with someone else, you have to make sacrifices."

"Come on, Jane. I told you I didn't pick the name. Jordyn didn't either. It was the stupid producers."

"I know, I know. I'm just razzing you. It's a good name."

"Well, knock it off," he said. "I'm sick over this whole thing. I feel like a fraud or something. Like a sellout."

"You're not a sellout, baby. It's only for TV."

"It's just that I miss you, Jane."

"I miss you too. You know what I did today? I sure wasn't getting my face powdered under any lights. I was walking my route and stepped in the biggest puddle of puke you've ever seen. Looked like hamburger meat and cottage cheese. And there was a trail of it leading to the culprit sleeping in a church doorway. Middle of the afternoon too. The smell followed me until I finally threw the shoes away and bought new ones."

"I'm sorry, babe. That sucks. But what were you doing writing tickets at a church?"

"It's on my route," she said. "I walk where they tell me to walk. But I do have a confession for you."

"Let me guess. You miss me so much that you voted for someone else, hoping I'd come home?"

"No, silly head. Although I do miss you. But it's just the opposite. As I was passing the church, I prayed for you to win if you're supposed to. Is that selfish and wrong?"

"Considering you had just stepped in a parishioner's puke, I think you were entitled to one selfish prayer. Are you going to watch the results show tomorrow?"

"I can't, baby. It's Thursday. I work night shift downtown. But Marj said she'd watch and call me with updates."

"Okay," he said. "I'll text you too if I can. Now I had better get some rest. I love you."

"I love you too. And good luck."

"Luck? I don't need luck. I've got your prayers."

Chapter 18

Jane was in the middle of writing a ticket when her phone rang. She slipped the ticket machine into her belt and answered.

"Did he do it? Wait. Don't tell me yet."

A full moon was rising between two buildings, and Jane looked up at it and made a silent wish.

"Okay, I'm ready now . . . Oh, Marj, I knew it. How did he look? Tell me everything."

By the time she ended the call, she was so overjoyed you'd have thought it was her smile the moon was reflecting. She sent Caleb a text, congratulating him. When she looked up again, the car she had been ticketing was gone. But she didn't care. She canceled the ticket and walked on, her feet almost skipping up the sidewalk as she went. She passed by expired meters without even noticing, too busy wishing everyone she came across a good evening, smiling at them with such genuine kindness that none could do anything except smile back.

A half an hour later, her phone rang again. It was a 206 area code from Seattle, and she assumed it must be one of her island friends calling to congratulate her after watching the show and recognizing Caleb. But as soon as she answered, she knew something was terribly wrong.

"This is Harborview Medical Center calling. Am I speaking with Jane McKinney?"

Hearing the words *medical center* erased the smile from Jane's face, and she stopped in her tracks and tightened her grip on the phone. Before responding, she looked up at the moon to make another wish, but the moon was gone.

❧

Marj buckled herself in and started the car. Then she sat with her hands on the wheel and looked at the dash as if she were confused about what to do next.

"Are you sure you're okay to drive, Marj?" Jane asked. "I've got time yet to catch a cab."

"I'm fine," Marj said. "It's just been a while."

She put Jane's car in drive, turned the blinker on, looked over her shoulder three or four times, and then finally pulled away from the curb. But by the time they reached the main road, she seemed to be getting the hang of it.

"So did they say it was a stroke?" she asked.

"They didn't know yet," Jane replied. "They were doing tests. They said it could be something called a TIA."

Marj nodded. "A ministroke."

"You're familiar with them?"

"Oh, yes," she said. "I've had one myself."

"You have? Oh, God, that makes me feel better. Not that I'm glad you've had one or anything. But you seem okay. What happened with you?"

"They gave me blood thinners and I quit smoking."

Jane eyed her suspiciously, knowing full well that she still smoked like a chimney.

Marj caught her look and shrugged. "Okay, I cut back my smoking. I do take the blood thinners, though."

"I just hope she's okay," Jane said, sighing. "I'm not ready for this. Not now."

They drove in silence for a while. It was still dark, and when a passing car flashed them, Marj searched for the lights.

"Right there on the blinker," Jane said.

Marj found them and turned them on. "How long will you be gone?"

"I'm not sure. But if you could water the plants on our balcony for me, that would be great."

"And your work? They approved you leaving?"

"I don't know. I left a message for my boss. I guess they'll have to be okay with it or else I won't have a job."

When they arrived at the airport departure entrance, Jane leaned over and hugged Marj, and they shared a silent look of understanding. Then Jane got out and retrieved her bag from the backseat, shut the door, and stood and waved good-bye, watching the taillights fade into the early morning gray.

❧

No sooner had the flight taken off than Jane felt sick.

She ignored the seat belt sign and went to the bathroom and retched into the toilet, then flushed it away. She wasn't sure if it was flying on no sleep and an empty stomach, or nerves. When she finished, she rinsed her mouth and splashed cool water on her face. The flight was nearly empty, and rather than return to her aisle seat, she took a window in an empty row, leaned against the wall, and tried to sleep. She kept rerunning her last conversation with her mother in her head.

She remembered driving away from the house and seeing her standing in the doorway obscured by the screen, and she remembered wondering if she'd ever see her again. Now she was wishing she'd stayed in touch. As miserable as she could be, the woman was still her mother.

Jane found herself wishing that Caleb were with her. He somehow always knew just the right way to comfort her. He would wrap her in his arms and make her feel safe. Last night when she had told him, he had offered to leave the show and come with her to Seattle. And she knew he had meant it. Thinking of him made her feel calmer, and she actually smiled as she finally slipped off to sleep, listening to the soft hum of the jet's engines just outside her window.

They were descending into Seattle when she woke. She lifted the window cover and looked out for familiar landmarks. All she saw was a wall of gray. Then they dropped beneath the clouds and into the rain and the wet runway came up slowly to meet them—touchdown, gray pavement rushing by in a blur, slowing, taxiing to the ramp, stopping. Back in Seattle again.

She hadn't bothered to check a bag, so she retrieved her carry-on and deplaned, then headed straight for the taxi line outside. It was odd watching through the water-specked windshield as the city of Seattle materialized slowly out of the gray, steadily clearer with each sweep of the wipers on the glass. She couldn't decide whether she wanted him to drive faster or slower, but it didn't matter because soon the hospital appeared out her window. The building was grayer than even the sky, except where it was punctuated with yellow-glowing windows. The rain clouds had dropped and the hospital rose up and disappeared into them as if the upper-floor residents already had some hold on heaven. She paid the fare with her credit card and thanked the driver. Then she stepped out into the rain with her bag.

It was surprisingly quiet inside, and her wet shoes squeaked loudly on the vinyl flooring as she walked to the help desk, then waited for the man there to look up from his computer screen. He directed her to the fifth floor, and two minutes later she was standing in front of a nurses' station.

"McKinney?" the nurse repeated. "Here she is. Room sixteen B. Could you sign in here, please? It's just down the hall there on your left, and there are gowns outside the door."

Jane took the pen and filled in her mother's name and her own, then wrote "daughter" under patient relationship. Some daughter, she thought. She located the room and put on a gown, and when she entered, she found her mother sleeping in the hospital bed. Her gray hair that was usually so perfectly done up was spread out on the pillow, and her skin seemed to hang from her thin face. She looked much older than Jane had thought she would, lying there with wires connected to her fingers and somewhere beneath her gown, so quiet and so still that the rise and fall of her heartbeat on the graph and the soft beeping of the oxygen machine were the only signs that she was in fact alive.

She was standing beside the bed gazing down on her mother when a nurse came in. He smiled at Jane and washed his hands in the room sink. Then he joined Jane beside the bed.

"She looks very peaceful now that she's sleeping."

"Is she going to be okay?" Jane asked.

"Yes, I think so," he said, pulling the chart up from where it was hanging at the foot of the bed. "The doctor should be around in an hour or so. She can tell you more."

"But she is okay, isn't she? You said that. I mean, she's going to wake up, right?"

"They gave her something to calm her down for the MRI. That's why she's sleeping now."

"So she was awake and talking earlier? Please tell me she was talking."

"She was talking well enough to tell me that she wanted a different nurse."

"That's odd," Jane said. "Did she say why?"

"She didn't say directly, but I got the impression that she wanted someone lighter skinned."

Jane felt a mixture of humiliation and relief. She looked down at her mother and shook her head and sighed. "Well, she must be all right then. I'm really sorry if she offended you. She can be that way."

"I've heard much worse," the nurse said with just the hint of a smile. Then he added, "She's actually my favorite patient now that she's sleeping. Why don't you relax and if I see the doctor, I'll let her know that you're here."

Jane's nap on the plane had not done much to make up for her mostly sleepless night, and she had just nodded off in the chair when the doctor came in and woke her.

"You must be the daughter," the doctor said, drying her hands and picking up the chart. "I can see the resemblance."

Jane sat up, then she stood. Then she wondered if maybe she should wash her hands too; she wasn't sure what to do. The doctor looked far too young to be a doctor to Jane. But she knew that Harborview had some of the best in Seattle. It was chilly in the room, and she crossed her arms for warmth and waited for the doctor to finish updating the chart.

"I spoke with the neurologist a little while ago, and it looks like your mother had a transient ischemic attack."

"Is that a stroke?" Jane asked.

"It can be a warning sign for one," the doctor said. "Do you know if there's a history of heart disease in her family?"

Jane shook her head. "I'm not sure."

"It looks like she scored well on the cognitive and motor tests. She doesn't have diabetes, so that's good. We'll get her on an aspirin regime and talk with her about diet and exercise, but I have every reason to believe she'll make a full recovery."

"When can I take her home?"

"We'll keep her one more night for observation, but she should be good to go as early as tomorrow morning."

Jane thanked the doctor and followed her to the front desk to claim her mother's purse. She opened it, got out her mother's health insurance card, and gave it to the nurse along with her mother's address and other information. She was putting the card back when she found a pack of Virginia Slims, the same brand Jane occasionally smoked, having picked up the habit when she was young by stealing them from her mother's purse. She tossed the cigarettes into the waiting room's trash can. Then she bought a cup of coffee from the machine.

Her mother was awake when she returned to the room. She took one look at Jane and her face fell into a frown. "What are you doing here?"

"Not exactly the welcome I was expecting, Mother."

"Let me have my purse," she said, struggling to sit up in her bed. "What are you doing with my purse?"

"You need to relax, Mom. I didn't steal anything out of your billfold. Although I did throw away your cigarettes."

"You did not."

"I sure as hell did. You had a stroke, Mom."

"I had a fainting spell."

"No, you didn't. You had a ministroke, probably brought on by heart disease, and you probably have heart disease because you smoke and you hardly eat and you never exercise."

Her mother opened her purse and looked inside as if to verify that everything was there. "I didn't realize you'd gone off to Texas to attend medical school," she said. "I don't need advice from my own daughter."

"I'll tell you what I didn't do. I didn't fly all the way back up here to be beaten down again by you."

Jane could hear the resentment in her own voice, so she looked out the window at the rain and told herself to relax, to remember why she was here. Then she looked back at her mother, determined to use a calmer tone.

"I'm scared for you, Mom. Really scared. And you should be scared too. This is a wake-up call."

Her mother looked up at her with her mouth pinched tight

and her eyes glassed over, as if she were doing her best not to cry. When she finally spoke, she said, "You need to go and see your brother. You need to tell him I'm okay."

"He's in jail, Mom. How would he even know that you're in the hospital?"

"Because I was visiting him when it happened."

"Oh, great. Can't we call him or something?"

"You know damn well we can't call him in the jail."

"But I don't want to go there, Mom."

"He's your brother, Jane."

"Yeah, for whatever that's worth. It's probably not even visiting hours."

"What day is it?"

"It's Friday."

Her mother glanced at the wall clock. "Friday hours are five thirty to seven thirty. You can make it if you catch a cab."

⁓

Her brother was waiting behind the glass when she walked into the visiting room. He looked as if he'd lost some weight, and his hair was cut short for once and he was clean shaven. She could tell he was nervous because he picked up the receiver from its cradle and held it to his ear before she had even sat down. She picked hers up too.

"Is she okay?" he asked.

Jane nodded. "She'll be fine."

He let out a huge sigh and looked up at the visiting room ceiling, mouthing, "Thank you."

"They said it was a ministroke. A warning sign."

"I was so scared, Jane. She was sitting right where you are now, lecturing me about politics or some shit, and she just went limp and dropped the phone. I went crazy in here. I mean, I was pounding on the glass. Then the door. The guards finally came in and tried to cuff me, and I paid hell getting them to even look through the window to where she was slumped on the ground. I almost caught a new charge. You sure she's okay?"

"Yeah, I'm sure. Back to her usual old self as soon as she woke up. I'll get her home and stay with her for a while. She needs to quit smoking and she needs to exercise."

"Good luck on either of those," he said.

"How are you?" Jane asked. "You look healthy."

"Shit damn. It must be all these cold sausage disks and Cheerios they feed us in here. I'm telling you, Jane, they don't fuck around at the King's Motel. High-class all the way, as I'm sure you saw from the concierge who checked you in."

He flashed a half smile. Then his expression turned serious and he adjusted his grip on the phone. "I'm sober, though, Jane. I am. And not just because I'm locked up either. You can score in here easy if you want to. But not me. I'm clean. No more blame game for me. And no more stinkin' thinkin' either. I've been doing step work, and we've got a Sunday meeting after service and everything. You'd be proud of me, sis. You would."

"I am proud of you," she said. "That's all I ever wanted for you. You know that. You're a good egg when you're sober, Jon. You're a rotten egg when you're not."

He looked down at the worn metal shelf in front of him and nodded. Then he took a deep breath and looked up again. "So, how are you, sis? How's life in the South? Mom said you moved to Texas with your gardener."

"He's not my gardener. But yes, I moved to Texas and we're great." She held up her hand to the glass and showed him her ring. "We're getting married."

"Holy shit, sis. No way. Congratulations. Really. Ain't that some shit? My big sister finally tying the knot. I guess Mom can quit telling her church friends you're a lesbian now. When are you doing it? I'd like to come if I'm not still in this damn cage."

"We haven't set a date yet. I'd love to have you there, Jon. But only if you're still clean when you get out."

"Shit, sis. I'll be clean. Clean and sober. I'm not drinking again for the rest of my natural-born life. And that's a fact. You can take that check to the bank and cash it right now."

"Well, maybe just do it one day at a time," Jane said.

She spent a few minutes telling him all about Austin, and he spent a few telling her all about the ninth floor of the King County Jail. Then a recorded voice came on to let them know that their visiting time was ending. They said their good-byes, and Jane promised to have their mother give him her number and her address so they could stay in touch about the wedding. She was about to hang up when he asked her the question she knew all along that he would ask.

"Sis, would you mind leaving a little money on my books? Mom was going to do it the other day but she had her thing, her ministroke, I guess . . . and . . . you know, it would really help me out. Maybe I'll get a new A and A book or something when I order my personals."

Jane smiled and said that she would. Although she knew damn well that the last thing he'd use it for was an Alcoholics Anonymous textbook.

❧

Her mother's house smelled of mothballs and bad memories. A kind of hopeless odor that hung in the air and clung to Jane's clothes. They had hardly walked through the door when her mother went straight to her room and closed the door, leaving Jane to fend for herself.

She took her bag to her old bedroom and paused with her

hand on the knob. She had not been inside since she'd left home at seventeen. She took a deep breath, then opened the door, and was met by twenty-three years' worth of boxes piled everywhere, even on top of the bed. It was as if her mother had used her room all this time as a dumping ground. A fitting idea, Jane thought, since all she ever did was dump on her.

She cleared the bed and stacked the boxes out of the way. Then she removed the bedding, shook it out in the hall, and remade the bed. When she finally lay down on the soft old mattress, she looked up at the popcorn ceiling and saw the same brown water stain that she had looked up at as a girl and tried to make into interesting shapes. Drifting continents and passing clouds. A dragon. A Cheshire cat. It had been her favorite pastime. Once she had even seen the face of God.

The stain was somewhat more faded, but there it was just the same. How long? Had there been a time before? Yes. She remembered the rainstorm that had brought it. She remembered waking up with water dripping on her face. She remembered running into her parents' room, afraid. She remembered the booze on her father's breath. She remembered his calling her a liar. She remembered her mother too, passed out on her wine. And she remembered creeping back into her room and sleeping in the closet on the floor, praying for the thunder and the lightning to pass. In the morning, the rain had stopped and the leak was gone, and she had begun to believe that maybe she had made it all up, that maybe she was just a scaredy-cat and a liar. But three days later, the stain had appeared.

Jane felt her stomach drop and knew she was going to be sick. She got up and hustled into the bathroom, lifted the toilet lid, and retched. She was kneeling on a shaggy sea-blue bath mat; the toilet seat lid had a matching blue shag cover and the seat itself was padded. The bathroom smelled heavily of the perfumed decorative clamshell soaps that filled jars on the shelf above the toilet, and the odor made her even sicker. She retched again, losing the contents of her stomach, and flushed it away.

She was numb and light-headed when she finally stood up. She took her mother's car keys, then left and drove to the nearest pharmacy. The lights were glaringly bright, the music too chipper for the depressing atmosphere. There were no other customers, and she was grateful for it.

She added some chips and some cotton balls to her basket, just to avoid being so embarrassed when she checked out. But she needn't have bothered because the clerk seemed to be in a Thorazine stupor as he rung her up. He didn't say hello or thank you, or even offer her a bag. She stuffed her purchase into her purse and left the chips and the cotton balls free for the taking on top of the trash can outside the pharmacy door.

Twenty minutes later, Jane was back in the blue perfumed bathroom, sitting on the padded toilet seat with her eyes closed and a prayer on her lips. She opened her eyes and saw a blue cross. It couldn't be. She reached for another test and peed on it. She waited, and she watched. Another blue cross. She looked at the claim on the box. *Over 99% Accurate.* She took out the last tester, but she couldn't pee again, and what was worse was that she knew she didn't even need to. She threw the tester across the small bathroom.

"Fuck," she said. "Not again."

Her mind raced away from her across twenty years of heartbreak and pain to when she had first found out she was pregnant with Melody. If she'd known then what had been coming for them both, she never would have survived the pregnancy. She almost hadn't survived losing her later.

She buried her face in her hands and cried. "Why? Why? Why?"

Later that night, she lay on her bed and looked up at the stain on her ceiling, trying desperately to shape it in her mind into some familiar face she might ask. Ask about the future; ask about the past. But her childhood faith had long since been lost in the real world, and all that remained in its place were bad memories and an old faded water stain.

PART THREE

PART THREE

Chapter 19

Jane's mother was late coming to the table for breakfast. When she did finally appear from her room, she was wearing her church clothes and smelled of Avon powder and perfume. She sat across from Jane, and Jane rose and retrieved hot water from the stove and poured her a cup of Earl Grey tea. Then she sat down again and watched as her mother selected a boiled egg from the bowl of them on the table, cracked it with her spoon, and peeled it, dropping the shell pieces onto her plate with tiny clinks that seemed to echo in the silence between them.

The clock ticked loudly on the mantel. The refrigerator began to whir. Jane sensed that they were both under some spell of speechlessness cast by the years' worth of things unsaid, the resentments of a life of regret, and as much as a part of her wished for some way to break this spell, a larger part of her wished to let it be and just run.

When the egg was peeled, her mother cut the tip off with her knife and salted it. Then she held it up as if to inspect it in the gray light coming in through the kitchen window.

"The rosebush looks to be doing okay," Jane said.

Her mother replied without looking away from the egg. "Marta's taking me to church, if you care to come along."

"Are you sure that's a good idea?" Jane asked. "I mean so soon after—"

"I'm fine," her mother snapped. "I had a little fainting spell and now I'm fine. And if the good Lord decides to take me, I hope he takes me at church, so that's where I'm going to be. If you want to come, you'll need to change."

"I think I'll pass. I was thinking of going to the island."

Her mother nodded, but she didn't look at Jane. Instead she picked up the shaker and salted her egg again, perhaps having forgotten that she had already salted it once.

"You may use the car," she said simply. "Since Marta's coming by to collect me, as I said."

"Thank you, Mother. That's very kind."

Her mother winced and set the egg on her plate as if being called Mother had made it suddenly hot in her hand. She picked up her cup and sipped her tea.

Jane watched the steam rise and run up around her mother's long nose. The mother she remembered was in there somewhere, hidden behind the mask of makeup and the thin skin and fine lines. Jane watched as she cradled her teacup with both hands, as if trying to absorb its warmth.

"I went once, you know."

"Went where?" Jane asked.

"To the cemetery."

"You did? To visit Melody?"

Her mother nodded. "It was a nice day and I just went. I brought pink scabiosas and pink tulips from Brenda Thompson's old shop. I think she would have liked them."

The thought of her mother visiting Melody's grave on her own softened Jane's heart. She was her grandmother, after all. Jane felt a lump in her throat, and she looked at the tablecloth in an attempt not to cry.

"Mother, there's something I need to talk to you about. Something important. If you don't mind."

When there was no response, Jane looked up and saw that her mother was gazing past her out the kitchen window, her mind somewhere else. In the gray light, Jane could see her eyes clouded with advancing cataracts, and she almost appeared to be already among the blind, seeing nothing but the past, and even that blurred by lies and by time.

"Mom, did you hear me? I need to tell you something."

Jane watched for a response but there was none. Then a horn double-honked out on the street, and her mother rose from the table as if responding to some command.

"There's Marta," she said, pushing in her chair. "I had better not keep her waiting or else someone will get our seats."

She disappeared down the hall, then reappeared wearing her big church hat. She paused at the door and turned back. "You don't have to stay, you know. I'll be fine."

"Do you not want me here?" Jane asked.

Her mother took a long time to answer. "I appreciate you coming. I know it's been a lot of trouble. But I just think you should get back to your own life."

Jane looked away from her and nodded, but she didn't say anything. Several quiet seconds passed, and she could feel her mother watching her from the door. She heard the door open, saw in her peripheral vision the wash of gray light, and then the door closed, snatching from her sight any and all hope of ever connecting with her mother in a meaningful way.

Jane sat and listened to the muffled thud of the car door shutting, followed by the purr of the car driving away. And she sat for a long time after, just listening to the dead quiet of the old house and staring at her mother's uneaten egg.

❧

Jane stood on the ferry deck and watched the island grow against the dark clouds stacked up on the horizon. It wasn't raining, but everything was wet as if it had recently been. The cold air felt good against her face, and she closed her eyes to listen to the familiar hypnotic hum of the ferry's engines, the quiet splash of water against its bow, and the call of seagulls in its wake. She couldn't tell if this felt more like a homecoming or a trip into the past, but either way she was happy to be alone for once. But she wasn't alone, was she? She had another life deep inside her, pleading its case against her fears, against her doubts, against her choice.

The announcement came for passengers to return to their vehicles, pulling Jane from her private thoughts. Her hair was tangled from the wind and her eyes were watering from the cold. She tossed her half-finished coffee into the trash and went inside and down the stairs to the vehicle deck. She started her car and angled the vent to let the heat blow over her numb cheeks. It felt good.

The ferry docked and she disembarked, driving up and out of the terminal and onto an island that had not changed. No, the island had not changed, she thought. But she had. The wet streets seemed to suck the color from everything until only gray skies and dark trees remained, and the scene out her windshield matched her mood as she drove toward the cemetery with a foggy head and a heavy heart. She slowed at the cemetery entrance with her blinker on, speeding up at the last minute and passing it by. Not yet, she thought. I'll go. I will. But not just yet.

The road led her around the island, providing peekaboo glimpses of the gray water through the trees, not unlike her fragmented memories flickering just beyond her conscious thoughts, always there like an old movie in her mind, despite her desire not to see them.

Jane found herself working her way slowly toward her old home. She feared it might already have been torn down; she feared that it hadn't been. When she finally arrived on her old familiar street, she found her house much the same as she had

left it, other than a different car in the driveway and new curtains in the kitchen window.

She put the car in park and sat looking out her windshield at
the house she had called home for fifteen years. What was this
place, really? she wondered. Just four exterior walls and a roof.
Just a rectangle of land on a big lonely planet, marked out with
two-by-fours and plywood by some cunning carpenter, topped
with composition shingles and skinned with slat siding painted
blue. But it was more than this. It was the place she had raised
her daughter, the place she had kept warm with hope and love
and dreams. It was a place filled with memories. And then it had
become the place she cried herself to sleep each night, wondering why her daughter had to die.

"Why, God, why?"

Caleb had come into her life here. And he had helped her to
heal. Then she had left it all behind to make a new life with him.
But now she wondered if perhaps she hadn't been running from
something when she followed him to Austin, running from a
place that had become too painful for her to face. She knew now
that you could never outrun your memories. The place might
be the trigger, but the past lived in her heart and in her mind.
Although perhaps a different future could live in her heart as
well—a different ending to a similar story, another chance to
make things right, a hope to someday heal.

Movement caught her eye, and she looked toward the door
of her old house and saw a mother and her young son step out.
As the mother turned to lock the door, the boy stood looking at
Jane from the step. His hair was as fine and blond as corn silk,
and he smiled innocently. The mother took his hand and led
him toward their car in the driveway. She didn't seem to notice
Jane, but the boy never did look away. Even when he was buckled in and they were backing out, his little towhead turned to

keep her in sight. Then he raised one small hand to the glass and the car was gone, taking with it Jane's nostalgia for this place.

It was someone else's hopes and dreams that lived here now—someone else's future, someone else's memories. She had been curious to see if Caleb's fountain remained in the backyard, but it no longer mattered. She put the car in drive and pulled away. She didn't look in the mirror. Perhaps because she knew there was no longer anything there to see.

She was driving back toward the cemetery on the main road when she saw a sign for Island Crest Assisted Living. The arrow pointed to a winding road that led up the island's central hill, and Jane slowed and took the turn.

What the hell, she thought, it was worth a shot.

The assisted living center was a sprawling single-level building built on top of a hill providing northwesterly views of the sound. The parking lot had a sprinkling of cars and several small buses with the center's logo painted on their sides. The air smelled of wet blacktop and of pine. She walked up beneath the portico and through the automatic glass doors to the lobby inside. It smelled of lemon floor cleaner and just a hint of disinfectant. She crossed to a circular welcome desk and addressed a man idly flipping through a *Sunset* magazine.

"Hello. I'm here to visit one of your residents. If she's here, of course. I'm not sure."

"Name, please," the man said, tossing the magazine and pulling his keyboard toward him.

"Mrs. Hawthorne. I'm not sure of her first—"

"Oh, her," he said, pushing the keyboard away without bothering to look anything up. "She's here, all right. Take a left there to the end of the hall. Then take a right. She's in room twenty-three F. And if she's not there, you'll probably find her hassling the nurses at their station."

Jane walked the long hall and turned as he had directed. The place was quiet and infused with fluorescent light, and it felt like a place where people came to say good-bye more than they did to visit. She passed open doors into rooms where she saw feet sticking out from blankets, pointing toward the soft blue glow of murmuring televisions. Talking heads lulling them toward death. She saw bulletin boards filled with cards and tables lined with flowers. She saw a man on the edge of his bed, rubbing lotion onto the stump where his leg had once been. She saw another man with his toothless mouth agape in dementia's telltale silent and final scream. She wondered if her mother would someday be in such a state and in such a place. She wondered if she herself would be. Perhaps sooner than any of us care to admit, she thought.

She came upon 23F and stopped. A small placard outside the door read: HAWTHORNE. A woman was sitting in a wheelchair, her head silhouetted against the TV. Jane knocked on the open door, but Mrs. Hawthorne didn't turn to look.

She reached up a hand dismissively and said, "Just leave it by the bed and I'll take it later."

Jane took a few steps into the room. "Hello, Mrs. Hawthorne. It's me, Jane. Jane McKinney."

The old lady placed her left hand on the wheelchair wheel and moved it backwards, then slowly turned the chair until she was facing Jane. She looked exactly the same, except maybe with a new touch of melancholy on her birdlike face. They looked at each other for a moment. Then the TV came on with a commercial for an upcoming documentary marking the fiftieth anniversary of the assassination of JFK. Mrs. Hawthorne glanced at the screen and shook her head.

"I just absolutely hate it every time I see that man's face on the television."

"You didn't like Kennedy?" Jane asked.

Mrs. Hawthorne dismissed the TV with a wave. "Oh, he was a fine president. Maybe one of the best. It's his hair I hate. It drives me to a rage every time I see it."

"You hate John F. Kennedy's hair?"

"Well, of course. It almost bankrupted us."

"And how did his hair manage that?" Jane asked.

"My second husband owned a chain of hat shops, and we couldn't get inventory fast enough. Hats, hats, hats. All the men wore them. Very classy look, I say. Then along came JFK with his wavy locks and that charming smile, and I'll be damned if every man in the union wasn't running around with his head as naked as the day he was born. It nearly ruined the country, if you ask me."

Jane had a hard time trying not to laugh. "Maybe you should name a goat after him."

The old lady chuckled too. "I did name a cat after him once, but that's a different story. How are you, dear? Come in, please. Sit down."

Jane took the only chair in the room, and Mrs. Hawthorne rotated her wheelchair a bit more so that they were facing each other. The room was simple. A window with lace curtains. An adjustable power bed. A chair. The TV. There was a small, plain dresser, its top adorned with an antique lamp that Jane thought she recognized from Mrs. Hawthorne's old house. Next to the lamp was a brass urn with a decorative lid.

"It seems nice here," Jane lied.

"Oh, don't give me that crap," she replied. "This place is a warehouse for the dying. Every week one leaves feetfirst, and a new one takes their place. The hallways fill with the families. All a-chattering too. Oh dear, you should hear their lies. 'You'll love it here,' they say. 'It will be fun, Grandma.' 'We'll visit all the time, Granddaddy.' Then they're gone and the next time you see them, they're back with the funeral van."

"Doesn't anyone visit you?" Jane asked.

"No one cares to come," she said. "No one except my one greedy son who's furious that I'm leaving my property to the state. They have instructions at the front not to let him in." She lifted her head and swung her eyes toward the dresser. "But I've got Jim and Carl there to keep me company."

"Jim and Carl?"

"My first and second husbands. I was widowed twice, you know. They're both in the urn there, waiting on me to join them. But you didn't come to talk about an old lady's slow crawl toward the crematorium. I see our man has put that ring he worked so hard for on your hand."

Jane looked down at the yellow diamond on her finger. Then she covered it with her other hand, because she worried that it might make Mrs. Hawthorne uncomfortable to see her wedding ring worn by someone else.

But Mrs. Hawthorne just smiled. "How is he?"

"Caleb's doing fine. He's in Los Angeles right now, playing his guitar and singing for a TV show. It's a nice break for him. I didn't know that I'd be coming today or I would have told him. I'm sure he would have asked me to say hello to you."

"No sense troubling a young man about an old woman," she said, passing her hand in front of her face as if to wave the idea away. Then she focused on Jane. "Tell me, my dear, how are you? I've seen happier faces in here on hospice nurses."

Jane sighed. She hadn't meant to; it just came out. She looked past Mrs. Hawthorne to the yellow lace curtains, and she tried to keep the tears from coming into her eyes.

"I'm just having a tough time, I guess."

When Jane let her eyes find Mrs. Hawthorne again, she saw

that the old lady was looking at her with her hands folded on her lap, as if waiting for more but in no way wanting to force it from her. There was a clear patience in her gaze, a sharpness of mind dulled only by a motherly compassion. It was something Jane had not seen in a long time, and it was comforting. She let down her guard and just spoke the truth.

"My mother had a stroke, so I left my job and flew home. But she doesn't want me here. And I guess I don't want to be here either. Caleb's busy filming his show. And I want him to be there. I do. It was even my idea. But I just feel cut off from everyone. I don't know if I should fly there or just fly home and deal with this alone. You see, I don't know if I can go through with this. Not again. I don't know if I'd survive. And if I tell him, I know I'll have no choice. I know how he feels. Oh gosh, I'm so sorry. I'm sure this makes no sense at all. Please, never mind my rambling."

When she finished, Mrs. Hawthorne lifted her clasped hands from her lap and leaned forward in her chair, resting her chin on them as she looked directly into Jane's eyes. "How long have you been pregnant, dear?"

The room blurred into a smear of yellow light, and Jane felt the tears slide down her cheeks. She opened her purse and fished out a tissue, dabbing the tears away as she spoke.

"I found out the other day. And I'm scared to death about it. I think that's why I came out here. To see Melody at the cemetery. To ask her if it was me. If it was my fault. The sickness, I mean. Alcoholism. Addiction. The disease. You see, I couldn't live through that again. I just couldn't."

"Melody is your daughter who passed away?"

Jane nodded. "Caleb told you?"

"Yes. We talked a great deal while he was working for me. Mostly he talked about you and how much he loved you."

Jane felt herself smile despite the tears. "Really? Did he say why?"

"He gave lots of reasons, I'm sure, but I was probably too busy watching his ass working in those jeans to even listen."

Jane couldn't help but laugh.

"Hey now, I might be old as dirt and damn near dead, but I'm not buried yet," the old lady said. Then she leaned forward and touched Jane's knee. "You'll be all right, dear. You will." Then she rose from the wheelchair.

There was a moment when she looked to be stuck, half in and half out, but Jane didn't want to insult her by helping so she waited and watched. She finally stood and reached for her cane. Then she shuffled over to the dresser and laid her hand on the brass urn. When she spoke again it was to Jane, even though her eyes remained on the urn.

"I was lucky to have had two men to love in my life. But two more different men there never were before and never will be again. If I tipped their ashes out, I wouldn't be surprised one bit if they poured into two separate piles on the floor."

She half turned, lowered herself onto the edge of her bed, and sat staring at the carved handle of her cane.

"Jimmy was my first and my one true love. But he was a wild man with a wild spirit. Never fall in love with a sailor, dear. Their hearts are quick to love, but there's nothing that holds them like the sea. And the only way they seem to be able to stand land is when they're drunk. He came home from the navy and surprised me with that ring you're wearing. Spent his entire inheritance on it. We had our wedding in a friend's backyard. Small but perfect. We rented a little apartment in San Francisco, and we made love day and night for nearly a year. Oh, did we make love. But it wasn't long before he was back out to sea. This time on a commercial ship. That's when I found out. I was alone and I was terrified too. I sent a telegram to their port to let him know. But I never heard back and I thought he hadn't received it. But he had. Oh Lord, I'll never forget that look on his face when he stepped off that ship and saw me."

She paused and looked down at the floor, and Jane saw her shudder beneath her shawl.

"He didn't say a word and neither did I," she continued. "He thought I'd lost the baby, and I guess I had. Three nights later, he was out drinking to ease the grief when he tried to break up a fight and took some bastard's knife in the gut. And just like that, I lost him too."

She brought her hand slowly to her chest, as if to comfort her own broken heart.

"It took ten years for me to see Carl for who he was. We had known him through friends. Not close, but from a distance. He said he had always loved me. And I grew to love him too. He was a good man. A quiet man. A loyal man. He had been widowed too and he had three daughters, then I gave him a son. I don't hear from the girls now that he's passed. But I wouldn't change a day of it."

There was a long pause while she stared up at the urn on the dresser.

"I'm not telling you all of this just to reminisce. I'm telling you because I was fortunate enough to have found what I needed in my life in two men. You're one of the even luckier ones who have managed to find everything in just one. That Caleb's a keeper, and I'd hate to see you break his heart like I did my Jimmy. He thought it was a miscarriage and I didn't tell him any different. But I always wonder what might have been."

Jane watched her, sitting there on the bed with the brass urn visible just above her shoulder. Everyone has their secret regrets, she thought, and maybe none of us will truly reconcile them until we're finally dead.

Mrs. Hawthorne rose on her cane. "There's something you should have to go along with that ring, but you'll have to drive me to my old house to get it. Do you have time?"

"Of course," Jane said. "I've got plenty of time."

Jane was pushing her wheelchair down the hall when a nurse stopped to ask them where they were off to.

"Just out for a little fresh air," Mrs. Hawthorne said.

They wheeled past the front desk and out beneath the portico. Jane helped Mrs. Hawthorne from the wheelchair and into the car's seat. She was light and frail, and her nails dug into Jane's arm as she held her for support. Jane was wondering what to do with the wheelchair when Mrs. Hawthorne told her she didn't need it and to just leave it there.

"They come out to collect them like shopping carts," she said. "We should hurry and go, though."

As Jane drove away, she looked in her rearview mirror and saw the wheelchair rolling down the sloped parking lot, with the man from the reception desk chasing after it.

"You weren't supposed to leave, were you?" Jane asked.

The old lady looked back and chuckled. "I'm not sure, but I'll be damned if I'll ask permission like some prisoner."

When they arrived at her old driveway, the first thing Jane noticed was that the mailbox that had read HAWTHORNE was gone. In its place was a PROPOSED LAND USE sign. Mrs. Hawthorne seemed to either not notice or not care as Jane passed it by and idled up the gravel drive toward the old yellow house.

There was a utility van in front of the house, and Jane parked next to it, got out, and went around and helped Mrs. Hawthorne from the car. The old lady leaned on her cane and looked up at the house, and they were each tilting so far left, woman and house, that Jane would not have been surprised if they had fallen over simultaneously. She held Jane's arm for support, and together they walked toward the porch and slowly climbed the steps. They stopped in front of the door and Mrs. Hawthorne leaned in to Jane, then lifted her cane up to touch a rusty horseshoe hanging above the doorframe.

"This horseshoe brought us over fifty years of good luck in this old house. Carl and I found it on our honeymoon and hung it up when we moved in. I want you to have it, dear."

"Are you sure?" Jane asked. "Don't you want to keep it?"

"And hang it at that geriatric hoosegow they've got me tucked away in? I don't think so. Besides, dear, it will bring me comfort knowing that it's hanging above another door where love lives. I'd like to believe some things just keep going on."

Jane looked up at the horseshoe. It was sad to think of this place being torn down. She remembered the first time she had come out here to try to sell Mrs. Hawthorne long-term care insurance. She remembered coming again with Caleb to pay for the goat.

She stretched up onto her tiptoes to pry the horseshoe free and was struggling with a stubborn nail when the door opened and a man ran into her and screamed. He jumped back into the house and fell flat on his behind. He sat there looking up at them and removed his headphones.

"You ladies scared the bejesus out of me," he said. "All the guys at the shop keep telling me this place is haunted."

"You had better hurry and tear it down," Mrs. Hawthorne said, "because if I die before you do, I might just come back and haunt it for real."

The man stood up and dusted himself off. "I'm just here pulling wire and fuses. Getting things ready for the wrecking ball. I take it this was your house, ma'am."

"Yes, it was. I came back because I forgot something."

He looked over his shoulder into the empty house. "There's not much here, ma'am."

"It's this horseshoe above the door, young man. Would you mind prying it free for us?"

He removed the horseshoe and gave it to Mrs. Hawthorne. Mrs. Hawthorne presented it to Jane. Then they thanked the worker and returned to the car.

Jane was helping Mrs. Hawthorne into the car when the old lady rested her hand on the open door for support and turned to look back at her house one last time. She seemed to be seeing the years unfold in reverse there on that old weathered porch, and Jane could have sworn that for a moment Mrs. Hawthorne looked young again. She closed her eyes and smiled. Then she lowered herself into the seat and didn't look again.

Back at the assisted living center, Mrs. Hawthorne refused to let Jane see her in. She said there was no point in both of them getting into trouble. "And besides," she added, "where I'm going, I had better get used to going alone."

So Jane pulled up to the edge of the portico and tried her best not to cry as they said their good-byes. "You'll come to the wedding, won't you?" she asked.

Mrs. Hawthorne's face crinkled into one big smile. "I wouldn't miss it for the world, dear. Here. Take this and write me down your address."

Jane took the small, worn address book and pen that Mrs. Hawthorne produced from a pocket beneath her shawl and wrote her address and telephone number inside. After she had handed it back, there was a moment when Jane thought they might embrace in the car, but Mrs. Hawthorne reached for the handle and opened the door. Jane got out and crossed around to help her, but she was already out and leaning on her cane.

Oh, the hell with it, Jane thought.

Then she wrapped Mrs. Hawthorne up in her arms and hugged her. She let her head rest gently on the old woman's shoulder and she was hugging not only her, but also her own mother, and Grace, and Melody. When she pulled away she had tears in her eyes. So did Mrs. Hawthorne. Jane wasn't sure why or where she got the courage, but she leaned in and kissed the old woman's cheek. Then she turned and crossed back to her open car door.

"Thank you, dear," Mrs. Hawthorne said, wiping away a tear. Then she smiled and added, "And you tell that Caleb of yours where to find me if things don't work out with you two."

Jane laughed and got in the car.

As she pulled away, she saw in her mirror Mrs. Hawthorne standing at the edge of the portico, watching her go. She saw the attendant come out with a wheelchair, and she saw the old lady wave him away with her cane.

Then Jane looked ahead and saw her no more.

≈

The sun was setting by the time Jane arrived at the island cemetery. She parked and got out, then breathed in the cool, moist air. She smelled cut grass, even though it was already fall.

She went first to Grace's grave. There were fresh flowers there, and she wasn't surprised, knowing how many friends she had. Jane looked down at the stone and at her friend's name etched there above the two major dates in her life—the day it had begun and the day it had ended. She knew it was the days between them that counted, and she thought about Grace's confession of regret.

Live the life I can't, she had said. *A life free from fear.*

She had expected to feel sad coming here. But she didn't. She felt as though her friend was in a peaceful place beyond both sadness and pain.

"I love you, Grace. I wouldn't have made it through losing Melody without you. I know that now more than ever. And I'm doing my best to follow your advice. To live a life without fear. But I am scared, Grace. I'm scared and I wish you were here."

She closed her eyes and bowed her head. She felt the last of the setting sun's rays on her neck, and a breeze swept across the cemetery and rustled her blouse. When she lifted her head again, the sky was painted in ribbons of pink.

She left Grace's grave and went to see her daughter.

There was no trace left of the flowers her mother had brought, but the stone was clean and the grass was green and clipped short. She didn't know what to say, so she sat down and leaned against the headstone and watched the light fade slowly from the sky. She put her hand to her belly, and she felt that there were three of them sitting there in the pink glow of that lingering sunset. Eventually, she reached into her pocket and took out the coin that had brought her and Caleb together, the coin her daughter had once held. She kissed it, then wedged it in the soil where the marble met the earth, pushing it deep to protect it from the mower. A tear rolled down her cheek, but for some reason she didn't feel overly sad.

When twilight dropped over that island cemetery, hung already in the east with stars, Jane was still sitting there in the shadows with her head leaned against the cooling stone. And had anyone at all been nearby, they might have also heard her humming Melody's favorite lullaby.

Chapter 20

Halfway across the hotel lobby Jane had to stop and check herself, wondering if she hadn't had a drink or two on the plane, because she was sure seeing double—identical twins in identical outfits everywhere. She continued on to the check-in desk.

"Can I help you, miss?"

Finally, Jane thought, someplace where people didn't call her ma'am all the time. Maybe she'd like L.A., after all.

"Yes. My name is Jane McKinney, and Caleb Cummings left a room key for me."

The woman searched through an accordion folder. "Cummings for McKinney, you said. Yes. Here it is." She handed Jane a key card, adding, "If you're here for the Double Trouble Convention, the bus will arrive in fifteen minutes."

Jane glanced behind her at the pairs of twins waiting in the lobby. Her hand moved instinctively to her belly. "Oh Lord, don't let this be a sign," she mumbled.

The housekeeping cart was in the hall, and it was clear that they had just been in the room because the bed was made and almost no sign of Caleb was visible when she entered. She closed the door and set her bag on the floor. Then she went to use the bathroom. It was strange looking at his toothbrush and his beard trimmer after all this time apart. She felt as though she were trespassing into a stranger's personal space. She freshened up and went back into the room. She opened the closet and saw his clean clothes hung neatly on hangers and a pile of dirty clothes beneath them on the closet floor. She kicked off her shoes, stripped off her pants and her blouse, and picked up a worn T-shirt from the pile and put it on. Then she drew the curtains closed, switched off the light, and curled up on the bed in the dark room.

She hadn't realized how exhausted she was—exhausted from the stress of attempting to care for her mother, exhausted from the emotional overload of returning home, exhausted from the battle raging inside her to tell or not to tell. She put her hands inside Caleb's T-shirt and pushed the cotton up to her nose, and smelled his scent before she drifted off to sleep.

Jane thought she was dreaming when she felt his arms wrap around her from behind. Then his lips were on her neck. Then his mouth moved up to her ear. He whispered her name and he whispered that he was glad she had come. Then he whispered poetic things she'd never dreamed before that she'd hear. He told her that he had things to confess. That he needed her more than anything else in this world or the next. That she was the star of his every dream, the meaning behind every heartbeat in his chest, and that his love for her grew with each and every breath. He told her he had loved her since the day they had first met and that he would love her all the days he had left. She felt his strong arms around her and his warm breath on her neck, and she let his words of poetry seep into her heart and into her soul. When he had finished confessing his love, she rolled over and brought her lips to his and they kissed. It was pitch-black in the room, but when she ran her fingers over his face, she could see clearly in her mind each of his beautiful features. And then there was his taste—familiar and exciting. She felt his free hand roaming her body, gently dragging his fingers across her skin, and some internally generated electricity from the mysterious workings of her heart raised the hairs on her arms and caused her legs to part.

Soon their naked bodies were pressed together and she felt

him slide inside her as if they had been made to fit together, and the only unnatural thing left between them was having ever been apart. For a few delicious minutes she forgot everything troubling her, everything weighing on her heart, and she let herself float there on that mattress, free as could be, feeling nothing but his desire deep inside her and his mouth on hers, both of them hungry with need.

When Caleb came it was with such force that he lifted his mouth away from hers and called her name. She gripped his forearms where they were planted on the mattress beside her, and she wrapped her legs around him and held him tight. And when she came, the mattress, and the hotel floor, and the floors below, and the very earth beneath them seemed to fall away as they spun a slow orbit around each other, their bodies entwined, revolving there in that dark room.

He finally fell to the bed beside her, and even in the dark, they were so connected that she could feel his smile. Jane scooted into the nook beneath his arm and rested her cheek on his naked chest. He reached his hand around and gently played with her hair.

"I missed you," he said.

"I can tell," she said, giggling. "I missed you too."

"Sorry I'm so late getting back. We were filming a car commercial at the studio."

"Well, look at you. So famous you're in a car commercial. Did they let you keep one?"

"Keep one? No. It's not the Oprah birthday show. We get paid scale, though. I'm not sure what that is, but everyone else was excited about it."

"Well, I'm sure they'll sell millions with you in the ad."

"Yeah, right," he replied. "Tell me what's up with you. You sounded kind of down on the phone before you left Seattle."

She wanted to tell him. She did. And she couldn't imagine a better time. But then she thought it might be selfish, that it might distract him from the show when he was so close to winning. And she also knew that once she spoke it out loud, things would never be the same between them again.

Tomorrow, she decided. She'd tell him tomorrow.

"Oh, my mother just had me depressed, as usual. But I'm fine now. Hey, why is it so dark in here? I can't even see your chest and I'm lying on it."

"Electrical tape," he said. "Want me to turn on a light?"

"No," she answered, hugging him. "Don't move. Let's lie here for a while. I like listening to your heart."

"Good," he said, kissing the top of her head, "because it's beating for you."

❧

The shrill ring of the hotel phone woke her. She felt Caleb roll over and she heard him lift the receiver, then put it back down. Jane closed her eyes and drifted back to sleep. When she opened her eyes again, the bathroom door was ajar and a beam of yellow light was bisecting the room. She heard the shower running. She rose from the bed, went to the bathroom, and pushed the door open. He had his arm up against the shower wall, his head bent beneath the stream of water. She remembered her trip to Paris with Grace, and she couldn't help but think that Caleb naked in the shower reminded her of a sculpture she might have seen there in the Louvre. She peeled his T-shirt off and went to join him.

It was her turn to hug him from behind, and when she did he turned his head to look at her and smiled, taking her in his arms, rotating her so the spray was on her back.

"Sorry to barge in," she said. "The door was open."

"Don't be sorry. I left it open as an invitation."

"Well, then, you should be sorry for waking me."

"You sure about that?" he asked, kissing her neck.

"Okay, maybe not."

He turned her around and pressed her naked body against the shower wall. Then his hands left her and she closed her eyes and waited with excited anticipation. When she felt his hands again, he was gently washing her back with a soapy loofah. He washed her shoulders and her arms. Then he knelt and washed her legs one at a time. When he had finished her legs, he turned her around and washed her front.

He hummed a beautiful tune as he worked, a melody she had never heard before, and he was so gentle with her, so absorbed in her body, that she felt truly worshipped. He finished and kissed her on the forehead. Then he moved her beneath the warm water to rinse off, and stepped from the shower and took a towel for himself off the rack. It was the simplest, quietest, humblest gesture of love she had ever experienced. Jane closed her eyes and tried to re-create the tune he had been humming, silently praying for the courage to say what she needed to say.

When she finished in the shower, she wrapped a towel around herself, took a deep breath, and went into the room. Caleb was just hanging up the hotel phone, fully dressed and ready to go. He stepped over to her, took her face in his hands, and kissed her.

"I've gotta run, baby."

"So soon?" she asked. "I was hoping to talk to you."

"I'm sorry, honey. We're filming interviews this morning as filler for the live show this week. Then I've got a rehearsal and a run-through with the music director at the set. But let's have dinner together tonight, okay? We'll talk then."

"Fine," she said, rising onto her tiptoes and kissing him on the cheek. "Go be with your adoring fans." Then she fell back onto the bed and held the back of her hand to her forehead, feigning exhaustion. "I'll just lie here in the room by myself and while away the day, wondering what to wear tonight, darling."

Caleb leaned down over her and whispered in her ear. "You just keep that towel on, and maybe we'll skip dinner and go right to dessert instead."

Then he grabbed his jacket and stepped to the door. "Oh shit," he said, turning back. "I forgot tonight is the charity auction dinner."

"That's okay," Jane told him, trying not to sound too disappointed. "I'll just see you after."

"No"—he shook his head—"you're coming with me. The dinner's here in the hotel ballroom at eight. I'll be back at least fifteen minutes before to get you."

"Fifteen minutes. Will you have time to even get ready?"

"My stylist will dress me at the set."

"Whoa there," Jane said, shaking her head and smiling at him. "Look who's a big shot with his own stylist. Now I'm really going to have to spend the day wondering what to wear."

Caleb grinned and blew her a kiss.

As soon as the door was closed, she missed him. Their reunion last night seemed already like a dream, and this morning had gone by far too fast. She hadn't even had a cup of coffee yet and her lover was already gone. There was a knock on the door and her heart leaped. Maybe his shoot had been canceled, or maybe he'd just forgotten his key. She rose to open the door. When she saw the smiling face behind the room service cart, she immediately let go of the door to tighten her towel and the door slammed closed on its spring hinges. She went and quickly put on a robe, then returned to the door and opened it again.

"I'm sorry," she said, stepping aside to let him in. "I wasn't expecting room service."

"No worries at all. Shall I just set it up here, then?"

He stopped his cart near the small desk and draped it with a white cloth, arranging the covered plates. He set out a pot of coffee. Then he poured fresh-squeezed orange juice into a champagne flute and topped it off with ginger ale and a slice of orange. She smiled to think that Caleb had arranged a virgin mimosa just for her. Then the man produced from somewhere beneath the cart a single long-stemmed red rose and laid it out on the cloth next to her breakfast.

By the time he turned to leave, Jane had fished a ten-dollar bill from her purse, but he waved it away.

"The gentleman already took care of that," he said, bowing slightly. "Enjoy."

Then he left her alone with her breakfast and her rose, and a heart full of admiration for the sexiest, most thoughtful man she'd ever met and was lucky enough to love.

◈

The warm sun washed down from blue Los Angeles skies and filtered through palm trees to dapple the sidewalks of Rodeo Drive. Jane felt as if she were walking in a movie. As if the director might at any moment call "Cut!" and the buildings would all suddenly be pulled down for the day and the streets rolled up. She passed a lime-green Lamborghini in a fire zone and a yellow Bentley double-parked. Oh, the fun she could have with her ticket book.

She stopped into the Louis Vuitton store just for kicks, and she was enjoying the patterns and smells of the leather so much that she let the salesperson think she was rich as he showed her every handbag in the place. She might have felt bad for wasting his time if she hadn't seen the prices of the purses he was peddling. When he finally left her to try his luck with another customer, she slipped out into the bright street again, laughing.

She found a boutique clothing shop at Rodeo and Wilshire, and when she entered the saleswoman nodded but left her to browse. There were dresses she could only dream of wearing, suits she'd have to be a CEO to afford. She found a rack of cute maternity wear, and she held one of the blouses up to herself in the mirror and tried to imagine what she'd look like. It had been so long, she could hardly remember.

"That color's perfect against your skin," the saleswoman said, appearing seemingly out of thin air. "Are you expecting?"

Jane blushed and said, "Yes. No. Maybe."

"Well, let's try a few on you and see how it feels."

Before Jane could protest, the saleswoman had taken two or three other blouses and a dress from the maternity rack and was leading Jane by the hand toward a changing room.

"Go ahead and take your blouse off," she said before disappearing into another room.

Jane considered making a dash for the door, but something about the lavender smell and the cool air in the shop made her want to stay. She took off her shirt and looked at herself in the mirror. She had lost weight these past few weeks, and she silently scolded herself for not eating better. She was examining her belly and trying to remember what it had been like when the saleswoman returned. She stood behind Jane and wrapped a stuffed pregnancy cushion around her midsection, then secured it with Velcro behind her back.

"This is about seven months," she said. "It should be perfect for that blouse." Then she left Jane alone in front of the mirror.

Jane took the blouse from the hanger, slipped it on, and pulled it down over the belly bump. Then she placed her hands on her hips and looked at her reflection. She turned for a side view. Now she remembered. Pain in her knees, swelling in her feet, bloating everywhere else. But she also remembered the soft kick against her palm, the slow turning in the night of that little life. The soft purple fabric did look good against her skin, as if maybe she were already glowing in that special way only a pregnant woman could. Maybe with Caleb's help and a lot of love, just maybe, she could do this again.

The saleswoman appeared, holding a glass of champagne for Jane, and asked, "What do you think?"

"You know what?" Jane said. "I really think I like it."

She took the blouse off and stood there wearing only her bra and belly bump, and read the tag dangling from the sleeve.

"Wowza!" she exclaimed, louder than she had intended to. "Who can afford to pay this much for something they'll only wear for a few months?"

"Most of our customers update their wardrobes that often anyway," the saleswoman said, offering the champagne glass to Jane. "Why don't you put on one of the others and I'll go grab some matching slacks?"

Jane shook her head and held out the blouse for her. "I'm sorry, but I don't think so. A person would have to have seventeen children to get enough wear out of that blouse to justify the price."

The saleswoman huffed and walked off, carrying away the blouse and the champagne. But Jane didn't care. Besides, she thought, what kind of person would offer champagne to a pregnant woman anyway?

When she had shed the belly bump and dressed in her own shirt again, she thanked the saleswoman and left the shop. Back out on the star-studded Beverly Hills street, Jane hopped a bus for Hollywood to find a consignment store and a dress she could afford.

It was five minutes to eight and Jane was just beginning to worry when Caleb strode into the hotel room wearing a tuxedo. She was so floored by how he looked, she couldn't say a word. Fortunately, he still had the power of speech.

"Wow!" he said, stopping to run his gaze up and down her new dress. "You look absolutely stunning."

"You think so?" she asked, turning for him to see.

"Think so? I know so. And if we weren't late, I'd strip off this suit and prove it."

"Thanks. You wouldn't believe it, but I got this dress for twenty-two dollars and the matching bangles for five bucks. But look at you. I like your hair slicked back like that. And this tuxedo you're wearing . . . so hot! I feel like I'm being escorted to a ball by James Bond. Maybe I should tuck my gun in my garter before we go."

"Are you really wearing a garter?"

"Oh, sure. I tell you I have a gun and all you care about is the garter. No, I don't really have either. I'm wearing Hanes pantyhose from Walgreens, if you must know. And I already can't wait to get them off."

Caleb stepped up and took her in his arms, then bent her back and kissed her. He looked into her eyes and smiled. "How about I take them off for you, right after dinner?"

He led her from the room to the elevator and down to the third floor, where tabletop bouquets of fresh flowers and silver balloons decorated the area outside the banquet hall. They stopped at the reception table and checked in.

"Plus one?" the woman asked Caleb, glancing at Jane as she handed him a bid card and an auction brochure.

"Yes," Caleb said, smiling at Jane. "Plus the only one."

They went inside and found their table, right up near the stage. Most of the guests were already seated, each table centered with an outrageous blown-glass arrangement, covered by white linen sprinkled with gold and silver glitter.

"So, what is all this for?" Jane asked, taking the seat that Caleb pulled out for her.

"It's an auction benefiting music programs for inner-city kids," Caleb answered, quickly adding, "Although I suspect its real purpose is to make the show look good."

Jane nodded to his bid card. "Are you bidding on something, big shot?"

"I'm supposed to bid on a vacation package, but I don't really have to buy it."

"Do you get to go on the vacation, though?"

"That's a good question, but I don't think so."

"Well, if you don't have to pay for it, and if you don't even get to go anywhere, what are you actually bidding on?"

"I don't know, babe. The producers put it in the auction just for show."

"Like a carnival shill or something?"

"I'm not sure what a shill even is," Caleb said. "And what do you know about carnivals?"

"You mean I never told you about the year I spent with Barnum and Bailey?"

He grinned. "No, what did you do for the circus?"

"I was a tiger."

"You mean you trained tigers?"

"No"—Jane clawed the air with her nails—"I was a tiger." Then she leaned over and kissed him gently and whispered, "And if you make a cougar joke right now, I'll hurt you."

A waiter came by with a tray of white and red wine and asked Jane which she would prefer. She turned her empty glass over on the table and told him neither but thanked him anyway. Then she noticed that there were two other seats at the table and she wondered who would be joining them. She had half of her answer a minute later when Jordyn walked in.

Her hair was swept up and pinned, and she was wearing a blue-sequined dress that would have given her the appearance of a mermaid princess if it didn't have a slit up the side that showed off her leg. Almost every eye in the place followed her to the table, male and female alike. Caleb was probably the only person who seemed not to notice Jordyn's entrance, and Jane couldn't help but wonder why. When Jordyn reached the table, she stood next to the chair on Caleb's other side.

"Aren't you going to pull out my chair for me?" she asked.

Without much more than a glance, Caleb reached over and yanked her chair away from the table. She gathered up her dress and lowered herself gracefully into the seat.

"Usually a man stands up when a woman approaches the table. And it's not a bad idea to compliment her dress either."

Caleb cast a curt smile her way. "Nice dress," he said tersely.

"Thank you, honey," she purred, equally sarcastic. "I just love your suit."

Caleb leaned back so she could have a clear view of Jane. "Jordyn, this is my fiancée, Jane."

Jordyn's face lit up into a smile. "Oh my God," she said. "All this time we're supposed to be rehearsing, and all Caleb ever does is talk and talk and talk about you. And I can see why. It's so nice to finally meet you."

"It's nice to meet you too," Jane said. "You're even more gorgeous in person than you are on YouTube."

Jordyn blushed, although Jane suspected that she could do it on command. "You're very sweet," she said, "but I'll confess I'd give up a month's worth of royalties for that dress you're wearing."

"Thanks. I got it at a consignment shop today."

"You're kidding. Which one?"

"Classy Closet on Fairfax."

Caleb's head turned back and forth as they talked, like some tuxedoed spectator following a tennis volley.

"You know what, darling?" Jordyn said, placing a hand on Caleb's shoulder and standing. "I'm going to go and sit next to your fiancée. No offense, but you and I've seen enough of each other, and she just seems so much more interesting."

She crossed behind Caleb and took the empty seat on Jane's other side. Jane wasn't sure what kind of perfume she was wearing, but it smelled divine.

"Thank you for lending me your man," Jordyn said. "He's been such a gentleman, really, and I just know I'd never have made it this far in the competition on my own."

"No need to thank me," Jane replied. She glanced over at Caleb, who appeared to be reading his auction brochure, but she knew he was really eavesdropping. "It's just good to see him chasing his dream."

"He's a real talent, that one," Jordyn said. "He's got the voice, the looks, and the heart."

"Yes," Jane answered with a smile, "he sure does."

Then Jordyn leaned in closer and lowered her voice. "Hey, listen, I hope you're not upset about how these producers are making things look between us. You know, not just as a duo, but as a couple. Because it's all just for show."

"Oh, I know," Jane said. "It's fine. Really. It is."

"Good. Because you should know that there's nothing at all going on with Caleb and me."

At this, Jane pulled back a little and looked at her. Jordyn seemed to have genuine concern in her expectant expression, but Jane didn't need a pronouncement of Caleb's fidelity from her.

"Honestly, Jordyn, I would never have even assumed there was something going on. And it's a little presumptuous of you to feel the need to offer me a denial. Especially when you seem to be tweeting and posting daily about how in love you two are. I'm not jealous, but I do have an Internet connection. So perhaps you're the one who needs to be reassured that there's nothing going on between you and my fiancé, and never will be."

Jordyn seemed more than a little shocked by Jane's candor, but before she could respond, a waiter appeared at her other elbow and asked if she wanted chicken or beef. She told him neither, that she'd made arrangements for a vegetarian meal. The waiter nodded, then tendered the same question to Jane.

"I'll have the beef, please," she answered. "And Caleb will have the same, won't you, babe?"

Caleb smiled and took her hand in his on top of the table. Jane cast one last glance at Jordyn and turned her attention to the stage. Minutes later, the MC came out and introduced the auctioneer, and the auctioneer introduced the first item: an old Martin guitar signed by Don McLean. He began the auction chant and the room erupted into a frenzy of raised bid cards.

When Jane looked back to the table, Panda, the young girl she recognized from Caleb's audition, was seated in the chair vacated by Jordyn when she moved. Panda seemed entirely out of place in a red dress with a yellow smiley-face T-shirt peeking out through the lace. She had a fresh streak of pink in her hair and a rainbow of bracelets tied on her wrists. She smiled at Jane and half waved, but the bidding was too loud to make a proper introduction. Then another girl in a BeDazzled denim dress rushed up to the table, obviously late. She had a head of curly blond locks and a vacant expression on her face as she searched the table for someplace to sit. But all four seats were taken. There was a pause in the bidding, and the new girl hooked her hands on her hips and huffed.

"Where am I supposed to sit?" she asked.

"Maybe you could take off your wig and sit on it, Carrie Ann," Jordyn suggested. "You've used enough hairspray, I'm sure it would hold you."

Panda's hand leaped to her mouth to contain a giggle, and Jane didn't know whether to cringe or laugh as well. She had had no idea there was such rivalry between the contestants.

"I see Garth over there," Caleb said. "You want me to ask him to get us another chair?"

"I'll ask myself," Carrie Ann said before she turned and marched off toward the producer.

The auctioneer started up again, this time hustling front-row tickets to the *Singer-Songwriter Superstar* finale. Jane noticed that there wasn't nearly as much enthusiasm from the bidders as there had been for the signed guitar.

"Well, now," Jane heard a deep voice say. "Who's this we have here with you?"

She turned and saw the producer smiling down at her and Caleb. Carrie Ann stood behind him with her arms crossed.

"This is Jane," Caleb said. "My fiancée."

The producer looked from Jane to Jordyn, then to Caleb. "But the cameras are here tonight."

"Yeah, so what?" Caleb asked with a shrug. "When aren't the cameras around?"

"Caleb, could I speak with you alone for a moment?"

The producer indicated with a slight tilt of his head a spot beside the stage. Caleb cast an apologetic glance toward Jane and rose to follow the producer away. As soon as they were gone, Carrie Ann plopped down into Caleb's empty seat. Her curls hadn't even stopped bouncing before she was pouring herself a glass of wine from the bottle the waiter had left at the table.

Jane suddenly felt very uncomfortable. She hadn't even

considered that maybe she wasn't supposed to be here tonight. Panda looked uncomfortable too, and when Jane looked over at Jordyn, she was almost certain that she saw genuine empathy for her situation in those big blue eyes.

"Let's go, babe."

Jane turned and looked up at Caleb. "We're leaving?"

"Yep. Fuck this place."

Jane glanced at the producer, standing behind Caleb with a scowl on his face. She took her linen napkin from her lap and set it on the table and stood. Her face felt flushed.

"I'll go, honey. You should stay."

Even though she was offering to leave alone, she hoped he wouldn't let her. But she never expected him to take her in his arms and kiss her right there at the table in front of the entire banquet hall, cameras, producer, and all. Then he took her hand and led her from the room.

They were waiting on the elevator when Panda came jogging up awkwardly in her red dress and her little heels.

"Panda, what are you doing?" Caleb asked. "Don't you go getting into trouble too."

"I don't care," she said defiantly. "I had to meet her."

"Meet me?" Jane asked, feeling somewhat confused.

Panda nodded. "He said you're getting married."

"We plan to, yes."

"Well, if you don't marry him, I'm going to."

Her little face was so sincere, Jane couldn't help but smile.

"You know what, Panda? If something happened to me, I couldn't imagine anyone else I'd rather he marry than you."

"Don't give her any ideas, Jane," Caleb joked. "She knows how to find the room."

Panda peeled a bracelet off her wrist and handed it to Jane. "Here, take this. It's a friendship bracelet."

Jane took the bracelet and worked it over her hand and onto her wrist, saying, "Thank you very much, Panda. I wish I had something to give you."

But when she looked up, Panda was gone.

"Could she be any sweeter?" Caleb asked.

"She's pretty sweet," Jane said. "But don't get any ideas. I'm still marrying you."

They rode the elevator back to their floor and walked the long hall to their room. Neither of them said anything about having left the dinner. Jane just assumed they'd let it go by. But as soon as they were inside the room, Caleb began packing his things into his duffel.

"Caleb, what are you doing?"

"I'm packing up to leave with you."

"Did that producer send you home because of me?"

"No, he didn't send me home. I'm leaving on my own. And I'm keeping their damn tuxedo too."

Jane grabbed his hand and stopped him from packing. "Caleb, you can't leave because of me."

"This has nothing to do with you."

"Yes, it does. You were fine until I arrived."

"I'm not fine, Jane. I'm tired of pretending. I'm tired of embarrassing you."

"I'm not embarrassed, Caleb. I'm proud of you."

"But proud of me for what, Jane? For lying? For selling out? For singing silly love songs to some girl I hardly know?"

He gave up trying to pack and dropped the duffel, then sat on the edge of the bed with his head in his hands. His hair had come loose and was hanging down.

Jane sat next to him, then leaned in to his shoulder and put her arm around his back. She knew in that moment that she couldn't tell him. Not here; not now. He was too close to success, and his dream was too fragile yet. And if she told him, he would leave with her for sure.

"Caleb, I love you. And I'm proud of you because you had the guts to show up to that audition, and because you found the courage to come all the way out here and give this thing your all. So what if you have to play this silly game with them? We each know who we love and that's what matters. You're too close now to quit."

He lifted his head and looked over at her. "You think so?"

"I do," she answered, nodding. "I do. And if you gave up because of me tonight, I'd never get over it."

"But they've got us working around the clock, Jane. I can't even spend any time with you and it isn't fair."

"It's okay, because I'm going home."

He turned to face her fully. "No, babe. You don't have to go."

"I want to, Caleb. I miss our apartment, believe it or not. And I need to get back and see about my job. I left for a family emergency, remember?"

"But you don't even like that job."

She reached and brushed his hair away from his face, letting her fingers linger on his cheek. "Well, you had better win this thing, then, so I can quit."

He smiled, took her hand in his, brought it to his lips, and kissed it. Then he stood and pulled her up with him. "Let's go out on the town tonight."

"Out on the town? You mean in L.A.? Right now?"

"Yeah. Wouldn't it be a shame to waste this tux and that dress? We'll pretend we're stars and we'll go dancing. Then I'll take you to Canter's Deli, where Sean took me."

Jane looked at his face, so sweet and so kind, the gentle man inside him always peeking out from just behind those haunting green eyes. She smiled.

"Okay. What the hell. But only if we can take a cab. These heels are killing me."

"Baby, I'm going to have the hotel order us a limo and charge it to the producer. I think it's the least he could do."

Caleb kissed her, then sat on the bed and picked up the hotel phone. He was waiting for the concierge to answer when she stepped in front of him and lifted her foot onto the bed beside him, then hiked up her dress, exposing her leg.

"Don't forget you promised to take these pantyhose off for me later."

He hung up the phone.

"Hey, what about our limo?" she asked cutely.

He leaned his head against her thigh, looked up at her like a puppy, and asked, "Can you tie a bow tie?"

"Yes," she said. "Why?"

He grinned and stripped off his bow tie. "Because Canter's is open all night, as is the car service."

Then he reached up under her dress and ran his fingers along the edge of her pantyhose.

"Hey now," she said, closing her eyes. "What are you doing in there?"

"I'm just checking your garter for your gun."

With his head still resting on her thigh, and his hand still inside her dress, she reached down and grabbed a handful of him through his suit pants.

"Whoa," he said. "What are you doing?"

Jane leaned her mouth down to his ear. "You checked for my gun, I'm checking for yours."

Chapter 21

Jane took a Capital Metro bus home from the Austin airport. The cheapest last-minute flight out of Los Angeles had had a two-hour layover in Atlanta, making it a long day of travel, and her mood was progressively worsening the closer she got to home.

The bus drove beneath darkening Austin skies that were heavy with clouds, and the early evening air was hot and muggy. She saw a young teen sleeping on the bus across from her, and when the boy shifted in his seat, exposing the inside of his arm on his lap, Jane could see purple track marks there. She wanted to wake him and talk to him, she wanted to take him home and clean him up, but she reached instead and pulled the cord for her stop. She stepped off with her bag and watched the bus drive away. Then she looked across the street for any sign of Marj, but the balcony was empty, the slider was closed, and the windows were all dark.

Inside her apartment, the air-conditioning was off and the air was stale and sweltering, and it smelled of the rotten kitchen trash she had forgotten to take out in her rush to leave. She thought she had asked Marj to water the plants on her balcony, but when she opened the curtains, the plants were as dead as any Jane had ever seen. A bad feeling crept over her, so she went out into the hall and knocked on Marj's door, but there was no answer. Jane was suddenly aware of how much she needed to talk to someone and of just how alone she actually was. She took her phone from her purse and dialed Marj, only to remember that she had a landline when she heard it ringing unanswered on the other side of the door.

She passed the evening drinking herbal tea and watching Lifetime movies on TV. It was a lonely night sleeping in her bed without Caleb—no one to whisper about love in her ear, no one beside her she could reach out and feel. Just Jane, alone again, and not even a yapping dog in the next apartment to distract her from her thoughts.

The image of the boy on the bus kept creeping into her mind. She remembered the night she had collected Melody from the hospital after her first OD. She remembered the promises Melody had made to never use again. And Jane believed now, as she had believed then, that Melody had surely meant to keep that oath with every bit of willpower she had possessed within her courageous young heart.

But willpower proved no match for the beast inside her, clawing away at her sanity in its attempt to kill her. And Jane knew all too well that a huge risk factor in that deadly disease was heredity.

She lay wide awake, staring at the dark ceiling and trying to wish the thoughts away. She found herself craving a cigarette for the first time in a long time. But even that seemed off-limits now, after her mother's stroke.

What was left? she wondered.

Grace's face seemed to appear from the shadows, and she heard her soothing voice saying, "Don't be a secret, Jane."

But Jane closed her eyes and chased the voice away with thoughts that would have seemed silly in the light of day.

Some secrets were just so hard to share.

∽

Jane walked into the restaurant, not quite knowing what to expect. It was cool and quiet and nearly empty inside, an expensive place for lunch. She stood at the hostess station until a young woman appeared.

"Table for one, ma'am? Or would you prefer the bar?"

"No. I'm meeting someone here."

"Oh, yes. He's in the dining room already. Right this way."

Jane followed her into the restaurant, walking over a bridge that crossed an interior koi pond, complete with little waterfalls and colorful lights. As they approached the table, he stood.

"Hello, Jane. It's good to see you."

"Thanks for making the time, Mr. Blanco. I appreciate it."

"Please, call me Manuel. Mr. Blanco makes me sound old."

"I feel the same way when people call me ma'am," Jane replied, casting a glance at the retreating hostess.

"Then I'll make you a deal to never call you ma'am if you never call me Mr. Blanco."

"I'll take that deal," Jane said, taking her seat.

She noticed Manuel inspecting her, and it made her a little uncomfortable.

"I like this new look," he said.

"What new look?"

He motioned up to his eyes, signaling that he was talking about her glasses. She blushed and took them off.

"They're for driving," she said, putting them in her purse. "I keep forgetting that I have them on."

Then she looked around at the swanky restaurant and at Manuel's suit. She was glad she hadn't worn her uniform, as she'd been planning to, since her goal in arranging a meeting was to get her job back.

"How is your mother?" he finally asked.

Jane sighed. "I'm so sorry for rushing off like that. The call came and I didn't know what to do. But she's going to be okay. It was a ministroke."

"I'm glad," he said. "And I understand. Family is family."

If he only knew, Jane thought, sipping her water. "How's your son?" she asked.

"Chandler's great. He's at football practice this afternoon. Thank you for being so kind to him at the meeting."

"He seems like a good kid," Jane said.

Manuel smiled proudly. "He is a good kid. And he really liked you, by the way. In fact, ever since we ran into you, we've been watching the singer-songwriter competition together." Then he leaned forward and in a quiet voice quickly added, "I'm sorry to bring it up."

"Why are you sorry?" she asked.

"It must be hard for you."

"Hard for me?"

"I just assumed it would be difficult," he said, picking up his menu. "Seeing what's happened. And on live TV too." He glanced up, as if to gauge Jane's reaction. "Listen, I can empathize. I've been dating younger people myself. It seems like everyone our age is taken. I met a girl on Match.com and brought her here, and you wouldn't believe me if I told you how she acted. It was terrible. When our food arrived, she took a photo of her plate and spent five minutes posting it to Instagram before we could even eat. And after guzzling two glasses of wine, she climbed onto my lap and took a dozen selfies of us. Is that what you call them? Anyway, everything's a hashtag with these kids. It's like it didn't happen unless they tweet about it. It isn't easy getting older and feeling left behind, is it? But we don't need to talk about your breakup if you don't want to." He closed his menu. Then he smiled at Jane. "It's nice being here with someone close to my own age."

"Caleb and I didn't break up," Jane said.

Manuel looked confused. "But I saw him and that other girl . . ."

"Jordyn? Yeah, that's just for TV."

"I don't know," he said, narrowing his eyes and shaking his head. "Their attraction looked pretty real to me."

Before Jane could say anything further, their server arrived to take their order. Jane was still stewing over his comment and could hardly think, so she ordered soup and a salad. When the server had taken their menus and left, she leaned forward in her chair and spoke with a clear, measured voice.

"Not that it should matter, but Caleb and that girl are not together. It's just some marketing ploy put on by the show's producers. I was just there with him; I should know. So I don't need to be patronized as if I'm some poor older woman who's been left by her younger lover."

"What do you mean, you were just there?"

"I mean I saw it with my own eyes. It's all made-up lies and trick photography."

"So you made up a lie about your mother having a stroke so you could go off to L.A.?"

"No, I wasn't lying."

"Then why were you there and not Seattle?"

"I just stopped in on my way home. Does it matter?"

He shook his head. "No. I guess it doesn't matter. Listen, Jane, about the job. We had to make other arrangements while you were gone."

"What other arrangements?"

"You were still in your review period, and you just up and left without approval."

"So you replaced me?"

"There was nothing I could do."

"Then why did you agree to meet with me?"

"Because I wanted to tell you in person. That's fair, isn't it? And after we met at the meeting . . . after I saw the show . . . I was thinking . . . you know . . . I thought maybe we could see each other personally . . . outside of work."

"Oh, I see. I'm the new girl in the Al-Anon group, so you

just thought you could take me out and buy me lunch and thirteenth-step me. Is that it?"

"No. It's not like that."

"Then you tell me what it's like."

"I thought I felt something between us."

"Do I have a job or not, Mr. Blanco?"

He looked at her across the table, and she thought she saw genuine sadness in his eyes. For what, she couldn't be sure. He gently shook his head and Jane stood up to go.

"Don't leave," he said. "I'm happy to just be a friend."

Jane reached into her purse and tossed a twenty-dollar bill on the table.

He appeared hurt by the gesture. "That's not necessary," he said.

But Jane had already turned and was walking away. She was crossing the koi pond when she slipped on the wooden bridge and nearly twisted her ankle. She knew he was watching, but she straightened herself up and continued on her way. When she got outside, a wind had come up and people were hurrying past with their hands up to hold their hair in place or to hold on to their hats. A newspaper went blowing by. But Jane faced into the wind and let her hair fly, marching back to her car. However, when she arrived where she had parked, she looked around, confused. Her car was gone. Then she noticed the ELECTRIC VE-HICLES ONLY parking sign. It was a free charging station.

Oh, the irony, she thought, if that's what irony even means.

She briefly considered going back into the restaurant and apologizing to Mr. Blanco, then asking for a ride to the impound lot. She knew she had been too hard on him and that it wasn't his fault that she was upset. But she couldn't face him again. And besides, she thought, it wasn't even losing the job that she was worried over. It was something else entirely.

She saw a bus approaching the stop across the street and she ran to catch it. She wasn't even sure where it was going, but she didn't care. Take me anywhere, she said silently to herself, climbing aboard, anywhere but right here, right now.

She slid a dollar into the pay slot and went and sat in the back. There were maybe a dozen other riders, equally dispersed among the seats so as to avoid any possible human contact. And Jane was okay with that. She sat and watched the scenery slide by outside her window and she thought about her life, about her hopes and dreams, about her losses and her disappointments. She wanted things back the way they had been, before she'd learned the news, back when she could leave the past in the past and not have a constant reminder growing inside her.

Above the bus windows were poster advertisements for iced coffee and cell phones and car tires, and Jane noticed one for Planned Parenthood. She got out her cell phone and went onto the website. Two bus transfers and an hour later, she was standing in front of the building.

Two picketers sat on the sidewalk next to homemade signs. They were eating sandwiches and they had an air about them of having given up. When they saw Jane, one of them switched his sandwich to his other hand, then picked up his sign and held it out for her to read.

YOU DON'T NEED BIRTH CONTROL,
YOU NEED SELF-CONTROL!

Jane resisted the urge to say something smart and walked past them to the entrance. The first door brought her into a vestibule with another locked door and a call box. She pressed the button and waited. She expected a voice to come on the speaker and she was wondering what she'd say, when there was a loud buzzing and the inner door popped open. The reception room was bright and quiet and clean. It reminded Jane of every other medical building she'd ever been in. The woman behind the counter seemed tired, but she was friendly enough when she asked Jane if she had an appointment.

"No," Jane said, "I don't. But I'd like to talk with someone about an . . . abortion."

It was a hard word for Jane to say, but the woman showed no reaction to hearing it as she handed her a clipboard of forms to fill out. She wrote out her insurance information and medical history, including the birth of her daughter, then handed the forms back and sat down to wait. There were a few others in the waiting room, but it wasn't a place for idle chitchat, so she picked up a copy of *Women's Health* and passed the time by reading an article on eating healthy for glowing skin.

An hour later, a young woman came out and called Jane's name, then led her into a back room. She said they needed a urine sample, and gave her a container and left her alone. When Jane had filled it, she knocked on the door as she'd been instructed, and a minute later the woman came back in. She checked the urine with a simple test strip and wrote something down on the chart.

Then she brought Jane to another room and introduced her to a doctor. He had beautiful brown skin and kind amber eyes. He said his name was Adam and asked Jane if she was okay talking with a male doctor; she said that she was. He offered Jane a seat. Then he sat across from her and spent a minute reading over her paperwork. The room was absolutely silent, not even a clock ticking on the wall.

"So," he finally said, setting the clipboard aside to look at her, "you have one child now."

Jane shook her head. "She passed away."

"I'm sorry to hear that," he said. Then he cocked his head slightly and asked, "And you don't want another?"

"I shouldn't be pregnant," Jane said.

"Were you using birth control?"

"I take the pill. I've taken the pill for years."

"Which one were you taking?"

"Ortho Tri-Cyclen."

He wrote this in her chart but didn't say anything.

"I missed a few days after I moved here. My pharmacy in Seattle had to fax my prescription down. But I doubled up. I read that you could do that. You can double up and it should work, right? I shouldn't be pregnant."

"Sometimes these things happen."

"But I shouldn't be pregnant, right?"

"I understand you're under stress, but I can confirm that you're pregnant. Have you stopped taking birth control now?"

"Yes. But it doesn't matter. I want to have an abortion."

"Are you sure?"

"Yes, I'm sure. I'm sure and I don't want to be lectured or talked out of it either."

He nodded gently and talked with a soothing voice. "We're not here to talk anyone into or out of anything, Miss McKinney. It's your life and it's your right. We're only here to promote your health."

"Good. Can we do it today?"

"No, we can't do it today."

"Why not?"

"Our scheduling, for one thing. But also the state of Texas requires you to undergo a sonogram and view the image at least twenty-four hours before the procedure."

"Can we do that today, then? The sonogram?"

"Yes, we can do that now if you'd like."

Jane said that she would, so he brought her into an exam room where they were joined by the girl who had taken her sample earlier. She gave Jane a gown and asked her to undress from the waist down.

"But don't you do the ultrasound on my belly?"

The girl shook her head. "It has to be a transvaginal sonogram at this stage."

Jane reluctantly undressed and put on the gown. Then she climbed onto the table and lay down with her knees bent as she was instructed. The nurse covered a probe with a condom, applied a coating of gel, and then handed it to Jane. Once it was in, the nurse helped guide it. The doctor stayed on the other side of Jane's knees and worked the machine.

"Texas law requires me to show this to you," he said, "but nobody here will tell if you'd rather keep your eyes closed."

"No," Jane said. "It's fine. I'd like to see."

He turned the monitor to give her a clear view. "It looks like you're about six or seven weeks."

"How can you tell?"

"The fetus is thirteen millimeters," he said, pointing. "And if you look close, you can see the heartbeat already."

Jane gazed at the black-and-white image on the screen, but it looked to her like little more than a clump of cells that she found hard to connect in any way with herself. But she could see the flutter of its tiny heartbeat. The ticking clock of a life just begun. And she knew in some strange and certain way that this little life, left to grow, had both the absolute power to bring her more joy than anything else on this planet, and the absolute power to bring her more pain than she could ever bear.

No, she thought, she couldn't bury another child and live. She could not and she would not.

"How does it work?" Jane asked. "The abortion."

"We'll give you a mild sedative to calm your nerves. And antibiotics and something for pain. Then we'll enter the uterus through the cervix and vacuum out the fetus."

"Would I have to watch then too?" Jane asked.

He shook his head and turned the screen away. "No, you won't have to watch."

Jane rested her head back on the cold table and looked up at the ceiling lights. The room seemed to be spinning and her mind was spinning with it. But it was her life, her choice.

⁓

The bus dropped Jane three blocks from the impound lot and she walked the rest of the way. The man behind the glass handed her a bill for almost two hundred dollars, even though they had towed the car less than a mile away and had had it less than a day. She paid with her credit card, signed away her rights, and went out into the lot to claim it.

It was dark when she arrived at the apartment building and Marj's lights were on. She went up the stairs to her door and knocked. Marj answered with a huge smile on her face.

"Hi, Jane! I saw the car was gone and thought you might be back. At least I hoped it hadn't been stolen. Come on in."

Jane entered with Buttercup close at her heel. She sat in a soft chair and invited the dog onto her lap, and sat running her fingers through his short fur.

"Would you like tea?" Marj asked.

"No, thank you," Jane said. "I drank two cups of coffee waiting on the bus."

"The bus?"

"It's a long story."

Marj took a seat next to Jane. "I need to apologize. I'm afraid your plants are dead." Despite looking apologetic about the plants, Marj was grinning like a schoolgirl in love.

"Those things were on their last legs anyway," Jane said. "But tell me what's new with you. You look so happy."

"Buttercup and I have been staying with a new friend."

"A friend?" Jane asked.

"Well, two friends, really. He has a Boston terrier named Hercules, and he and Buttercup get along like long-lost twins."

"Oh, Marj. This is great news. Where'd you meet him?"

"I owe it all to you," she said. "I've been hiding away in this apartment for years, but you got me out and going to that meeting, and we met two weeks ago Saturday. He's a widower too. I know it's kind of fast to be shacking up, but neither of us is getting any younger, if you know what I mean."

Jane smiled. "Yes, I do know what you mean."

"But what's going on with you? You look upset. I hope it's not the plants."

"It's not the plants," Jane said, looking down at the dog in her lap. "Marj, I need to ask you a big favor, but you can't tell anyone about it. Especially not Caleb."

"Okay. Sure. Anything."

"I need you to drive me to the clinic tomorrow."

"The clinic. Oh dear Lord, Jane. Are you sick?"

Jane looked up at her and shook her head. "I'm having an abortion."

Marj seemed to be caught completely off guard by Jane's statement and she sat with her lips trembling slightly, as if she wanted to say something but couldn't get it out. When she did finally speak, it wasn't what Jane was expecting to hear.

"But . . . but . . . I'm Catholic, Jane. I can't do it."

"Catholic? I've never seen you once go to church."

"That's neither here nor there. I was baptized."

"So you're judging me?"

"I'm not judging you, Jane. I just can't take you."

"This is ridiculous," Jane said. "You're not the one having the abortion, Marj."

"I said no. And that's final."

Jane felt Buttercup tense beneath her hand at the change in tone of Marj's voice. Then he scurried off of Jane's lap and ran and jumped onto Marj's. Jane rose from the chair, hesitating long enough to dispel any hope she had that Marj might change her mind, then she turned to leave the room. She was halfway down the hall when she stopped and came back.

"It isn't fair of you to even think you can judge me, Marj. I don't care if you're the pope. You've been to meetings. You know what this disease does to people. My father, my mother, my brother. My sweet little girl. I buried my daughter, Marj. I dropped the first handful of dirt on the casket myself. You've been hiding in this apartment here for years because you lost your husband. I saw you when you thought you were going to lose your precious dog. Well, imagine losing your child . . . your baby. Imagine it, Marj. Can you even? You do that and if you still think I'm some sinner, then you can take your judgment and go to hell for all I care."

Jane was crying by the time she finished, and Marj and Buttercup were both staring at her with wide eyes. Jane turned and marched from the apartment. She pulled Marj's door closed behind her and stood for a moment in the hall. She considered briefly going back in to apologize, but she decided now wasn't the time. Instead she went into her own apartment and sat down on the bed and had a good long cry.

An hour or more had passed when she heard a tapping on her door. She rose and went to the bathroom to wet a cloth and wiped the running mascara from her eyes. Then she went to answer the door. Marj was standing there in her robe with an apology written on her face and Buttercup cradled in her arms.

"What time should I be ready to take you tomorrow?"

Chapter 22

Caleb barged into the rehearsal room with three copies of his song that he had typed up and printed in the hotel business center. He handed one to the music director and one to Jordyn.

"What's this?" the music director asked.

"It's the song we're singing tomorrow."

"But that's not what Garth—"

"I don't care about Garth," Caleb interjected, cutting him off. "It's this song or no song."

"But this is just lyrics and tab."

"That's why I brought you a copy. Jordyn and I can either sing it acoustic, or you can write sheet music for the band."

The music director turned to Jordyn. "Are you on board with this?"

Caleb watched her to see if she would fight it or go along. She glanced down at the song he had handed her, and then she looked up at the music director and smiled.

"I think it would be nice with at least some keyboard on the bridge."

The music director threw up his hands and walked out of the rehearsal room with Caleb's song. Jordyn placed her copy on the music stand and picked up her guitar.

"Well, what are you waiting for, Romeo?" she asked. "We had better get to rehearsing if we're going to have this song down by tomorrow's show."

Caleb smiled and grabbed his guitar.

They practiced harmonizing for hours, and when their time in the rehearsal room was up, Carrie Ann strutted in with her rhinestone-encrusted guitar and her backup band. They could hear her yodeling almost all the way to the elevator.

"I don't really care if we win or not," Jordyn said, "as long as she doesn't."

"You really don't like country, do you?" Caleb asked.

"Oh, I love country. I just hate Carrie Ann."

In the elevator, Caleb took his phone from his pocket to check for messages from Jane, but his phone battery was dead.

"What's the matter?" Jordyn asked after he sighed.

"Jane accidentally packed the wrong charger when she left, and hers won't fit my phone. Now I'm out of juice."

Jordyn took Caleb's phone from his hand and glanced at the plug. "You can use one of mine."

"You've got an extra?"

"Are you kidding me? Paige is a social media pro on the road. She packs me backups for my backups."

When they arrived at Jordyn's room, Paige was working on one of the laptops. Jordyn asked her for a phone charger, and she retrieved one from a bag and handed it to Jordyn without even glancing at Caleb. Then she scooped up her iPad and her purse and left the room.

Caleb watched her go. "I get the feeling she really doesn't like me."

"It's not you she's mad at," Jordyn replied. "It's me."

"Well, you two should make up so she can stop throwing daggers my way. She hasn't even said two words to me. What did I ever do to her anyway?"

"I'm guessing she's tired of responding to tweets about you all day," she said. "We've got a few hours yet before our fittings. Let's rehearse."

"I should go charge my phone."

"Just plug it in here."

Caleb plugged his phone into an outlet to charge. Then he sat next to her on the bed to run through the song again. When they had finished, he noticed Jordyn staring at him with a curious look on her face.

"What?" he asked, embarrassed. "You don't like the song?"

"I've never seen you insecure about your music before."

"This one's important to me. That's all."

"You really love her, don't you, Caleb?"

"Yes," he said, smiling, "I do."

"Well, it's a great song and I'm proud you're letting me sing the harmony with you."

The way she was staring at him made him feel shy and he looked away. Then he noticed the Skype home screen up on one of her laptops, and he got an idea.

"What do you need to Skype someone?" he asked.

"Just an e-mail or a name."

"Could you do me a favor? You remember my roommate, Sean, from the preshow? He was madly in love with you, and I know he'd just die if you Skyped him."

"Sure," she said, getting up from the bed and sitting down at the computer. Then she looked up at Caleb and grinned. "Should I go topless and really shock him?"

～

It was the day of the live show and they were on the studio soundstage doing a dry run when Caleb got to the chorus line of his song and froze. He looked at Jordyn, but she just shrugged and shook her head as if it were news to her as well.

"Who changed this?" Caleb asked.

The music director took off his headphones and looked up from the sound booth at Caleb. "What's that?"

"I asked you who changed this."

"If you've got an issue, take it up with Garth."

Caleb took the sheet of music off the stand and carried it backstage. He found the producer going over the evening's shot sequence with the director, and he reached between them and slapped the sheet of music down on the folding table they were using as a desk.

"What the hell is this?"

"Looks like your song for tonight," the producer said.

Caleb glared at him. "Did you change it?"

"What does it matter who changed it?" he asked. "This is what you're singing."

"This is bullshit, Garth. And you know it. The song is 'Jane's Harmony,' not 'Jordyn's Harmony.'"

The producer picked up the song and held it out to Caleb. "Yeah, well, get over it, kid."

"I'm not your kid, pal, and if you think I'm singing this tonight, you're dead wrong."

The producer's expression changed from annoyance to anger. He glanced at the director, and the director took his list from the table and walked away. When the director was out of earshot, Garth looked back to Caleb.

"You listen to me, you little punk. I've been putting up with your attitude since day one and I'm sick of it. Now, if you want a shot at winning this thing, you had better just suck it up and start going along with the program."

"You can't change my song," Caleb replied. "It isn't right."

"You had better read your contract again, young man. I'm the producer and I can change anything I want to."

"Fine, then," Caleb said, half surrendering, "let's go back to the other song. The one we originally rehearsed."

"Sorry, kid. It's too late for that. We've already recorded the backup track and timed the show. This is the version you're singing now." He forced the sheet of music into Caleb's hand. "And don't forget it's live on a twenty-second delay, so if you try any fancy stuff onstage, I'll cut it and overplay the backup vocals singing Jordyn's name."

Caleb looked at the producer's fat face, at his beady eyes darting left and right in their deep sockets like some sadistic narcissist sizing him up. It was the same look he'd given Caleb when he had pulled him from the table and told him Jane had to leave the charity dinner. She had looked so disappointed that night leaving the banquet hall, even though she had done her best to cover it up. And he knew this public charade of him and Jordyn being a couple must be taking its toll on her. The thought of her hearing a song he'd written especially for her sung for Jordyn instead was just too much.

Caleb held the sheet of music up in front of the producer's face and ripped it in two. Then he turned to walk away.

The producer laughed. "I'll just show photos of you two rehearsing and have Jordyn sing it herself live," Caleb heard him say.

He stopped, turned, and walked back.

The producer had a queer little smile on his face, but it disappeared instantly when Caleb kicked the folding table next to him and sent it flying on its side across the floor. Papers were still fluttering to the ground where the table had been when Caleb stuck his finger in the producer's face.

"You dare play even one bar of that song and I'll hire a crackerjack attorney and spend every penny I earn for the rest of my life suing you and this show. You got that?"

Garth looked more than a little frightened, although Caleb wasn't sure if it was because of his threat to sue or because his finger was just inches from the man's bulbous nose.

"You signed a contract waiving your right to sue," he finally squeaked out.

"Yeah, and I signed a nondisclosure agreement too. But you can shove your contract up your ass because I'm sure the media would love to hear about how you made all this shit up between Jordyn and me just for ratings."

The producer stood there looking at Caleb's finger and trembling with rage, but it seemed he had nothing left to say. Caleb turned and walked away, this time without stopping. Jordyn and the sound engineer were waiting at the edge of the stage, and it was clear they had been listening. Jordyn followed Caleb as he collected his guitar and closed it up in its case.

"Are you really leaving?" she asked.

Caleb stood up, guitar case in hand, and looked at her. "I should have left a long time ago."

"But what will they say?"

"They'll think of some lie, I'm sure. They always do."

"Not the show, Caleb. The fans. What will they say?"

Caleb looked at her there and she suddenly seemed a sad spectacle, standing on that big empty stage. All that poise, all that sex appeal, and none of it real. It was all nothing but an act she put on to please the cameras and some nameless crowd of fans in some virtual world.

"Maybe you should try telling them the truth, Jordyn. You might be surprised how accepting people can be."

"What's that supposed to mean, Caleb?"

"It means I'm sick and tired of these lies. Of hurting the one woman in my life that I really love. And you know what? You should be too."

"I don't know what you're talking about."

"Oh, yes, you do."

And with that, he left her standing there, walked off the stage, and crossed the studio, heading for the main exit. Before he walked out the door, he stopped and looked back one last time at the fancy Hollywood set and at the empty seats that once held his fake but adoring fans. Jordyn was still on the stage, just watching him, but he was too far away already to make out the expression on her face. He had expected to be sad when he left, but now that he had decided this was it, all he felt was relief. He had been caught up in the glamour and the lights and he had let himself hurt the one person he loved more than anything in the world. Now it was time to make things right.

Caleb turned away from Jordyn and the stage, pressed the door open, and walked from the dim studio into the golden glow of the bright Los Angeles sun. And he knew then that things were just as they should be again—just him and his guitar on his way home to make love to his best friend.

❧

Caleb dialed Jane from the terminal while he was waiting on his plane, but it went straight to her voice mail before it even rang. He had no idea what they'd say on the live show about his being gone, and he didn't want her to find out that way anyway. But it didn't seem like the kind of thing you could get across in a text either. He knew once he was in the air he wouldn't be able to get ahold of her at all, so he dialed her again and settled on leaving a voice mail.

"Hi, babe. I just used the credit card you gave me to buy a ticket home. I'm at the airport waiting to board. It's a long story, so call me if you get this. I love you. I'll see you soon."

Twenty minutes later, he was still sitting there staring at his phone and hoping it would ring when he heard the call to board his flight. He stood and hoisted his duffel over his shoulder and got in line. A man tapped him on the back.

"Hey, fella," he said when Caleb turned around. "Aren't you that guy from the singer-songwriter show?"

Caleb nodded. "Yeah, I'm him."

"Man, oh man, I knew that reality TV was all bullshit. They

say it's live, but here you are standing in line with me at the airport and the show's starting right now."

Caleb followed the man's eyes over to the waiting area and the bank of ceiling-mounted TVs just in time to see the burning sheet of music fade to the *Singer-Songwriter Superstar* logo. He stepped out of line and walked over so he could watch and hear above the chatter in the terminal.

The announcer bounded onstage with his usual charisma to start off the show. Then, before introducing the finalists, the camera panned close in on his face and his expression turned so suddenly somber it was hard to imagine anyone anywhere believing it wasn't scripted.

"I have some sad news to share with you all tonight," he said as if delivering a eulogy. "One of our favorite contestants has had a family emergency and had to leave the show early to return home. We'd like you to join us as we say good-bye to Caleb Cummings with this farewell montage."

The TV cut to a montage of Caleb's time on the show, beginning with his audition and leading up to their rehearsal just the day before. But even though the montage was set to Caleb's music, there was no clip of him and Jordyn rehearsing "Jane's Harmony." Probably because of his threats, he thought, but for whatever reason he was grateful.

Interestingly, the only nostalgia he really felt as he watched his experience in L.A. flash on the screen was for the time he had spent with Sean. Caleb laughed when he saw a clip of the two of them singing, both wearing eyeliner. The editors had gone light on his and Jordyn's fake relationship, probably to soften the blow of his leaving for whatever fans the two of them had, and Caleb figured she'd be okay without him just the same.

The call came again for his plane to board, and Caleb was turning away when the montage ended and the camera showed Jordyn sitting on a stool in the spotlight with her guitar.

"Here to help us say farewell to Caleb," the announcer crooned, "is his own partner, Jordyn, who has requested to sing a very special song."

Caleb stepped closer to the screen.

The camera zoomed in on Jordyn's face, and she seemed to Caleb not to be on the TV at all, but rather she seemed to be staring through a window into the airport with her eyes focused on him. Then her expression seemed to soften, and she smiled into the camera and spoke.

"I need to set the record straight. I feel very fortunate to have had the chance to get to know Caleb and to write music with him for the few weeks that we had together on the show. But you all deserve to know the truth. Caleb and I were never a couple. Caleb is engaged to be married to a woman in Austin who he is madly in love with. I've met her and I can see why. And tonight, I'm here to tell the world that so am I. So this song is dedicated to my friend Caleb, and to the love of my life, who's backstage listening right now. This is for you, Paige."

She took her guitar pick from the strings and began to play and sing a gorgeous love song that Caleb had never heard before but that she had obviously written for Paige. Caleb would have liked to listen to the entire thing, but the final boarding call came over the speakers and he turned and walked away, leaving her singing on the TV.

He smiled all the way down the ramp and all the way onto the plane. And he was still smiling when the wheels left the runway. He smiled for Jordyn and for himself and for Jane. He smiled because he knew all three of them were finally free.

⁓

Caleb swung into the first row of empty seats he came to. He put his guitar in the seat next to him and his duffel on the floor between his feet. Then he pulled out his phone and dialed Jane for the fifth time since he'd landed—straight to voice mail, again. He was worried how she might take his leaving the show, especially after she'd gone to all the trouble she had to support him while he was there.

He leaned his head against the cool window and watched the headlights pass by outside. The bus rocked back and forth and so did his estimation of himself—one moment a quitter, the next a hero. He was excited and nervous at the same time. So much so that he missed pulling the cord for his stop.

He got off the bus four blocks away and jogged with his bag and his guitar back toward the apartment. The night air felt cool against his face, and his mood was lighter with each step he took closer to home, closer to Jane. As he approached the building, he noticed that the apartment lights were off and the curtains drawn. There was a faint light on in Marj's bedroom, but otherwise her windows were dark too.

By force of habit, he stuck his hand into his jeans pocket for his keys, forgetting he'd been so long away from home. It took him a few minutes to fish them from the bottom of his duffel, and then he unlocked the door and climbed the stairs two at a time.

The apartment was dark when he entered. Not one light on anywhere. He set his guitar and his duffel on the floor, quietly closed the door, and stood for a moment just listening. He wondered if he should be worried. Then his ears adjusted, tuning out the street, and he heard the ocean waves from the bedroom sound machine and he figured Jane must already be asleep.

Caleb walked to the bedroom and pushed open the door. He could see her face in the green glow of the bedside alarm clock. She looked like a little girl. He feared if he woke her in the dark she might be frightened, so he reached and switched on the light. She stirred, but she didn't open her eyes. He stood for minute and watched her sleeping. Her hair was tied up and she had one arm bent and resting on the mattress beside her pillow. She was the most beautiful thing he'd ever set eyes upon.

Jane's lids flickered, then opened, her eyes slowly coming to focus on him standing in the doorway. He had expected to see surprise, but he almost thought he saw sadness wash over her face.

"Caleb—?" she said, his name almost a whisper. Then she pushed herself up until she was leaning on her elbow. "What are you doing here? Did Marj call you?"

"No, baby. Why would Marj have called me?"

She didn't respond right away, so he stepped into the room and sat on the edge of the bed.

He gently touched her cheek. "Are you okay? What's going on?"

"I'm okay," she said. "Why are you home?"

"Aren't you happy to see me?"

"Yes, I'm happy. I'm just a little confused."

"You must not have watched the show." When she shook her head, he continued. "I had a fight with the producer and walked off. I'm sorry if you're disappointed in me."

"Oh, honey," she said, pulling his hand to her lips and kissing it, "I could never be disappointed in you. I'm sure you had good reason to leave."

"Thanks, baby. But what's going on with you? You said you thought that Marj might have called me. Why?"

"There's something I need to tell you, Caleb."

When she said it, she looked away from him, almost as if she were ashamed.

"What is it, babe? You know you can tell me anything."

"I meant to call you, but I took the wrong charger home."

"I know. Mine was dead for a while too. It's okay. Every-thing's okay. What do you need to tell me, Jane?"

She sat up a little more and looked at him. Then she looked down and picked idly at a loose string in the comforter.

"It's just that I've been overwhelmed and terrified and deal-ing with things all alone here. Then when I was in Seattle, I visited the cemetery . . . and . . . and . . . well, you know what happened to Melody as well as I do. So when I got home I went . . . I mean, today I had Marj bring me . . . well, it doesn't matter anymore, I guess . . . because . . . well . . ."

"What is it, baby? Just tell me."

She stopped picking at the blanket and looked up at him. "Caleb, I'm pregnant."

The worried look on her face seemed so removed from the news and how it made him feel that he was sure he hadn't heard her right.

"Did you just say you're pregnant?"

She bit her lower lip and nodded.

Caleb didn't know whether to cry or hug her or scream. He stood from the bed and ran from the room. He threw back the curtains and opened the living room slider, then stepped out onto the balcony and screamed at the top of his lungs for all of Austin to hear.

"We're having a baaaaaaaaaaaaaby!"

Then he ran back into the room, caught Jane getting out of bed, picked her up, and spun her around. He got ahold of himself after three or four revolutions, then he set her down carefully and crouched and placed his hands on her belly, before looking up at her.

"I shouldn't spin you like that," he said. "It isn't good for the baby."

"It's not made of glass, you dork," Jane said, smiling down at him and caressing his hair. "Now stand up here and let me give you a proper kiss to welcome you home."

He stood and wrapped his arms around her, and said the first thing that came into his mind. "I'm going to be the best father in the world."

Jane looked into his eyes, and he could tell by her smile that she believed him.

"I love you, Caleb Cummings."

"I love you too, Jane McKinney," he replied. "Which reminds me, we had better hurry up and get married or our kid's gonna have two last names. And we need to start making a list of first names too. I like Hunter, or even Tristan. You should like Tristan because of your Tristan-and-Isolde thing with the dresses."

"Tristan? What makes you think it's going to be a boy?"

"Of course it's going to be a boy," he answered. "I can just feel it. But I'm not stuck on Tristan. I've always liked Trevor and Tyler too. I don't know why they all start with *T*."

"Oh, shut up already and kiss me," Jane said.

And not wanting to upset her in her condition, Caleb stopped talking, brought his lips to hers, and did just that.

Chapter 23

Jane sat on the apartment couch with a blanket and a bowl of buttered popcorn on her lap, idly popping kernels into her mouth while she watched the commercials.

"Hey," she called, "the show's coming on again."

She heard the microwave chime, and Caleb came over and refilled her bowl with a bag of freshly popped corn. Then he sat down beside her to watch.

"If you want me to gain any sympathy pounds," he said, "you're gonna have to share this batch."

Jane brought the bowl of popcorn between them, and they each took turns grabbing handfuls while their eyes were glued to the screen. The show's host called Panda and Carrie Ann out onto the stage with him. Carrie Ann looked extra coiffed and confident; Panda looked slightly disheveled and shy.

"Do you think Jordyn's upset that she didn't make it through to the finale?" Jane asked.

"I doubt it," Caleb said. "She never wanted the recording contract anyway. I think she was in it for the free publicity."

"Well, she sure got that."

A man walked out and handed the host an envelope. Then there was a drumroll and the stage lights dimmed, the two remaining girls now standing in the wash of a spotlight.

"America has voted," the host said, "and I'm proud to announce the winner of the first national *Singer-Songwriter Superstar* competition, and the recipient of a half-million-dollar recording contract. And our lucky winner is . . ." He paused to tear open the envelope, then looked straight into the camera and said, "The winner is Amanda Wyatt."

Panda appeared to nearly collapse onto the stage, she was so shocked to hear her name. Then she turned to hug Carrie Ann, but Carrie Ann was busy looking around in disbelief.

The announcer pulled Panda over into his spotlight and held the microphone in her face. "How does it feel to be the Singer-Songwriter Superstar?"

She blinked her wide eyes into the camera and smiled her charming, girlish smile. Then, without warning, she snatched the microphone, rose onto her toes, spun around once, smiled into the camera, and simply said, "It feels fantastic!"

Jane reached for the remote and clicked off the TV. When she looked over, Caleb was smiling as if he had just won.

"I'm glad it was her," he said.

"You're not sad it wasn't you?"

He shook his head. "I like seeing people who are really good at what they do get rewarded for their talent. Especially if they're also humble."

Jane could tell he was genuinely happy for Panda, but she couldn't help but notice a flicker of disappointment in his eyes.

"What about you now, honey?" she asked.

"What about me?"

"I haven't seen you even open your guitar case once since you've been home. You know, just because we're having a baby is no reason to give up on your dream."

"I'm not giving up on my dream," he said, smiling. "I'm just trading it in for a better one."

"But you don't have to trade, Caleb. I've done this before. You always find ways to get by. I've got a few leads for work, although they might want me to wait until after the baby's born to start. But I have savings left from selling my house."

"No way," he said. "You're saving that money. Mr. Zigler's giving me overtime at the warehouse, and he said I could maybe move up in a few months to delivering. That pays more. And Jeremy's got a line on a cheap pedicab for sale that we might go partners on."

"A pedicab? Are you kidding?"

"No. I'm serious, Jane. We'll fix it up and take turns working nights when I'm not at the warehouse. It'll be good exercise and we can make great money."

"Caleb, you don't have to work pedaling a bike cab."

"I plan to support this family doing whatever I have to do."

"Well, when will you have time for me and the baby?"

"There'll be plenty of time as long as I'm not wasting it on music. Now you see? I'm trading a dream for a better reality."

He looked so adamant that Jane knew arguing further would be of no use at all. Instead, she set the popcorn bowl aside, opened the blanket on her lap, and motioned for him to join her.

"Come here, lover, and let me put my arms around you."

He scooted up next to her, leaned his head against her side, and placed his hand on her belly. Jane played with his hair. After a while, he looked up at her and smiled.

"I can feel it," he said. "I can feel the baby move."

"That's just the three bags of popcorn I ate settling," Jane replied, smiling down on him. "You won't feel the baby until the second trimester, honey."

Caleb looked so cute with his hair tousled and that crooked smile on his face that she cupped his chin in her hand and leaned down and kissed him. His lips parted for her, and he reached up and put his hand on her cheek. When they finally pulled away long enough for her to speak, Jane looked into his eyes and did her best to smile flirtatiously.

"Let's go make love," she said.

"But I don't want to hurt the baby."

"You won't hurt the baby."

"Are you sure?"

"Dr. Oz said it was okay."

"Didn't he also say to rub coffee grounds and coconut oil all over yourself?"

Jane laughed. She kissed him again just for being cute. "Just take me into the bedroom and make love to me."

Caleb smiled and rose from the couch, then bent and picked her up in his arms and carried her off toward the bedroom.

"Am I heavy?" she asked.

He grinned down at her in his arms. "You might want to lay off the popcorn."

"I hope you're joking."

"I'm joking."

"Good," she said as he laid her gently down on the bed. "Because I'm only getting heavier from here on out."

Caleb peeled off his shirt and straddled her. "That's okay," he answered. "I like my ladies thick."

"Ladies?" she asked. But before he could answer, she reached behind her and grabbed a pillow and hit him so hard he fell off the bed.

"You better watch it," he said, getting up and crawling back on top of her. "I'm not above handcuffing a pregnant woman to the headboard."

Even though the idea kind of turned her on, she thought better of hitting him with the pillow again. Instead she reached up and wrapped her hands around his neck, pulling his lips down to hers.

∽

Jane stopped at the red light and watched as a troop of small angels and demons and one tiny little pink fairy princess trotted across the street. They all had smiles on their painted faces and orange plastic pumpkins filled with candy swinging from their little hands.

"They're cute, aren't they?"

"We always waited until dark to go trick-or-treating," Caleb said. "Not broad daylight in downtown. And I used to bring a pillowcase, not a pumpkin. You can't fit enough candy in those things. What's happening to this world?"

Jane looked over at him and laughed. "You might think differently about trick-or-treating when you have a daughter."

"You mean, when I have a son."

"Would you be disappointed with a daughter?"

"Of course not," he said. "I just have a feeling it's a boy."

"Well, we'll keep it a surprise then."

The light turned green and Jane drove on.

"Won't you tell me where you're taking me, baby?" Caleb asked. "I don't understand why I had to leave early from work or why the need for all this secrecy."

"Just sit back and relax, my little goblin. You'll see."

Ten minutes later, Jane pulled up in front of a house just a few blocks south of Sixth Street. She noticed Caleb looking out the car window at the property, desperate to find out what all of this was about. But other than the white van in the driveway and the black metal fence, there was nothing unusual about the outside of the house.

"I hope this isn't a costume party," Caleb said, "because neither of us is dressed up."

"Sure we are," Jane replied, joking. "I'm Snow White and you're Grumpy from the Seven Dwarfs. Now, stop being such a brat and try to enjoy the surprise."

Caleb reluctantly got out of the car, following Jane as she led him up to the door. She knocked and almost immediately a man opened it. She stepped inside and when Caleb followed, she turned to watch his expression as he took in the space they had entered.

"Jane, this is a recording studio."

"I know," she said. "And not just any recording studio either, but the best one in all of Austin. Isn't that right, Dave?"

Dave had just closed the door, and he dropped his head and blushed as he responded, "We were voted the best, yes. But that was last year." Then he reached out his hand to Caleb. "Nice to meet you, Caleb. I'm Dave. Or sometimes people call me Davie or David or even dickhead, depending on how late we've been recording. I'll be your producer."

"My producer?"

"That's right," he said, sweeping his hand out to take in the studio. "This place is all yours for the next two weeks to lay down your album. Jane here tells me most of the songs are already written. She showed me clips from the show, and I gotta say that I'm already a fan, man."

"Album?" Caleb asked, looking at Jane. "My album?"

Jane smiled. "Your album, honey."

"That's right," Dave said. "And we've got a great lineup of contract musicians to back you up too. Some of the best in Texas. The studio has guitars, basses, pedals, amps, pianos, drums, and lots of vintage synths. I record digital and analog. Then I'll be working with Sammy on your postproduction. Oh, and I forgot to tell you, Jane, but Rebecca said she'd love to shoot Caleb for the album cover and Julia will design it."

Caleb looked around the studio again.

"I don't understand what's going on here, Jane."

"You heard Dave," she said. "You've got everything you need to record your album."

"But who am I recording it for?"

"For your fans, silly. Don't you know that since the show ended you've got over fifty thousand fans on Facebook and half that many already on Twitter? We don't need that show's contract to release an album. Do we, Dave?"

"No way," he said, shaking his shaggy head. "In fact, a lot of traditionally signed artists I work with are dumping their labels and distributing straight through iTunes and Amazon. Shit, you're both from Seattle, right? Well, then, you've heard of Macklemore, I'm sure. He's not signed. And I hear rumors him and Ryan Lewis might be nominated for a Grammy this year."

Caleb walked to the control room and looked through the big window into the live recording room. Jane stepped up beside him. She saw his eyes settle on his guitar case, already there waiting for him beside a microphone and a stool.

"This is great, Jane," he said. "It really is. But I can't do it. I have to work."

Instead of answering him, Jane stepped aside.

"No, you don't."

Caleb spun around when he heard Mr. Zigler's voice. "What are you doing here, boss?"

"I'm not your boss anymore," he said.

"You're not?"

"No, I'm your partner. Jane and I believe in you. And so do a lot of other people. And when you believe in someone, you invest in them. So we're investing in you. Now all you have to do is put in the time and the talent, and make an album you're proud of. We'll take care of the rest."

Caleb started to say something, but Mr. Zigler held up a hand and cut him off.

"Jane told me how you feel about receiving charity, so I'm here to tell you that we intend to get every penny back plus interest. Now, trust this old man when he tells you not to say another word and to just nod that you'll do it, and grab that young lady there and hug her."

Caleb nodded and Jane could see he had tears in his eyes. Then he grabbed her and wrapped her in his arms. He was still hugging her when he spoke softly in her ear.

"Thank you, Jane. I love you so much."

Then he turned to shake Mr. Zigler's hand, but Mr. Zigler ignored the offer and hugged Caleb himself instead.

"Whoa," Caleb said with a smile when Mr. Zigler finally let him go. "Do you hug all your business partners like that?"

"Only the cute ones," Mr. Zigler said with a wink. "In fact, getting to hug Jane there was half the reason I went along with this deal. Now, I've got to get back to the warehouse and hire two men to replace you, so you had better get busy recording."

"I better get going, myself," Jane said, joining Mr. Zigler as he walked toward the door.

"You're leaving me too?" Caleb asked.

"I sure am," she said. "I've got an appointment to keep."

"An appointment with who?"

"With a pint of Ben and Jerry's and *Dancing with the Stars* on the DVR," she answered, leaning in and pecking him on the cheek. Then she said, "See, sometimes it's nice to be the boss. You just call me when you're done, baby."

The last thing Jane saw before she turned to follow Mr. Zigler out the door was Caleb smiling at Dave and shaking his hand. With just that little glimpse of a grin, she knew that everything would work out just as it should.

∽

The album dropped eight weeks later on the Friday after Christmas. They threw a huge party at Sherman's to celebrate. Mr. Zigler had the booths closest to the stage reserved for friends of Caleb and for his employees, and true to his word, he served a custom brew of bottled beer bearing Caleb's likeness on the label, offering up all the proceeds to a youth alcoholism charity. He had even had T-shirts printed up to match the album cover, and his wife was selling them at a table along with actual CDs. Jane couldn't remember a time when she had felt so excited and so happy.

The drummer hit the cymbals to get everyone's attention and the room fell silent. Jane watched the stage as Caleb came out to join the band. He scanned the crowd with a huge and happy grin on his face. Then his eyes settled on Jane. The way he looked at her, it was as if she were the only person in the place. Then he leaned in to the microphone and spoke.

"I'd like to dedicate my first song, in fact the entire night, to the woman who made all of this possible. The woman I love more than anything else in this world. To my future wife, to the mother-to-be of my child, I dedicate this to you, Jane. Thanks for always believing in me. I call this one 'Jane's Harmony.'"

Then he lifted his Jane guitar into place and played a sweet melody. When he sang out the first line, his voice seemed to come from every direction in the room, as if he were singing from somewhere already deep inside Jane's heart.

> *A lonely melody*
> *Sung out in the cold*
> *A broken plea*
> *To heal a tortured soul*
> *I came to her grave*
> *Thought I was alone*
> *I prayed anyway*
> *I sang my heart's only song—*
> *That song, that song, that song*

That brought you to me
Oh, that lonely melody.

I stood in the rain
I made my final vow
Then an angel came
And took me home
Fear chased me away
But love's never wrong
You found me that day
Singing your song—
Your song, your song, your song
That brought you back to me
Oh, your lovely melody.

Now from Austin's sunny days
To Seattle's rainy scene
Across all the long-lost ages
And the valleys in between
Through all the coming years
Our love goes on and on
Through a thousand happy tears
I'll be singing our song—
Our song, our song, our song
That set our hearts free
Oh, our sweet harmony.

Because, baby, you see
You just have to believe
That from sunlight and still waters
To hailstorms and high seas
I'll love you when it matters, baby

The way I pray that you love me
If I live a thousand years
Or even a thousand lives to be
I'll spend them all with you, baby
Singing Jane's harmony.
I'll spend them all with you, baby
Singing our sweet, sweet harmony
That sweet harmony.

Chapter 24

It was late on a Friday night at the end of January, and a dusting of snow lay on Austin's deserted streets. It seemed the unusual freeze had chased even the most ardent inebriates in for the night. But despite the lack of takers, Caleb pedaled on into the cold, looking for a fare. He liked the quiet and the way the yellow streetlights dulled the colors from his sight, and he liked the feeling of an honest day's work in his tired legs.

He heard music spill out of a bar, and then it went quiet again as the door closed. A moment later someone shouted, "Hey, rickshaw boy, over here!"

He circled back and pulled alongside the curb.

"Colder than a well digger's ass out here," the man said, climbing into the pedicab seat. "Thanks for picking me up."

"You bet," Caleb said. "Where you heading?"

"Littlefield Quarters, on Sixth and Brazos."

Caleb nodded and pedaled off up the street. He could hear the man humming a tune behind him and it was nice to have some company, even if only for a few blocks.

"How about this snow?" the man asked after a while.

"I'm from Washington, so it doesn't bother me much."

"Well, it seems old Mother Nature sends us just enough every few years to let people know who's in charge. I'll bet you're not setting any tip records tonight."

Caleb turned and looked at him and shook his head. "No, I'm sure not."

"Hey," the man said, "aren't you that guy who was on the TV show? The singer-songwriter contest deal."

"Yep, I'm that guy," Caleb replied, not entirely happy to have been recognized.

The man scooted forward in his seat, lowering his voice as if to avoid being overheard, although there was no one about. "I thought you released an album, dude. There were flyers all over town."

"I did," Caleb answered. "About a month ago now."

"And you're riding around in a rickshaw?"

Caleb turned and looked at him and shrugged. "I've got a baby on the way to support. Whatever it takes."

"Shit," the man said, sitting back again. "That's rough."

Caleb pulled up to Littlefield Quarters, and his fare stepped out of the pedicab and took out his wallet.

"What do I owe you?"

Caleb waved it off. "Ride's on me."

"You sure? I gotta pay you something."

"It's fine. Really. I was heading this way. Besides, night like tonight, I'm just happy to have some company."

Caleb nodded good-bye and pulled the pedicab away from the curb to pedal off toward home. He was a half a block away when he heard the man shout after him.

"Thanks, dude! I'll download your album."

Caleb smiled and thought to himself, Sweet. Now I only need to give away another hundred thousand or so free rides and I might have myself a music career.

He stopped at the all-night convenience store on their block and purchased a pint of Chunky Monkey for Jane, her Ben & Jerry's flavor of the week, and a pint of Chubby Hubby for himself. Then he rode the rest of the way home, chained the pedicab to the apartment fence, and went inside to the one thing in this life he loved even more than music.

❧

Jane was on the sofa, dividing her attention between her laptop and the Super Bowl pregame show on TV, when her shriek brought Caleb running in from the kitchen in a panic. He looked at her, then at the TV.

"What are you screaming about? The game hasn't even started yet, babe, and you just made me dump your guiltless guacamole dip all over the kitchen floor."

"Not the game," she said, ignoring the TV and waving him frantically toward the computer on her lap. "You won't believe this, honey. Come and look."

Caleb flopped down on the couch next to her and followed Jane's finger pointing at the screen.

"No way," he said, taking the laptop. "Let me see this."

Caleb refreshed the browser and looked again. "How is this even possible?" he asked. "Was it Jordyn's tweet about my album to her fans?"

"That," Jane said, "or it could have been her Facebook post. Or her YouTube video. Or Panda's blog about you." She leaned over and kissed his cheek. "Or maybe it's just a really great album, baby, and it took a while to catch on."

"But I'm up next to Lorde on the chart. I don't believe it."

"I didn't either," she said, "but look here." She reached and clicked on the other browser, then pulled up the iTunes sales report.

"Holy sh—" Caleb glanced over at Jane's belly, remembering that little ears were just beneath the bump there, and caught his comment short. "I mean, holy guacamole. Almost seven thousand downloads just today."

Jane hit the refresh button. "Almost eight thousand now."

Caleb refreshed the browser again and more downloads appeared. He had a huge smile on his face even as he shook his head in disbelief, and he was so completely absorbed in the good news on that little screen that he didn't even appear to hear the knock on the apartment door.

Jane rose from the couch and went to answer it. Buttercup rushed inside between Jane's feet, and Marj and Bill stood in the doorway, holding an enormous party sandwich and a plate of homemade cookies.

"Come on in," Jane said. "The game's about to start."

"We thought maybe it already had," Marj said, stepping inside, "what with all the screaming we heard over here just a minute ago. What did we miss?"

Jane nodded toward Caleb on the couch. "Caleb's album is halfway up the iTunes Top One Hundred chart."

"Oh, sweetie," Marj said, hugging Jane. "You two deserve this so much."

"Congratulations, Caleb," Bill called into the living room.

Caleb looked up from the laptop. "Oh, thanks, Bill. I still can't believe it."

"Well, it's a great album, so I'm not surprised." Then Bill took Marj's hand in his and looked at Jane. "We have some good news of our own. Tell them, honey."

Marj smiled and held up her hand, showing off a ring. "Bill and I are getting married."

"Oh my God, Marj! This is so great. Caleb, they're getting married. Come see the ring." Jane took Marj's hand and looked at the ring. "It's so beautiful, Marj. Wait a minute. You're not pregnant too, are you?"

Marj laughed. "At my age? Don't be silly. But I want you to be my maid of honor."

"Only if you'll be my matron of honor," Jane said, placing a hand on her growing belly and adding, "since you'll probably beat us to the altar."

Caleb closed the laptop and put it away. After everyone had

fixed themselves a plate, they all sat down on the couch to watch Denver kick off to Seattle for Super Bowl XLVIII. Jane had a plate of goodies on her lap, her lover on one side, her friends on the other, and her home team playing the biggest game of the century on the TV in front of her. She was as happy as could be.

Then Caleb put his arm around her and kissed her head, and said, "The only way today could be any better, baby, is if the Seahawks actually win."

Win or lose, Jane couldn't imagine the day getting any happier. Until she felt their baby kick, and suddenly, it did.

∽

They were driving to the house when one of Caleb's songs came on the radio. He pulled the car over to the side of the road and sat looking at the station's call letters on the radio's display, as if he couldn't believe what he was hearing. Jane sat in the passenger seat, grinning with pride.

"Did you do this, baby?" Caleb asked.

"Me and Mr. Zigler did it, yes. It's just the local Austin stations for now, but we hired a radio promotion company and we're hoping to get more airtime soon."

Caleb was still smiling when he pulled back into traffic. "Who knew you had such a head for business."

"It helps a lot when the female station manager sees your picture on the album cover."

Caleb laughed. "Are you pimping me out to sell albums?"

"Not yet," she said. "But I might when it comes time to sell tickets for your tour."

Caleb reached over and took her hand in his as he drove. "You know there's no one in this world or any other for me except you, don't you, baby?"

"Even right now? As pregnant as I am?"

"Especially right now."

Jane smiled and looked out the window as they turned onto their new street. Their agent was already there waiting when they pulled up. Caleb jumped out and went around to help Jane from the car. Then they walked hand in hand across the street and met their agent at the gate. He reached into his pocket and held out the keys to their house. Caleb looked at Jane, but she nodded for him to take them.

"The owner had no problem with the two-year option to buy at the agreed price," the agent said. "I put a signed copy of the lease-option agreement on the counter."

Caleb shook his hand. "I appreciate that, Vincent. If things keep going well with the album, maybe we'll buy it sooner rather than later."

"We can do a walk-through, if you want," Vincent offered.

Caleb looked at Jane, but she smiled and shook her head.

"I'm sure everything's fine," she said. "Thanks for all your work. You've been great."

After Vincent drove off down the street, Jane and Caleb surveyed their bungalow. It was small but perfect. A white picket fence, a green lawn with a shade tree, a covered porch. But the real reason they had fallen in love with it was a backyard that was almost too big to believe. And not one blackberry shrub anywhere in sight.

Caleb opened the gate and led Jane up the walk by the hand. He had just put the key in the door when Jane put her hand on his and stopped him. Then she opened her bag and took out Mrs. Hawthorne's horseshoe.

"We have to hang this above the door first," she said, handing the horseshoe to Caleb. Then she retrieved from her bag the small hammer-and-nails kit she'd picked up for just this occasion.

Caleb put the keys in his jeans pocket, took two nails, and put them in his mouth. Then he took up the hammer with one hand and lifted the horseshoe above the door with the other and centered it.

"Which side up?" he asked, mumbling through the nails.

"I think the open side up," Jane said, remembering how it had been. "That way the luck won't spill out."

When the horseshoe was in position, Caleb was stuck for a moment with the horseshoe upheld in one hand, the hammer in his other hand, and no way to get the nails from his mouth. He looked to Jane, but she laughed, enjoying his predicament. He grinned, obviously appreciating the silent joke between them. Then he put the hammer in his back pocket and took up a nail and held it and the horseshoe in place with one hand, then retrieved the hammer from his pocket with the other and nailed the horseshoe into place. Jane watched this with great wonder, curious how it was that men managed such things but couldn't seem to get the cap back on the toothpaste.

Caleb handed Jane the hammer and she put it back in her bag. Then she took his hand in hers, gazed up at the horseshoe, and smiled for Mrs. Hawthorne.

"Let's just sit on the steps for a minute before we go in."

They sat down on the upper step and looked at their yard. A butterfly fluttered just above the grass. A squirrel ran across the lawn and up the tree, setting birds there to squawking. A breeze rustled the leaves. It was a perfect spring afternoon.

"You know," Jane said, "before Melody and I moved into our house on the island, we sat on the porch and said a prayer."

She felt Caleb squeeze her hand. "We can say a prayer."

"But it's been a long time."

"All the better, then," he said.

Jane closed her eyes and listened to the birds and to the breeze. Her mind wandered back across all those years to her and five-year-old Melody sitting together on the steps of their first home, looking up at snow clouds gathering in the gray Washington skies. She could almost feel the cold on her cheeks. She missed that little girl, and she knew she always would. She whispered a prayer. The same prayer. And then she was back on the porch with Caleb, the Texas sun warm on her face and Caleb's hand warm in hers, and she knew that the prayer had already been answered.

She rose and Caleb rose with her.

He unlocked the door and pushed it open. Then he turned, took her bag from her and set it down beside the door, and scooped her up into his arms.

"Am I really heavy?" she asked.

"Not at all, babe," he answered hoarsely as he strained beneath her weight.

And Jane knew it was the only time he would lie to her, and she loved him for it. Then he kissed her before he carried her through the door and into their home.

~∾~

Caleb paced in the waiting room, mumbling wild prayers and pulling at his hair. Sweat glistened on his brow and when he clawed his fingers through his hair, his hands were shaking.

He leaped at the doctor as soon as he appeared. "Is she okay now? Can I go back in?"

"We need to do a cesarean section, but you can scrub up and come into the operating theater. The anesthesiologist is there with her now."

The doctor led Caleb down the hall and into a room, where they both washed their hands and arms, then put on gowns and caps. When they walked into the operating room, Caleb saw Jane on the table and his heart skipped a beat. There was a half curtain suspended from the ceiling, blocking the lower half of her body, where two nurses and the anesthesiologist were busy working. Jane's face was pale and her hair was drenched with sweat. But she smiled when she saw him.

"Hi, honey," she said. "How are you holding up?"

Caleb returned her smile as best he could, brushing a loose strand of hair away from her face. He looked at her with such concern, it nearly broke her heart.

"I'm holding up okay," he finally answered. "How are you doing, baby?"

"I'm all right. They gave me a spinal and I can't feel my legs. They say they might remove my appendix if it looks infected."

"Both of them?" Caleb asked, slightly panicked.

Jane couldn't help but laugh. She reached up a finger and poked his nose. "You're silly. Appendix isn't plural. A person only has one."

"But if you only have one, don't you need it?"

"No, I don't need it," she assured him. Then she looked at him in his gown and hat and said, "You know, it's too bad you don't even know what an appendix is, because you would have made a really cute doctor."

"I'll be happy to just be a really cute father," he told her.

He took her hand in his and Jane could feel that he was shaking with nerves. She looked into his sweet green eyes and she wished she could somehow reassure him that everything would be fine, but she was in need of reassurance herself.

The anesthesiologist's head appeared above the curtain. "Can you feel that?"

"Feel what?" Jane asked.

"That's the answer we want to hear," he replied.

Then the ob-gyn joined the others, and they were all there working and talking beyond the curtain for a while—nothing urgent, just a quiet murmur.

Time seemed to pass in strange intervals to Jane.

She looked up at Caleb and waited and wished and prayed.

"I'm making the uterine incision now," she heard.

Then there was a lot of tugging and pulling, so much that she thought she might be ripped beneath the curtain, and she squeezed Caleb's hand to her chest and looked into his eyes. A minute passed, maybe two. Then she heard the most beautiful sound in the world. She heard her baby cry. Her heart filled with joy and her eyes filled with tears.

She felt Caleb's lips on her forehead.

"Congratulations," the ob-gyn said from beyond the curtain. "If you look to your right, you'll see your beautiful baby girl on her way to the warm room."

Jane lifted her head slightly and blinked away the tears just in time to catch a glimpse of the nurse carrying their baby from the cold operating room into the attached warm room. Then she leaned her head back onto the pillow and closed her eyes, and thanked God and the universe and modern medicine and the doctors and the nurses and her sweet, sweet Caleb, the father of her healthy child. When she opened her eyes again, she saw that he was crying too.

"I can't believe it, Jane," he said, shaking his head. "I'm so happy, I can't believe it."

She squeezed his hand. "I couldn't have done it without you. And what did I tell you about painting that room blue?"

He smiled and wiped away a tear. "Maybe she'll like blue."

"Maybe she will," Jane said. "Maybe she will."

Several minutes later, while the doctors closed her incision, the nurse came out and called Caleb into the other room. He looked at Jane, hesitating.

"Go ahead," she said. "Go see our little girl."

It seemed like forever, lying there being stitched up and watching that door. Then Caleb reappeared with the largest smile she'd ever seen on his handsome face, holding a tight bundle of blankets in his arms. He walked to the bed and gently held their baby up for her to see.

It was the most darling little face Jane had ever set eyes on. She reached her arms out to take her from him, but then hesitated and looked to the nurse who had followed Caleb out and was standing behind him. The nurse nodded that it was okay. Jane's arms were trembling, and Caleb helped guide the baby until Jane had her cradled to her breast.

They were quiet there together for several minutes. A new family on one side of the curtain, the doctors finishing up their miraculous work on the other.

"I guess now we'll need to come up with a name," Caleb finally said. "All the ones I had picked out were for boys."

Jane looked at Caleb. He seemed both older and younger than he had just minutes before. As if he'd taken on a new responsibility for something very important, but in the process had shed some sense of responsibility for everything else. She decided that fatherhood looked good on him.

Then Jane looked down upon this perfect little life in her arms, this miracle that she and Caleb had created together.

"Her name is Harmony," she said with a smile. "Harmony Grace Cummings."

"You don't want her to have your last name too?"

Jane looked up at the man she loved and smiled. "No. Because as soon as she's old enough to walk me down the aisle, we'll be making an honest man out of you."

Caleb smiled. "Harmony Grace Cummings it is, then," he said.

And then he bent over the bed and kissed them both.

Epilogue

Three years later, the cars were lined up on the street for three blocks in both directions, and the laughter coming from the backyard was so loud that the courier didn't even need the address or the white and purple balloons on the gate to find the place.

He straightened his tie and knocked on the door. When no one came, he knocked again. At last it opened.

"You're just in time," the woman said. "Come on in."

"Oh, no," he replied. "I've only come to make a delivery. Is Miss Jane McKinney here?"

"She's busy right now. I'm Marj, how can I help you?"

He bent and picked the box up from between his feet. "I have a delivery for her."

Marj reached for the box, but he pulled it away, saying, "Miss McKinney needs to sign."

"Can't I sign for her?" Marj asked. "It's an important day."

"I know it is," he said, "but this is an important delivery and it needs to be signed for by her."

"Wait here, then," Marj said, pulling the door closed.

When the door opened again, a beautiful woman wearing a lavender lace Renaissance dress and a matching flower in her hair smiled at the courier and said, "May I help you?"

"Are you Jane McKinney?"

"I am for another few minutes," she said.

"I'm with the law firm of Douglas and Cooper, and we're making a delivery on behalf of the Seattle attorney handling Mrs. Hawthorne's estate."

"Her estate? I knew she had passed, but . . ."

"Yes, she left instructions for this to be delivered today."

He handed Jane the box. It was heavier than it looked. She set the box just inside the door, then took the pen he offered and signed the delivery receipt. He folded the paper, slipped it into his breast pocket, thanked her, and left.

When the door was closed, Jane knelt and pulled back the tape, then opened the box. It was filled with packing peanuts, and on top was an envelope. She opened it and removed the letter, written in a shaky script.

> *Dear Jane:*
>
> *I know I'm showing up unannounced, and with two husbands to boot, but a promise is a promise. I hope you and Caleb won't find us a burden on your special day. Feel free to pour us out into any old Texas river after you've said "I do." Or keep us on your mantel. Either way, I've enclosed a small token of my sincere appreciation for the kindness you and your thoughtful, hardworking man showed to a lonely old woman.*
>
> *If I've learned anything worth passing on in these ninety-three years, it's that life is filled with questions, and love is the answer to every one of them. So I wish you lots of luck, but above all else, I wish you lots of love. And don't you dare be at all sad over me—I'm starting my new life as well.*
>
> *Faithfully yours forever,*
> *Mrs. Nancy Lou Hawthorne*

There was a check inside, and when Jane unfolded it and read the amount, she nearly fell over. Then she reached into the box and pulled the brass urn up from the packing peanuts. She couldn't resist looking underneath it, and sure enough there was an old yellow piece of masking tape with faded writing that read: *1949—$9.85*. Jane chuckled. Who would have thought that the woman who knew the price of everything she'd ever bought would end up being so generous?

"What do you have there, baby?"

She looked up at Caleb; he was holding their daughter in his arms. He had never been more handsome than he was today, wearing linen pants with a sash and a puffy white silk shirt. And Harmony had never been cuter, either, her hair curled, her big green eyes filled with wonder.

"It's Mrs. Hawthorne," Jane said, nodding to the urn in her hands. "She showed up for the wedding after all."

Caleb smiled. "She sure was a special woman."

"Yes, she was. And she sent us a wedding gift too. A check."

"Really? That's unexpected. How much was it for?"

Jane grinned. "Let's just say we'll be paying off the house sooner than we thought."

Caleb raised his eyebrows. "Wow. Does this mean we can go on a honeymoon after all?"

"I think it means we can run off to Venice and kiss beneath the Bridge of Sighs."

Caleb adjusted Harmony in his arms, then leaned in and kissed Jane, saying, "I can't wait."

"Daddy's kissing Mommy."

Caleb pulled away and looked at Harmony and smiled. Then he looked back to Jane and said, "We came to find you because Harmony here is ready to walk you down the aisle. Aren't you, sweetie?"

Harmony nodded. "Yes, Daddy."

He held Harmony out for Jane. "Why don't you trade me, baby, and I'll go and find Mrs. Hawthorne a seat in the front row."

Jane swapped the urn for her daughter, kissing Caleb in the

process. "Don't put the urn next to my mother," she warned. "She has strong opinions against cremation."

"I wouldn't do that to Mrs. Hawthorne anyway," he said, grinning and carrying the urn away.

Jane and Harmony watched him go. Both were smiling. Then Jane turned with Harmony in her arms and looked at their reflection in the foyer mirror. They wore matching dresses and had matching lavender begonias in their hair.

My God, Jane thought, how lucky can one woman be?

When Jane stepped from the house into the backyard, the band began playing a simple but beautiful instrumental version of "Somewhere over the Rainbow."

Jane looked at all the faces of the people turned around in their white chairs. Among them she saw Marj and her husband, Bill. She saw Caleb's music friends and the warehouse workers. And she saw her mother, sitting next to her brother, Jon, who was finally out of jail and, at least for today, sober. She saw Mrs. Hawthorne's urn glinting in the sun. And she saw their new neighbors, desperately chasing down their kids, who had abandoned their chairs to play a game of tag around the tree in the corner of the yard. She saw Mr. Zigler in his best Sunday suit, standing proudly beneath the arch he had helped build, his mail-order license in his pocket, ready to marry them. And she saw Caleb beside him, looking very much indeed like a prince.

She and Caleb smiled at each other, fifty feet of grass the only thing in the world left between them. Then Jane set Harmony down on the lawn beside her and squatted to look into her daughter's green eyes.

"Do you know that I love you more than anything else in the world, sweetie?"

"I love you too, Mommy."

"Will you take me to your father now so I can marry him?"

Harmony smiled, her curls bouncing as she nodded. "Daddy showed me how."

Jane stood and took her daughter's tiny hand in hers. Then she leaned her head back and closed her eyes for a moment. The sun was warm on her face and the music played beautifully in her ears. She could almost feel her friend Grace and her daughter Melody smiling down on them today.

Jane opened her eyes and looked ahead at the man she loved, where he waited for her beneath an arch covered with a garland made of flowers. Then she smiled down at her daughter and nodded.

"I'm ready now," she said.

Harmony took the first confident step toward the altar and Jane followed, walking down the grassy aisle toward her future.

What boundaries would you cross
for true love?

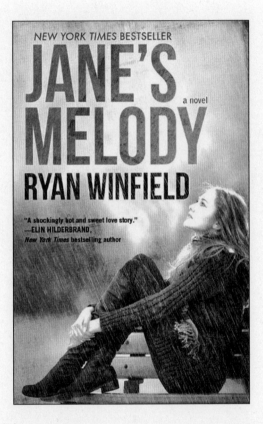

Discover the beginning of Jane and
Caleb's love story in *Jane's Melody*,
available from Atria Books.